The Devil's Son

*Cap Hatfield and the End
Of the Hatfield and McCoy Feud*

ANNE BLACK GRAY

Woodland Press, LLC

Published by

Woodland Press, LLC

Chapmanville, West Virginia • USA

Copyright © 2012 Anne Black Gray

ISBN 978-0-9852640-0-0

SAN: 2 5 4 – 9 9 9 9

 See Woodland Press, LLC on FACEBOOK
See our website: www.woodlandpress.com

CAP HATFIELD

AUTHOR'S NOTE

When I was a child, my mother and her sisters often spoke fondly of their Uncle Cap. One Easter, when they were children, he gave my aunts baby ducks and my mother a baby rabbit, by far the nicer gift in her estimation. Mother told me Cap was "your Granddaddy's friend." Since Granddaddy was a reserved, well spoken man, a West Virginia mayor, state senator, and judge of the circuit court at one time or another, I pictured my mother's uncle as a man with similar traits and disposition. Cap died six years before I was born, denying me any opportunity to know him personally.

Years later, as an adult, I learned that "Uncle Cap" was Cap Hatfield, notorious killer and right hand man to his father Devil Anse Hatfield, during the infamous Hatfield-McCoy feuds. It seemed impossible that Uncle Cap and Cap the killer could be one and the same. *The Devil's Son* is the result of my efforts, long after my mother's and aunts' deaths, to discover how Cap made the great transition he seemed to have made and, concomitantly, how the Hatfield-McCoy feud ended.

After reading histories, memoirs, two master's degree theses, and numerous old newspaper articles, I began to put a story together, a story that was never totally clear because information was sparse about many of Cap's adventures, sources conflicted concerning names of sparring parties and dates of events, and very little was written about motives and interpersonal relationships. In fact, some tales and films portrayed the Hatfields and McCoys as cartoonish, irrational figures. To put together a coherent story, I had to re-create motives and conversations and provide scenes of life inside the Hatfield family. When data were sparse or conflicting, I chose words and actions that fit the flow of lives and the changes in them. That is, I have written a novel, not a history. The characters, events, and settings in southern West Virginia and northern Kentucky in the 1880s are actual, but conversations and details of some events are fictional.

I have traced the flow of Cap's life as though mapping the course of a river I have never seen and never can see. There are good, detailed maps of some portions of the river and stretches where no information at all is available or where sources conflict. Because a river is prevented from excursions that defy physical laws, such as gravity, one can draw a reasonable likeness of its course between known points. I have mapped some of Cap's life in just such a way, making informed guesses about its flow between known events.

Past Alive

I love historical fiction.

When the raw material of the past, in all its complexity and ambiguity, is forged into thrilling tales to which we can relate and from which we can learn, the past truly comes alive. Even when it's unbelievable, as in a certain popular series in which a heroine at the dawn of the human species singlehandedly invents everything from fire to the missionary position, historical drama can be riveting. And when it's believable—well researched and finely crafted, as it is in *The Devil's Son*—historical fiction is some of the most compelling reading available.

As a West Virginian, I especially enjoy historical drama about major events from our state's past—everything from the Matewan Massacre and the mine wars to the Monongahela Rye that graced the tables of the Czars—the state's history is rich with stories of slave revolts, the captives of Indians, tunnels and silicosis.

In *The Devil's Son*, author Anne Black Gray gives us the result of her own look into her family's past, the stories her mother told her as a child. As Anne says, when she was young in Logan County, West Virginia, she used to hear stories about "Uncle" Cap, who had been a friend of her grandfather's. Her grandfather had been "a reserved, well spoken man" and a "West Virginia mayor, state senator, and judge of the circuit court," and she assumed Uncle Cap must have had some of those same qualities, though she never met him. Later she read about the feared Cap Hatfield, second son of Devil Anse, the man who, more than anyone else, history considered the party most responsible for the famous Hatfield-McCoy Feud.

Instead of choosing to disregard either historical record or family lore, Anne set out to determine the truth that could be behind both reputations. How could the man who brought her mother a baby bunny as a gift be the same man history sometimes refers to as a "heartless cutthroat"? She researched the topic for years, and supplemented that research with conversations and memories of people in her family and surviving members of both clans. She worked to determine the truths behind the events, to both learn and intuit the story as it might have actually happened. Along the way, she became one of America's leading experts on the Hatfield-McCoy feud and was interviewed by the History Channel for a documentary on the feud.

The result of her efforts is *The Devil's Son*, a true historical drama. In *The Devil's Son*, Anne Black Gray weaves a nuanced story with the ring of truth; she unfolds complex historical events that could have given rise to both reputations. I think of *The Devil's Son* not as a fictional take on the Hatfield-McCoy feud, but as a compelling truth, true in the way that eternal stories are true, not only true to the facts as they are known, but true to the minds and hearts of humans. *The Devil's Son* is more than a novel, it is a myth in the grandest sense.

In the storytelling culture of Appalachia in general and West Virginia specifically, it's about time we see the Hatfield-McCoy feud as more than litigation and gunplay. Some full measures of anger and bloodthirst and offended honor there surely must have been, but these do not make the feud comprehensible. *The Devil's Son* gives us a story that makes sense of the historical record by presenting real, three-dimensional human beings, acting not irrationally but for logical reasons that we recognize as reasonable motivations. *The Devil's Son* presents a tale that is by turns tragic and inspiring; Gray's novel both squares with the historical record and tells a tale we can believe.

Despite what you might have heard, the people engaged in the world's oldest profession are not courtesans selling comfort, but bards telling tales. Storytelling is the world's oldest form of social discourse. All this jabber about history and truth aside, read *The Devil's Son* for what it is—a dynamic epic that compels us to live in the world of southern West Virginia as it was more than 125 years ago, treating readers to historical drama at its best.

Geoffrey Cameron Fuller
Writer-editor

ACKNOWLEDGMENTS
FROM ANNE BLACK GRAY

I want to thank my fellow readers and writers for your support and thoughtful commentary: Trudy Armer, Shirley Friedman-Chase, Mary Kummer, Ethel Schwartz, Scott Edwards, Cat Hulbert, Robyn Joy Leff, Pat Lohr-Williams, Roark Whitehead, and Cheryl Woodruff. And thank you, my husband Ed Gray, for your devotion and dogged dedication, reading every page of the manuscript and its revisions almost as many times as I have. Finally, I thank editor Geoffrey Fuller for his careful attention to detail, his creative contributions, and his collaboration in our search for words used to express the often strong feelings of Appalachian people of the nineteenth century.

I am also indebted to the following books and their authors: *Pills, Petticoats and Plows*, Thomas D. Clark; *An American Vendetta*, Theron C. Crawford; *The Tale of the Devil*, Dr. Coleman C. Hatfield and Robert Y. Spence; *The Feuding Hatfields & McCoys*, Dr. Coleman C. Hatfield and F. Keith Davis; *Social History of Logan, West Virginia, 1765-1928*, M. A. Thesis by Mary Bland Hurst; *The Hatfields and McCoys*, Virgil Carrington Jones; *The Rise of Education and the Decline of Feudal Tendencies in the Tug River Valley of West Virginia and Kentucky*, M. A. Thesis by Homer Claude McCoy; *A History of Logan County*, Henry Clay Ragland; *The Hatfields and McCoys*, Otis K. Rice; *The Museum of Early American Tools*, Eric Sloane; *History of Logan County, West Virginia*, G. T. Swain; *The Land of the Guyandotte*, Robert Y. Spence; *Big Sandy*, Jean Thomas; *Feud: Hatfields, McCoys and Social Change in Appalachia, 1860-1900*, Altina L. Waller; *West Virginia, a History*, John Alexander Williams.

A NOTE ON THE LAUNGUAGE
OF *THE DEVIL'S SON*

The author and the editor of *The Devil's Son* took some liberties in the interest of vivid storytelling. For instance, the salty language used liberally by Cap and company is genuine, where possible, and where not either conforms to the standards of the day or has been eliminated because it sounds wrong to the modern ear: What was once a scalding curse meant to scandalize and dominate the hearer has become a punchline, appropriate only in cartoons (dagnabbit!).

In addition, the English spoken by nearly everyone in *The Devil's Son* has certain characteristics that, while deviating from Standard English, was consistent throughout the region. When such nonstandard pronunciation and word usage appears in literature, it is often noted with apostrophes and other typographical devices meant to call attention to its nonstandard nature. For precisely this reason, in *The Devil's Son*, words that were commonly pronounced in particular ways are written as if that pronunciation were standard: Taking is spelled takin, as it is pronounced, rather than takin', which calls unnecessary attention to itself. Got to is spelled gotta, ain't is spelled aint, and so on. The speakers of the mountain dialect were not consciously dropping g's, they were merely speaking as those around them spoke. These conventions may look odd to the reader at first, but the spellings quickly become as "normal" as the "nonstandard" pronunciations were in Cap's world.

Lastly, one of the people around whom *The Devil's Son* was woven was named Phamer McCoy. Or Pharmer McCoy. Historical records are unclear. The same is true of several other names of the people who lived on all sides of the Hatfield-McCoy feud. Obviously, though, where multiple spellings existed in the historical record, the author had to choose just one to use. She did.

WHAT OTHERS ARE SAYING
ABOUT *THE DEVIL'S SON*

"Never before has an author so vividly captured the drama, action and character of what stands as America's most famous feud. Anne Black Gray has dared to step beyond the "legend" surrounding the Hatfields & McCoys. *THE DEVIL'S SON* now stands as the benchmark book on this subject." —**Mark Cowen**, director/producer, Emmy®-nominated HBO documentary, *BAND OF BROTHERS: We Stand Alone Together.*

"A vividly imagined and engrossing novel that ably fills the gaps of history, like chinks in a cabin wall, and brings the mountain wilderness, the Tug Fork, and the Hatfield-McCoy feud boldly to life." —**Dean King**, author of the national bestseller *Skeletons on the Zahara* and the forthcoming *The Feud: The All-American, No-Holds-Barred, Blood-and-Lust Story of the Hatfields and McCoys.*

"I grew up in southern West Virginia, and heard about the Hatfields and McCoys all my life. I thought I knew the story. Until I read *THE DEVIL'S SON*, I'd never thought of Devil Anse and Cap Hatfield as real people, with thoughts and dreams beyond revenge and killing. Their lives weren't just brutal, but vital and heroic, and this book about them is truly engrossing." —**Karin Fuller**, award-winning author and syndicated newspaper columnist.

"Anne Black Gray combines extensive historical research and compelling storytelling to make *THE DEVIL'S SON* a historical thriller of the highest order." —**Brian J. Hatcher**, author and editor of *Mountain Magic: Spellbinding Tales of Appalachia.*

"Anne Black Gray brings lots of color and excitement to the saga of America's most infamous feud. Her attention to detail makes the story of the latter days of the battle between these clans a riveting read." —**Brad Crouser**, author of *Arch. The Life of Gov. Arch A. Moore, Jr.*

"*THE DEVIL'S SON*. Accurate history that is an absolute joy to read! I would have taken keener interest in American history had every book under that category been written with such narrative flair!" —**Michael Knost**, author and editor, winner of the 2009 Bram Stoker Award for *Writers Workshop of Horror*.

"Riveting. Anne Black Gray skillfully brings to life one of the great stories of Appalachian history. *THE DEVIL'S SON* is a very powerful and entertaining story." —**F. Keith Davis**, co-author of *The Feuding Hatfields & McCoys*, and author of *The Secret Life* and *Brutal Death of Mamie Thurman*.

"Anne Black Gray's book, *THE DEVIL'S SON*, and her startling rendition of America's most historic family blood feud is the real McCoy. It's family values on steroids." —**Raamie Barker**, senior advisor to West Virginia Governor Earl Ray Tomblin and descendant of Uncle Dyke Garrett.

Chapter 1

To attack, they'd have to come across here. Cap ran his gaze down the steep slope that dropped off behind the family's mountaintop fort, through barren tree limbs to the gleaming, ice-covered Tug, then across the river to the flat shore deep in snow on the Kentucky side. He scrutinized the trails heading down cliffs on the other side of the river a half mile away. He listened to the total silence of an empty land blanketed in snow. There was no one out here but himself—not on foot, not on horseback, no animal bigger than a rabbit or a squirrel, no prints of mountain boots or hooves in the new snow or on the river ice.

At a flash of red in a tree below, he raised his Winchester. It was only a cardinal.

After all these years he was still on edge every time he came here, the very spot where the McCoys had crossed the river and killed Cousin Bill. Laughing and grinning, Bill had left the Hatfield cabin one morning and had come home a corpse in a blanket, his face slashed open and his teeth cut out to force them from a McCoy neck. His cousin was no quitter, had fought on after his ammunition was gone, after he'd plunged his knife into McCoy flesh, after he'd lost most of his blood through the bullet holes that riddled his body, then fought to the last with his hands and teeth.

The McCoys had crossed and were sneaking through summer woods grown thick with leaves and underbrush when they'd happened on Bill. Today, with the trees barren of leaves, the river frozen to silence, and all the animals hunkered down in the cold, no one could come within two or three miles of the fort without being seen or heard.

Turning to face the fort, Cap heard the small movements of his feet as loud crunches in the snow and wondered if the men inside, only about a hundred feet away, had heard him and would call out for him to identify himself. No one did.

He wished he could assure Nancy their world would always be this peaceful so their child-soon-to-be and his stepson Joey might grow up without fearing for their lives. He and Nancy often had; Nancy's former husband, Joey's father, had died from gunshot wounds.

Of course, it was no surprise the McCoys weren't out here on New Year's Day. They'd have drunk themselves stupid seeing 1887 out and 1888 in and wouldn't be watching the river or anything else.

Stopping just short of the fort's door, Cap sucked in a breath so fast the cold air hurt his throat, surprised he hadn't realized before this moment that New Year's could be his lucky day. He could take advantage of this emptiness, cross the river into Kentucky and ride on through the woods to catch Randall McCoy and his boys at home, celebrating. He could put Nancy's fears to rest forever, as well as his mother's. This could be the opportunity of a lifetime.

Not that death was a punishment Cap wanted to inflict on anybody. Sadly, death meant not only the end of the victim, but a never-to-be-forgotten loss to his family. Still, it would be worth the sorrow if he ended all the warfare on both sides of the river forever. Even Randall McCoy's kin deserved to live in peace, and they couldn't with that old son of a packsaddle always stirring up trouble.

Cap felt excitement course through him, like a jolt of whiskey. He'd come up with a way to eliminate the gravest of all dangers to his family, a way no one else had thought of, a way that was certain to succeed. He had a way to replace the fear in his wife's and mama's eyes with happiness and gratitude.

But that didn't mean Pappy would go along with his plan. Pappy had ordered everyone to come here to resupply the fort's arsenal and to choose up for lookout watches over the Kentucky and West Virginia sides of the river, not to go raiding into Kentucky. Cap would have some persuading to do. Getting Pappy to change his mind to favor someone else's plan over his own was never easy.

He told himself to settle down and think. His father must see him as a man with a thought-out plan, not the hot-headed kid he'd once been—getting himself shot in the leg in a bar brawl and other such foolishness. If Pappy had been paying attention, he'd already seen how much more settled and thoughtful his favorite son had become now that he was twenty-three, married, and a father-to-be. And he must have some idea of this son's military potential. Cap often felt a kinship, a similar way of thinking, to the Roman Caesars and Confederate generals he'd read about. Like them he'd come to realize he had the head of a leader of men on his shoulders, possibly the head of a general.

Pappy was bound to listen to his idea. It should be easy to convince him the McCoys would sooner or later force the Hatfields to raid into Kentucky to save their lives and their honor and that no time to invade would ever be better than today. For five years no McCoy had shot at, knifed, or murdered a Hatfield. But now they'd once more started up the taunts, the threats, the crowing about their marksmanship over in Kentucky, in the streets of Pikeville. His cousin, who was married to a McCoy, had heard it. The Hatfield men bringing timber to the mills on the Ohio River had heard it. Cap had even read in the Louisville newspaper of their boasting about using their new rifles on the Hatfields.

He knew how to answer those threats. Don't wait for an attack. Strike first. Old Randall, his remaining sons and nephews were just two hours ride from where he stood. From here, he could see the trail leading up the cliffs and into the woods towards their farm.

Cap took a deep breath of biting, cold air, pulled open the fort door and let it shut behind him as he stomped the snow off his boots. He propped his Winchester against the wall and hung his coat on a peg beside the others.

He greatly admired this fort. In his teens he'd helped Pappy design and build it, every log a foot across, the solid oak door a foot thick to stop any bullet. There were no windows to weaken the protection of the walls, only gunports chiseled wider on the inside than the outside to give defenders a wide shooting angle. Grease-covered cooking pots and kettles littered the fireplace where embers flickered and died, and tracked-in mud and melted snow lay in clumps on the dirt floor. But against one log wall clean, well-polished rifles leaned and boxes of ammunition were neatly stacked.

Six men seated on benches around the puncheon table had their eyes on him—his younger brother Bobby Lee, cousins smart Elliot and dumb Cotton Top, Uncle Jim, and Tom and Charlie from the logging crew. His older brother Johnse, slouched on a dirty mattress on the floor, ignored his arrival.

At the head of the table, Pappy sat in the fort's only chair. Lips, almost hidden between bushy black beard and mustache, were pursed tight. Steely gray eyes beneath shaggy eyebrows returned Cap's scrutiny.

Brushing his hands briskly together, Cap stood facing his father from the other end of the table.

"Where you been?" Pappy asked. "We been waitin for you."

"Lookin things over." Cap would approach Pappy as carefully as you coaxed the big bull in the pasture into the barn if you didn't want to be run through. "It's dead quiet. No one's out there and no one's been out there since the snow came down last night."

Pappy's buzzard beak of a nose twitched and pointed downward. "No surprise."

"There's somethin I want to talk to you about. You know Randall and his boys have new rifles and they've been braggin they're gonna use em on us."

"Randall's a old bag of wind." Pappy chuckled. "All the same, we'll keep watch over the river for a while."

"Think about it." Cap took a couple of cautious steps towards Pappy. "New rifles. Where'd them McCoys get the money for new rifles?"

"Don't know. Kind of worries me."

"And why are they carryin on like that after five years of peace and no trouble from us?"

"You'd think they'd know better'n to contrary us," Pappy said. "They paid a terrible price for the killin they done in the past."

"You know what I heard?" Cap stared right into Pappy's eyes. "Randall's braggin he'll kill *you* with his own hands and cut a slice of meat from your body and roast it over hot coals. Are you gonna stand for that?" He couldn't see how Pappy could ignore such an insult. A sign of weakness like that invited attack.

Pappy stroked his beard in thought. "You might think it'd be a smart thing to make Randall pay for them words. But if Randall's just shootin off his mouth like usual and I went after him, I'd look like a fool. Can't let that happen. Not in these mountains."

Cap edged a little further down the table, closer to Pappy, who was now leaning back in his chair and gazing into the rafters. "Do you want to wait and see what they do with them rifles? Give em a chance to do somethin we'd need to get even for again?"

"We'll keep a close watch on em. They come over here and they'll feel some hot lead."

"We can make sure they don't come. You know they been drinkin all night and won't be on the lookout. We can cross over and take em out, easy." Cap searched the faces around the table for support. "We aint used this fort for nothin but a loggin camp for five years. You fellers want to live here week in and week out?" He pointed to the muddy floor and a pile of dirty mattresses and blankets. "That's what'll happen if the feuds start up again."

"Heck, no," Uncle Jim said.

"I aint gonna live here." Cotton Top made a face.

Tom Chambers shook his head from where he stood on the hearth, kicking the remains of a last burning log, scattering sparks into the room.

"Get out of that fire, Chambers," Pappy said. "One of these days you're gonna burn this place down."

"Then let's make sure we never have to." Cap wasn't going to let Chambers and the fire become a distraction. "Let's ride into Kentucky and end this before it can get started. What do you say?"

To a man, they turned to Pappy.

"Cap's makin good sense, Anse." Old Uncle Jim was the only one with the guts to speak up. "Before you know it, them whoresons'll sneak over and bushwhack us."

Johnse raised his head and smirked at Cap. "When they come over, they'll be lookin for me first." Just last week when Johnse had gone over to Kentucky peacefully, to visit his wife's kin and to sell a little of his famous whiskey, a McCoy had pointed a rifle right at his head and bragged he had a bullet with "Johnse Hatfield" on it.

"You can see what's comin next," Cap pushed on. "We can't just sit and wait for them to pick a time and place to murder us. We don't want no more orphans in this family."

Uncle Jim thrust a bony finger in Pappy's direction. "Anse, they're carryin on just like they did before they stabbed and shot your brother. And left him for dead."

Cap looked around the room for more support, but no one gave an opinion one way or the other. Only he and Uncle Jim were willing to get crosswise of Pappy. Jim never hesitated to speak his mind, probably because he was older than Pappy and had been in the War with him.

Pappy traced his finger along a gouge in the table. "This table's gettin all banged up."

"The table!" Cap spit on it. "We got more important things to talk about."

"*You* tellin *me* what's important?" Pappy squinted up at Cap. "You aint in no position to do that."

Cap gripped the edge of the table, right next to Pappy. "We got a chance to get shed of Randall, maybe a couple of his boys, on a day when they won't be good for nothin."

Pappy closed his eyes and pressed a hand to his chest. "Wonder if the children is gonna come down with the grippe all over again like me?"

Cap froze. This was some kind of trick. Pappy'd had the grippe a month ago, around the first of December, but he'd seemed to be over it. He was probably going to start twisting and turning, ducking and dodging. Cap never knew how to argue with him when he got that way.

"You're not sick. You been out in this weather. You rode five miles to get here."

"For sure, I'm not up to goin after McCoys today." Pappy forced a little cough. "Just not up to it."

"You're not up to it." Cap took a deep breath and leaned on the table toward Pappy. "Let me go into Kentucky after Randall McCoy. All my life you raised me to fight for this family. I want to do that. Right now, today, when it counts."

Pappy unfolded himself from the chair and stood up. He rubbed the shiny Confederate captain's pin, big as a silver dollar, that was always on his shirt collar. "I got the grippe, but I aint dead nor dyin. I aint ready to resign my command here."

Rage clutched at Cap's throat. He tried to calm himself. He edged slowly right up to Pappy until his head of black hair was level with Pappy's, his gray eyes even with Pappy's.

"You was exactly my age." Cap reached out and touched Pappy's pin with two fingers. "Twenty-three when you wore that pin and led your regiment during the War. And you wasn't near as well-trained as me."

Pappy gave a little cough and thumped his fist on his chest.

"Let me lead these men into Kentucky now! Mama would want me to and so would Nancy."

"Better get me a Bateson's Belfry." Pappy hacked and spit into the fireplace. "First sign the grippe's got a holt of me and you're about ready to bury me alive, you bein in such a hurry to take over."

"You got no right to talk to me like that!" Bateson's Belfry, an iron bell mounted on a coffin for its occupant to ring if he was being buried alive!

"I got a right to talk to you any way I want to," Pappy said. "Now sit down and shut up about all this goin into Kentucky." He pointed to the chair at the head of the table. "I'm through with it."

Cap slumped into the still-warm seat.

"That's better. Now, what I'm tellin you to do is to keep a lookout. Get down by the river. See if anybody's been crossin over."

"Go on home." Cap held his head with his hands. "I'll take care of things."

"I don't want nobody hurtin my family. Don't you let em sneak up on us."

"I won't." Cap didn't think he could tolerate much more of Pappy instructing him as though he were a child. "What about. . ." Cap jerked his head in Johnse's direction. His brother, still drunk from last night, had been drinking all day and would be no help at all.

"Johnse stays with you. Watch over him."

Cap clenched his teeth. He always had to watch over Johnse.

"You're in charge now." Pappy's face softened and became a sly smile. As he left, he let in a gust of icy wind, chilling the room.

Chapter 2

Everyone sat listening to Pappy's footsteps crunch down the snow-covered path to the horse barn.

"You're ready, but your Pappy aint about to give up the reins," Uncle Jim said. "You might as well get used to waitin, 'cause you're gonna have to wait until he's dead or pretty near to it."

"We're takin a terrible chance not goin after the McCoys today." Cap rubbed his throbbing temples with his thumbs. "And it's humiliatin to just sit here and do nothin. Humiliatin!"

"Try lookin at it your Pappy's way," Uncle Jim said. "He don't want to see the best part of his life disappear. Bad enough he's not captain of the Logan Regulars like he was in the War. He aint about to give up bein captain of the Hatfields."

"I don't think Pappy's the man he was when he led the Regulars. He's almost fifty years old now. He thinks things over and over and over, waitin for what, I don't know. We'll never get another chance like today."

Uncle Jim screwed up his face and pulled on his beard, which was downright skimpy compared to Pappy's bushy one. "He could be right, you know. Wouldn't be the first time Randall McCoy was all fuss and feathers and no fight."

"Gettin rid of Randall and his boys would sure make loggin easier this spring." Cousin Elliot had a good head on his shoulders and was worth listening to. "We wouldn't have to waste men on guard duty. We could put em to work. And remember how, a few years ago, we had to jump off them logs into the river when we was under fire? We lost half our timber in the Tug. I'd be happy not to see them days again."

"Why the heck didn't you bring that up when Pappy was here?" Cap glared at Elliot, even though he knew why. Elliot had long ago decided there was nothing to gain and everything to lose in arguing with Pappy.

"We've been told to scout around, so let's just go do it," Charlie Carpenter said. Charlie had joined Pappy's logging crew two years ago. He was so good with an axe and a saw it was hard to believe he'd been a schoolteacher before he'd ridden into the mountains where there were no schools. And Charlie was pretty handy with a rifle.

"What do you say, Cap? You're in the captain's seat now," Uncle Jim said.

At the needle in Jim's words, Cap winced. "Maybe we'll get lucky and find Randall layin in wait for us down by the river."

Uncle Jim snorted. "If I know Randall McCoy, he aint out freezin his butt off. He's inside by a warm fire, with a jug."

"We're the only dumbbutts out here." Johnse was now sprawled flat on his back on the filthy mattress.

Cap turned his head away from Johnse to hide his sorrow and disgust at his brother's condition. "Come on. Let's move out." Picket duty instead of an attack! He wanted to get this chore done and go home.

Each man grabbed his hat, coat, rifle, and cartridge belt. Cap had to hold the door open and call out "Johnse!" before his brother reluctantly joined them. Outside the cold air bit into their flesh as they filed down the path to the horse barn, which was built on the side of the mountain away from the Tug where anyone trying to steal or shoot the horses would have to pass close by the fort first.

Boots and hooves clatter-clanked on the hard frozen earth as each man, his breath a puff of smoke in the frosty air, untied reins stiffened with cold and mounted his horse. Cap shoved his rifle into its saddle holster, right by saddle bags stuffed with ammo. Nine-and-a-half pounds of wood and steel, loaded with eighteen cartridges, his Yellow Dog Winchester repeater was almost a part of his body.

As was his horse. Once atop Traveller, Cap rubbed the horse's shaggy winter-coated neck and got a head-turn in reply. "We'll ride down to the river and look things over. Goin down Thacker Mountain in sight of Kentucky shouldn't be no problem today. All the same, ride quiet and keep your eyes and ears open."

They rode into the woods, single file, a line of coonskin caps and black floppy hats bobbing along the trail, rifles poking out from saddle holsters, bandoleers of cartridges strapped over their coats. Around them, leafless branches stretched their bony fingers up from dense stands of oak and maple. Snow dusted the ground and clumped on fallen logs and outcroppings of stone.

Cap pulled up beside Tom Chambers. He pointed to the pitch torches Tom had tied behind his saddle.

"What you got them things for?"

"You know I don't like to ride in the dark." Tom scowled at Cap.

Cap dropped back, shaking his head. They weren't going to be out here after dark. Chambers liked to set fires, plain and simple. He liked to be ready for any opportunity that might come up.

He rode up to Cousin Elliot. "It's gonna eat at me a long time, missin our big chance to stop the McCoys today."

"You had me sold. I was seein myself, lyin on my back on a log raft, floatin down the Tug, happy as a June bug, not a worry on my mind."

"Hah!" Cap snorted. "I see myself lyin on my stomach on that raft, re-turnin McCoy fire."

"One of these days some McCoy's gonna get lucky," Elliot said. "And pick one of us off."

Cap rode back and had a few words with Bobby Lee, Cotton Top, and Charlie Carpenter. Nobody was happy about the prospect of rafting logs down the Tug under fire. They might have to resort to doing it at night, dodging other logs, shoals, islands, and the river bank in the dark.

When they came to an overlook of the Tug, Cap raised his hand to get the men to halt. Far below, the river gleamed like gun metal, snaking its way between Kentucky and West Virginia. He squinted into the low winter sun to study the ford and the switchback trail up the cliffs on the Kentucky side. Not a dang soul out here.

He took off his gloves and flexed his fingers anyway. The trigger finger had stiffened. If they should be lucky enough to spot the enemy, he wanted to be ready.

"Let's go," he half-whispered. At his motion the riders began winding down the switchback trail.

He was in charge of scouting today. But it looked like he'd never get to be the leader he was meant to be. Pappy had come home from the War and put his captain's cap on his two-year-old head, not on his older brother Johnse's. That's how he'd come to be called Cap instead of Bill or Anse after the William Anderson Hatfield he'd been named at birth. He'd known as long as he could remember that he was Pappy's favorite.

Johnse was Mama's boy. When Pappy was away at the War, Johnse had spent his first four years alone with his mother and never quite took to Pappy. Even though Johnse was older than Cap and the natural choice for Pappy's next in command, Cap had been chosen over him.

Being the favorite should have counted for more. No matter how many times Pappy reined him in, he always thought the next time would be differ-ent, but it wasn't. The first wretched upset had been the aftermath of the hog trial in 1878. He was fourteen then. The trial was held on the Hatfield side of the Tug because that's where the hog in contention, a razorback with long skinny legs, an ugly sharp snout, and rough brown fur, had turned up. Fattened up on beechnuts and acorns, such pigs were worth a lot because they made fine nutty tasting pork chops and bacon.

* * *

"No room inside for anybody that aint part of the trial!" Justice of the Peace, Deacon Anse, stood blocking the door to his cabin.

While Pappy was saying "Good afternoon, Anse," Cap tried to slip by the Deacon and get inside. But when Pappy said, "You heard the man," he turned and ran for a window. Lots of people were coming to this trial and he didn't want anyone else, especially a McCoy, to get in his way and keep him from seeing it, not when he'd never seen a trial before. And not when the Hatfields were sure to win.

He lucked out and got the best window. He could see all the men inside sitting on the Deacon's kitchen benches and some crates—Floyd Hatfield, who was accused of stealing the hog; Randall McCoy, who claimed the hog was his; witnesses for and against Randall and Floyd; Deacon Anse; the twelve jurors; and a nervous, fidgety hog tied to a table leg.

Cap watched everyone inside settle down before the Deacon ambled in, black suit and white shirt with a stiff collar signs he had authority over the other men in their overalls and mountain boots. Deacon Anse's whole name was Anderson Hatfield, just like Pappy's, and they both had titles—Deacon Anse because he was fair and respected, and Devil Anse because he was feared and respected. Fair was good, but fear, Cap knew, counted for a lot more.

"Look at them two." He jabbed Johnse with his elbow and pointed to Pappy and Randall McCoy, sitting side by side. Pappy's beard jutted in front of him and his broad strong hands lay on his knees mere inches from the Winchester propped against a nearby wall. Old Randall McCoy's faded red mustache drooped over a weak, nervous mouth.

"You, Randall McCoy, accuse this man, Floyd Hatfield, of stealin this here hog?" Deacon Anse opened the trial.

McCoy's effort to look important by perching on his crate like a proud rooster and preening his moustache made Cap laugh. Randall was a sniveling sissy, always complaining, usually about something he'd made up like this hog-stealing charge. Mama always said Aunt Sally had a lot to put up with in that cantankerous old goat. She liked Aunt Sally in spite of who she'd married.

"I surely do," McCoy replied. "Found my pig at Floyd's when we was visitin my wife's sister. Bad luck, her bein married to that thief."

Three of Randall's sons hooted from one of the windows.

"Dumbdungs," Cap called out loud enough for them to hear. "Think you're so big? You aint nothin."

"And you, Floyd Hatfield, claim the hog is yours?" Deacon Anse went on.

Floyd, dark brown hair neatly combed, wearing a cleaner shirt than Cap had ever seen on him, sat up straight. "'Course it's my hog! He's got my mark on him."

"I seen Floyd mark his ear myself." Cap's cousin Bill spoke up. "Floyd's boy throwed the pig to the ground and Floyd cut his mark."

"Liar! Floyd stole that pig." It was Tolbert McCoy, Randall's oldest son, shouting from another window. At twenty-eight, he was the same age as Bill, but half the man in Cap's estimation.

"Come in here and say I'm a liar!" yelled Bill, his hand on the hilt of his hunting knife.

Cap leaned out of the window to see if any McCoys were heading inside for Bill. If they did, he was ready to fight at his cousin's side.

"Shut up, you outside there!" Deacon Anse yelled. "I can't hear the evidence with all this hollerin."

"I brung my cousin Bill and my cousin Anderson to tell you that's my hog and that's my mark on his ear," Floyd said. "My wife'll tell you the same thing if you want her to come inside."

"We heard Bill and I'll listen to Anse," Deacon Anse replied. "But leave your wife out of this, her bein a sister to Randall's wife. I'll not allow your quarrel to make trouble between sisters."

Cap agreed. Fair enough, no need dragging women into the argument.

"That Floyd's mark, Anse?" the Deacon asked Pappy.

"Dang right. It's a peculiar sign Injuns made on rocks around here. Aint no one else got one like it."

"Bill and Floyd put that mark on after they stole him," Randall said.

"We all turn our hogs out to forage," said the Deacon. "And we all put our own mark on them. Where's your mark on this one, McCoy?"

"It's hid by Floyd's mark. Look and you'll see." Randall, with his sixteen-year-old son Calvin's help, got hold of the hog and held it still.

The twelve jurors and the Deacon crowded around.

"Look here." Randall displayed the notches cut in the hog's ear. "Here's Floyd's marks. And here's mine down amongst em, pretty near spoilt by Floyd's."

"There aint no marks in this ear but mine," Floyd said. "The rest is damage done from livin in the woods."

"The heck you say!" Randall stomped a booted foot on the floor.

The hog squealed and peed on Deacon Anse's clean wood floor. Cap burst out laughing along with everyone else, Hatfields and McCoys.

"Darned hog! My place is gonna stink like hog piss for a month." Deacon Anse glared at Randall.

Randall scowled at the Deacon. "You been against me right from the start."

"Let's grab our hog and take it home!" Phamer McCoy yelled from a window.

"Shut up, all of you!" Deacon Anse glared at the windows and door. "I want this jury to get busy."

"You Wall Hatfield, Elias Hatfield, Jim Vance, Mose Chafin. . ." He pointed to six of the Hatfield kin. "And you Sam McCoy, Selkirk McCoy, Asa Harmon. . ." He designated six McCoys.

"I picked this jury—six Hatfields and six McCoys—fair and square. They'll decide the trial, not me and not you." He pointed around at the spectators standing outside.

Pappy always said Deacon Anse was a smart man. He'd lasted longer as Justice of the Peace than anyone else, and he'd never been shot at on account of people being unhappy with the way he ran a trial.

"Floyd Hatfield has went and stole our pig," Randall said. "And them two. . ." He pointed a trembling finger, first at Floyd, then at Cousin Bill. "Is total outright liars."

Bill jumped to his feet and charged at Randall, only to be blocked by Deacon Anse.

"Sit down," the Deacon said. "This here's a trial, not a fight."

"No man's gonna call me a liar and get away with it," Bill shouted.

"Get over to t'other side." Pappy walked over to Bill and pointed to the cabin wall across from where Randall was sitting. "Let's get on with this trial."

With a sulky look, Bill did as he was told.

Pappy had told Bill the right thing to do, Cap supposed. If a fight broke out, they might never finish the trial and see his family win. They could fight after the trial.

"I been tryin to make out this here hog's mark," one of the jurors said. "Can't find none but Floyd's."

Several of the crowd gasped. It was Randall's cousin Selkirk McCoy, going against his own kin right out in public.

Cap, like everyone else at this trial, knew Selkirk was in a tough spot. For the past few years Selkirk had earned a better living than lots of people in the mountains by working on Pappy's logging crew. He often stayed on the West Virginia side of the Tug for several days at a time. But, still, he was a McCoy.

"Look closer, Selkirk," Randall said. "You got McCoy eyes."

"I can see for myself, Randall, without you tellin me," Selkirk retorted. "I say there aint but one mark on that hog."

Onlookers shouted their opinions from the windows and door.

"Shut up!" Deacon Anse bellowed. "The jury will now make a decision. I charge you to take your duties seriously. You must decide on the basis of the evidence and on what you know to be fair, not on the basis of your feelings and family ties. And do it quick so we can all quit wastin our time on this stinkin ugly pig!"

Not decide on the basis of family ties! Like Pappy said, the law was full of tricks you had to watch out for. What kind of man wouldn't stick by his family?

"How many say that's Floyd's hog?" Deacon Anse queried.

All six Hatfields and Selkirk McCoy raised their hands.

"How many say he's McCoy's?"

Five McCoys raised their hands.

"That settles it. Floyd, take your hog home."

Cap whooped and wheeled away from the window. Hatfields all around the cabin were laughing and slapping each other on the back.

Randall McCoy came storming out of the cabin, eyes down, the corners of his mouth set in a pout. Selkirk had only gotten to the doorway when Randall turned and pointed at him as though his finger were the business end of a rifle. "You got a nerve callin yourself a McCoy. You are the enemy of the Mc-Coys."

The next thing Cap knew, Cousin Bill was face to face with Randall. "Now who was you callin a liar? Your own cousin says that's Floyd's pig."

"You're a liar," Randall snarled. "You and the rest of the pig-stealin Hatfields. Come on, boys. Let's get out of here." He motioned to Tolbert, Phamer,

Calvin, and young Randall.

Bill made right for Randall, but had no chance to get near him. Tolbert lowered his head and ran hard at Bill, butting him off his feet and knocking the breath out of him.

The whoreson! Cap ran to jump on Tolbert, but got stopped in his tracks. Someone had grabbed the shoulder straps of his overalls. He swung to slug his opponent. It was Pappy. He'd better not make another move.

"I don't aim to get into no fight today," Pappy said gruffly.

Still holding onto Cap, Pappy went on. "Tolbert McCoy, get out of here before I let this wildcat son of mine loose on you. He's a mean one and he'll tear your head off. Wouldn't want to see that happen to you."

"Let me at him!" Cap let out a roar, raising his hands with his fingers curled like claws, making like a cornered bear.

Trying to catch his breath, Bill got slowly to his feet.

"Stay away from the McCoys, Bill. If they want to fight, let em go home and fight amongst theirselves." Pappy turned to Randall. "We won this here trial fair and square. Now go on home and quit stirrin up trouble."

"Fair and square! You won this here trial 'cause you brung all your men, every one of em armed, and scared Selkirk McCoy, who we all know to be a yellow coward, into goin against his family. I don't call that fair and square. Selkirk'll stay on your side of the river from now on if he knows what's good for him."

As the McCoys rode away, Cap had a notion to fire his rifle over their heads a few times, but Pappy was in charge here.

On the way home, Pappy rode up beside Cap. "I aint about to let nobody get knifed or shot over a dang ugly pig that's ours anyway. I pick my times and I pick my places for my fights. You gotta learn to do that. What do you think would of happened to me and my men in the War if we'd wasted men and ammunition on every tom-fool quarrel that came our way!"

Cap fought back tears. All he'd done, what he always did, was stand up for his family the way he should.

* * *

Although there'd been a lot of caterwauling, no Hatfield or McCoy before or on the day of the trial had done actual harm to the other. But the hostilities begun there had grown so fierce over the ten years since the trial that many of the people present on that occasion, including Cousin Bill, had met violent deaths. Things hadn't changed much for Cap in those years. Pappy was still training him, teaching him, yet never allowing him to be the leader he was meant to be. Today would have been perfect for him to be the one to end the feud, and here he was on lookout, a job that even Cotton Top could do.

Halfway down the switchback to the river, Cap halted the men before emerging from the trees into full view of anyone on the Kentucky shore. Once more he neither heard nor saw a soul. He was doomed to inaction when action could do so much. In only a few minutes they were back in the partial protection of leafless trees and scattered boulders.

* * *

There were times when Pappy's trust in him had raised Cap's expectations. Like when he was eighteen and they'd stood with Uncle Jim beside a creek, planning to build a sawmill. The springtime creek was running fast, swirling to the edge of a steep fall where it plunged down the mountainside, carrying branches, small trees, and a struggling young raccoon in its muddy waters. Cap reveled in the roar and the chilling spray on his face and arms.

"Listen, Cap." Pappy had to shout to be heard. "If we build a sawmill we can turn our timber into lumber right here and sell to everybody in these mountains. We won't have to float logs down the river to the mills on the Ohio. Folks around here won't have to go all that way for boards and beams. With a mill, I'll have cash to pay the crews and buy supplies every spring without borrowin."

Cap grinned at Pappy with admiration. Many local families had been forced to sell their land to bankers, well-to-do store owners, and eastern mining and timber corporations when they'd been pressured with debt suits and heavy taxes that mountain people didn't know how to deal with and couldn't pay. Men in the county seat of Logan were after Pappy's land, too, bringing phony suits for illegal lumbering and unpaid taxes, trying to drag Pappy into court until his cash well ran dry. A sawmill of their own might bring the Hatfields more money than any of the Logan businessmen were making.

"You're the smartest man in the mountains!" Cap shouted, with only a shade of dishonesty. He'd seen signs he was beginning to outstrip his Pappy.

"I want a band saw for my mill," Pappy shouted back. "They got one in Catlettsburg that turns out lumber ten times as fast as a circular saw. They're sayin you need a big river to make it work, but maybe a big enough dam can turn our creek into a big enough river."

Cap had noticed that a band saw, which had the potential to enrich the Hatfields, was about the only part of the modern world Pappy gave a darn for. He'd have nothing to do with reading and the new ideas about sending all children to school. He always said he'd tell his children everything they needed to know and that books and newspapers were mostly lies. He didn't like the new towns with as many as three or four hundred people crowded in together, making rules about where your animals could roam and what you couldn't do or say on the streets, and laws telling you how you had to behave on Sunday, like no spitting or swearing near the church. When Cap and his brothers decided to shave off their beards, Pappy had ridiculed their new-fangled foolishness.

"Peck brothers have a fifteen-foot drop for their mill," Cap yelled. "Said they wished they'd of made it higher. And they're only grindin grain, they aint powerin a sawmill."

"How much we got to dig out to get a eighteen-, twenty-foot drop?" Pappy had seen for himself the size of Peck's mill.

Cap handed Pappy a long cord rolled around a stick, then fastened together five sections of wood dowel by screwing them into each other. He'd had the Logan carpenter make each section four feet long. He tied one end of the cord Pappy was holding through an eye in the end dowel and sloshed down the muddy embankment alongside the waterfall. Keeping the cord horizontal over the tops of intervening bushes, he raised the twenty-foot pole until it was vertical and the cord was as level as he could eyeball it.

"To here," Cap shouted to the men above him. "This is where we have to start diggin into the mountain."

"By gum, you're good. Mark it!" Pappy said.

Cap felt his face go hot with joy at the well deserved admiration in Pappy's eyes. He could figure with numbers like no one else in the family. He was downright smart and he knew it. He jammed the bottom dowel into the soft, wet earth before climbing back upstream on the slippery creek bank.

"We'll bring a crew, maybe a dozen men, down here in August, dig it out, and pile up a good stone dam." Pappy turned to Uncle Jim. "How long you think that'll take?"

"With a dozen? A week or so."

"And then what? Who's gonna run this fine sawmill?" Cap grinned at Pappy.

Uncle Jim put his arm over Cap's shoulders. "I'm thinkin of a feller that knows timber and has got a good head."

"Captain of the sawmill," Pappy said. "Want to give it a try, Cap?"

"Yes, sir!" Cap answered like an officer in the army. "We'll have a sawmill like no one around these mountains ever seen before."

Running a sawmill when he was eighteen! His future would be guaranteed, free from worries about hanging onto land and owing people money.

"What about that band saw?" Uncle Jim said. "How we gonna get our hands on one of them things?"

"I'll go down to Catlettsburg and find out where they bought theirs," Cap answered. He wanted Pappy to see he could be counted on to plan for everything they'd need. "I reckon I'll get the carpenter in Logan to give us a hand on the mill wheel. He'll lay the thing out on paper, and me and the crew'll do most of the hammer and saw work."

It started to drizzle, a warm rain from the soggy late spring sky. A haze of misty water hung over the creek. Cap could see where the mill wheel would turn, the huge wheel going round and round through the mist, groaning and straining under its load.

"I can see our wheel spinnin," he shouted and waved. A rainbow spread a perfect arc over the creek.

"I see it, too," Pappy cackled. "Like a spinnin wheel spinnin gold."

"Dream of gold at night, have good luck in the mornin." Cap repeated the old saying. "It's a good luck sign for the mill."

"No more money worries next year." Uncle Jim was laughing. Cap hardly ever saw him look so happy.

"We'll buy ourselves some fancy suits in Logan, store-bought frocks for Mama and the girls," Cap said. "We can even go to Ohio and take a ride on a train."

"Now who'd want to do a thing like that?" Pappy snorted. He'd seen one down by the Ohio. "A body can ride a horse or drive a buggy hisself, but no one knows who's sittin up there drivin that train!"

"Wonder why nobody else thought of buildin a sawmill," Cap said.

"Most folks just wait for what comes to em," Pappy replied. "Them old preachers teaches em to be that way. Predestination they call it. Accordin to them, our lives is all decided before we're born. My religion teaches me I'm predestined to get what I go after, and I'm predestined to get nothin if I don't work for it."

Cap didn't think much of the Primitive Baptist predestinators either. As far as he could see Pappy's religion nearly always worked for him, while the primitives who sat back and waited for God to show them what He had in mind were still waiting. The Primitives said theirs was the way of God and Pappy's land trading and selling timber was the way of the Devil.

"Had a argument with a predestinator t'other day," Pappy said. "I told him if Abraham, that feller in the Old Testament, hadn't of used his free will, Jesus wouldn't never of been born."

Jim grinned. "How you figure that, Anse?"

Cap laughed. He and Uncle Jim knew good and well the point to the story would be how Pappy had outsmarted the predestinator.

"Well, it's like this." Pappy's eyes twinkled. "If Abraham would of sacrificed his son Isaac, there wouldn't of been no need of having Jesus sacrificed for us, no need of Jesus hisself. 'Course God told Abraham, at the very last minute as I recollect, he didn't have to kill his son. And Abraham spared Isaac. But he used his free will. He could of gone ahead and kilt the boy and then there'd of been no need for Jesus. He would of never been borned." Pappy guffawed and slapped his leg. "Feller just stood there, his mouth a-gapin. Didn't know what to say."

Cap contemplated the mud at his feet. Pappy had picked a story about a father sacrificing his favorite son.

* * *

Cap's sawmill ambitions had been frustrated for five years now. When Pappy had sought a permit for a dam, the judge had informed him that the signatures of his downstream neighbors who used creek water for their crops and livestock were required. "You illiterates would know what the law says if you'd learn to read," the judge had sneered. Pappy had hired a lawyer to prepare the document, and they'd finally collected the signatures. Now all they lacked was the money to build the dam and mill.

Cap yearned for that mill. As things stood, he was left wondering if Pappy would have actually let him take charge of such an important job.

One by one, the men emerged from the trees onto the flat, snow-covered river shore. Its voice choked with ice, the river was silent.

Cap rode back and forth along the bank, examining the ground. "All I see is rabbit tracks where they was just hoppin around with nothin after em." If the rabbits had been running from a hunter or a dog, their toenails would have dug deeper into the snow. "Ice aint broke in. No one's been down here." His heart sank. He'd been clinging to the slim hope that they'd encounter at least one McCoy.

"What'd you expect?" Uncle Jim said. "It's New Year's."

"Maybe we ought to take a look on the other side." Cap pointed across the river. "They could of come over there and decided not to cross."

"We got nothin but enemies over there, Cap," Uncle Jim said. "And if you'll remember, a few of us got Kentucky warrants out for us."

"You see anyone with a warrant?" Cap laughed.

Uncle Jim grinned. "Have we ever seen a sheriff out here?"

"We can't do our job right if we stay on this side." Cap searched Uncle Jim's face for agreement. Every step closer to the McCoy place increased their chances of encountering the enemy.

"This'd be the first time I been to Kentucky in almost five years." Jim seemed to be agreeing to go.

Cap nudged Traveller forward onto the ice. It held. "Injun file!" he called out.

Johnse balked. "I'm not goin."

Uncle Jim slapped Johnse's horse on the rump to get it started. "We're gonna take a look, that's all."

Soon the eight of them were strung out across the frozen river, easy pickings for a rifleman hiding over in Kentucky.

Chapter 3

On the other side, Cap rode up and down the shore at the bottom of the cliff. There were no hoof prints, no footprints. He peered up the cliff side trail, then turned to Uncle Jim. "I say we ride into those woods and look around."

"Pappy's gonna kill you," Johnse said, his eyes suddenly open and alert. "He told you to come down here and look things over. That's all."

"That's all I'm doin. Lookin." Cap glanced around at the others. Bobby Lee saluted—he'd do whatever Cap told him to. Tom Chambers was grinning like he'd heard a joke. Charlie Carpenter fingered the butt of his Winchester, looking ready but not exactly eager. Cousin Elliot, always a cautious man, said he'd agree to going a little farther up the trail. Cotton Top was gazing absently around, humming to himself.

Johnse looked Cap in the eye, drew his pistol and fired into the air, setting the horses to whinnying and bucking.

"Goldarn! They'll hear that all the way to Randall's," Cap yelled. He charged towards Johnse.

But Uncle Jim rode between them. "You put that thing away."

Johnse shoved the pistol back into its holster. "Sorry. Accident. Just checkin it out."

If Pappy hadn't ordered him to take Johnse along, Cap would have told him to turn around and go home.

"Let's get goin," Jim said. "I'll watch him."

Cap tapped Traveller's side and headed up the cliff side switchback. When they reached the top without encountering any sign of another person, Cap could see no reason why they shouldn't ride a bit further in the direction of the McCoy cabin.

As they began winding along a narrow trail, surrounded by trees and boulders, Cap trotted up beside Uncle Jim.

"I'm thinkin we outnumber them," Cap said. "For sure Randall and Calvin will be there. Calvin's a good shot. But the only other son of Randall's livin in these parts, the only one that ever had any sense, is Jim. He probably went home by now, if he was ever there for New Year's in the first place. Randall's nephews—well, I figure Jeff has a good time when he's drinkin, maybe Sam would come along, and I don't know about Bud. Even the McCoys get tired of his temper. The most that'll be at Randall's is six, probably only four, and maybe only two."

"And we got eight," Jim said.

"We got eight and they don't know we're comin. We'd catch em un-awares. Do what we gotta do and be back in West Virginia before anyone in Kentucky knows what happened." Sheriffs from the two states were supposed to enforce the law in the Tug Valley, but they almost never travelled over the mountains from their county seats. They sure wouldn't be out here, getting in the way, today.

"I was thinkin," Jim said. "About your Pappy's last words as he was leavin—'You're in charge now.' He was puttin you in command of these men. Not for good. He aint ready for that. Just for today. That's as far as he could go."

"He was just handin me a chore, like I was a little boy."

"I think he's tryin you out. He wants to see what you do when you're on your own."

"You think so?" Cap's heart was beating faster, his body burning like it was on fire, his head ready to explode. "We could settle this once and for all."

"Some days I stand on my farm, lookin over into Kentucky, wishin I'd get a clear shot at Randall. I believe the rest of the McCoys would stay away from us if it wasn't for him." Uncle Jim rode to the head of the column, stopped the men in a quiet, snow-covered meadow and lined them up.

Cap halted Traveller in front of them.

"Seein as how our enemy's asleep at the watch—not a sign of any of em out here—I've decided to attack. We're goin after Randall McCoy and any of his boys that's there with him." He liked the commanding ring to his voice, felt he came by it naturally. "We'll start this year out right and end the killin of our men for good."

He stared at Johnse. By promising to end the killing, he'd hoped to get Johnse behind the raid.

"Pappy's gonna knock your head off." Johnse was enraged.

"I want you all to swear," Uncle Jim said, "that you will not leave Kentucky until we've finished off Randall McCoy."

Cap shivered. He watched the solemn faces—Bobby Lee and Elliot grim, Tom and Charlie determined, Cotton Top eager.

"Mama aint gonna like this neither," Johnse blurted out.

"Mama don't like her boys gettin shot at," Cap said, suspecting Mama wasn't his real reason for balking. But still he could see Mama twisting the bottom of her apron if she heard what they were planning to do.

"Swear," Jim said. "All of you swear."

One by one they swore, except for Johnse.

"If we go back on our word, may Hell be our grave," Cap added. "Let's go serve up McCoy a fine supper of lead!"

He rode erectly in front, leading his men to meet the enemy, running through plans in his head as any general worth his salt would do. The best strategy was to wait to attack after dark. He'd yell out for Randall and his men to come out with their hands up. If there was no surrender, he'd have to order heavy gunfire to drive the McCoys away from the windows and gun ports, then charge the place and batter a door open. There was no way McCoy could escape.

Not being a part of any official army, he'd never get a captain's pin or a captain's hat for what he was about to do. Maybe a scar from battle. A small scar. One he could point to and say, "I got this the day we ended the feuds forever."

As he'd been taught from an early age, he'd protect his family, no matter what he had to do.

* * *

He was eight and Johnse was ten when Pappy had said, "Let's see how many terrapins you boys can find."

With the summer sun warming their skin and their bare feet in the soft warm earth, he and Johnse ran through the tomato and cucumber patches, picking up turtles with squares of black, brown, and yellow on their backs, playing a game of who could find the most. They piled them at Pappy's feet, and he herded the ones that tried to get away.

When they could find no more, they grinned and looked up at Pappy. He picked one up, legs and head weaving in a struggle to escape, and dashed it against a tree stump. Its shell split open and guts and blood gushed out. "That's one terrapin aint gonna eat our crops no more."

Johnse burst into tears and cried out, "We didn't know you was gonna kill em." Cap felt faint, his eyes stung and his stomach heaved.

Then Pappy reached down, picked up a terrapin, and handed it to Cap. "Do it, son."

Cap looked down at the weaving head with its bright, beady eyes. He looked up at Pappy—maybe he was only joking. But Pappy's face was set, his nose hooking insistently out over his bushy beard. Cap heaved the turtle, heard a sickening splat, and saw the turtle's blood and flesh spurt out, its front legs still twitching. He willed himself not to throw up.

Johnse had run away. But Cap had helped Pappy smash terrapins against a tree stump until all were dead. With each turtle, Cap had felt more strongly about the rightness of what he was doing to protect the family garden and less about how much the turtles wanted to live.

* * *

Cap glanced back at the line of men strung out behind him and shook his head as Johnse sipped from a shiny brown jug hanging from his saddle. His brother, whose handsomeness had once made grown women fidget, had become a shaggy mess from too much whiskey and bad living. Pappy ought to give up on trying to make a soldier of Johnse. He already had one good soldier-son who never let him down.

Cap had always been proud to fight for his family. What a difference there was between the Hatfields and families headed by weak men, frightened little rabbits, too scared to defend themselves, who sooner or later lost everything because the law was never around to protect them. If they went running to a mountain preacher for help, the preacher only made them fear God and the Devil instead of other men. He and Pappy would have none of that—they always made sure fear was their ally, not their enemy.

Chapter 4

After they'd picked their way down the steep side of one last hill to the edge of the clearing where the McCoy cabin stood, Cap reined in Traveller. Taking great care to be quiet, he and his men dismounted. They tied their horses well outside the clearing and huddled together.

"We'll sneak around and surround the cabin before dark," Cap said. "Come over here, and we'll see how things are laid out."

Peering between trees in the waning sunlight, they saw they were at the bottom of a slight rise below two cabins connected by an open passageway. Smaller structures were scattered about the cabins. Snow blanketed the ground and partly covered tree stumps in the clearing and crop stubble in a garden. Cap turned to Johnse. "What's in them cabins?"

Johnse shrugged. "I aint been here for a few years."

"We could use your help, Johnse!" Cap pointed to the cabin on the right. "What's that one?"

"It's the main cabin, where they cook and eat. There's a couple of beds in the loft."

"Smoke's comin from the chimney, so someone's in there," Cap said. "And that one?" He pointed to the left.

"Sleepin cabin. Beds and bunks."

"Where can we hide 'til it gets dark?"

Johnse dug at the snow with the toe of his boot.

"Come on. Don't quit on me now, Johnse." He didn't like to force Johnse to deal with painful, conflicted memories, but he needed to know the facts if he was going to conduct a good raid.

Johnse let his gaze wander around the clearing, then pointed to a rough-hewn board structure.

"That's the corn crib. Someone could hunker down behind it. Chicken coop and pig pens are over there." He pointed to the left. "But there's nothin in them things to keep a bullet from goin right through. The smokehouse down this way is where I'd want to hide. Somebody with the guts to run for it could get behind the outhouse or the stone well up close to the cabins."

Cap saw the need to cover four doorways—the two opening onto the passageway and the two on the other side of the two cabins.

"Seein as you like the smokehouse, I want you and Uncle Jim to hide behind it and cover the passageway door of the sleepin cabin." Uncle Jim would keep an eye on Johnse. "You wouldn't mind shootin Randall if he come out that door, would you?"

"Roseanne always hoped he'd come around to treatin her like a man should treat his daughter." Johnse sighed. "But he didn't."

"Here's your chance to get even, Johnse." Cap hoped more anger than sympathy would run in Johnse's veins tonight. "When it gets dark, I'll holler for Randall and his boys to come out and give theirselfs up. We'll give em a chance to surrender, but if they don't come out right away, I'll call out two more times and you fellers call out right after me so's they'll know we got a lot of men surroundin em."

Cap nodded to Tom Chambers, whose shaggy hair hung almost to his eager, shining eyes, and Charlie Carpenter who was listening intently. He told them to position themselves where they could cover the rear sleeping cabin door.

"Remember, if they come out peaceful, we don't do nothin." Cap watched their faces to be sure they'd heard him. "Don't shoot unless I say, but if I say, get any man that comes out that door."

Tom held up two of his pine torches. "What about these?"

"Hang onto em. We might fire the cabins if we can't get em out no other way. But we're gonna warn em first, and we aint gonna hurt no women or children. Understand?" He paired Tom Chambers with Charlie Carpenter because Charlie was more of a thinker. They'd balance each other.

Next Cap turned to his cousin Elliot and younger brother Bobby Lee. Robert E. Lee Hatfield was six feet four inches tall and weighed almost three hundred pounds, a hard man to hide. He could shoot, but never went looking for a fight. And he never challenged Cap's position as Pappy's favorite son, even though he was next to Cap in age. He assigned them to the back door of the main cabin.

"No shootin unless I say," he reminded them. "My aim is to get Randall and any grown men he has with him without hurtin no one else." Cap patted Elliot on the back. Elliot was tough and always kept his head in the face of danger.

When he turned to Cotton Top, it was already getting dark. "You and me'll get behind the corn crib and cover the passageway door to the main cabin."

Cotton Top, his white-curled head bobbing, made funny little snorts. Cap liked having Cotton Top along. Everybody, including the Widow Mounts who'd adopted him, said he was a half-wit, but he did what he was told and he was a good shot.

"You're a good man," he told Cotton Top. "Just don't shoot or do nothin unless I tell you to."

"I'm your man, Cappie."

Cap winced. Nobody but Mama called him Cappie. It was not a suitable way to address a commanding officer in front of his men.

"We'll get that whore's son McCoy and be home by mornin, rid of the McCoys forever," Cap assured everyone. He waved them off to their positions. Carefully, quietly, they stole away and disappeared into the darkening woods.

He led Cotton Top around the clearing to the corn crib, which was about fifteen feet long, about half that thick, and high as Cap's head—perfect cover.

Cap's heart pounded as he peered around the side of the crib at the main cabin that seemed suddenly very close in the light of a half moon. Low in the sky, the moon cast shadows behind structures and trees—long, dark shadows that could easily conceal a man. Near the cabins last night's snowfall had been trampled on, revealing that the McCoys had spent the day here. Little specks of light were beginning to show around the shuttered windows. Except for the soft snuffling of the pigs across the way and the sound of horses breathing and chomping in the barn, the area was quiet.

Cap pulled off his gloves to free his hands for the trigger and reload pump, then flexed his fingers. This was the hardest time of all, waiting. But it was important to hold their fire and follow the plan. He wanted no slip-ups today. The moon had risen higher when he saw the passageway door of the main cabin open.

"Aim, but hold your fire," he said to Cotton Top. They made out four figures, whose shapes showed they were wearing long skirts, heading across the passageway cluttered with barrels, probably holding pickles, cheese, cabbages, and the like.

"Women and girls goin to the sleepin cabin," Cap said. He heard voices, but made out no words except "Allifair," the name of one of Randall's daughters Cap had known all his life. It looked as though Randall's womenfolk were now in one cabin, the men and boys in the other. Their mission had just gotten simpler.

When he'd allowed enough time to be sure everyone had gotten to his post, he took a deep breath. It was time to call out the McCoys.

Rifle shots exploded from Uncle Jim's and Johnse's post by the smokehouse. A jar in the passageway smashed open.

"You horse's rear!"

That was Uncle Jim hollering. Johnse must have fired, dang him. He hadn't hit anything that mattered.

Cap had to act fast to get back on plan. "Come out, Randall McCoy, and surrender yourself and your men as prisoners of war, and we'll spare your women and children." His voice boomed over the clearing. Everyone inside and outside the cabin must have heard him.

He waited, but no reply came from the cabins.

"He comin out?" Cotton Top called.

Cap pulled on Cotton Top's arm and told him to hush.

"Not over here," Bobby Lee answered.

Cap ground his teeth. Why didn't they shut up?

No sound at all from the cabins. Even the pigs and horses had stopped snuffling and snorting. Cap could hardly bear the pounding of the pulse in his head.

"Goldarn em! Let's see if a little fire'll get em out!" Tom Chambers yelled from somewhere on Cap's right, which was not where he was supposed to be.

"No!" Cap shouted. "Don't do nothin until I say!"

Shots came from the main cabin and pinged through the trees surrounding the clearing.

"Come on out with your men, Randall!" Cap yelled. "We don't want to hurt none of your women and children." He rested his rifle barrel on a tree branch and trained it on the cabin door.

Several bullets shot in his direction answered him. He returned fire at a window where the shutter was open a crack and he'd seen a flash.

Cap lowered his rifle when someone dashed towards the back of the main cabin.

"No!" Cap shouted when he saw it was Tom Chambers, his pitch torch blazing, lighting up the snow-covered clearing. But Chambers leaped onto a stack of firewood piled against the house, pulled himself onto the roof and began torching the shingles. A shot blasted from inside the cabin. Silhouetted by flaring flames, Tom screamed and held up his hand, revealing that all the fingers had been blown away. He rolled off the roof and thudded to the ground. The roof was ablaze.

A boy's voice from inside called out, "That's all the water!"

Tom got up and staggered away from the cabin, into the woods.

"Use the buttermilk from the churn," a woman's voice shouted from the sleeping cabin.

A churn of buttermilk wasn't going to be much help putting out a fire. At any moment Randall and his men would be driven outside.

"Move in on em!" Cap yelled.

He and Cotton Top ran in a crouch toward the cabin, then ducked behind the stone well when they saw the passageway door of the sleeping cabin open.

The flickering light of flames lit up the doorway where two girls in long nightgowns stood.

"Cap Hatfield, I heered your voice," the taller girl said. "I know you're out there."

"That's Allifair,"Cap growled to Cotton Top. "She knows I'm here, and she'll tell the law I kilt her pappy."

"I'll take care of her!" Cotton Top said. He dashed over, shoved his rifle against the terrified girl's breast and pulled the trigger. There was a loud roar and Allifair fell at the feet of the other girl, arms and legs thrashing. Cap heard Allifair's blood gurgling as it gushed, dark and foamy, through a large hole in her nightgown.

"You idiot!" he bellowed at Cotton Top.

"They kilt Allifair," the little girl shrieked.

Cap rushed up to face the child across Allifair's now motionless body. Wide-eyed and trembling, she stared at him and Cotton Top.

"Don't shoot me," she cried. "Please don't."

Before Cap could answer, Randall's wife Sally pulled the child aside and confronted them.

"You murderers!" she screamed.

"Get back inside, old woman," warned Uncle Jim, who'd come running up.

Sally McCoy looked down at her feet where Allifair lay.

"You kilt my girl!" She lunged at Cap.

"It wasn't me." Cap dropped his rifle to catch her in his arms, but she never touched him. Uncle Jim whacked her in the side with his rifle butt, sending her sprawling to the ground.

"For Christ's sake, Jim!" Cap yelled. Had Jim gone mad?

"She might have had a gun or a knife."

"I aint got no gun nor no knife, Jim Vance," Sally cried, crawling towards her daughter's body. "Allifair! Sweetheart!"

29

With a powerful blow, Uncle Jim whacked his rifle butt into the back of her head. Sally McCoy lay motionless, face down beside her daughter. "That'll quieten her."

Cap knelt by Allifair. Her body was now entirely red with blood and very still. He felt for the artery in her neck, listened for her breath, touched her eyelids, called out her name. Allifair was dead.

"You deaf? Didn't you hear me?" Cap yelled. "I said no women and no children, Cotton Top!"

Still on his knees, he turned to Allifair's mother, putting his face near hers. "Sally, Aunt Sally," he called to her, stroking her face. It was still warm, but Aunt Sally didn't answer, didn't move.

"Didn't mean to hit her so hard. But we can't be botherin with the old woman," Uncle Jim said. "We got to do what we come here for."

Cap shook his head, trying to clear his mind. They hadn't come here to kill Aunt Sally and her daughter. They'd come to kill Randall McCoy. If they didn't kill him and whoever else was in the other cabin, this woman and her child would be the only deaths they'd inflicted tonight.

"Look over there!" Bobby Lee was pointing.

Cap leaped to his feet and spotted someone racing away from the main cabin.

"It's Calvin," Bobby Lee said. "Headin for the corn crib."

"Shoot him!" Uncle Jim yelled.

In a fusillade of bullets, Calvin pitched forward. He lay still.

Then, in the opposite direction, Cap spotted a man running only a few feet from the edge of the clearing. Time for one shot. But in a thunderous roar of falling logs, the near wall of the burning cabin collapsed and the man escaped into the woods.

"That was Randall, I know it was," Cap whispered. "I'll find you, Randall McCoy, if you hide in Hell!" he shouted. "Get Tom's torches and light em. We're gonna hunt that mule dung down."

"No!" Uncle Jim said. "We can't cross that clearing, we can't light up no torches. He'll pick us off one by one."

"Well what are we gonna do?" Cap shouted, his voice hoarse with rage. "Let him go free?"

Cotton Top was standing over Allifair's prostrate body. "Now she can't tell on you, Cappie."

"Didn't I tell you no women and children?" Cap dropped his rifle and seized Cotton Top by the shoulders. "No women and children!" He flung Cotton Top onto the snow beside Allifair.

"I done it for you, Cappie," Cotton Top whined from where he lay.

"You all heard me." Cap was trembling.

Johnse came up and stood with his eyes averted from the bodies.

Uncle Jim turned on him.

"This is your fault," he snarled. "If you'd of waited for orders before you shot, we'd of got Randall, not his children."

"I didn't shoot no children, and I didn't hit no women," Johnse shouted. "You think I'd harm Roseanne's mama and sister?"

"Look at this!" Cap pointed to Allifair, the gaping hole in her chest bubbling a red froth. "Look!" Speaking through teeth that chattered even as he tried to clench them, he jabbed a finger towards Aunt Sally, lying face down in the snow. "You're to blame for this. You and Cotton Top and . . ." He searched Uncle Jim's face for some kind of explanation for what he'd done to Aunt Sally.

Johnse jammed the butt of his rifle into the snow. "I didn't shoot neither one of em. How can you be blamin me for this when I didn't want to come over here in the first place?"

Cap looked around at Uncle Jim, Elliot, Bobby Lee, Cotton Top, Charlie Carpenter, and Johnse. He didn't know where Tom Chambers had gone. He didn't know whether to protect the family or hunt the enemy. Should he pull into the woods for the safety of his men or should he pursue Randall? Did he have a right to risk his men's lives? Everything was clear earlier today, everything was a muddle now.

There might still be a way to save this raid. "Let's go into the woods, all of us together and search for Randall. We'll stay out of the clearing, and we won't light no torches."

Cap took a last look at the bodies of the two women, hoping for a miracle, a sign of life. But a bloody nightgown with flung-out arms and legs was all that was left of Allifair, while Aunt Sally lay unmoving with her face pressed into the snow, her fingers stretched toward her daughter.

He was trudging through the snow toward the woods when he heard small voices calling for help. He turned around. The main cabin had nearly burnt to the ground and the fire was heading along the passageway roof toward the sleeping cabin where two little girls in nightgowns stood by the doorway.

He ran back and confronted the children. "Is anybody else inside?"

When they shook their heads no, he picked up a child under each arm and carried them screaming and struggling all the way across the clearing to the barn.

"Stay in here," he said, depositing them on the hay. "The fire won't come this far." He left them holding onto each other and sobbing.

Snow clouds slid over the moon, but flames lit the clearing, the smoke-house, the corn crib, and the well. The air smelled of burning wood and pine tar. Embers and ashes fell around him as he passed the cabins, one burnt to the ground, the other half consumed. By the time he met his men in the woods, it was too dark to see much of anything.

They'd only stumbled about a hundred yards through snow-covered underbrush in search of Randall when they came across Tom Chambers. Cap forced a shot of Johnse's whiskey down his throat, ripped Chambers's shirt to make a sling for his arm, lifted him into his saddle and tied him there.

Chapter 5

Cap rode sweep in the rear, watching Tom Chambers's limp and moaning form, tied into the saddle, flip-flopping every which way. Riding into Kentucky he and Chambers had both felt like a man and a half. Now, coming back, Cap had shrunk to half a man and Chambers would never be whole again. He, Pappy's son, had led a raid that had killed a woman and her children and let the man they'd come for get away. How could he live with himself after today? He was lower than a barn rat, lower than a flea on that rat's behind.

With his great military mind, why couldn't he have come up with a plan that would work? If only he'd left Johnse in the woods to watch over the horses and taken Chambers's torches away from him. He and the rest of the men should have crept silently up to the cabin, waited for the womenfolk to go to the sleeping cabin, then begun firing without calling out for a surrender in voices that would be recognized. When they'd gotten close enough, they'd have fired at the windows and doors of the main cabin until they were splintered and shattered, run up, aimed inside and killed Randall and Calvin, nobody else. He smashed a snow-laden tree branch with his gloved hand so hard his hand ached.

He repeated how it should have gone over and over to himself until it seemed almost as if the raid had happened that way. Leave Johnse with the horses, take away Chambers's torches, don't call out so his voice could be recognized, burn no cabins, shoot only Randall and possibly Calvin. Do no harm to Allifair and Aunt Sally, who could have spent the rest of their lives in peace when their father and husband was no longer starting trouble.

Cap could only console himself that he hadn't actually shot anyone, hadn't hit anyone, hadn't ordered any killings. In fact, he'd ordered his men *not* to kill women and children. Cotton Top had murdered Allifair, Uncle Jim had gone crazy and hit Aunt Sally too hard, Cap didn't know who'd shot Calvin, and Johnse had started all the shooting that never should have happened. He wasn't as guilty as any of them.

And now that he thought about it, he realized that no one alive had seen any of their raiding party, let alone witnessed a shooting. Randall probably hadn't gotten a clear view of Cap or any of his men and could only guess which Hatfields had been out there in the dark. Allifair and her mother had seen him and Uncle Jim and Cotton Top, but they were both gone. The little girls he'd rescued, whoever they were, didn't know him. And he'd make sure they never got the chance to see and identify him. He and his men were in the clear as far as the law was concerned. Not a living soul could say otherwise.

So he hadn't killed anyone and couldn't be identified. But he had led this miserable raid, and whatever the outcome of the battle, the commanding officer got the praise or the blame. When Pappy found out what had happened tonight, that would end his dreams of someday becoming head of the family.

He couldn't explain Uncle Jim's vicious attack on Aunt Sally even though he understood the source of his uncle's rages. Jim and his sister, Cap's grandma, had grown up despised by their rich kinfolk back in eastern Virginia because their mother had had her children without marrying. All Jim's and Grandma's rich and snooty relatives called them bastards, wouldn't have anything to do with them or their mother and let them nearly starve in poverty. Jim and Grandma eventually found themselves a home in the mountains along the Tug where young women accidentally having babies was no great sin. After Grandma married Grandpa Eph Hatfield, the Hatfields took her and Jim into their family. Jim had never forgotten or forgiven—he loved the Hatfields and hated anyone who threatened them.

Uncle Jim rode up beside Cap. "It's a swivin shame we didn't do the job by ourselves," he said. "We'd of got it done."

"We swore an oath we wouldn't leave Kentucky till Randall McCoy was dead. What about that!"

"I reckon we're liars," Jim said.

Cap couldn't argue with that. "What about Johnse? Did he shoot when he did to warn the McCoys that we were out there?"

Jim thought a moment. "He was powerful fond of Roseanne. He most likely didn't cotton to the idea of killin her pa and her brother. And, after all, his wife is first cousin to Roseanne and all her brothers and sisters."

"His wife." Cap shook his head. "I still don't know why Johnse married Nancy. She's not only a McCoy, but she's the worst of their lot."

"Could be he thought he'd end our families' quarrels."

"Could be." Cap reckoned a better guess was that Johnse had decided to show Pappy he could marry whoever he wanted. "He might have thought he was gettin another Roseanne."

"Randall had a lot to do with her dyin the way she did. And your Pappy, Cap. He's part to blame, too.

"And Pappy." The only big fault Cap held against his Pappy in all these years was how he'd dealt with Johnse and Roseanne McCoy.

Cap called ahead to Johnse to give the groaning Tom Chambers another shot of whiskey. He was beginning to realize he couldn't go home to his wife now. If he wanted Pappy to get the true picture of what had happened, he must tell the story himself, today, making sure Pappy knew he wasn't the cause of the deaths of Randall's children and the burning of his house.

"Your Pappy will be thankful to hear Aunt Sally can't tell on any of us," Jim said.

Cap didn't think Pappy would be thankful they'd killed a woman. When he talked to Pappy, he had to do more than merely construct excuses and flimsy defenses for what had happened. The death and destruction was so bad he had to make up for it somehow. "I want to tell Pappy that you and me'll go out, just the two of us, and get Randall before he has a chance to come after us. Keep our oath, make honest men of ourselves."

"We could do that."

"Then that's what I'll tell Pappy when I get to his place. Agreed?"

Cap heard Jim chuckle. "Your Pappy's gonna be ready to hang us both, Cappie. Better we hang together."

Cap winced. That was a mongrel boy's joke. He urged Traveller forward until he caught up with Johnse. "Did you shoot first to warn the McCoys?"

No answer.

"Then you did."

"Get away from me," Johnse said.

"I'm gonna give you a chance to square things up for what you done to this raid. Next few days, you talk to your wife. Find out where Randall's gone. Let me know." Since Johnse had been crazy enough to marry a second McCoy woman, they might as well make use of her.

Johnse remained silent.

Cap shook his head. Johnse had gone nowhere but downhill since he'd lost Roseanne.

Chapter 6

Roseanne McCoy rode into Johnse's life on Election Day, June 10, 1880.

Cap felt happiness spread all over him as he, Pappy, and Johnse rode up to Jerry Hatfield's place in Kentucky. Everything he'd wanted to see was there—baskets and trenchers of food piled on long picnic tables, boys his age playing horseshoes, and pretty girls in bright print skirts and dresses. Other West Virginia Hatfields had come too—Uncle Ellison and Aunt Sarah, Uncle Elias and Aunt Betty, Uncle Jim and Aunt Mary, Floyd and Esther, and lots of cousins. Mama and the younger children had to stay home because the baby was sick, but she'd sent along gingerbread, applesauce, and pickles with her men.

Cap could hardly wait to get off his horse and get started. But first things first. He had to help unload Johnse's whiskey jugs that hung from their saddles and line them up in a row near the side of the road. At elections Johnse always made a lot of money selling his whiskey. For a few minutes, Cap watched and admired his brother.

"Come and get the best whiskey in the mountains," Johnse called out. "It'll put a sparkle in your eye and a spring in your step. Cure your children of worms and your husband of cantankerousness, Ma'am. Some men will praise God, some will feel their manhood as never before. Come buy Johnse's lovely concoction. Only a penny a pint, a dime a jug." Johnse's blond hair and wavy mustache shone like liquid gold in the sun, his voice as smooth as honey, and his smile as sweet.

Men ran across the field to do business with Johnse. Cap could only guess whether they bought from his brother because his whiskey was the best or because they liked doing business with him, basking in his charm.

Tagging along with Pappy, Cap stopped by the wooden table where ballots were stacked by a tiny American flag. When Pappy asked Frank Staton to read the list of candidates to him, Cap peeked over his shoulder to see if he could make any sense out of the printing. Not only couldn't he read a word, he couldn't even tell one letter from another except H for Hatfield, the letter he'd often branded on the ends of logs ready to float down the Tug. A boy about eight or nine picked up one of the ballots and began to read words like *sheriff* and *governor*, and Cap felt ashamed. At eight the little fellow could read, while at sixteen Cap could only stand there and feel stupid.

Pappy wasn't embarrassed that he couldn't read. He nodded his head approvingly at each name Staton read until he heard Abner Caldwell was down for county sheriff. "You don't want no Pikeville feller for sheriff," Pappy said to Bud McCoy. "Vote for Matt Ferguson. He's from the Tug Valley, one of our people."

Bud squinted at Pappy. "None of your business who I vote for," he said. "Matter of fact, it's none of your business who's runnin for sheriff in Kentucky."

Bullcrap, Cap thought. Pappy wouldn't want to see a sheriff elected who was serious about collecting federal revenue taxes and Bud knew that. What was probably eating at Bud was that Pappy always looked over everyone's ballots after they voted, found out who they voted for, and let them know if he agreed or not. He wouldn't harm a soul or change their ballot, but some people were afraid of being on bad terms with Pappy and he knew it. In order to make his influence felt he went to every election he could in the Tug region.

As Cap left the voting table and headed for the horseshoe pit, Pappy called out, "Stay away from the McCoy boys, Cap."

Cap scanned the clearing around Jerry Hatfield's cabin. Jerry, a distant cousin whose branch of the family had lived in Kentucky for nearly a hundred years, was heading across the clearing, jug in hand. Randall Junior, Phamer, and Calvin McCoy were drinking with their cousins. Old Randall, Aunt Sally, and Tolbert weren't there. And, lucky for him, none of the McCoys was pitching horseshoes.

Cap watched and waited until the game they were playing was over.

"I can beat any of you!" he yelled out.

"Oh, yeah?" Jimmy Chafin strutted up to Cap. "Prove it."

When they started taking turns slinging horseshoes at the stakes, one of the boys claimed it was his horseshoe that lay around the stake and Cap's that lay in the dirt. Cap punched him hard in the shoulder and got punched right back. Cap slugged with all his might, enjoying the smack of his blows landing on the other boys and theirs landing on him. Fighting was half the fun of horseshoes.

Then two Kentucky men sat down on tree stumps, took out fiddles, and began playing dancing music. Cap had another boy pinned to the ground, but suddenly lost interest in fighting. He got up and brushed the dirt off his shirt and overalls before going over to where the dancing was starting. Girls liked boys better when they were clean and had combed their hair.

He saw Johnse was down to a last few jugs, smiling and laughing with three girls who giggled and swayed, hoping to interest him in asking them to dance, and Tolbert McCoy was just riding up with his sister behind him on the saddle. Roseanne's long black hair fell from red ribbons and hung to her waist. Her eyes glowed as black as her hair. Her skin was cream-colored and looked as soft as Mama's down quilt. No wonder everyone talked about her beauty and her way with boys.

Tolbert jumped off the horse and helped Roseanne down. Carrying a wooden basket, its handle over her arm, she flounced her violet skirt with little red flowers.

"Peach pie." She smiled at each of the boys gathered to admire her. "Made it myself. I wonder who'll share it with me."

When Johnse joined the group, leaving his whiskey, laughing, joking, getting up close to her, Cap stifled the warning he knew Johnse would resent. *Don't make a fool of yourself over a McCoy tart, brother.* But he wondered what it would feel like to touch Roseanne's face, to kiss her mouth, to watch her flirt and smile at him. To eat her peach pie.

He felt a tug on his arm.

"I just love fiddlin and dancin." It was red-headed, big-busted Meribeth from his side of the Tug. "Don't you, Cap?"

"I sure do." He grabbed her hand and led her over to join a Virginia reel. At least one girl was hanging around him instead of Johnse. They joined in the reel, dosie-doed, allemanded and passed their partners on the left and right, brushing their bodies against each other as often as Cap could arrange it, bare arms touching, her willing fingers twining with his from time to time. For half the afternoon they took time out only for eating when he could snuggle close to her and share trenchers of ham, gingerbread, potato salad, cookies, and whatever else they could lay their hands on.

"Let's find a shady spot," Cap said, guessing she probably knew he was looking for more than shade. Holding hands, they sauntered down a path into the woods. But at the sound of low voices and giggling, Cap feared they weren't going to have the place to themselves. Through the trees, he saw two figures squirming on the ground. Tiptoeing up to a large tree, he and Meribeth peeked from behind it.

Johnse and a long-skirted girl lay on the ground, writhing and kissing, their arms wrapped around each other. When Johnse raised his head to murmur soft words, his face flushed and perspiring, Cap saw the girl was Roseanne McCoy. The bodice of her dress was open and her breasts were bare.

"Holy crap!" Cap couldn't believe his eyes. "Johnse must be drunk *and* crazy."

"He's crazy all right," Meribeth said. "Over Roseanne."

"You're beautiful, Roseanne," they heard Johnse say. "I want you more than anything in life." Roseanne just smiled and lay back on the grass.

Cap knew he had to do something—fast!

"I see what you're doing, Roseanne McCoy," Meribeth called out, beating him to it. "And I'm gonna tell."

"You slut! You snitch!" Roseanne yelled, her fingers fumbling in their haste to button the front of her dress.

Johnse leapt to his feet before Cap could get back behind the tree. "Get on out of here, Cap."

"You'd better get back before Pappy starts lookin for you," Cap said.

"I'll kill you!" Johnse yelled and threw a half-full jug at him.

"Come on, Meribeth." Cap dragged the objecting and complaining Meribeth back up the path out of the woods. "Don't you dare say nothin about this." He gripped her arm hard. "You hear me?"

Smirking, but nodding her consent, she pulled her arm away and ran over to her family.

Cap headed straight for Pappy and began jabbering with nothing in mind except distraction. "I stayed away from the McCoys," he announced.

Pappy nodded and kept on walking.

"I heard a lot of talk about them." Cap stopped right in front of Pappy. He managed to keep Pappy occupied with concocted stories about the Mc-Coys until Roseanne and Johnse finally came out of the woods, when he ran across the clearing to intercept them. It was obvious from their flushed faces and adoring eyes that they had been sharing more than a picnic basket.

"Where's the fiddles and the dancin?" Roseanne was clinging to Johnse's arm.

"Dancin's over." Cap pointed to two fiddlers tucking their instruments into pasteboard cases.

"Where's Tolbert?" Roseanne looked around the clearing where men, women, and children were saying goodbye to each other and packing empty baskets and leftover food into saddlebags.

"Tolbert left," Jerry Hatfield said. "He said he wasn't feelin good and Phamer would take you home."

"I don't see Phamer neither." Roseanne shrugged, her eyes searching for an explanation from the others around her.

"Seems like I saw him ridin out a while ago," Esther Hatfield said.

"They left me? My dumb brothers left me? How am I supposed to get home?" She turned a pleading face to Johnse.

Crazy Johnse put his arms around her and kissed her. "You'll just have to come home with me."

"You can't do that, you idiot!" Cap saw Pappy approaching from across the clearing.

"You scared of Roseanne because she's a McCoy?" Johnse challenged Cap. "I aint. She's my sweetheart."

Pappy strode up and stood before the couple, scowling.

Cap clenched his fists until his fingernails cut into his palms. Johnse was going to catch it now.

"Johnse, I might go home with you if your Pappy says it's all right." The way Roseanne smiled at Pappy, she was almost flirting with him.

Cap couldn't believe she could say such a dumb-head thing. Didn't she know the trouble she and Johnse were in?

Pappy smiled back at her. "Of course you must come home with us. I see you have stolen my son's heart."

Cap thought the mountains—his whole world—had cracked and would fall apart.

Johnse gave Roseanne a kiss and climbed on his horse. "You can ride with me."

Cap broke into a sweat of fear for Johnse. Pappy must be playing with him and would explode any minute.

Instead, Pappy offered Roseanne his clasped hands as a step to boost her onto the saddle behind Johnse. Declaring Pappy was such a gentleman, Roseanne accepted and soon they were all riding off toward West Virginia.

As Pappy rode along, giggling and talking to himself, Cap wondered if he'd gone loony from too much whiskey and the hot afternoon sun. He rode up beside Pappy.

"How come you're lettin Johnse bring Roseanne home like this? I don't want no McCoy in our house and neither do you."

"Can't think of nothin I want more." Pappy was still giggling. "What wouldn't I give to see Randall's face when that old fart gets the news that I have his precious Roseanne. He'll crap boulders. Welcome to my house, Roseanne." Pappy slapped the horn on his saddle and laughed out loud.

"Johnse doesn't think this is a joke. He's crazy about Roseanne." Even as he tried to persuade Pappy not to make his brother the butt of a joke, Cap knew it was too late to change anything. They were well on their way to West Virginia with Randall McCoy's daughter. Clever Pappy had seized this opportunity to hurt and humiliate an old enemy without firing a shot.

"Johnse is serious today. Tomorrow's another day." Pappy started chuckling again. "We'll probably hear Randall carryin on all the way over in West Virginia."

True, Johnse could soon tire of Roseanne. But suppose he didn't? Cap was sure that right now Johnse was so smitten by Roseanne he couldn't begin to see what Pappy was up to. And why, all of a sudden, was Pappy willing to rile up the McCoys?

As they approached home, a full moon painted the field, barn, and cabin in shades of silver and gray. Colorless and motionless, the world lay frozen and dead, waiting for dawn to revive it. Even Roseanne's dress and the red of her ribbons looked nearly black, her creamy skin and rosy cheeks a uniform gray. Yet, dismounted and heading toward the cabin, Roseanne captured Cap's eye with her hip-swinging stride and swishing skirts, her raised chin and billowing hair, black one instant, a sparkling of silver threads the next. It was as if the moonlight had stopped all other life for the moment to devote itself to showing off Roseanne.

But Roseanne, all the while holding his hand, clearly belonged to Johnse.

Pappy pushed open the cabin door to a silent home. Everyone was asleep.

"Roseanne can sleep in one of the empty bunks," he said. "Give her some kivvers, Johnse."

Pappy went up the ladder to the loft where he and Mama slept with the baby, while Cap, Johnse, and Roseanne headed for the door to the sleeping room.

In the dark, Cap pulled off his boots and overalls and snuggled under the soft, warm quilt Mama had made for him.

"I can't find the spare kivvers in the dark," Johnse whispered loud enough for Cap to hear. "But I got plenty on my bunk. Why don't you crawl into bed with me, Roseanne?"

"I don't know if I ought to do that, Johnse," she whispered back.

"You could take my bunk, and I'll sleep in one of the empty ones. I probably won't get too awful cold."

"I don't want you to be cold."

"Then come and keep me warm."

"We'll keep our clothes on?"

"Can't keep my boots and pants on and you can't keep your dress on, Roseanne. Not enough room."

"I guess you're right," she giggled. "I'll slip off my shoes and my dress."

He should have kept his face to the wall beside his own bunk, but Cap rolled over ever so slowly and quietly and squinted through partly closed eyelids toward Johnse and Roseanne. With only a trickle of light from the embers of the kitchen fire seeping under the door to the bunk room, he couldn't tell how much clothes they had on, let alone what Roseanne's body looked like.

"All right, I'm in," Johnse said. "Now just slide in beside me. Oh, Roseanne!"

"Are you warm enough, Johnse?"

"Not quite. Roll over and hold me tight."

"Why, Johnse Hatfield, what has happened? You're all hard like the barrel of a gun!" Roseanne's voice squealed louder than her previous whispers.

"I surely am, Roseanne. You're so sweet. I want you so bad."

"I want to see."

"I can't show you now. It's too dark. But here, you can feel me. Only, whisper quiet. Cap might still be awake."

Cap faked some heavy breathing and snoring while he listened to the moans, grunts, and gasps from Johnse's bunk. He tossed and turned, trying to picture what they were doing. What if Pappy knew what they were up to?

Pappy was smart. He must have guessed.

After their morning chores, Cap and Bobby Lee returned to the kitchen to find Johnse at the table with the younger children. Roseanne, still in her election day flowered skirt and blouse, was frying bacon and hot cakes. Cap's eleven-year-old sister Nancy Belle was dipping coffee from the pot she'd swung away from the fire. In charge of her smoothly run kitchen, Cap's little Mama, her hair already done up in a neat bun, sat and held the still whiny Baby Elias to her shoulder. It took more than a whiny baby to upset Mama, and evidently it took more than finding Roseanne McCoy in her house when she got up in the morning.

"Bobby Lee, this is our guest, Miss Roseanne McCoy." Pappy's face beamed from where he sat at the head of the table, the light from the fire reddening his cheeks and glinting off his eyes.

Bobby Lee nodded and plunked himself on the bench beside Johnse.

"Roseanne's gonna sit there," Johnse said.

"That's my place." Bobby Lee scowled at Roseanne.

"They're sweethearts," Pappy said. "Give her some room."

Cap sometimes missed the early days when where to sit was never a problem, a time when he and Johnse and Bobby Lee had the cabin and their parents to themselves. Now there were five more children and everything was getting so crowded Pappy had added more bunk beds, pegs for clothes, and soon they'd be needing a longer table and benches.

"You can squeeze in next to me," Roseanne said, as Nancy Belle and her smaller sister Mary handed out the bacon and hotcakes. "I'd be happy to sit between two such fine-lookin men as you and Johnse. You're a very fetchin feller, Bobby Lee."

The seating worked out fine. Bobby Lee grinned shyly at Roseanne, obviously enjoying being squeezed in beside her. And you'd have thought she was a favorite daughter, the way Pappy was treating her. Cap wondered what Mama was thinking about Pappy's messing around with Johnse and Roseanne.

"You'd better get word to Roseanne's family," Mama said. "They must be terrible worried."

Cap hoped his mother was figuring out the best thing to do.

"I'll ride over and tell Floyd's wife first thing this morning, Levicy," Pappy said. "She'll get word to her sister."

From his expression, you couldn't tell, but Cap would bet Pappy wanted to let Aunt Esther know where Roseanne was so she'd tell her brother-in-law Randall.

Holding the baby on her hip, Mama brought more hotcakes from the skillet to a wooden platter she set on the table. "Take Roseanne with you," she said. "So's Esther can see for herself we're not forcin her to stay."

"And take a chance Randall and his wife is stoppin by Esther and Floyd's? Why, they might steal her away from Johnse."

"You know Randall don't stop by there ever since the hog trial." Mama laughed at such a notion.

"I don't want to see Aunt Esther. I want to stay here with Johnse." Roseanne kissed Johnse on the cheek.

"Then it's settled. I aint takin no chances with these young folks' happiness." Pappy looked so earnest that Cap began to wonder if it was possible that he'd been won over by Johnse and Roseanne.

Only a couple of days after Pappy's visit, Roseanne's Aunt Esther knocked on the cabin door and Cap let her in. Not even bothering to take off her coat, Esther settled herself into a rocking chair beside Mama, who was shelling peas into a bowl in her lap.

"My sister left word Roseanne had better come home right now. There's no tellin what Randall will do if she don't."

Gleeful as a crow that had snatched the best piece of fruit from another bird, Pappy hopped around the cabin on his long skinny legs and cawed.

"You can't take Roseanne away from my son. She needs his lovin," Pappy cackled. "And I believe she's taken a shine to my hospitality."

Cap returned to churning butter for Mama, pounding the paddle as hard as he could. Pappy had no business using Esther to taunt Randall. If he were Pappy, he wouldn't do such a mean thing to his brother and Roseanne. He wouldn't drive Randall McCoy crazy.

"Roseanne's out pickin blackberries with Johnse," Mama told Esther. "I wish they were here so you could see how happy they are."

"It'll break her mama's heart if Roseanne don't come back," Aunt Esther said.

"Anse." Mama stared at Pappy until she was sure she had his attention. "Roseanne should go see her mother. If she and Johnse are really in love, they can keep seein each other. Aunt Sally and I would see to that."

"Roseanne wants to stay here. You heard her say so. How can we throw her out, Levicy?"

"That's true, Esther." Mama sighed. "She didn't even want to visit *you*. She's really stuck on our Johnse."

Cap stopped churning for a minute. "Why don't you stay until Johnse and Roseanne get back?" he said.

"I wish I could, but I need to get on over to my sister's. What am I gonna tell her?"

"Here, Esther." Pappy picked up a full pie tin. "Take some cherry pie with you. Share it with Randall. Roseanne made it just this mornin."

Mama sighed and shot Esther a look that meant she wished Pappy wouldn't behave like this.

"Tell Randall we sure are enjoyin Roseanne's pies," Pappy giggled. "And tell him we're tickled to death havin Roseanne among us. This here's her pretty red hair ribbon." He grinned and twirled the ribbon in the air.

"No wonder they call you Devil Anse," Aunt Esther muttered.

By the end of the week, all the Hatfields liked Roseanne. She played freeze tag with the four little ones, tickled them till they squealed, fussed over them when they had small hurts, and separated them when they got into fights. She dragged Mama's sewing machine out of the corner, made a calico dress and underthings for herself, and helped Nancy Belle learn how to get the foot treadle and the cloth speed working smoothly together. She picked flowers and put them in a jar on the table, wildflowers from the woods—sparkling bluebells and pink and white trilliums.

Every day Johnse's happiness impressed Cap more. Johnse sang the Billy Boy song: "Can she bake a cherry pie, charming Billy? She can bake a cherry pie quick as cat can wink an eye." He left out, "But she's a young thing and cannot leave her mother." Johnse always seemed to have his arm around Roseanne, and she must have kissed Johnse's face and hair a hundred times a day.

Cap decided he was ready for a love affair like Johnse's. All he needed was a girl.

He noticed that only Mama sometimes looked grim, especially when Pappy sent word to Randall through friends and relatives that his son Johnse was taking great pleasure in Roseanne McCoy's company. Cap had always caught crap for being too ready to provoke a fight. If what Pappy was doing wasn't fight-provoking, then what was? And he was working his mischief without cause. The McCoys hadn't bothered anyone for a long time.

Next day, Deacon Anse came by to say that Randall McCoy wanted Roseanne to come home right now.

Roseanne very respectfully answered, "I don't want to go home."

The Deacon sighed and clasped his hands on the table as though he were about to pray. "I'll give it to you straight. If you don't come home today—you can ride with me—your Pappy says he never wants to see you again."

"Pa'll get over it," Roseanne said. "He has a temper, but it blows over after a while."

Deacon Anse still looked troubled. "You're breaking your Mama's heart."

"Well, that's the worst of it. I miss her, too."

"Your pa's talkin about shootin Johnse or any Hatfield he lays eyes on.

We don't need any more of this feudin." He turned to Pappy. "Anse, send this girl back home. She's young—she don't know the trouble she's causin."

"Tell Randall not to get so het up. These young folks are happy. You can see for yourself."

"I don't want to grieve Ma and Pa," Roseanne cried out. "But I love Johnse." She squeezed Johnse's hand.

Mama looked up from her pea-shelling. "I think you should go home for a visit, Roseanne. Mend your mama's heart. And don't worry. You'll always be welcome here."

"But, Mama, what if they don't let Roseanne come back to me?" Johnse whined.

Pappy stroked his beard. "Randall might never let Roseanne come back. I believe she should stay here."

Cap, who'd grabbed a leftover breakfast biscuit, felt it stick in his throat. How could Randall get over his temper with Pappy constantly taunting him about Roseanne? Mama kept rocking her chair, holding baby Elias against her shoulder and soothing him.

"Please stay, Roseanne," Nancy Belle pleaded. "You're like a big sister to me. I aint never had a big sister before."

Little Elizabeth buried her face in Roseanne's lap and hugged her knees. "Don't go," she cried.

Roseanne looked at Cap.

"Stay with us. We want you to. Long as you're happy," he answered. It seemed the right thing for Johnse and Roseanne, even though he was still worried about what Pappy was up to.

"Tell Ma I miss her, but my place is at Johnse's side," Roseanne said.

Johnse had that so-happy-he-was-balmy look he always had on his face these days. "Today Roseanne and me are goin to Williamson to sell some whiskey. I'll take all my money and spend it on her."

When Cap returned from a corn-hoeing at a neighbor's farm late in the afternoon, Roseanne was wearing a new dress and showing it off out by the picnic tables. It was pale green with white flowers and dark green ribbons here and there, white eyelet lace on the neck and the ends of its long sleeves. Cap didn't know what to say, she was so beautiful, like a woman a man might see in his dreams.

"I aint never seen such a dress in all my life," Mama said. "Store bought, all ready to go, like it was made for you."

"Spent all my whiskey money on it," Johnse bragged. "Almost all of it. Look what I brung you, Mama."

He set a ball of cord on the table and opened a bag of little wooden pegs. "Them's clothespins. You string the cord between two trees and then take your wet clothes and fix em to the cord with these pins so's they can hang there and dry."

"What keeps em from fallin off?" Nancy Belle asked.

"Here." Johnse gave one end of the cord to Bobby Lee and the other to Elliot, who was only eight and had to stand on a tub to keep his end as high as Bobby Lee's. Then Johnse took off his shirt and attached it to the clothes line with two clothespins.

"Aint they wonderful?" Roseanne said to Mama. Above their heads, summer birds with new young ones chirped, down by the creek chiggers sang, growing loud and silent in perfect unison. The honeysuckle, covered with pale yellow sweet-smelling flowers, was climbing over the fence around the chicken coop and racing up the path toward the cabin. To Cap, it was as if the world was making itself beautiful for Roseanne and Johnse.

Mama laughed. "All the women hereabouts will be covetin my clothespins."

"Such a simple idea." Cap admired the cleverness of a man who could invent this clothes pin. "I should of thought of it myself."

Everyone went in to supper as happy as Cap had ever seen his family. The shutters were open so that the breeze carried the scents of honeysuckle and green growth of every kind into the cabin.

"Just look at Roseanne," Pappy said. "Pretty as a blowth of flowers on a spring day."

Cap winked at Nancy Belle and she smiled back. She was his favorite sister.

"Pretty enough to make a man a fine wife." Johnse was beaming.

Everyone at the table grew silent.

"Of course Roseanne and me intend to marry," Johnse said.

Roseanne twined her arm with Johnse's and smiled happily.

At the other end of the table, Pappy pushed his food away and leaned forward. "Marry? Marry?"

"I'm eighteen." Johnse looked proud and handsome. "Time I was settlin down."

"Maybe so. But first you got to find yourself a decent wife."

Roseanne's smile vanished.

"I found one." Johnse's jaw was set and his eyes didn't waver from Pappy's.

"You're jokin. This here aint about marriage. This here's about havin a little fun."

"I aint jokin." Johnse's face turned bright red. "I want to be Roseanne's husband and the father of our children."

Cap's heart was in his throat. He could never imagine telling Pappy he was going to marry a McCoy.

"Oh, Johnse!" Mama's eyes were shiny with tears.

Pappy stood up at the head of the table, his beard jutting out from his chin at the angle Cap knew always meant trouble. "You aint hearin right. I said we're just funnin here."

"We want to get married." Johnse's voice was now wavering. "Roseanne would be a fine wife."

Roseanne's glare was like gunfire aimed at Pappy.

"Disgrace!" Pappy roared. Little Elizabeth started to whimper. "No son or daughter of mine will ever marry a McCoy! Not one drop of McCoy blood shall flow in my grandchildren's veins."

Cap dropped his gaze to the table top. He couldn't look at Johnse or Roseanne.

"How can you say that!" Roseanne cried and ran from the cabin, a teary-eyed Johnse stumbling after her.

"No marriage and that's that," Pappy called out after them.

Cap watched Mama. She didn't look angry, but the love light and admiration she nearly always had in her eyes for Pappy had dimmed. Cap knew what that meant. Mama would never contradict her husband in front of the family, or anyone else, but after she'd thought things over a day or so, if she still couldn't line her thinking up with Pappy's, she'd begin telling him little by little what was bothering her. Most of the time, she'd succeed in changing his mind. But he guessed Mama would find it hard to persuade Pappy this time.

After Pappy left to look at a horse he was thinking of buying, Johnse and Roseanne returned to the cabin. Johnse sat hunched, eyes on the kitchen table in front of him. Beside him, Roseanne held his hand.

"I think it'd be a good idea if I talked to Aunt Esther about takin her back home." Mama laid a gentle hand on Johnse's shoulder.

"All that crap about not wantin to break my heart! " Johnse snarled. "He don't care nothin about my heart. He's got one thing on his mind—prankin Roseanne's pa."

"Don't you disrespect your Pappy." Mama smacked Johnse's shoulder with a wooden cooking spoon. "I won't stand for that."

"We can't stay here no more," Roseanne said. "We're gettin out of here right now." She headed for the bunk room, Johnse shuffling after her.

Cap helped Mama tote her pots to the wash shed. That was the only comfort he had to offer her.

In a few minutes, Johnse and Roseanne returned to the kitchen, carrying mill sacks stuffed with clothing. Johnse had draped his winter coat over his arm.

"You don't need no coat, Johnse." Cap didn't want to see his brother packing up to leave for so long he'd need a coat.

"I'm leavin, Cap." Johnse's jaw was set with determination.

"Where are you gonna stay?" Mama asked.

Cap felt bad, knowing how much of Mama's heartstrings were tied to Johnse.

"Somewhere else!" Roseanne's voice was tight with desperation. "Sorry, Mama Hatfield. Thank you for all you've done for me. I'll miss you and the children." She hugged Mama, Nancy Belle, and Elizabeth. "And you, too, Cap. Of course I'll miss you."

It was a week before anyone heard from Roseanne and Johnse. One morning, when Pappy was out of the house, Mama confided in Cap. "I heard from Aunt Esther. Johnse took Roseanne to her Aunt Betty's in Kentucky. Betty's gonna take her in."

"What about Johnse?" With all the kin they had around the Tug, Cap wasn't worried that Johnse might not have a place to stay. He wanted to go see him.

"He's been stayin here and there with some of your cousins. He sees Roseanne just about every day. I think it's better he and your Pappy stays apart for a while."

From time to time, word of Johnse and Roseanne reached the family. Even though Aunt Betty was only a few miles down the road from Roseanne's ma and pa, the word was that neither of them ever came to visit her and that her ma was grieving terribly. It tore at Cap's heart that Pappy never mentioned either Johnse or Roseanne. After all Johnse was his son, not his favorite, but his son.

The uneasy peace was broken one night when a woman's pounding and screaming at the cabin door woke everyone up. Cap pulled on his overalls, ran out of the bunkroom, and grabbed his rifle from the gun rack. Pappy, holding a lantern up high, opened the door. Roseanne was there, her face tear-stained and badly scratched. At first, she could only gasp for breath.

"Come quick!" she pleaded between sobs. "It's my brothers, Phamer and Jim and Tolbert. They caught Johnse comin to see me. Pa come, too, and said he wants to see Johnse die for what he done to me. I'm afraid they're gonna kill him."

Inside the house, where all the children had gathered in their night clothes, Roseanne caught her breath enough to tell how her pa and her brothers had taken Johnse away from Aunt Betty's, down the road toward the Pikeville jail. She'd ridden through the woods in the night so fast the bushes and branches had whipped and scratched her.

"I'm goin after him," Cap said without waiting for Pappy's reaction. He was going to save Johnse with or without Pappy's help.

"Anse." That's all Mama needed to say.

"They aint gonna take my son." Pappy set down the lantern and grabbed a rifle from the rack. "Let's go."

So Pappy still regarded Johnse as his son. Cap got his Winchester, too.

"This aint a McCoy trick to get us into a ambush is it?" Pappy faced Roseanne.

"It aint no trick, you old fool!" Roseanne screamed. "And this aint my fault or Johnse's. If you and Pa had of stayed out of everything, Johnse and I'd of been happy and we'd all be safe from harm. You're a pair of old fools, you and Pa, messin and meddlin in other people's lives."

"You call me a old fool, and I'm off to save your Johnse's neck?"

"Old fool!" Roseanne screamed at Pappy's back as he and Cap headed toward the barn.

It looked that way to Cap, too, but he intended to keep his opinion to himself.

Cap and Pappy drove their horses as hard as they dared in the dark, gathering Hatfields from every cabin they passed. By the time they splashed across the Tug at dawn, they had a dozen men and more were being rounded up.

Pappy stopped on the Kentucky side. "If we find the McCoys and Johnse aint with em, shoot every one of em. Shoot to kill."

Cap would bet if he'd said that, he'd have been called hot-headed and trigger-happy.

"Wait a minute, Anse," Uncle Elias said. "Let's see how serious this really is. They may just want to rattle Johnse a bit."

"I told you what Roseanne said. Randall's fixin to murder my son."

"He don't hardly do nothin he threatens."

"This could be a ambush," Pappy replied. "Ride quiet. Be ready to shoot."

Cap hoped Uncle Elias would have a chance to talk some sense into Roseanne's father and brothers. Roseanne deserved the Hatfields' respect. To save Johnse's life she'd ridden through the night without any heed to her own safety.

Not long after dawn, they—there were thirty of them now—were riding down the road to Pikeville, surrounded by pine forest, when they rounded a bend. There were about a dozen McCoys camped on the ground. Randall McCoy was standing in the middle of the road, his rifle pointed right at Pappy.

"Stay where you are, Devil Anse," he said. "Or I'll blow your goldarn head off."

Cap and the others reined in their horses. Only Pappy inched toward Randall, who stood his ground.

"Where's my son?" Pappy said.

Cap spotted Johnse sitting under a tree, outside Randall's line of fire, not even tied up, and pointed him out.

"Hatfield!" Randall's oldest son, Jim, yelled. "Let me handle this in peace." He approached his father. "Come on, Pa. No need for that rifle."

Still aiming at Pappy, Randall McCoy stepped away from his son.

"We got you outnumbered, McCoy," Pappy said.

Johnse stood up and two McCoys immediately pointed their rifles at him. "I'm goin home now." He took a couple of careful steps toward Pappy's horse.

"Not another step, you goldarn varmint," Randall barked at Johnse, all the while keeping his rifle aimed at Pappy. "You're gonna pay for what you done to my Roseanne."

"Roseanne's in love with Johnse." Jim McCoy stood between Pappy and his father. "They got thirty men, we got a dozen. We all stand to lose a lot of blood."

Johnse kept walking toward Pappy, ambling forward until he reached Pappy's side and suddenly yanked Pappy's rifle from its holster. "I don't want no shootin," he said.

"You fool!" Pappy shouted. "You want to die at McCoy hands?"

Crazy Johnse! Pappy was about to claim him as his son again.

"Just get me out of here and leave everybody be," Johnse said. He emptied Pappy's rifle shells onto the ground.

Jim, the only one of the McCoy brothers Cap thought had any sense, nodded. "Take him and leave."

Cap watched Pappy for a signal. But Pappy was only gawking at Johnse who was stashing the rifle in a saddle holster and mounting his horse that had been grazing nearby.

When Randall McCoy lowered his Winchester, his son Jim took the opportunity to take the rifle and empty it of ammo.

"He ruint Roseanne." Randall's eyes still had their ferocious glint. "He's got to pay for that."

"Roseanne's just fine, Pa. We're all just fine," Jim said.

As Cap rode off with his family, on the road toward West Virginia, he heard Randall still shouting threats at their backs. He was relieved when they rounded the bend to ride among the pine trees, out of sight of the McCoys.

A while later Pappy spoke. "Only way we'll ever be safe from them dang McCoys is to get rid of Randall. I can see that now. Makin trouble for us is the only pleasure he gets out of his miserable life. He aint gonna quit till he makes us kill him, Cap."

And you could say Pappy got considerable pleasure out of making trouble for the McCoys, Cap said to himself. For some reason, Pappy found it completely fitting to use Roseanne to taunt Randall McCoy till he was about out of his mind, while he, Cap, was always called a hothead for starting a fight with a McCoy. Some day he'd figure out what the difference was in Pappy's mind.

One thing was sure. Pappy hadn't counted on Johnse and Roseanne falling in love. He'd hurt his own son.

Cap wondered when and where he would be told his part in killing Randall.

Johnse returned home and lived there for months, occasionally slipping out to meet Roseanne, always in West Virginia, or so he said. He brewed whiskey and drank a lot.

One day, when Deacon Anse dropped in on them during midday dinner, his favorite time for visiting, the whole family heard his announcement. "Roseanne gave birth to a baby girl, Johnse. You're a father."

"And I'm an uncle." Cap was proud, as though he'd actually done something.

"Our first grandchild, Anse." Mama smiled.

"Not *our* grandchild," Pappy said. "That there's a McCoy."

Johnse ran out the front door. In a few minutes, Cap heard his horse galloping away. "He'll be okay. Not even the McCoys would shoot a man comin to see his new baby," he whispered to Mama.

Mama waited for a few days, till Pappy was out hunting, before sneaking off to Kentucky to see her granddaughter. "Don't you go tellin your Pappy and start up a ruckus," she warned Cap and the children. "He has enough on his mind without worryin about what I'm up to." She took a little crocheted blanket she'd used for her last two babies.

When Mama came home late in the afternoon, she put the blanket back on a shelf. Her eyes were sad and red, like she'd been crying.

"The baby's dead," she said. "Roseanne said it took sick right after it was born. Looked like that child never had no will to live. She said Johnse saw it once before it passed on."

Mama rocked herself in the rocking chair. Cap sat nearby and held her hand. "Maybe that baby was never meant to be born."

"Poor little thing." Mama looked so sad.

"You don't have to worry about me, Mama. I'll never marry a McCoy. I won't have no McCoy babies."

Chapter 7

Johnse's romance with Roseanne had left Cap's number one position more secure than ever until today's fire and killings in Kentucky. Now he doubted the day would ever come when he'd lead the Hatfields.

Just after a silvery sun rose over the mountain ridge, Cap led his ragtag army across the Tug into West Virginia. With no goodbye, Uncle Jim took the first trail off to his cabin and Cotton Top, nursing his hurt feelings took the second. Charlie Carpenter had Tom Chambers ride home with him to care for his mangled hand. Cap assigned Bobby Lee and Cousin Elliot to keep watch at the fort until he could send relief. They'd have to be extra vigilant for Mc-Coys coming across looking for revenge.

"You got to find out where Randall's at," Cap said as Johnse headed for his place. "You owe us that." Johnse didn't answer. Although it had been several years since Roseanne had joined their daughter in death, Johnse's pain over his losses never seemed to end.

Now alone, Cap began talking to himself as he rode a frozen, rutted trail up the mountainside. "Don't shoot till I tell you, Johnse. That's what I told him. And what does he do? He shoots a pickle jar and gives us away. I said no women and children, and Cotton Top blows a hole in Allifair and Uncle Jim whacks Aunt Sally and kills her. I told Chambers no fire, and he burns the cabins down."

Cap smacked the saddle hard enough to sting his hand and cause Traveller to kick his hooves up. If only things had gone the way they should! "I left Johnse in the woods to watch over the horses," he said aloud for his ears only. "I took away Chambers' torches. We crept up to the main cabin without a sound till we began firin. We shot out the windows and doors till we could get a clear shot inside. Then we killed Randall and left Allifair and Aunt Sally unhurt, their home unburnt."

That's how the raid should have gone, could easily have gone, if it hadn't been for Johnse, Cotton Top, and Chambers.

But Allifair, Calvin, and Aunt Sally were dead, a fact he couldn't change, no matter what he wished for or what excuses he made. Their deaths were his fault and he did not deserve Pappy's pardon. He did not deserve the sun's light and warmth. He did not deserve food or drink in his belly. Nothing could atone for the deaths of a woman, her daughter, and her son. For this, no rest would ever come to him.

There was only a small hope for partial redemption. He must reverse the worst of his mistakes by destroying Randall McCoy. Afterward, he'd erect carved tombstones for Aunt Sally, Allifair, and Calvin and see that their graves were kept up and flowers put on them.

When he prodded open the door to Pappy and Mama's cabin, everyone was seated around the table, eating breakfast. A kerosene lantern atop Mama's sewing machine and a hearthfire lit the room, which was shuttered against the New Year's cold. High overhead, laundry hung like a hangman's victims from clothes pins attached to cords.

Mama, in a faded blue calico frock that bulged over the baby who would soon be joining the family, was bringing fresh-baked biscuits from the hearth. Bacon sizzled in the huge blackened skillet sitting on the coals. In spite of himself, Cap's stomach and mouth yearned for those biscuits and bacon. He hadn't eaten since the previous morning.

"Mornin, Cap," Pappy said from his place at the head of the table. "You're here early."

Lips pressed tight, Mama only nodded at him as she added coffee to the iron pot hanging over the fire. Cap loved the way Mama always got so serious when she was busy cooking and getting out the family meals. "Now don't be botherin me," she'd say. "I got to keep my mind on what I'm doin here." Then, once she'd set out the steaming food, her face would relax and her smile would reach out to everyone at the table. Nancy Belle, Mary, Elizabeth, Elliot, Elias, Troy, and little two-year-old Rosie were digging into breakfast, leaving an available place near Mama's end of the oil cloth-covered table.

"Sit down and tell us your news." Pappy drummed his fingers rat-a-tat-tat on the table, his great beak of a nose jabbing the air. That nose had always filled Cap with awe—it could point in accusation, chop in anger like a hatchet, or curve down like the beak of a waiting buzzard.

Cap sat down and reached for one of Mama's hot biscuits. "We went down by the river like you said. Wasn't no sign of nobody." Maybe he should make something up, say they'd come across several McCoys with rifles.

Pappy grunted. "Wouldn't surprise me if you didn't see em. Even if they was there."

"We had a suspicion. Somethin wasn't quite right. That's why we crossed over."

"Crossed over? What do you mean crossed over?"

"On the ice."

Pappy tugged at his beard. "Kind of risky goin over there."

Mama sat down by Cap. "How's Nancy?"

"She's fine." At least she was fine two nights ago when he'd last seen her. Mama and Nancy claimed they were in a race for whose baby came first.

"Nobody on the Kentucky side?" Pappy popped half a buttered biscuit into his mouth.

"Nope. Nobody." Cap glanced uneasily at Mama. "Not one lookout between the river and Randall's place." He would let his miserable story out a little at a time.

"Hold on a minute." Pappy held up his hand. "From where you was, down by the river, how would you know what was on the trail between you and Randall's?"

"We took a look," Cap said, stomach tightening and hands sweating.

Pappy gripped the edge of the table. "I never told you to go over to Randall's."

All the children had become silent, their heads turning first to Cap, then to Pappy and back.

"Give Cappie a chance to explain, Anse," Mama said. "Let's hear what he has to say before you light in on him."

"You put me in charge," Cap said. "I decided to size up the situation." Pappy would see, had to see, that this was a reasonable line of thinking.

Pappy raised his hands as if to appeal to God. "Why can't I have one son that follows my orders? I said look around by the Tug."

"I did. Then I decided to look further."

Pappy's gaze drilled into Cap. "You went all the way to Randall's place? You and everyone I left you with at the fort?"

"Yes." He'd barely begun his story and already Pappy was whipsawing him.

"Well?"

It wouldn't be long before Pappy and everyone else from around the Tug heard what had happened to the McCoys and their cabins. Cap's only chance to save himself with Pappy was to tell his version right now, when he didn't want to think of the raid, let alone talk about it.

"There was smoke comin out of the chimney. Snow was trampled around the cabin, so we knowed they was there and they'd been there a while."

"I aint gettin a good feelin about this." Pappy's eyes glinted under shaggy brows.

56

"I decided we'd surround the cabin and yell out for Randall to surrender." Cap wished he could stop here. "First thing I knew Johnse started shootin—after I just finished tellin him not to. You shouldn't of sent him with me."

"I sent him with you to be a lookout!" Pappy shouted. "Only a idiot would send him after Randall McCoy."

"Poor Johnse," Mama mourned.

"He didn't hit nothin but a jug of pickles," Cap said. "That one shot he got off started the McCoys shootin at us."

Pappy's face had gone almost purple. "You went against my orders and picked a fight!"

"You put me in charge and you always said a man should think for himself."

"Think!" Pappy bellowed. "What you done don't pass for thinkin." He rubbed his chin and shook his head. "What a bunch to go into Kentucky with. You took Cotton Top and Tom Chambers and Johnse?"

Now that Pappy put it that way, Cap couldn't believe he'd done such a stupid thing. "Everyone you left me with."

"Well, what come of this squirrel-brained prank of yours?"

"Like I said, Johnse started shootin and the McCoys started shootin back."

"They hit any of our men?" Pappy's eyes were sparking fire.

"Nope. It was after dark. The way I planned things, they couldn't get a shot at us unless we ran out in the open. From behind cover, I yelled out for Randall and his men to come out and surrender so no women and children would get hurt. Didn't figure I could go wrong with that." He now knew how that could go wrong and what he should have done instead. The more he talked, the more he realized how stupid he sounded.

Pappy snorted. "You know Randall McCoy aint got the guts to do a thing like that."

"Next thing I knew Tom Chambers was headin for the cabin with a couple of his torches. I yelled 'Stop! No fire!' But he had fire in his hands and fire in his heart. He jumped onto the roof and torched it."

"You got the McCoys out in the open. You must of got off a few shots at somebody then."

"Only McCoys that come out was Allifair and a little girl." Cap looked around the table. Everyone had stopped eating except two-year-old Rosie who was feeding herself with her fingers.

"Mama," Cap whispered in her ear. "There's some things I don't want these children to hear."

"Nancy Belle, take the children back there and stay until I tell you to come out." Mama pointed to the bunk room door. Nancy Belle started to protest—after all she was eighteen. "Now!" Mama pointed toward the bunkroom, and they left.

The worst was left for only Mama and Pappy to hear. "Allifair said 'I heerd your voice, Cap Hatfield. I know you're out there.'"

"Stop the raid. That's what I'd of done right then." Pappy slapped his hand on the table. "She could finger you if you kilt anyone."

"It didn't go that way." Cap glanced sideways at Mama, who had gone to her rocking chair. "Before I could say a thing. Cotton Top up and shot Allifair. She's dead."

"Oh, no!" Mama covered her face with her hands. "Poor little Allifair never had nothin to do with these troubles."

"That's a bullet through my own heart." Pappy stabbed a bony finger into his chest.

Cap felt his face go hot. "I told Cotton Top not to shoot no women or children. I told him! And it gets worse. When Aunt Sally come out to see what happened to Allifair, Uncle Jim swacked her with his rifle butt to get her out of our way. We still had to get Randall."

"What happened to Aunt Sally?" Mama's voice could barely be heard, like a whisper.

"She tried to get up, so Jim hit her again. He didn't mean to hit her so hard."

"How bad?" Mama said.

Cap stared into the fireplace. He wished he were somewhere else, anywhere else.

"Tell me," Mama demanded.

"She's dead, too."

Over and over, Mama shook her head as she pressed her hand to her belly. "Sally was a kind-hearted woman, and she loved her children as much as I love mine."

"A woman and her child." Pappy held his head in his hands. "I feel as if I have the weight of a ox on my back."

"Tom Chambers' fire burnt the cabins down to the ground." Cap could scarcely find the courage to go on. "The McCoys shot all the fingers off his right hand from inside the house." By generating some sympathy for his men, Cap hoped to divert Pappy.

"The fire must of drove Randall out," Pappy said. "You got him then?"

"We saw somebody and a couple of the men fired. But it turned out it was Calvin that got shot."

"What about Randall? Tell me about Randall."

Cap took a deep breath. "He snuck out of the house and run into the woods."

"You mean," Pappy bellowed. "You mean he got away?"

"Couldn't help it. The cabin fell in from the fire just when he was runnin. But he didn't see any of us, so the one good thing is that there aint no witnesses alive to talk."

"That may save you from a necktie posse."

"Johnse is gonna find out where Randall went. Soon as we find out, Jim and me's goin back out to get him."

The smell of burning bacon made Cap turn his head toward the fireplace and a neglected skillet. Mama made no move to save the bacon.

"Johnse aint natured for shootin and fightin, Cap," she said. "Especially not with the McCoys. You know that. And now. . ."

Cap could finish Mama's sentence. *Now that Allifair, Aunt Sally, and young Calvin had been killed, Johnse's sadness would only deepen.*

Pappy hurried over, yanked the smoking skillet off the coals and flung the burnt bacon into the fire. "Sons is supposed to be natured to obey their parents. Ours aint, Levicy. Ours have disgraced us."

Cap searched Mama's face for a sign of forgiveness. Mama wiped away tears with her apron and stared down at her lap.

"I have disgraced this family," Cap said. "You got a right to be vexed with me."

"Vexed with you?" Pappy glared at him. "How could I be vexed with you when all you done is let Randall get away, let your men kill his wife and children?"

"I can't undo what's already done. But I'm tellin you I didn't kill no one, I ordered them not to kill women and children. And that's the truth. Anyhow, I'm gonna make up for one of our mistakes. I'll get Randall McCoy. You told me yourself that someday we'd have to kill him."

"You don't understand the first thing about leadin men and conductin a war. A officer has to control his troops, he has to be in command. You never knew what Cotton Top or Johnse or Tom Chambers was gonna do. You put the wrong men in the wrong places. You had no business goin over to Kentucky, and I aint about to let you run off and make more dumb mistakes."

"You have to. Who else you got?"

"Since when do you tell me what I *have* to do!" Pappy bared his teeth in rage.

"Let's move back away from the Tug, get away from these troubles." Mama's eyes were pleading with Pappy. "Get ourselves shed of this shootin and killin."

"See what you done," Pappy said. "Your Mama wants to move away from her home. And why is that? She knows Randall's gonna want blood for what you done today. That's why."

Mama went to Pappy and hugged him to her. They held onto each other, little Mama a foot shorter than Pappy, swaying back and forth, groaning and sighing. Cap's chest tightened, and tears threatened to form.

"Our boys okay?" Pappy asked without letting go of Mama.

"All fine except Tom Chambers."

"The McCoys. Who's left besides Randall?"

"Two little bitty girls. I took them to the barn where they'd be safe."

"Now how come they're still alive? How come my son, the child killer, didn't get em all?"

Mama let go of Pappy.

"Captain Anderson," she said, using his Army title the way she always did when she had something to say on a serious matter. "I am sick to death with fearin for the lives of my husband and children and my neighbors. I want to get us a place as far from Kentucky as we can."

"No!" Cap shouted. "I can't let them McCoys drive you out. I *won't* let them."

"You aint no sicker of this war than me." Pappy suddenly looked like a tired, sad old man. "But I don't fancy movin away. Don't like the idea at all. It's a sign we've gone weak."

"Our baby's due next month." Mama patted her stomach. "I don't want it born into this fightin and shootin."

Pappy perched on the edge of a bench, frowning. "I'll take you and the children down to my brother's place in Logan, Levicy. Till you have the baby. Got to admit it aint no way to have a baby—bullets flyin around. And they will be flyin. The McCoys are for sure gonna want to get even."

"You are the sire of my children and the love of my life, Captain Anderson," said Mama. "I could never love nor admire anyone more. But I wouldn't admire you a whit less if you decided to pick up and move away from here for good." She turned to Cap. "You oughta think of movin yourself and Nancy away from the Tug, too."

"I can't run away, Mama. Nancy and Joey can go to Logan with you for a spell, but I got to stay out here and finish up with Randall."

"I don't want to hear no more of what you're gonna do." Pappy's voice was as quiet as a catamount's whimper right before it struck its victim. "You're goin home now." His voice rose to a screech. "I don't want to hear you've been any farther from your house than to feed your horses or milk your cow until I tell you what you're to do!"

Mama said, "Go look after your family, Cap. That's the best thing for now."

Pappy strode to the cabin door and held it open.

"Go! Get out of here! I don't want to look at your dumbdung face. I don't want to hear no more of your stupid ideas."

Cap grabbed his coat and stumbled out into the snow and cold air of the gray morning. He got his horse and headed home.

Home. Where he'd have to tell the whole story all over again.

Chapter 8

Taking his time trudging up the icy path from the barn to the cabin, Cap tried to think of how to put the best light on the raid when he told Nancy. But his mind was too tired to think. He'd been up for two days and a night with no rest. And on the way home from Pappy's, he'd had to round up two men to spell Cousin Elliot and Bobby Lee at the fort. He pushed the door open to stare into the barrel of a pistol.

McCoy! No time to grab his gun. He thought he was dead.

The pistol lowered and he saw Nancy's blue eyes.

"I thought it was your footsteps comin up the path." Her voice was shaking. "But I wasn't dead sure."

He took the pistol from her hand and laid it on the kitchen table, then held her close, felt the hard round knot of the baby, the warmth of her face pressed to his. "Don't worry. I'm here now." As he stroked the soft waves of her hair, her shaking eased. She pressed her head to his shoulder. He couldn't explain why, but he, too, felt safer now, being with her. He loved her for that and suspected she knew of the effect she had on him.

She kissed him on the mouth. "You been gone so long. What happened?"

"Trouble. Lots of it." His throat tightened. She'd already had three miscarriages trying to have their baby. And now she'd have to hear how he'd let a woman and her children be murdered, how their husband and father would be looking for revenge.

"Why, you're all wet." Nancy started unbuttoning his coat. "Take off them soppin clothes and put on some clean, dry things before you catch your death. We'll talk after Joey goes to bed," she whispered. She pulled off his coat and shirt, and he took off his boots and socks and climbed out of the cold, wet blue jeans.

Joey stood peering at him from behind the washroom door. "Mama was scared it wasn't you out there."

"For all you know, Joey, Saint Nicholas was there." Cap laughed as hearty a "Ho, Ho" as he could manage. Six-year-old boys shouldn't have to fear who was coming to their house.

"Get washed up, you two," Nancy said more loudly than she had to. "I got a nice supper cookin."

Cap put on a clean shirt and pants and soft Indian moccasins. He and Joey washed their hands in the tin basin Nancy had set out. So tired he could barely sit at the oil cloth-covered table, Cap drank in the warmth and orderliness of his home. A fire burned steadily at the hearth, and a bright kerosene lantern lit one shelf where Nancy kept her dishes and cooking pots and delft and another that held their collection of books and magazines. Potatoes sizzled in a skillet, and he caught whiffs of a pan of fresh-baked cornbread and beans cooking in the big iron pot hung over the fire.

Joey was just tall enough so that all of his freckled face with its large blue eyes and protruding front teeth showed above the table top.

Nancy took their plates—actual china plates, not wooden trenchers like most mountain people used—one by one to the fireplace where she heaped on fried potatoes, cornbread and lots of green shucky beans.

"I hate shucky beans." Joey scrunched up his nose.

Cap's opinion of the tough, brown beans lying in ambush inside green pods wasn't much better.

"Why, Joey Glenn," Nancy said. "You picked those beans yourself, strung em up and hung em over the fireplace to dry. You should be proud of them."

"Did you find ole Randall?" Joey asked. "Was he out by the fort?"

"He wasn't out by the fort."

"Would you shoot him if you found him?"

"I don't want to talk about it." *Ever*, Cap told himself.

"You gotta shoot him." Joey stabbed a bean with his fork and glared at it. "You said we'd never be safe if we didn't get rid of that ole varmint."

"Those are things for grown-ups to worry about, Joey," Nancy said. "Not little boys. Now eat your supper."

"Shucky beans!" Joey sneered. "Why don't we have pork chops instead of dumb ole shucky beans?"

"We can't always be eatin pork chops." Nancy put her hands on her hips, but smiled at her son in spite of herself. "What we got hangin in the smoke house has to last us till the hogs are fattened up again, end of the summer."

"I'm gonna die before summer if I don't get some pork chops," Joey whined. "I'm gonna die from eatin shucky beans."

Cap couldn't help smiling.

"Shucky beans, shucky beans, feed em to the pup. Shucky beans, shucky beans make me throw up," Joey chanted.

Cap began giggling.

"Shucky beans, shucky beans, stir em with a frog. Shucky beans, shucky beans, throw em to the hog."

Joey squealed and rolled the brown bullet-like beans around on his plate with his fingers.

Cap laughed until his sides were hurting. He couldn't stop himself and tears came, tears he tried to cover with his hands, then tried to hide by putting his arms on the table and laying his head on them. There was no hiding so much misery—he sobbed until he ached, an awful thing to do in front of his wife and child, who needed him to be strong. He was ashamed to be such a poor excuse for a man.

When he'd finally stopped shaking, he raised his head. Nancy and Joey were staring into their plates.

"Eat your beans, Joey," Nancy said.

Joey stuffed his mouth full and began chewing.

After Joey went to bed downstairs, Cap and Nancy climbed up to the loft and snuggled under a heavy quilt. With no fireplace in it, the loft was never warm in winter despite the stone chinks covered with clay that Cap and she had crammed between the logs. Nancy, in her flannel nightgown, lay in Cap's arms. She reached around to stroke his back under the shirt of his long johns.

He knew better than to use his exhaustion as an excuse for not talking. He had to tell her what had happened. "It didn't start out like much. Pappy put me in charge of the men and said to watch out for McCoys comin across the river."

"What about your Pappy? What'd he do?"

"Went home, said the grippe was still hangin onto him."

Joey's voice called out "Papa" from below.

"What's he want?" Cap said.

"To know he's safe, that we're all safe."

Cap got out from under the quilt to stand by the bed and felt the cold right through his long johns. He climbed down the ladder to find Joey sitting on his small bed in the corner by the hearth.

"Someone's out there." Joey pointed to the door.

"No one's out there. Go back to sleep."

"I heard someone sneakin up."

Cap pulled back Joey's quilt. "Go back to sleep, son. No one's out there."

"There is. I heard him."

"Okay. Put your boots on, Joey." Cap pulled his on and lit the kerosene lantern.

Outside, as their feet crunched on snow and patches of ice, Cap raised the lantern high to throw its light as far as possible. One by one, oak trees, poplars, snow-covered tree stumps, the chicken coop and barn appeared in the glow.

"No one's sneakin up. Not even a footprint in the snow, except for mine, Joey."

That was now. How long would it be before Randall McCoy rounded up a posse and came across the river looking for revenge? Pappy would post lookouts at the fort, but there were times when snow and darkness could hide a few men, and there were other, more difficult, seldom-used places to cross.

"You scared em away, Papa." Joey looked up at him. "They're scared of you."

That's what Cap had always hoped, that his enemies would have enough sense to fear him. But a need for revenge could overpower good sense in any man.

Climbing back into bed, he told Nancy how he'd had to show Joey there was no one lurking outside the cabin. He didn't tell her he was sure there soon would be.

In the dark, he couldn't see her face as he told her the whole awful story of the raid. She gasped and said, "Oh, Cap" in surprise when she heard how Johnse had fired too early, in anger at Tom Chambers firing the cabin, and in rage and anguish at learning Cotton Top had shot Allifair and Uncle Jim had bashed Aunt Sally.

"Nancy, I can't get the sight of that bleedin girl and her poor dead mama off my mind." He lifted his head, then smashed it back into his pillow. "Over and over I told them 'No women and no children.'" He buried his face in Nancy's hair, but couldn't stop the aching sobs racking his body.

"You went out there to protect Joey and me and your brothers and sisters." She was wiping her tears with her sleeve.

"I thought I couldn't miss. Catch Randall and his boys on New Year's while nobody was on the lookout, then high-tail it back to West Virginia. The end of our troubles. Dad-blame it! Now I gotta go back out and find that horse's rear."

He rolled onto his back, so furious he could scarcely catch his breath. "Pappy says he aint havin no part of me huntin down Randall and messin up again. He ordered me to go home and stay here! He ordered me!" He wanted to see Nancy's face, but could barely make out the outline of her head against the pillow.

"That's one thing, maybe the only one, me and your Pappy agree on." She poked a finger into his chest. "I don't want you goin after Randall neither."

"If we don't get him first, he'll for sure come after us."

"There's no end to that. Somebody's always got to get even with the last harm the other one did. I want to move away from here. So does your Mama. If we all move down to Logan, that'll put an end to the fightin."

"And let the McCoys drive us out of our homes? What kind of man would I be to let that happen?"

"Trouble is, you can't see more than one kind of way to be a man. On account of your Pappy's always drummed it into you that you have to fight and put fear into the hearts of anyone even thinkin of givin the Hatfields trouble. Like you're all soldiers in a war."

"It's a man's duty. . ."

"You mean your Pappy says it's a man's duty."

He smashed his fist into his pillow. "Leave me be. Why can't you just give me some peace? That's what I need."

"I'm your wife, Cap." She stroked his forehead the way he always liked. "I'm here for *you*, not for your Pappy. You don't have to keep doin everything he says. You're a grown man. You got a mind of your own."

"Some kind of mind! Look what happened when I decided not to listen to Pappy—a dead woman and dead children."

"That's because you *did* listen to him. All those years he kept on teachin you that you have to make war to look after your home and family. Well, he's wrong about that. Dead wrong."

Exhausted, Cap let himself sink into the feather bed. He had a wife and a father who never seemed to agree on anything, which was more than he could bear right now. Nancy had stopped stroking his head, but was still hovering over him.

"Let's move away from the Tug, Cap. In Logan we wouldn't have to worry about the McCoys. I want to raise our children where it's safe. Where there's a school."

"School? Pappy never wanted us to go to school." Why was she bothering him with these crazy ideas when he was too weary for even the smallest conversation?

"This isn't going to be Pappy's child and neither is Joey." She was still at him, wouldn't quit.

Their child. He didn't want Nancy to lose this baby. She'd already lost three—one for Randall Junior, one for Phamer and one for Tolbert, all executed by the Hatfields. Now two more dead McCoy children needed to even the score. If she lost this baby, it would be his fault.

Under the quilt, he reached for her hand. "I'm too tired to think straight."

"You haven't slept in almost two days."

He wanted to hold Nancy tight, but was already dreaming of their baby being snatched away by a bloody Allifair McCoy he didn't have the strength to fight off.

Chapter 9

Cap's eyes snapped open in the dark. His body may have collapsed, but his mind was racing. He'd left Allifair and Aunt Sally lying dead, side by side in the snow, Calvin by the corn crib. He should have covered the bodies before he left. He could still go back and do that.

In the dark, he could hear Nancy breathing, but couldn't see her. Pulling back the quilt, he was about to step onto the loft floor when she mumbled something and snuggled up to him. If he got out of bed, he'd have to tell her why.

Now that he was more awake, he realized going back was a bad idea. Randall had probably come out of the woods by now and found the three bodies and the two little girls in the barn. In the morning, he could go to Uncle Jim's place and they'd make plans to go after Randall before he could revenge himself. But Pappy had told him to stay home. Nancy wanted him to stay home. That wasn't quite right. What she really wanted was to move to Logan, to have some peace.

To be left alone and have some peace. That's why Grandpa Eph's parents had come to these mountains in the first place. In Virginia, Grandpa said, they fined you for cussing or not going to church, they jailed you for not paying your taxes. They taxed people so much that you could end up having to borrow from a rich man and then having to work for him to pay him back with hardly enough wages to starve on. And the rich men had help keeping you under their thumbs—the government, the church, schools teaching you it was your duty, the only honorable path, to do as you were told. So the Hatfields had come to the mountains to get away from all that. They just wanted to be left alone.

But who'd believe that? Over the last few years, the *Louisville Courier* had paid reporters to write outlandish stories about Hatfield men shooting not just McCoys, but every dead body that turned up with a bullet in it in West Virginia and Kentucky. "A vicious beast who won't rest until he's driven every decent man from West Virginia," some dumb fool had written about Pappy. "Illiterates whose only use for a newspaper is for gun wadding," another had written about the whole Hatfield clan.

Illiterate! He *could* read. Nancy had begun teaching him before they'd gotten married.

The rumors were so bad that some folks said he'd killed Nancy's first husband so he could marry her, when it said right on the death certificate that Joe Glenn's business partner had shot him. The truth was Cap had happened to find Nancy and little Joey when they needed a man to protect them.

That was almost six years ago. He reached over and lightly touched Nancy's hand. Some nights back then, when he'd floated home, full of his pleasures with Nancy, Pappy'd wanted to know what they were up to. "I'm learnin to read," he'd said. It had tickled him to hear Pappy mutter, "Dang waste of time." He giggled to himself. It still tickled him.

Now he was happy with a house and family of his own. Theirs was a good house, built in only five days with the help of neighbors and kin, just like the house-raisings where he'd helped other new families. The men pitched in to cut the logs, notch and stack them, put in doors and windows, and nail on the roof shingles. The women gathered around to cook for the men. There was food and fiddle music and dancing every night.

Nobody could have a house-raising along this side of the Tug if the Mc-Coys came over looking for revenge.

Still breathing deeply, Nancy stirred. The only way the world would ever be safe for her and their children would be for Randall McCoy to be taken out of it.

It was morning and there was enough light seeping in around the edges of the loft shutters for him to see the difference between Nancy's pale skin and dark hair. She opened her eyes.

"You're wide awake, Cap," she said softly, sleepily.

"I been thinkin."

"What?" He could make out her smile.

"I been thinkin about takin you and Joey to Logan."

"Oh, Cap." With a pregnant woman's grunt, she rolled over and hugged him. "What all can we take with us?"

"Before you start packin, I got to talk to Pappy. He ordered me not to do nothin he don't tell me to. I gotta see him first."

"Cap!" Nancy seized his shoulder and shook him. "This is our life, not your Pappy's."

"I got to talk to him." He didn't know how to make Nancy understand about himself and Pappy.

Chapter 10

He reckoned this was the best time to talk to Pappy—in the early afternoon, just after dinner, when there was a chance he'd be full and content. Standing outside the cabin with his ear pressed to a shutter, Cap listened and sniffed cooking aromas—bear meat, his favorite. The children were chattering and Pappy was quiet, a good sign.

He crunched through a light layer of snow to the front door he'd always entered by barging in. Maybe he should ease it open today or go around through the sleeping room and come in that way. No matter which way he considered, he envisioned Pappy bellowing at him.

Gently, with the tip of one finger, he pushed the door open and came inside behind where his brother Elliot was sitting. Mama was at the far right, Pappy at the far left end of the table.

"What are you doin here?" Pappy said.

The children stopped chattering and turned their eyes toward Cap.

"Nancy's time is gettin close. She wants to go to Logan."

"Your Mama, too." Pappy glared at him for a moment. "That's your fault."

Cap's head was beginning to ache and his ears to ring. "I want to take her and Joey to town as soon as we can get packed."

"Bring all this trouble down on us, then run to Logan with your tail between your legs," Pappy said.

"It's for Nancy and Joey and you know it." Cap's voice was getting louder in spite of his efforts to control it.

"The truth of it is Nancy's goin to Logan to look after you." Pappy sneered.

"Just like I'm goin down there to look after you, Anse," Mama said.

The children laughed.

Mama stood up and began clearing the table. "We'll see you and Nancy and Joey in Logan, Cappie."

Two days later, Cap and Nancy were packed for a stay at Uncle Elias's and Aunt Betty's. It had taken that long to squeeze everything into their saddle packs and talk to a neighbor on the next hill about feeding their pigs and chickens while they were gone. With two horses and a mule carrying six large saddle bags, he and Nancy had made room for a few books and magazines

—biographies, histories and women's romance stories—as well as their clothes and Joey's. Nancy had tried to talk him into leaving behind "that stupid book that claims the South won the War and has the Capitol in Washington surrounded." But it was the only book Pappy liked read to him, and Cap figured he'd take every chance he could find to cajole Pappy into a better frame of mind.

They set out for Logan in mid-morning. Cap rode Traveller, while Nancy sat sidesaddle on their fat old mare and Joey, his little legs sticking almost straight out, was astride the mule.

What a wretched, miserable day it was when a man had to flee his home to protect his wife and child, particularly when his own foolish actions had roused the enemy that would soon be after them. As Cap rode along to the plod-plod of horse hoofs and the squeaky voices of leather saddles and saddle bags, the sun rose high in the sky, its glare reflecting painfully off the snow into his eyes. His ears were so cold they hurt. The sun was too bright, the shadows too dark, bird calls, too shrill. He let his chin droop to his chest, half closed his eyes, and tried not to see, hear, or feel anything.

It was three hours before they came down out of the mountains to arrive at Frank White's clapboard store.

"We'll stop at Frank and Mary's, rest a spell and get some grub." He jumped down from Traveller to help Nancy off the mare. He was surprised how easily the bulging Nancy climbed down. But she always was naturally strong and graceful.

"Look, Joey." The cheeriness in Nancy's voice helped to ease Cap's gloomy mood. "Look at the cardinals." She pointed to a bright red male and a wood-brown female pecking dried corn off a snow-dusted porch rail. From a window ledge inside the store, a yellow tom cat stared through a glass window at the birds.

"He aint comin out in this cold after no bird." Joey laughed.

"Mrs. White won't want us trackin snow and mud into her nice clean store," Nancy warned Joey. They scraped the snow off their boots on a mat in front of the door.

"Not one speck of dirt and no commotion," Cap said. "Pappy told me how before the War, when he was young and kind of wild, Mary's mother used to close the store, shutter the windows, and hide in the house out back when him and his men rode into town. They knew she was there, but they left her alone." When Mary heard about the New Year's raid, would she close the store to him?

"Well, we won't be wild in Mrs. White's, will we?" Nancy hugged Joey's shoulders. "Then she'll be happy to see us."

Inside, a pot-bellied iron stove warmed the room. Two kerosene lamps hanging from the ceiling lit shelves and counters stacked with dishes, bolts of cloth, pills, boots, and books. Barrels of flour, pickles, salt, and nails stood on the floor, where mattresses rolled up and tied with yellow cord were also piled. Cap had to duck his head to keep from bumping into the buckets, tackle, and iron pots hanging on cords from the ceiling. Two young girls sat reading by the window where the cat crouched.

"Afternoon, Frank." Cap stepped up to the counter. Frank White was tall and broad-shouldered, but you could see the store owner in him—white skin, slim hands, not much in the way of getup and go—different from men who lived in the mountains.

"Cap Hatfield! What are you doing in town?" Frank didn't sound very friendly. "We heard there was some trouble." Frank pulled a pair of overalls off the shelf and laid them on the counter.

Was he talking about the raid? Cap tried to keep a poker face.

"Trouble? What are you talkin about?"

"There's been some talk about a ruckus over in Kentucky."

Cap grimaced. "I guess you know more'n I do." Frank had heard something.

Mary White promenaded up to the counter in her elegant fashion, developed, rumor had it, by hours spent every week walking with a book balanced on top of her head.

"Mary! How beautiful you look," Nancy said.

Cap had to admit Mary did look pretty in a long blue and green flowered skirt and starched white blouse, a cameo brooch at her throat. He'd never seen Mary in a homemade gingham or calico dress that women like his wife wore.

"Why thank you, Nancy." Mary's voice wasn't warm and friendly either.

"I'm takin Nancy to Uncle Elias's place to wait for the baby," Cap said. "Thought we'd stop by to visit and warm ourselves, have some grub."

"You're a bit late, I'm afraid. Nothing's left from dinner, and I haven't yet started supper." Mary pursed her lips together.

Cap caught the aroma of food cooking and felt his temper rising. Mary White could never be accused of saying an impolite word, but she was skilled at getting her dislikes across without words.

When Frank opened his mouth to speak, Mary turned sharply to her husband.

"Sorry, folks," he mumbled. "Looks like we're all out."

"You can sit for a minute, Nancy, if you've a mind to." Mary pointed to the worn wooden chairs around the pot-bellied stove.

"We don't need your chair or your fire, thank you," Nancy said. "Come on, Cap. Come on, Joey." She headed for the door and Cap followed her.

Joey, who'd been talking with the girls, ran after them. "Them girls don't believe I can read," Joey said. "Their mama told em Hatfields can't read and write, and we're hooligans. So I read a whole page. I showed them!"

"You read real good, Joey." Nancy gave him a hug.

"Mary White and her high-falutin ways!" Cap snorted. He almost wished he'd done something to upset Mary, like spit tobacco on her floor or swear a blue streak in front of her.

"They said you and Grandpa Anse aint nothin but trouble, Papa," Joey went on. "Their mama hopes you get put in jail so's there won't be no more fightin 'round here."

"She's ignorant, talkin like that," Cap said. "She don't live down by the Tug where McCoys could come over from Kentucky real quick and get her if she didn't fight back."

"Mary White has no manners at all," Nancy said. "Tellin stories to scare little children! Nobody's gonna get your Papa or Grandpa Anse."

Cap wondered about the rest of Logan. The Whites had apparently heard something about the New Year's raid—he didn't know what—and the news would have spread throughout Logan. An attitude toward the Hatfields would have formed. Maybe two attitudes—for and against.

As for some sheriff or constable getting him or Pappy—no way! Nobody would dare lay hands on either of them. All the same, he'd keep his eyes open and ears to the ground when he got to town. It paid to know who your friends and enemies were.

They took the rutted road, iced over in spots and muddy in others, from White's store, between steep mountains and into Logan. Down in the valley where the low sun couldn't reach and ice clogged the Guyandotte River, it was cold and dark in the middle of the day.

There wasn't much room in Logan, which Cap guessed was never more than half a mile wide, so the houses were squeezed together on little plots. He didn't want to live in a place like this where neighbors were closer than his outhouse and pig pen at the farm.

At the edge of town, the homes were log cabins separated by split rail fences. But as they rode on, they came to wood frame houses with picket fences painted white or brown. A few places were fancy, two or three stories high, surrounded by wide porches and railings, with more columns, arches, towers, and windows than you could count. Those were the houses of rich businessmen.

A man Cap didn't recognize, with a hat pulled down over his ears against the cold, came out of one of Logan's three taverns and trudged along the crunchy cinder walk flanking the street, drawing the sweet, stale smell of whiskey and beer along with him. Two women in coats down to their booted ankles, clutching packages wrapped in brown paper and string, picked their way from one stepping stone to another placed to help people cross the street muck of mud, melting ice, and manure. They glanced at Cap and his family, then quickly looked away. At the court house, several men watched them ride by. Cap knew them all, but only one tipped his hat. A mountain man Cap had occasionally had a few drinks with clatter-clomped in mountain boots along the new section of boardwalk fronting the barber shop, timber office, tannery, and shoe store, eyeing him warily.

Some of these people had never approved of the Hatfields. Now he had to worry about the rest, too.

In front of the Buskirk Hotel, Cap spotted John Floyd, an old friend of Pappy's and Secretary of State to Governor Wilson, a splendid sight in a long, black coat and derby hat bought in Charleston, the state capitol, where he and his wife got all their clothes. Floyd's handsome face, smooth as a woman's, was set off by a fine slim nose and dark brown eyes under softly arched eyebrows. Rumor was he went to the barber's for a shave twice a day, every day, to hear the local news and gossip he said was important to a politician. Floyd would know what was being said about the Hatfields. Cap dismounted, tied his horse to a rail, and hurried to meet him.

"Cap! How the heck are you?" Floyd clutched his arm. "I'm relieved to see you and your family looking well." The way the man gripped Cap's arm and searched his face made Cap uneasy. Floyd waited until two women had passed out of earshot, then spoke softly into Cap's ear. "I heard about the posses."

"What posses?" Cap blurted out, neglecting to keep his voice low. It would be impossible for Randall McCoy to bury his dead and round up a posse in only four days.

"Didn't you hear? The McCoys are getting up posses to go after you and your father and any other Hatfields they can lay their hands on. Perry Cline's backing them."

"Perry Cline!" Cap snorted. "That lily-livered toad?"

"According to my informants, Cline's been running around Kentucky hollering about some unfortunate affair on New Year's. He's been buying arms for the McCoys for some time and now he's got the Governor of Kentucky to offer a big reward for catching Hatfields."

"So that's how the McCoys got new rifles! Where are they lookin for us? Not over here in West Virginia?" Keeping his voice low this time, Cap glanced up and down the street.

"With the money they're offering, I expect there will be posses and bounty hunters in the hills and on our streets any day now."

Floyd's news was like a blow to Cap's gut, not to mention his plans for going after Randall. Randall wouldn't be traveling alone, but with a small army. And it was no longer true that killing him would end the feud, now that Cline was providing arms for posses and the Kentucky governor was offering rewards. Over only four days since New Year's things had gotten a lot more dismal.

He pointed to Nancy and Joey. "We're bringin the women and children to Logan."

"Good afternoon, Nancy." John Floyd tipped his derby.

"I'm hungry," Joey said. "We didn't get nothin to eat at the store."

"Perhaps you'd like to take your son over to Whited's." Floyd pointed to the boarding house down the street. "They usually have something extra on the fire."

"Good idea." Cap suspected Floyd was about to bring up some matters he'd rather Joey, and maybe Nancy, wouldn't hear. "We'll talk later," he told Nancy.

"Better watch your back, Cap," Floyd whispered. "Some folks in Logan favor calling on Governor Wilson to send the state militia down here to run you Hatfields out of Logan County."

"State militia!" This sounded like what Joey had heard from Frank and Mary White's girls.

"But you shouldn't worry too much about that." Floyd winked. "I'll be sure to remind the Governor of the great things Hatfields have done for him. And for me."

Floyd, who owed his Secretary of State position to Wilson, was no more grateful than he should be. Pappy had always seen to it that Logan County voters picked the ballot with Wilson for governor and Wilson's men for State Senator or Assemblyman. He and Pappy, well armed with revolvers and rifles to prevent election day violence, would stand guard over a table where ballots for one party were stacked on one side and ballots for the other party on the other. When Pappy pointed out the right choice, almost every man voting would pick his ballot from the Wilson pile. A few fellows grumbled and complained, but almost no man voted contrary to Pappy's wishes.

"That rag of yellow journalism, the *Louisville Courier,* says Sally McCoy claims you shot her daughter Allifair and her son Calvin, Jim Vance beat her with his rifle butt, and armed Hatfields burned their cabins clear to the ground," Floyd said. "I know that can't be true, but some folks around here are believing it."

"Sally McCoy's alive?"

Floyd searched Cap's face. "Why wouldn't she be?"

Cap was relieved, worried, and shocked. Sally McCoy was alive, but she had her facts wrong. "I didn't kill no one." He hoped his short answer would do for now. Surely Floyd wouldn't want to hear the whole story right now, in the middle of the street.

Floyd doffed his hat to two passing women. "Maybe Randall told her to pin Allifair's death on you."

"Sometime I'll tell you my opinion about what happened on New Year's." Cap couldn't bear to tell his miserable side of the story right then.

Floyd nodded, silently, as Cap had hoped he would. If you were a friend of his, he usually contented himself with your decision about what you would or would not talk about. He'd find out some other way.

Jim Nighbert, a land owner and agent for Cole and Crane Timber, passed by on the boardwalk, eyes glaring at Cap from a sallow, heavily bearded face, his black coat bulging over his round belly.

"There's a man you'd better watch out for," Floyd said.

"My Uncle Elias says Nighbert considers himself the biggest bug in the Logan cornfield."

Floyd laughed. "He's a 'varmint,' to use one of your father's favorite words. But listen Cap, have you and your father ever considered moving to Logan? Elias likes it here, away from all the trouble."

"Let them danged McCoys chase us off our land? You know me and Pappy better'n that, John Floyd." Floyd was letting him know he suspected there was something to the stories in the *Courier*. Maybe not exactly what was described in that rag, but something.

"Sometimes it's better to cut your losses rather than lose everything you have. Even General Lee came to realize that."

"But Lee was losin. We aint."

Floyd raised his fine eyebrows. "The tide of battle has turned, Cap. Kentucky's posses and bounty hunters are now the hounds, and you're the rabbits and it'd be a good idea to look for a safe hole to hide in. As far from the border with Kentucky as you can get."

"There aint no McCoy can make me run like a scared rabbit!" How could John suggest such a thing?

Floyd sighed and shook his head. "I said posses, not necessarily legal ones, and bounty hunters, people that will get paid for catching or killing you. Lots of people, way beyond a few McCoys. Here, take my copy of the *Courier* and read what they're saying." He pulled a newspaper from his coat pocket and handed it to Cap.

"You're a good friend, John." It looked like he'd have to forget about going alone after Randall, but he and Pappy didn't dare give up their homes and timberland. What would they do to earn a living down here in Logan, where there was no timber and they were feared and hated by so many? "I appreciate your advice. Pappy and me'll think it over."

"Let me know if you need my help." Floyd appeared relieved. "I'll always stand by you and your father as you've always stood by me. And there are others in Logan like me." He pointed to Doc Rutherford's sign across the street.

"Thanks, John." Cap admired Floyd's ways with people. Many politicians would have run for cover, would have had nothing to do with the Hatfields, after what the *Courier* had printed. But John always found a way to make everyone feel like a friend, no matter whose side they were on in a quarrel. He could be friends with the Hatfields and the Nighberts at the same time and knew how to make his actions backing one side acceptable to the other when he needed to.

Cap knocked at at Whited's door and told the hired girl he'd come to pick up Nancy and Joey. He didn't want to risk asking to go inside and being turned away by a Hatfield fearer.

The three of them rode in silence. Cap wanted to tell Nancy that Aunt Sally was alive, but not where he'd have to shout it from his horse in the middle of a Logan street. Searching the faces of people they passed, he thought he saw hostility everywhere. But a bunch of frightened townspeople who'd worked themselves into a dither wasn't nearly as much to worry about as posses and bounty hunters.

He'd learned from Floyd that Perry Cline was not only calling for posses to go after his family, but was supplying the McCoys and others with arms. Cline was a lawyer and businessman, supposedly one of the richest men in Pikeville, who always stuck to town, riding a fancy carriage between his brick office building and big white mansion. You wouldn't catch Cline on mountain trails out beyond the Kentucky mountains down by the Tug. What was he joining up with the McCoys for?

Revenge for something that happened years ago? Many times Cap had heard Pappy tell how Cline had lived and timbered in West Virginia just like the Hatfields, about ten or fifteen years ago, in the 1870s. Cline's holding had been large—three thousand acres of oak, poplar, and beech—but he hadn't been satisfied with cutting his own trees and had logged on Pappy's much smaller piece of land, too. After a court made him pay Pappy back, Cline tried to get even by cutting more Hatfield trees. Finally, the Court awarded Pappy Cline's deed to hold in trust for the whole three thousand acres, which Pappy decided entitled him to timber anywhere on that land. He used a crew armed with rifles to chase Cline and his men out. Claiming he feared for his life, Cline had fled to Pikeville where he had relatives living near Randall McCoy. Mama and Pappy eventually built their home on the "Cline" property.

There could be a connection here. Cline wanted revenge or wanted his land back.

Chapter 11

Frantically trying to think how he'd present Floyd's bad news to the family, especially Pappy, Cap led Nancy and Joey toward Uncle Elias's and Aunt Betty's place. He had to let everyone know about the posses and bounty hunters, but he yearned to avoid enduring more blame, especially from Pappy.

"There it is." He pointed out a white wood frame house constructed of smooth, planed boards. It was a box, a two-story crate for people, from which windows with glass in them stared out like eyes. Lined with shrubs, a path led from the front gate through a picket fence to a porch that sheltered two rocking chairs. A vision of his own cabin standing free in a field with trails wandering past boulders, trees, and wild blackberries passed through his mind. Since they'd moved to Logan, Uncle Elias and Aunt Betty were living more like townspeople than mountain folks. The only thing that made Elias's house any different from his neighbors' was four beaver pelts nailed up to dry on a wall under the porch roof.

Cap helped Nancy and Joey down and tied the horses and mule to a hitching rail before entering what Aunt Betty called her yard, which she didn't want trampled by horses, cows, or pigs. That and the fact that her neighbors all had fences were the reasons for hers.

Inside, Uncle Elias, Aunt Betty, their two youngest children, Cap's sister Nancy Belle and brother Elliot were sitting around the fireplace with Pappy and Mama. Everyone but Pappy said a warm hello and Aunt Betty almost swept Joey off the floor, making him squeal with delight when she shouted, "Bear hug!" Then she sent him outside with her children to sled in the snow.

Except for the cherry wood rocking chair Mama had settled in, the cane bottom chairs and wooden kitchen table were the kind of furniture Cap was used to. And the family used a stone fireplace for cooking and heat just like mountain people. But the room's white plank walls, a narrow wooden staircase leading to the second story, and glass in the windows said this was Logan, not the mountains. The place gave Cap the uncomfortable feeling that Uncle Elias and Aunt Betty were slipping away from the family.

Betty resembled Mama—short, dark-haired, and dark-eyed. Uncle Elias was tall, barely short of Pappy's six feet, deep-chested and powerfully built like his brother, but his nose arched slightly, not threateningly like Pappy's formidable beak. Cap thought Elias looked like a watered-down version of Pappy.

Pappy, tamping tobacco and fiddling with the stem of his pipe, never looked up to greet him and Nancy.

"Where'd you put the rest of the children?" Cap asked Mama.

"We handed them around here and there. Your uncles Smith and Patterson don't mind takin them and Joey in, but they don't want nothin to do with no wars. So they want you and your Pappy and Johnse and Bobby Lee to stay away."

"They're treatin us like we're a bunch of mad dogs." His own uncles! "What's the matter with them?"

Pappy's head jerked up. "What's the matter? You killed Randall McCoy's wife and children and left him alive to go squawkin all over Kentucky about it. That's what's the matter."

Cap stepped over to the fireplace and kicked hard, knocking a partly burnt log back into the center of the fire. "I never touched Allifair or Calvin or Aunt Sally. If I hadn't of had to drag Johnse and Cotton Top along I would have gotten the job done right."

"And if my aunt had of been a man she'd of been my uncle," Pappy snorted. "You aint got no other word but 'if.' Must be the only word they got in them books you read."

With a swish of her skirts, Cap's sister, Nancy Belle, stood up in front of Pappy and tugged so hard on the bottom of her quilted jacket that it made a snapping sound. "It aint Cap's fault. You always hold Cap to blame when anything goes wrong."

Cap could have hugged Nancy Belle. Unlike Mama, who supported just about everything Pappy said and did, Nancy Belle always spoke her mind. Of course, Mama understood Pappy, whose father had been mean and harsh with him, leaving Pappy with a very thin skin when it came to criticism. If she disagreed with him, she would speak to him in private, softening him up first.

"Wouldn't be no McCoys around if you was after em, Nancy Belle." Pappy chuckled. His favorite sister could talk back to Pappy in a way Cap could never get away with.

"I feel safe with Cap around." Nancy Belle stared down at Pappy.

"You think you know so much." Cap's skinny little fifteen-year-old brother Elliot sneered. "We aint all that safe." He tilted his chin sideways and up in a way they all thought was to make up for being short and having three big tall brothers.

"Well, you aint never fought nobody," Nancy Belle shot back. "So how would you know?"

"Nancy Belle!" Mama glared at her. They all knew Mama hoped to keep Elliot out of the fighting.

"Mama's right to shush us," Cap said. "We got to take care of our troubles and quit arguin amongst ourselves."

"Sit down and shut up," Pappy said. "I'm sick of listenin to you."

"But Cap's right." Uncle Elias was coming to his defense. "Enough of this arguin."

"You know what he done?" Pappy leaned toward Elias and pointed to Cap.

Elias nodded. "I know and I'm tired of hearin about it."

Mama went to Pappy's side and laid her hand on his shoulder. "Hollerin at Cap aint gonna help, Anse. What's done is done."

Pappy bit his lip, patted her hand and continued glaring at Cap.

Cap knew he was in for more trouble when Pappy got today's bad news. But maybe he could shift some of Pappy's rage to the *Louisville Courier* reporters. He pulled the paper from his pocket, spread it on a table by a lantern.

"I got some lies and bad news to read to you."

Pappy snorted. "Never mind he can't take a simple order, my son can read a newspaper." He shook his head and rolled his eyes.

Elias grimaced. "Don't run him down for readin, for God's sake. Readin makes a lot more sense than fightin."

Cap wondered what it would have been like to be Elias's son instead of Pappy's. He cleared his throat. "Are you gonna listen or not?"

"Of course," Elias said.

"Don't make no nevermind to me." Pappy lit his pipe and drew on it.

Cap began to read aloud the story that filled the front page of the paper. "It starts out 'A Murderous Gang, A Terrible Story.' They got pictures somebody drawed of me and Uncle Jim and Johnse and you, too, Pappy, with rifles, lookin like we're about to gun somebody down. Under my picture it says 'Murderous Fiend.'"

Cap felt sick. The burden of being a child killer was settling on his back and he feared it woud stay there for the rest of his life. "I didn't kill nobody," he said softly.

He looked at Nancy, whose happiness at being in Logan had faded from her face.

"Well, let's hear the rest." Pappy's voice brought Cap out of his thoughts.

"It don't get no better." He read on. "It says Randall found his wife and brung her to Pikeville in his wagon with two little girls sittin half froze beside their grandma."

"Are they sayin Sally's alive?" Pappy's voice dropped almost to a whisper.

"Alive and talkin."

"Poor Sally aint never been the cause of these troubles between our families." Mama's eyes were tearing. "I'm glad she lived."

Cap read how Aunt Sally had told reporters Cap shot Allifair and Calvin "in cold blood."

"I never did nothin to her." Cap was getting desperate to stamp out this lie. "Aunt Sally was inside her sleepin cabin when Cotton Top shot Allifair. She couldn't of seed who done it."

"What'd I always tell you?" Pappy said. "Them folks that write books and newspapers'll write any lie for money."

For once, Cap was glad that Pappy was aiming his rage at a newspaper.

"Sally's callin Uncle Jim 'that evil Jim Vance'," Cap read on. "She's sayin he clubbed her with his rifle as she tried to go to her dyin daughter. That part's true."

"Jim's got a quick temper," Uncle Elias said. "Still, I never thought he'd hit a woman."

Cap had more news. "The paper says Aunt Sally was frost-bit real bad and might die soon and add another murder to the list of Hatfield crimes."

"My heart aches for her," Mama said. "She must be cryin her eyes out for Calvin and Allifair. And her home's gone, too."

"She's tellin the whole world who was there on New Year's," Pappy said. "And addin some that wasn't there at all. Save your tears for our boys."

"All tears is the same, Anse. No matter whose children they're for."

"She's callin Cappie a *murderer*, Levicy." Pappy's voice had a knife edge to it.

In spite of everything, Cap felt a little relieved. It looked like Pappy might be thinking of him as a valued son again. He read aloud how people in Pikeville were helping Randall and Aunt Sally out with food and clothes and a place to stay. The Hatfields were reviled in Kentucky, and wanted for the murder of children, he was the most hated of all.

He hated himself, hated the vision of bloodied Allifair that went everywhere with him.

The rest of the article told how Perry Cline was donating money for guns and ammunition to arm posses dedicated to hunting down Hatfields. Besides the McCoys, many other Kentucky citizens were volunteering. The Governor of Kentucky was offering a $2700 reward for the arrest and delivery to the Pikeville jail of any Hatfield involved in the New Year's raid or the murder of three McCoy boys in 1882.

"That wasn't murder!" Pappy stomped his feet. "Them boys done the murderin. Everybody knows that. They was *executed* for murder."

"What do you expect from a Kentucky newspaper, Anse?" Uncle Elias gave his brother a you-should-know-better look.

Pappy frowned. "Cline's behind all this. He's probably been waitin all these years to get even with me over that land."

"Cline was settin the McCoys on us," Nancy Belle said. "Then waitin to pounce like a big old cougar pitty-pattin up behind us, lickin his chops."

"If they didn't use the New Year's raid for an excuse, they would have found another," Nancy added. Cap would be forever grateful to his wife and sister for these words.

Pappy looked at Cap. "Don't know what we're gonna do about them posses. They daren't come over here to Logan, but they're probably fixin to cross the Tug. Takin our logs down the river's gonna be near impossible this spring."

Pappy was beginning to talk family problems over with him again as though he realized there was no one else who could help him except the son he'd trained to take his place some day.

"I got a little bit more to read." The article finished with the news that Special Deputy Frank Phillips of Pikeville had been assigned the duty of "bringing these criminals to justice."

"Who the heck's that?" Pappy asked.

"He's got a mean reputation as a bully over in Kentucky," Uncle Elias said. "Likes to shoot at men's feet and make em dance like he heard gunfighters do out west."

Pappy frowned. "We got to find out how many men they got in them posses and what their orders are."

Cap took a deep breath. "We got a big job ahead of us and we ought to sit down and think about some plans." He hoped it would matter to Pappy that he wanted to think and plan instead of carrying on about gunning down McCoys the way he would have in the past, although that's what he intended to do after he'd thought and planned.

Chapter 12

That evening John Floyd summoned Cap, Pappy, and Uncle Elias to the town meeting room in the courthouse. Uncle Jim was coming, too, as soon as he left Aunt Mary at a cousin's house.

"He wants to know what really happened on New Year's," Cap said on the way. "I'll bet you anything."

"Naw, he don't," Pappy answered. "He knows all he needs to. By now, John's figurin out how to get us out of this mess whilst stayin in tight with the likes of Nighbert. He's got a real knack for politickin and he'll be wantin to enjoy hisself with his ability."

Uncle Elias chuckled. "You know your man, Anse."

In the meeting room, a lantern lit the table where they were to sit and cast a glow into the shadows surrounding the rows of benches.

"How many people you got in Logan now?" Cap was surprised at the size of the room.

"More than three hundred," Floyd said. "Three thousand in the county."

That was way too many for Cap. They'd get in his way if he lived down here, which he never intended to.

Uncle Jim entered and stomped the snow off his boots. "Phillips got Selkirk McCoy."

"I don't hardly believe that," Pappy said. "Where'd you hear that?"

Cap knew Randall had wanted to get his hands on Selkirk ever since he'd backed the Hatfields at the hog trial. But Selkirk had moved to West Virginia a long time ago and stayed there.

"Phillips and about thirty others—I guess mostly McCoys—come across the Tug, snuck up on Selkirk whilst he was squirrel huntin and carted him off to the Pikeville jail. Heard it from Sally McCoy's sister, and she oughta know."

"They can't come over into West Virginia and kidnap a man!" Pappy slapped his hand hard on the table. "That's against the law."

"Well they done it," Jim said. "And they'll get two thousand and seven hundred dollars for bringin him in."

"Governor Wilson and I will certainly have something to say to the Governor of Kentucky about that!" Floyd raised his voice as he did when he made public speeches. "An incursion and kidnapping in our sovereign state, encouraged by financial reward. Intolerable!"

"You'll see to it they hand Selkirk over?" Pappy asked.

"Wilson and I will certainly do our best. Let's hope Governor Buckner cooperates." Floyd hesitated. "I need to pass on something I learned today from my barber who overheard someone talking to Jim Nighbert. A railroad's going in down by the Tug."

"That so?" Pappy gave Floyd a puzzled look.

Floyd nodded. "It's not settled yet whether the railroad is to go up the West Virginia or the Kentucky side of the river. So, before the news becomes public knowledge, everybody in the know is trying to grab up land on both sides. Towns and businesses will spring up along the railroad and they all want to be in on the boom times."

"Then my land—our land." Pappy pointed at Cap and Uncle Jim. "It's gonna be worth a heap of gold."

"Nighbert's figured that out and has gotten a step ahead of you. He's gathered up all the Judases he can find who will swear in court that you owe them money. He's putting together one big lawsuit, big enough, he hopes, to force you to sell your property out by the Tug to settle. Then good old Nighbert will pounce on your land and buy it."

"Danged vulture," Pappy snarled.

"Everybody knows Pappy pays his debts!" Cap exploded. "Nobody in Logan will believe that hogwash."

"All Nighbert needs is a few fellows hungry enough for their shekels of betrayal to swear to a false oath in court," Uncle Elias said.

"Land and money." Floyd shook his head. "Men like Nighbert and Perry Cline would never dream of carrying a gun or even getting their boots muddy on the back roads. But they'll egg others on to do their dirty work, offering money and glory in exchange." Floyd said the suit was being brought for a total of $613.31 and showed them a list of the plaintiffs. He feared Nighbert and his gang would succeed as long as they stuck together and no one squealed on anyone else.

Pappy swore he owed none of those men a penny, and he couldn't lay his hands on that much money without selling some of his property. "John, this is the worst fix I've ever been in. They're after my sons, my men, my money, my loggin business, and my land. They want everything I got except my wife and babies. How am I gonna pay $613 if Nighbert wins? If I lose my timberland and can't make no money, how am I gonna pay for guns and ammunition to fight off them posses and for lawyers when I'm sued?"

"We got to get back to timberin," Uncle Jim said. "That's all there is to it. No way around it."

"You was raised on bear meat, Jim," Pappy said. "So you aint never gonna give up on nothin. But tell me how we're gonna do this timberin with bullets flyin around our ears."

"There's a couple ways we can go." Seeing his chance to earn back Pappy's esteem, Cap grabbed at it. "We can pull back from the Tug a while and hope this blows over. But that'll leave our homes unguarded. We can sell our land and move down here. But how will we timber then? Or we can get up our own posse, go after Phillips and his men when they come over here and run em out. I'm in favor of that."

"I'm inclined to go after them posses, too," Pappy said. "But first I got to figure out what I can pay for."

For years Cap had kept track of Pappy's business debts, costs, and income in books Nancy had once sold in her store. Pappy would have to rely on him to figure out what he could pay for, a perfect opportunity to demonstrate his worth and unique value.

For an hour or so, Cap calculated at one end of the table while Floyd read to Pappy and Uncle Jim about the raid from an Ohio newspaper. Cap was pretty sure they had twenty-five men they could count on, could probably get ten more, who'd have to hole up in the fort or camp out by mountain trails until they'd wiped out enough of the posses to force Phillips and the McCoys to give up. For that they'd need rifles, ammunition, and food for everybody for as much as six months because it might be impossible to cut timber or hunt or grow crops this year, and their smoke houses, root cellars, chicken coops, and barns might be looted. When everything had been added up, Cap found that for just the first month they'd need to buy twenty rifles, thousands of bullets, and enough food to fill a lumber wagon. That would cost nearly three hundred dollars.

"Whooee!" Pappy sat back and whistled. "That's just about all the cash I got. And we aint even got to hirin lawyers."

"If we man the fort and patrol our land, we'll run out of money by the middle of spring even if we use every dollar we have amongst us." Cap couldn't argue with his own figures. "Our best move is to go after them now, try to get it over quick."

Pappy ran his fingers through his beard. "Might take us a while to catch up with them Kentucky varmints."

"We better get started now," Cap replied.

"I want the fort manned and patrols out by our land every hour of the day and night until we get our livestock, our food, your Mama's sewin machine, her dishes, everything down to Logan with us. Get all our belongins out of reach. Then we'll have a go at wipin out them posses."

Cap liked this plan, his plan really, and was glad Pappy admired it as much as he did. "If we can do that, if their losses are heavy enough, Cline and Phillips'll have to give up."

Floyd tapped his fingers on the table. "Just make sure you stay out of Kentucky. Governor Wilson and I won't be able to help you if you're captured over there."

"Nary a one of us will be settin foot in Kentucky. Them's my orders." Pappy shook a finger at Cap like any parent would shake his finger at a naughty child.

Cap hated that finger.

Chapter 13

The next morning Cap mounted Traveller in a cold, heavy fog where he couldn't see more than a few feet and the hoofbeats of the horses around him were muffled. He and Pappy and Uncle Jim wanted to get to their homes out by the Tug early, ahead of any Kentucky posses, to fetch all their livestock and belongings back to Logan. On the way out of town they rounded up Bobby Lee, Charlie Carpenter, and five cousins, good dependable men, enough to pack and carry out a lot of goods on their horses. They borrowed three mules from Uncle Smith in Logan and a hauling sled from Pappy's place. They'd box up the chickens and drive the ox, cows, and hogs along the trail as best they could.

Within a few minutes they were in the snowy, leafless woods, peering into the fog and listening intently. No one expected posses or bounty hunters on the Logan side of the mountains, but it was smart to be cautious. All Cap heard was the plod-plunk of horseshoes in snow. They saw no other riders and only a few cabins before crossing the mountains and coming down on the Tug side. Descending through the fog, they made out Ralph Steele's cabin and barn.

Pappy reined in his horse, held up his hand, then put a finger to his lips, apparently listening for something. The only sounds Cap heard were horses stomping and nickering in the barn.

Dismounting quietly, Pappy hitched his horse to a tree and motioned the others to do the same. Cap strained to see or hear what Pappy seemed to have seen or heard. But he heard only restless horses in the barn and saw nothing but a wisp of chimney smoke rising from the cabin and blending into the fog.

"Hear them horses?" Pappy whispered.

Of course he heard them. That's what you'd expect to hear when the Steeles were home, which the chimney smoke said they were.

"There's three of em and Steele aint got but two," Pappy said. "And they're frettin because they aint used to bein in Steele's barn."

Cap could have kicked himself. If he'd been leading, they'd have ridden right past this cabin. Shame and envy. He was beside himself.

Catching sight of Cap's distress, Pappy allowed a quick smirk of superiority to pass over his face. "I'm gonna take a look at them horses," he whispered. "Stay here. Keep out of sight."

Pulling their coat collars up high against the cold dampness, Cap and the others huddled under the snow-laden branches of a pine tree. Pappy was back in a minute. "Them horses aint from around here. They sure aint Steele's."

"McCoys!" Cap kept his voice low in spite of his excitement. What a stroke of luck if they caught Randall McCoy today.

"McCoys, a posse, bounty hunters." Pappy said. "We'll know in a minute. We got ten men and there's only three of them. I want you to spread around the cabin." Pappy directed everyone to positions in back of the cabin, to the left and right and watched until they were in place. Only Cap stayed with Pappy behind the pines.

"Come out with your hands up!" Pappy shouted from behind a tree. "I'm Devil Anse Hatfield and I got forty men out here."

Grunting, stumbling, and scraping sounds came from inside the cabin, but no one answered. Cap strained in vain to hear a voice, although he wasn't sure he could identify Randall's or any other McCoy's if he heard it.

"You're surrounded," Pappy called out again. "You best come out here where I can get a look at you. With your hands up."

"You best go on your way!" a voice called from the cabin. "We aint comin out."

"That's not Steele," Uncle Jim called out to Pappy. "That aint nobody from around here."

And that wasn't Randall McCoy. But Cap wasn't ready to give up hope. There were two other men in there.

"There's only three of em and they got the shutters closed over the winders," Pappy told Cap. "They can't see us, so you and me's gonna run up and break down the door. Pass the word along for everybody to run in behind us."

After waiting long enough for the message to have gotten around, Pappy held his rifle in front of himself and Cap imitated him.

"One, two, three," Pappy counted and they dashed toward the cabin, turned sideways at the last moment, and slammed their shoulders against the heavy plank door. With a crash of splintering wood, the door broke from its hinges and flew across the room with Cap and Pappy right behind. Hatfield men instantly ran in to fill the one-room cabin. By the light of a dying night fire, Cap saw three men with raised hands, none of them a McCoy or anyone else he knew.

"Where's Steele?" Uncle Jim barked at the prisoners.

"Don't know who you're talkin about," a tall lean man with dark, greasy, slicked-down hair said. Cap could tell from the peculiar way he talked and the store-bought jacket and pants he wore that he wasn't from the mountains. The other two with britches tucked into their boots looked like mountain men, but weren't from around here either. Their unkempt beards and clothes said they'd been on the road a few days.

"Who're you?" Pappy pointed his Winchester at the man's head.

"I'm Dan Cunningham. You got no business bustin in here without a warrant, Devil Anse."

"You got a warrant for breakin into this house?" Cap wasn't going to let Cunningham get away with that warrant hogwash. Posse members or bounty hunters, these men had no stake in the Tug Valley feuds. They were here for the money or just for the heck of it, buzzards and vultures out to feed off the embattled Hatfields.

"Didn't break in," Cunningham sneered. "We knocked politely and when nobody came to the door we looked inside."

"You got any more men around here?" Pappy asked. "Randall McCoy? Frank Phillips?"

Cunningham laughed. "They left for Kentucky yesterday with the Mahon brothers—three of em."

Phillips's posse had come into West Virginia and kidnapped three more Hatfield kin right out from under their noses.

Pappy seized Cunningham by the jacket front and slammed him against a wall. "Where they takin em?"

"Pikeville," Cuningham sneered. "You can't catch up with em. They been in Kentucky half a day by now."

Pikeville. Then there was no hope of getting them back.

"Anything happens to the Mahon brothers and you fellers will pay for it in blood," Pappy said.

Cunningham didn't flinch, but the other two looked worried.

"Get their guns." Pappy let go of Cunningham. Then he had Bobby Lee and Charlie Carpenter search the cabin loft, the wash shed, and outbuildings. They found no one.

"What do you think we ought to do with these varmints?" Pappy looked to his men, standing across the room from their captives, rifles pointed at them like a firing squad.

"Can't let em go," Uncle Jim said.

"Shoot em and be rid of em." Cap's cousin French Ellis had never been known to shirk his duty when it came to killing.

"I want that one." Cap aimed his rifle at a beady-eyed weasel. He wanted to see how scared their prisoners would get.

"You're playin with us," Cunningham said. "You aint gonna shoot us, are you, Devil Anse?"

Pappy grinned. "You aint much good to us dead. We can't trade dead bodies for Selkirk McCoy or the Mahon brothers. Mr. Cunningham, I think we'll take you fellers to Logan."

Cap lowered his rifle.

"What do you mean take us to Logan?" Cunningham's other sidekick, a big, brawny fellow without much smarts showing in his eyes spoke up.

Pappy looked the man up and down, seeming to find nothing pleasing about him. "I'm gonna take you to Logan and lock you up in the pokey."

"That's kidnappin," the prisoner replied. "Do that and you'll be wanted for kidnappin on top of murder."

Cap had a good laugh at that. "And what about Selkirk McCoy and the Mahon brothers? I believe what happened to them's called kidnappin."

"Wrong," Cunningham said. "Mr. Phillips is in charge of a legal posse, deputized by the Governor of Kentucky."

Cap laughed again. "Legal? Deputized? You and Phillips aint deputized to do nothin in West Virginia and you know it."

"Tie em up," Pappy ordered.

Cap and Bobby Lee tied the three prisoners' hands in front so they could ride their horses.

"You're Cap Hatfield, aint you?" Cunningham said as his wrists were being bound. "Devil Anse's number one son. We got a murder warrant for you."

Pappy stomped over and shoved his face next to Cunningham's. "Any man lays a hand on my son's gonna answer to me."

Cap clenched his jaws. A treasured son was a good thing, but it rubbed him wrong that Pappy hadn't said something more like "My son can take care of you any day."

They took the captives outside at gunpoint, then brought their horses from the barn and forced the three men to mount. Pappy took Cap and Jim aside. "With the rest of the posse on the way to Pikeville, I think we got a day or two before they come back across the river. We'll haul these three to the

Logan jail and be back out here by morning."

Uncle Jim nodded. "Might be we can trade em. Otherwise, I'll be burned if they're worth the trouble of haulin em in."

"Let's get movin," Pappy said. "I want to get to Logan before dark."

Pappy let the others ride ahead, hanging back to have a word with Cap. "Think you learned anything about handlin a skirmish today?"

Cap's face turned hot. He kicked Traveller's side and joined the line of men on the trail.

"You got a chance to watch me and learn a few things, son," Pappy called out from behind him. "You'd do well to pay attention."

Cap kicked Traveller again, riding as fast as he could along the muddy, rocky trail until he was far enough from Pappy to be out of earshot.

Two hours down the trail they maneuvered their horses carefully down the steep, icy bank of Little Creek.

"There's ten of you and three of us," Cunningham said as they stopped at the creek side. "If we'd of had better odds, you'd be on the way to jail instead of us."

"We would of taken you in anyhow," Pappy said. "You aint much good at bounty huntin."

"Been a detective for twenty years," Cunningham said. "I can take you on any day. Just give me a chance one on one with you, Devil Anse."

"Might do that." Pappy's grin was wide enough to show a row of teeth between his heavy beard and mustache.

Look out, Cunningham, Cap thought.

As Cousin Elliot started across the creek, his horse spooked at the thinning ice snapping and cracking beneath its hooves. Elliot finally coaxed it along and Cap got Traveller to cross, but the other riders decided it was safer to get off and lead their horses through the knee-deep, ice-encrusted creek rather than risk being thrown into the freezing water.

Except for Pappy. His horse danced back and forth in the snow at the creek edge until Pappy got down. "Cunningham, come get my horse," he ordered.

Cunningham stood where he was on the opposite bank.

Cap prodded Traveller over close to Cunningham. "Get on over." He pointed to Pappy.

Slowly, hands still tied in front of him, Cunningham waded Little Creek, then led Pappy's horse across.

"Now come get me, Cunningham," Pappy called out.

"What do you mean 'Come get you?'"

"Come back over here." Pappy pointed to the ground at his feet.
Cunningham waded across.

"You're about to get your chance for one on one," Pappy said.

"Can't fight with my hands tied up." Cunningham held out his arms.

"Who said we was gonna fight? I got some fine-lookin boots here and I aint aimin to get em wet. You're gonna carry me across—one on one." Pappy laughed and hopped around, flapping his arms like a crow.

"I aint."

Uncle Jim raised his rifle and pointed it at Cunningham's head.

"You just turn around, and I'll hitch myself up." Pappy climbed onto Cunningham's back, wrapped one arm across Cunningham's chest, his legs around his prisoner's waist and with his free arm held his Winchester over Cunningham's head. "One on one. Just like you wanted."

Cunningham grunted and struggled across the creek carrying Pappy, whose bushy beard hung down to Cunningham's eyes as he called out, "Giddiup, mule!" Cap reckoned Pappy's hee-haws could be heard all the way to Logan. They had to be deafening in the purple-faced Cunningham's ears. Pappy wasn't about to shoot his victim, but tormenting him half to death was a fair substitute.

Uncle Jim nearly fell off his horse laughing, while the others watched in amazed silence. Deciding it was time to let Pappy know he was behind him all the way, Cap let rip a loud roar of what he hoped sounded like laughter, even if it didn't feel like it. When he saw Pappy's eyes glisten in appreciation, he forced himself to keep on.

After they'd crossed, Pappy eased himself off Cunningham's back and danced a little jig, his coat tails flapping. He pointed to his boots.

"Aint they purty?"

Wet and shivering, Cunningham spat on the ground. "Frank Phillips aint gonna think this is funny."

"Tell Phillips to come on over." Pappy chortled. "You and him'll make good cell mates."

By now, Cap supposed Cunningham was about as angry as he'd ever been in his life. Being humiliated by Pappy could drive a man crazy.

On the way to Logan, Cunningham carried Pappy across two more creeks, erupting into floods of profanity each time. Cap began to have doubts about how smart all this humiliation was. If he was only a bounty hunter before today, Cunningham was now a Hatfield-hating enemy.

It was nearly nightfall by the time they rode into town. Lanterns and oil lamps were just being lit in houses with glass windows, their lights glowing through the fog. The courthouse, the only brick building in Logan, the only brick building Cap had ever seen outside Catlettsburg on the Ohio, housed the jail on one side, with four cells on the ground floor and four on the floor above.

Men watched curiously as Pappy, Cap, and Cousin Elliot herded the three prisoners across the frozen, rutted yard, up ice-covered stone steps and through the front door. The jailer's office, opening off the entrance hallway, was so small that Pappy had the rest wait outside, except for Bobby Lee who was sent to fetch John Floyd.

A lantern threw a bright light on a rough-hewn, unpainted table and gun rack, the only furniture in the office of the jailer, Jim Chafin. The walls and floor were of solid stone, cut from a Logan quarry, as were all the cells on the ground floor. No one had ever escaped from these stone cages with bars of iron on their doors and windows.

"We caught these three varmints hidin out in Ralph Steele's cabin," Pappy told Chafin, who was Cap's cousin on his mother's side. "They's part of a Kentucky posse illegally in our state for the purpose of kidnappin. Bein as we know that's against the law, we did the sheriff a favor and brung em in."

"*This* is kidnapping!" Cunningham complained. "Draggin us in here— that's against the law."

Chafin didn't reply, never even changed the expression on his leathery face, but pulled a Winchester out of its rack. "Git!" he said to Cunningham, pointing to the door. "How about givin me a hand, Cap?"

Cap followed him down a hallway and locked each of the captives in a separate cell with a key from Chafin's ring. He'd never before been inside the jail, but now saw first-hand how cold and dark it was in the stone cells. Only a trickle of light from a street lamp seeped through the barred windows.

"Governor Buckner'll hear about this!" Cunningham grasped the bars to his cell as if to choke them.

"Let Buckner know we might consider lettin you go if he frees our men." Cap had an idea, one of his best. He could write to Buckner offering to trade these three for the four Hatfield men held in the Pikeville jail.

When he returned to Chafin's office, John Floyd was there, elegant as ever in black coat and derby hat.

"Who you got back there, Anse?" With his thumb Floyd indicated the direction of the row of cells. As they all sauntered down the hall to the first cell, Pappy told Floyd how they'd captured the prisoners.

"Part of Phillip's gang of kidnappers, are you?" Floyd peered in and wrinkled his nose as though he smelled something bad.

"You aint got no charges to hold us on," Cunningham said. "We never did nothin but ride around the beautiful snow-covered mountains enjoyin ourselves in the great out of doors."

"Charges? Attempted kidnapping. Attempted murder. That sound right to you, Anse?" Floyd raised his eyebrows and smiled at Pappy.

"Kidnappin and murder!" Cunningham yelled. "That's a lie, you son of whoredung!"

"And using vulgar language." Floyd shook his head as though deeply offended. "Keep a record of every time he opens his mouth to use foul language and disturbs the serenity of this peaceful establishment," Floyd said to Chafin.

When Cap, Cousin Elliot, and Pappy left the jail with Cunningham's fuming and raging—no profanity—ringing in their ears, Floyd followed them into the street.

"Cunningham wants out real bad." Cap shook his head and chuckled. "Why don't we help him out? I'll write a letter to Cline and Buckner offering to trade him and his pals for Selkirk and the Mahon brothers."

Pappy nodded. "Good idea."

Cap tried not to show the elation he felt at those two words.

Floyd put his arm across Pappy's shoulder, something only two or three men outside the family would dare to do. "You have more trouble, Anse. Didn't want to say anything about it in front of your prisoners."

"Don't need no more trouble, John."

"They have your brother Wall in the Pikeville jail."

"My brother never wanted no part of any of these troubles."

Pappy suddenly looked old and tired. It sent shivers through Cap to see Pappy look that way.

"He aint never shot at no one," Cap blurted out. He couldn't believe they'd haul Uncle Wall in. Wall was a man who kept the peace and abided by the law even when it made no sense to do so.

"They're charging him with those killings in '82," Floyd said. "Same for Selkirk McCoy."

Pappy groaned. "Wall never killed nobody. Nor did Selkirk."

"They pick up anybody they can and make up the charges as they bring them in, Anse."

Cap doubted they'd ever get the record straight over in Kentucky. Shooting the McCoy boys in '82 was not murder. It was an execution, a punishment for murder committed by the McCoys. Back then, Wall had seen capturing the McCoys as morally justified and legal, but he'd refused to take part in executing them without a proper, legal jury trial. Wall was a strange man who valued the law too much to commit an illegal act, no matter what the provocation.

"How'd they get him, John?" Pappy's voice was weak and low.

"You'll be surprised. Wall sent Phillips a message that he'd surrender and stand trial, that he believes that Kentucky, like all of the United States, is under the rule of law, to which he is subject and by which he abides. Then he sat at home and waited for them. Phillips picked him up yesterday."

"If we'd of gone up to the Tug a day earlier, we could of stopped em from takin Wall." Pappy's shoulders were sagging.

"He wanted to go, Anse." Floyd squeezed Pappy's shoulder. "He said he'd been a Justice of the Peace a long time and believes in doing things by the law."

Pappy snorted. "I believe in doin things by the law, too. But there aint no law in Kentucky. Cline and Phillips is in charge over there. The law's gonna do whatever they say."

"Seems like Uncle Wall could figure that out," Cap said. "He must of forgot about Great Grand Uncle Abner."

Cap had heard Abner Vance's story many times. When a young man named Horton, who was betrothed to Vance's daughter, returned her pregnant, saying "Here's your heifer, you take care of her," Vance had shot and killed the fellow, then fled into the mountains of western Virginia to hide from the law. His son tried to persuade him to go back and stand trial, lest he spend the rest of his life hiding out. Abner argued that the Horton family dominated in that part of Virginia, and he was not apt to get a fair trial, but his son was convinced everybody in the county sympathized with Abner and he'd get off with a jail sentence for manslaughter, rather than being hanged for murder. Abner finally consented and was prosecuted by a Horton attorney and judged by a jury full of Hortons. Poor Great Grand Uncle Abner was convicted of murder and hanged. Over and over Cap had heard the lesson to be learned from this story: It's not safe to fall into the clutches of a government held by unfriendly hands.

"It's the principle that's always mattered to your uncle," Floyd said. "To him, the finest thing he can do is to guide his actions by his principles."

"Principles is only worth somethin if everyone around you agrees to live by em," Pappy said. "Them folks in Kentucky aint gonna pay no heed to Wall's principles. He aint gonna get no better trial than Uncle Abner."

"I'll speak to Governor Wilson," Floyd said. "Sic him on the Governor of Kentucky. Buckner's got to at least pretend he believes in the rule of law."

Cap watched and listened, envious of the respect Pappy and John Floyd had for each other.

Chapter 14

Uncle Elias had a little barn back of his house where Cap, Pappy, and Uncle Jim unsaddled their horses and fed them.

"Wish I was havin supper at home," Pappy said on the way up to the house. "Elias is a good brother, puttin us up, but I want to go home. My horse don't like it in Logan neither, too many noises he don't know nothin about makes him skitterish."

Cap felt skitterish himself in this town. But when he pulled open Elias's back door, the mouth-watering aromas of pork chops and corn pone greeted him. And shucky beans. He smelled shucky beans cooking with bacon fat.

Nancy came over and kissed him.

"Sit yourself down, Cap. We'll have supper and then I'll tell you what I've been doin today." She helped him off with his coat.

What she'd been doing! What about what he'd been doing? Cap thought this was a peculiar way to greet a husband who, as far as she knew, had been in the mountains all day hauling their belongings and chickens and pigs. She didn't seem at all interested in what they'd been able to bring back and had no idea about Cunningham.

When Cap sat at the table, Aunt Betty's orange cat, Pumpkin, rubbed up against his leg. Out by the Tug, Mama had once had a cat that caught mice in the barn, but a fox had gotten it. Pumpkin, on the other hand, had grown fat and sleek in Logan's safety.

"You need help puttin your belongins in the shed after supper?" Uncle Elias asked Pappy.

"Don't have nothin to store." Pappy told Elias about Uncle Wall turning himself in and about capturing the three bounty hunters.

"When it comes to the law, Wall's like a young swain blinded by a pretty woman," Elias said. "Only Kentucky law's a lot more dangerous than any woman I ever knew."

Mama put a bowl of mashed potatoes in front of Pappy. "I am sick to death of all this worryin and fightin." She plunked a pot of shucky beans in front of Cap hard enough to make a thud. Cap's eyes were on Aunt Betty, who was carrying pork chops on a fancy white, blue, and gold crockery platter. Between Frank and Mary White's store and the Logan Mercantile, it looked like Aunt Betty was buying just about everything she laid eyes on.

"We had a break today, Mama, catchin some of Phillips's men," he said.

"I'm gonna write a letter to Governor Buckner and offer to swap prisoners." He felt a paw with sharp claws on his knee.

Elias looked up from the plate he'd been spooning corn pone onto. "What makes you think they'll trade five of ours for three of theirs? Them three aint even kin or neighbors to nobody over there. They're just detectives wantin some of that reward."

Cap slipped Pumpkin a few of his shucky beans.

"Fellers like them are gonna keep comin long as there's a big reward out for every one of us they bring in," Pappy said.

"We're sittin over here worryin about our lives and our homes." Nancy folded her hands atop her belly. "Them folks in Kentucky aint worryin a bit."

Pappy shook his head. "Cline and Buckner's handin out blood money to the McCoys and a whole lot of other varmints. Aint nobody givin us money. Pretty soon, if we can't cut timber and float it, I'm gonna be hurtin bad."

"Who's interested in a way to keep the posses in Kentucky and our money in our pockets without no fightin?" Like a buzz saw, Nancy's voice cut through the conversation.

"You got some black magic?" Uncle Jim asked. "You been up to Witch Mountain?"

Nancy laughed. "To get the witch's power, you have to stand on top of that mountain with one hand on top of your head and the other on the bottom of your foot whilst you say 'I consign all that lies between my two hands to the Devil.' In my condition, I can't hardly do that."

"I'd do it if I thought it'd work," Pappy said.

Pumpkin meowed. Shucky beans weren't good enough. Cap dropped a pork chop bone with meat clinging to it onto the floor, and Pumpkin purred as he gnawed on it. Out by the Tug, he'd often had to deny Joey pork chops and insist he eat his shucky beans.

"You all quit your jabberin," Aunt Betty said. "Nancy's got somethin serious to say."

"Aunt Betty and Mama Levicy and me went to see John Sergeant today," Nancy said. "That feller that's been buyin and sellin land around Logan."

"You can talk to Sergeant all you want." Pappy shook his head. "But you aint talkin for nobody but yourself. I aint never gonna live in Logan. I aint makin no deal with John Sergeant."

"I don't want to live in Logan neither." Cap wanted that understood right now.

"Could be as bad as livin in Virginia," Uncle Jim said. "And there's no timber in Logan."

Nancy put both hands on the table and faced Pappy across from her. "I aint talkin about livin right here in Logan. I'm talkin about livin far enough from the Tug to get away from posses and the McCoys."

"What's wrong with Logan anyhow?" Uncle Elias said. "You got three brothers livin here already, Anse, and nobody's shot at any of us in a long time."

"And where will you be, Elias, if I sell out and move over here where I don't have no timber?" Pappy said. Uncle Elias had always worked with Pappy's timber crew, before and after he'd moved to Logan.

"Mr. Sergeant's very interested in our land by the Tug," Nancy said. "Cap's and mine, Mama's and Pappy's, Bobby Lee's, and Uncle Jim's and Aunt Mary's."

Cap grunted. "We know why. The railroad." He heard Pumpkin burp.

"My land aint for sale," Uncle Jim said.

"I told em to count you and me out," Aunt Mary said. "Our cabin and our farm's our whole world."

"Mr. Sergeant said he'd give us a real good price," Mama said, as Cap watched Aunt Betty set out two pies. They were chocolate cream pies baked at Whited's boarding house where they had a big iron step stove with an oven. Cap, who was very fond of cream pies, had to admit that life in Logan had some advantages over life in the mountains.

Pumpkin meowed again, but Cap was not about to share his cream pie.

Pappy snorted. "Them speculators figure they got me like a pack of hounds with a bobcat up a tree. They aint gonna give me no good price."

"Now listen." Nancy raised her voice in defiance. "Sergeant says he can sell us a lot of land down by Main Island Creek, fifteen miles outside Logan, almost as much as all of us together got out by the Tug. And I talked him into throwin in enough money for us to build new homes and for Pappy to take care of that lawsuit that's comin up."

Pappy jumped up from his seat and began to flit about the room. "Now why would he do that?" he bellowed. "I'll tell you why. Because he's in cahoots with Perry Cline. That's why."

"He'll do it because he wants land down by where the railroad's goin in," Nancy said. "He's a speculator, lookin for a chance to get rich."

"For sure, you don't have to worry about no railroad goin in out by Main

Island Creek," Aunt Betty said. "We aint even got one comin to Logan. No need for it."

"That's right, Aunt Betty." Nancy reached over and patted her arm. "No railroad, fifteen miles from Logan and forty miles or more over the mountains from the Tug. Aint nobody gonna bother us out there." A smile brightened Nancy's face. "Sergeant said he'd trade us four hundred acres of good bottom farmland along the creek and more than four thousand acres of oak, poplar, and beech all over the mountains behind it. We'd own the headwaters of Beech Creek that runs to the Tug, so you can cut timber and float it down like you always done. How does that sound?"

Pappy glared at Nancy. "If your enemies don't have no fear of you, if they know you'll run like a scared bunny rabbit when you should be fightin for what belongs to you, they'll set upon you and take what you have. And with a reward offered for catchin you, they'll never stop comin. We aint leavin our homes. We aint runnin away."

"Captain Anderson," Mama said. "You have always taken loving care of me and our family. This here's a chance to raise this child away from wars." She patted her belly. "We can pay off them law suit folks. We can live and you can do your loggin in peace. There aint much more I could want from this world."

"Cap, I hear tell they got great big fish in Main Island Creek," Nancy said. "You and Joey'd like that."

"There aint no fish big or tasty enough that I'd want to forsake my home for it." Cap was beginning to be irritated by Nancy's persistent pushing. Didn't she hear Pappy say they weren't moving away from the Tug?

"It's a lot easier to grow crops on flat bottom land instead of a steep mountainside," Aunt Betty added.

The women must have spent the day talking over Sergeant's offer until they'd become of one mind about it.

Pappy stood up and strode to the head of the table beside Uncle Elias's seat. He ran his eyes over every man and woman in the room. "I aint lettin the whole world see me turn tail and run from my home. That's the final truth of all this. Levicy, you can stay in Logan with our children and the baby till I get rid of them posses. Then we're goin home and we're stayin there."

"I know you got yourself all worked up about this," Cap said to Nancy. "But you'll have to tell Sergeant he aint got no deal. Hatfields don't scare off as easy as he was thinkin."

"When we was livin out by the Tug, I couldn't sleep nights," Uncle Elias said. "I was always lookin over my shoulder for someone sneakin up on me. Call it bein scared, bein a fraidy-cat if you like, Anse. It don't matter none. It don't take nothin away from what we—me and Betty and your brothers Smith and Patterson and their families—got in Logan. We got a good life—peace, a house with glass windows, stores and good neighbors close by."

"You got good lives in Logan on account of we're out there by the Tug cuttin timber and fightin off the enemy," Pappy said. "If we move down near here there won't be nothin to stop them posses. We got to hold our line at the Tug."

Nancy sighed. Cap saw resignation on his wife's face, but behind her eyes her mind was busy. He suspected he'd hear about this matter again.

Pumpkin, his tummy full, stretched and went to lie in front of the fire.

Chapter 15

In the morning, after Cap deposited his letter to Governor Buckner at the mail post in the Buskirk Hotel, he and Pappy set out to fetch belongings and live-stock to Logan with the same group of men that had captured Cunningham and his henchmen. The fog had disappeared. A low yellow winter sun was trying unsuccessfully to warm the frozen earth.

Of all the women and girls, only Aunt Mary chose to tag along with the men.

"Why don't you stay down here in Logan, old woman?" Uncle Jim said to her. "You're only gonna get in my way out there."

"I'm packin up my own pots and pans and clothes and things, you old fool," Mary snapped back. "I aint lettin you mess with my belongins. Lord knows what you'd come back with."

When Jim and Mary squabbled, Cap stayed out of it. Always fussing and arguing, they'd gotten along somehow for almost forty years.

At a trail crossing in the mountains, the riders split into groups, heading for their homes near the Tug. Cap rode with Jim and Mary to spend the night at their house and help them pack before going on to his cabin, where they'd meet up with Uncle Elias and two of the Dempsey boys. Around noon, they came down a trail toward a creek where a raccoon was lapping water from a hole in the ice.

"Hold it." Jim reined in his horse, raised his rifle and shot the raccoon dead. The sharp crack of the shot exploded, then echoed from the mountains.

"Consarn it, Jim!" Cap's ears were still ringing. "Anyone within a mile of us heard that."

"See what I got to put up with, Cap?" Aunt Mary fumed. "Any posse huntin in these mountains knows where we're at now."

"You better quit your yappin," Uncle Jim said. "Bad Frank Phillips'll hear you."

Cap held up his hand. "Hush now!" he warned. They sat for five min-utes, listening. Not a twig snapped, no horse snorted or whinnied, no rifle was fired. "I guess no one else is out here." He was relieved.

"My heart's still a-poundin." Aunt Mary laid her hand on her chest.

Jim scooped up the dead 'coon and laid it across the front of his saddle. "Supper," he said.

"You think I'm gonna cook that thing for your supper!" Mary said. "I got better things to do. Besides a 'coon that big's gotta cook for hours, after it's skinned."

"Breakfast then. Cook it for breakfast. You are the contrariest woman!"

Mary rode on in silence. But Cap knew she'd cook it. This was just the way it always was with Aunt Mary and Uncle Jim.

After they reached the cabin, Cap fed their pigs and chickens, while Uncle Jim skinned the carcass and Mary began packing. They stayed close by the cabin, away from the field that overlooked the Tug and could be watched from the Kentucky side.

"We'll stay down by Logan for a spell," Uncle Jim said to Aunt Mary. "But I aint never sellin this place."

Aunt Mary stopped packing a saddlebag and gazed out the cabin door across the frozen, snow-dusted tobacco and corn stubble in their field. "We lived here pert-near thirty years. Raised our children here. I know every piece of this farm like I know the flesh and bones of my own body."

Jim smiled a small smile. "I'd rather die happy out here than live in misery in Logan."

"Nancy and Mama will get over the idea of movin to Logan as soon as we get rid of them posses," Cap said. "Just wait and see."

Spending the night on a mattress downstairs while Aunt Mary and Uncle Jim slept in the loft, Cap lay awake half the night, getting up to look outside every time he heard a noise. All that summer after the McCoys had forded the river to kill Bill Staton, he'd been afraid, like Joey was now, that someone out to get him was just outside the door. He was eight then. Now here he was, at twenty-three, afraid there might be someone out there.

Uncle Jim had understood Cap's eight-year-old fears. One day Jim had cut the end of a long, thick grapevine loose from a tree so it could swing out freely over a hillside.

"It'll swing all the way over the creek, Uncle Jim," Cap had said, staring down at the water eight or ten feet below. "What if I fall off?"

"You won't." Jim grabbed the vine and swung out over the creek, his long legs kicking every which way as he laughed. "See," he said when the vine returned him to Cap's side. "It's like flyin."

"You go with me and hold onto me, Uncle Jim."

But Jim put Cap's hands on the vine, saying, "It aint real flyin unless you do it yourself."

Cap stomped his foot and screamed, "I can't!"

Uncle Jim let go of the vine in Cap's hands and stood back.

There was no use arguing anymore with Uncle Jim. If he wanted to fly, he'd have to go by himself. The minute he lifted his feet and wrapped them around the vine, he flew through the air, high above the creek, like a bird. It was the most wonderful, exciting thing he'd ever done, but he didn't want Uncle Jim to see how pleased he was. When he let go of the vine, he tried to frown. Jim tried to scowl back, but the two of them ended up laughing.

Back at the cabin, Cap told Aunt Mary how he'd swung on a grapevine out over the creek all by himself. "Humph!" was all she replied. But the twitch at the corner of her mouth and the shine in her eyes had said she was proud of him.

The raccoon simmered in an iron pot over a low fire all night long. Low as the fire was, Cap still worried about the wisps of smoke that must be rising out of the chimney and how close a man had to be to see them. Although it was unlikely that posses would roam the woods at night, Cap stepped outside into the moonless dark several times to look and listen.

After he and Jim pushed the table and benches well away from the open window, out of the line of rifle fire, they had a breakfast of corn pone and the tastiest, most tender, raccoon Cap had ever eaten. Every few minutes Cap got up to stick his head outside and look around. Now that it was daylight, he could see across into snow-covered Kentucky, but not down below where the Tug was. Even though they'd smothered the fire once the raccoon was cooked, he worried someone might have seen the smoke earlier.

Uncle Jim looked at the pile of things Aunt Mary had packed and shook his head. "We can't carry all that in one trip. We'll take some of it over to Cap's this mornin where there's more men to help and come back for the rest this afternoon."

"I'll ride out first," Aunt Mary said when they'd gotten their saddle bags onto their horses and were mounted. "Phillips and his gang aint interested in catchin a old woman and anyhow I'm a lot quieter than you fellers. I'd spot them before they spotted me."

Mary rode off down the trail. A few hundred feet behind, Cap and Uncle Jim followed along the ridge above the frozen Tug—sometimes coming into full view of the Kentucky shore in brilliant sunshine, sometimes plunging into woods thick with snow-covered trees and shrubs. In open places, the sun was melting the snow so their tracks would soon disappear. But in the woods anyone could easily see which way they'd gone. Cap kept his Winchester across his lap and listened.

Uncle Jim began to mumble and swear. "That 'coon's givin me a bellyache, Cap. He's gettin back at me for shootin him."

Cap laughed. "Glad I didn't shoot him. I'm feelin just fine." He clucked to his horse and headed up the steep side of Thacker Mountain. Traveller slipped and lurched a couple of times as he picked his way up the rocky trail covered with snow and ice.

"This here 'coon's fit to be tied." Uncle Jim sucked in his breath and either choked or coughed, Cap couldn't tell which. "He don't like this ride one bit. Son of a whore!"

"He'll get tired pretty soon and leave you be." Cap didn't know what to make of Jim's strange sounds. He seemed to be having trouble getting his breath.

"I'm havin a heck of a time," Jim said as the horses continued up the steep trail. "My guts is all tied up in a knot, and I'm about to vomit. I got to stop and get off."

Cap had never seen Uncle Jim in this kind of trouble. Even though Jim was sixty, he could usually ride all day. With a knife or bullet wound if need be.

They weren't quite to the top when Jim slid out of the saddle and stumbled over to sit on a boulder where he doubled over and rubbed his belly. "I shouldn't of ate this dang 'coon. He won't quit kickin and fightin." Vomit shot out of Jim's mouth and landed in the snow.

Cap sat beside him, trying to figure out how sick Jim was. He could hear Aunt Mary's horse still plodding ahead. The next instant he heard her horse heading back toward them. Cap stood up to see her come into sight, her eyes wide and hair flying. "They're comin up the mountain!" she screamed. "A whole passel of men. And they all got rifles."

Cap grabbed his Winchester from its saddle holster. "How far down the trail?"

"They're smack dab behind me." Then she noticed Jim doubled over and the vomit staining the snow. "What's the matter with you?"

"My belly's on fire. It's that 'coon you cooked."

"Cap and me aint sick. You must of ate too fast. Now get up on your horse and let's ride out of here."

"I aint up to ridin." Jim looked up at his wife. "I'm gonna stay here and fight."

"You can't," Mary said. "There must be fifty of em."

"You get on back down that mountain, old woman." Uncle Jim waved weakly at the trail they'd just come up. "You'd best go with her, Cap."

"You can't stay," Cap said. "I'll help you up into your saddle."

Men's voices, the words not yet clear, reached them. They heard the sound of horses' hoofs slipping and stumbling on the treacherous trail.

"Go!" Uncle Jim said.

"Jim!" Mary cried out, tears in her eyes. "Cap and me can't leave you here!"

"Don't go on like that. I aint worth it."

"Do what he says," Cap urged her. "I'll look after him. Get goin now while you can."

Mary leaned down from her horse and put her shawl over Jim's shoulders. "Here, you'll need this. You're shiverin bad."

"Don't know why you waste your time on me," Jim said. "Nobody else would."

"Nobody else knows you like I do." Tears trickled down her cheek.

"Time to go, Aunt Mary." Cap slapped her horse on the rump and it headed down the trail carrying its weeping burden. He moved his and Jim's horses a little ways off the trail, out of sight.

Just as he got back to Jim's boulder, Sam McCoy came into view about thirty yards away on foot, leading his horse down the slippery trail. Uncle Jim raised his rifle and shot Sam's horse, which fell screaming and kicking onto the trail.

"Dang this coon!" Jim swore. "Made me miss."

Cap saw Jim prop his rifle on the boulder in front of him and aim it. But before he could shoot, Sam McCoy leaped head first off the trail and over the side of the mountain, tumbling and crashing through the brush and rocks below. Jim shot the flailing horse in the head to put it out of its misery.

Cap plunged across the trail into the woods, worked his way in among the lower branches of a large pine, and leaned against the rough, wet bark. There was always a chance he and Jim could pick the posse off one by one as they came to the high point of the trail. They were both carrying bandoleers of cartridges, enough to reload their repeaters fifteen or twenty times.

He soon had a clear view of the rider following Sam and shot. The man fell off his horse and lay motionless in the icy slush on the trail.

The next rider jumped off his horse to drag the fallen man off the trail into the woods. Cap shot at him as he dragged, but missed. The horse spooked and dashed pell-mell down the trail past Uncle Jim. From up ahead came sounds of footsteps and branches being snapped.

"Who's out there?" a voice called out and Cap wondered if it was Frank Phillips. "Surrender now and we won't have to kill you," the voice said. Cap saw underbrush moving and heard feet scrambling. There were a lot of men and they were spreading out through the woods.

"You want to surrender, Cap?" Jim moaned. Vomit spewed from his mouth into the snow.

"I will if you will." Cap hated the idea, but figured that was about the only way to save Jim's life. It was plain to see Jim couldn't run or hide or dodge a bullet.

"I'm stayin put. I'm gonna die today anyway. But I have every intention of takin a few of these varmints with me."

"Then I'm stayin, too," Cap said. He began shooting everywhere he saw movement. Twice he heard men groan after he'd fired.

Bullets began pinging off trees, rocks, and frozen earth. Cap heard what he guessed was Phillips shouting orders to spread out and flank him and Jim. Cap shot at a man dashing between trees and missed, letting Phillips's men know where to aim the next barrage. He ran through waist-deep underbrush to a spot behind a pine with dense foliage.

Jim had no place to hide and couldn't run. He heard Jim grunt and turned to see him lose hold of his rifle and clutch his belly. Blood oozed from between his fingers.

"I'm comin over to look after you," Cap said trying to stop his teeth chattering from fear for Uncle Jim. He slowly began to edge through the pines toward Jim.

"They've kilt me." Jim's voice was faint. "No sense in you gettin kilt, too. Get goin whilst you can." Blood was running over Jim's legs, spilling down the boulder and dripping onto the trail.

A bullet whizzed by Cap just as he got from behind a tree.

Jim's face, now ashen, contorted with pain. He was gasping for breath. Maybe Phillips wouldn't kill a badly injured man. Maybe there was a chance of bringing help in time to save Jim.

"Want my cartridges?" Cap asked.

"Nope. Can't use the ones I got."

"I'll bring help. Try and hold out."

"Good boy, Cappie." Jim tried to smile. "I think this bullet kilt that ornery old 'coon. He's finally givin me some peace."

"I'll be back." Cap crouched and dashed through the underbrush as Jim, without being able to aim, fired his rifle to give him cover.

"You had enough, Cap Hatfield?" someone yelled.

They'd seen him! Cap scrambled toward his horse through the underbrush. With all the snow and ice and rocks, he kept losing his footing as he plunged downhill, nearly falling, catching his coat in a tangle of vines, jerking free of it, running and sliding as bullets whizzed around him and smashed into nearby trees.

Then the shooting stopped.

"We see you, Jim Vance," Cap heard a voice say. "Come out and surrender."

A shot rang out.

Cap leaped onto his horse. He heard one more shot before he rode for his life.

"Uncle Jim! Uncle Jim! Don't die!" he said to himself over and over.

Underbrush lashed his face. He welcomed the pain.

"Uncle Jim, don't die!" he screamed as he rode out on the ridge above the gleaming Tug, half a mile from where he'd left his uncle.

"Don't die, die, die," came the echoes from cliffs across the river.

He pictured Uncle Jim, clutching a grapevine, swinging free of the earth.

Chapter 16

The next day, in the gloom of early evening, Cap and Pappy rode into Logan with Jim's corpse. They'd found him sitting upright, propped against the boulder where Cap had left him, a bullet hole in his forehead. The posse had stolen his Winchester, cartridges, boots, saddlebags, and horse. They'd even taken Aunt Betty's shawl and the coat Cap had left in a mountain bramble.

For a while Cap and Pappy hadn't touched the body. "Jim and me went through the War together," Pappy said. "We been loggin and livin close by one another ever since. Twenty-seven years side by side."

Cap feared Jim's death would be even harder on Pappy than on himself.

"I could always trust Jim," Pappy said.

Cap nodded. "With anything." Pappy had trusted Jim to oversee timber cutting, floating log rafts down the Tug to market, and collecting money from lumber yards. He'd always confided in Jim about his plans to attack or defend against their enemies, and counted on Jim to be by his side when the Hatfields had to fight.

"I learnt to trust Uncle Jim when we was lumberjackin," Cap said. He and Jim would face each other from opposite sides of a tree trunk four to six feet across, swinging their axes in a steady beat of iron clanging on wood, filling the air with flying chips. One slip in the rhythm, a moment of carelessness or an act of rancor, and their axes would have come together to fly off in who knew what dangerous, or even fatal, direction. With Jim, the rhythm had always been steady.

Above anybody else, Cap supposed, a man would miss someone he could trust.

"Jim always said he'd been lucky in life once he left Virginia," Pappy said. "But good luck has to be sooner or later followed by bad. His luck run out on him yesterday."

It didn't seem like Pappy was holding Cap to blame for leaving Jim up here to die alone, which relieved his feeling of guilt somewhat.

They had wrapped Jim in a blanket, tied the blanket with yellow cord, and hung the corpse across the empty saddle of a horse they'd brought with them. To avoid Phillips and his men, Pappy had decided not to try holding a wake and burying Jim on his farm, where he'd always said he'd wanted to lie. For now they'd bring his body back to Logan.

At dusk they neared town.

"Let's see if we can get Jim to Elias's without nobody takin notice," Pappy said. "Don't want word to get around we're losin good men to Phillips."

Out on the street, they saw only a storekeeper and his young helper closing the Mercantile, and old Major Ellis ambling their way.

"Should be easy," Cap said. "Just stay across the street from the Mercantile and salute Ellis as we go by. He's gonna salute back and we won't have to say nothin to him." Major Ellis had kept alive what he said was his wartime rank all these years and always expected it to be recognized.

Cap rode ahead and saluted the Major, who, instead of returning the salute, held high what Cap realized too late was a small torch on a long stick. At a touch of its flame, a street lamp's wick flared into brilliant light, shining like a sun on Pappy, Uncle Jim, and the two horses.

"What the frig!" Pappy exploded. "Whose side are you on, Ellis? You lightin me up so someone can take a shot at me?"

"No, sir. Just doin my duty." Major Ellis slapped his thigh and wheeled to march on down the street.

"Remember them street lamps we saw shinin near Uncle Elias's?" Cap said. "I reckon Ellis lights em."

"We gotta get away from the consarned thing." Pappy kicked his horse's side and arrived at the next lamp just in time for it to light. Now the store keeper and his helper and two women with packages turned to stare at Cap and Pappy and the blanketed object on the third horse. Idlers from the court-house steps, heading for the tavern, trailed by a group of women of a low sort, stopped to gawk, too.

"That a body you got there?" yelled out a woman in a once fancy, but now dirty and rumpled dress. "A dead body?"

"Found this man up the road," Pappy said. "Sick near to death. Said he'd ate a bad 'coon. The danged critter must of kilt him."

"If a 'coon kilt him, then how come there's blood?" the boy from the Mercantile said.

"None of your business, boy," Pappy snapped.

Of all people, Jim Nighbert, with his wife-to-be—the divorcee Vicie Fowler—on his arm, strolled into the light of the street lamp, their faces bright against the shadows behind them.

"Devil Anse, what have you been up to?" Nighbert demanded. "Who is that dead man?"

111

A crowd began to gather. Cap felt trapped.

"Mind your own business," Pappy snarled.

Cap heard a man in the crowd say, "Devil Anse has kilt again."

"I aint no killer!" Pappy spit on the ground. "If I was natured to be a killer there is many a man I could have picked off from the brush. I've been a hunter and trapper for years. I know every foot of these mountains. Don't you suppose I've had plenty of chances when I was under snug cover to pick off some fellers I thought had no business bein where they was? I didn't do it because I am not that kind of man."

There was no answer from anyone in the crowd. Pappy had spoken from the heart, and everyone here had to believe what Cap knew for a certainty to be the truth.

Cap spotted John Floyd working his way through the crowd.

"Pardon me, ma'am," Floyd said as he approached Pappy. "Pardon me, sir."

Then Floyd did what no one else had dared to do. He pulled back the edge of the blanket and had a look at the body.

"Why this is your Uncle Jim Vance," Floyd said. He turned to the crowd. "Anse and Cap are bringing a sad burden into Logan."

The game was up, but Cap would wait for Pappy to speak first.

"Phillips and his posse caught up with Jim," Pappy said.

"Where?" Floyd looked hard at Pappy. "Surely not in Kentucky."

"No, sir. It was on Thacker Mountain. Jim and his wife and Cappie was ridin along when Jim took sick. He couldn't ride no more, couldn't get away and the posse come upon him."

"Crossed the border and murdered one of our citizens, did they?" Floyd was addressing the whole crowd now. "How do you folks like that? Invading the sovereign territory of the State of West Virginia!" Floyd turned his head slowly, letting his gaze pass over each person pressing in around him.

"I'm sorry Phillips kilt Jim Vance," said a woman in a blue wool bonnet tied primly under her chin. "And I don't much like the idea of him comin into West Virginia. But I doubt he'll bother himself with any of us unless he thinks we're in cahoots with the Hatfields."

"Good point," Nighbert said. "We'd all feel safer if Cap and Devil Anse left Logan. What are they doing here anyway?"

Floyd held up his hand. "I've known the Hatfields all my life. They've never harmed a soul in Logan. They've only fought to protect their land, our land, from those marauding villains from Kentucky who have nothing better to do than making war. We ought to be helping these good people."

"I am not a quarrelsome man," Pappy said. "I always pay my debts, and I do not take what does not belong to me."

Cap saw people around him nodding their heads in agreement. Not many local citizens could make the claim that they always paid what they owed, and Pappy was known throughout Logan County for that honorable trait.

Nighbert cleared his throat. "John, you might have a point about who's defending and who's attacking. I'm not saying either way. But when people in Charleston and on the East Coast read about this Hatfield feud, nobody wants to invest around here. Some of us stand to lose a whole lot of money."

"You sat here in Logan nice and safe, Nighbert, while Jim was out there fightin off them posses and dyin!" Cap shouted. If he'd been anywhere but the middle of Logan, he would have made Nighbert pay for being such a jackass.

Nighbert crossed his arms over his chest and looked like he was intending to hold his ground.

"Do you think only Hatfields are in danger from these marauders?" Floyd said. "Ha! I for one would not care to go fishing or hunting down by the Tug. Would you, Nighbert?"

Nighbert glowered from under heavy black eyebrows and rocked back and forth on his heels and toes.

"Or surveying," Floyd continued. "Surveyors are needed for the railroad that will be going in along the Tug. And for laying out towns with businesses we are all hoping will follow. But who'll want a surveying job if he has to constantly fear for his life on account of Kentucky posses?" He looked around. "Which one of you wants that job? Which one of you wants to work and live on our state's border as the Hatfields have?"

How John Floyd was inflaming the crowd made Cap nervous because in the recent past these same people had gotten themselves worked up in opposition to the Hatfields.

"Your point's well taken." Doc Rutherford, Pappy's old friend who'd delivered most of his children and mended many of his crew's timbering injuries, spoke up. "Isn't that so, Nighbert? Why, those railroad men might decide to put their tracks on the Kentucky side of the Tug if they think our side's too dangerous. A fine situation that would be."

"Of course, I wouldn't like to see problems with the railroad," Nighbert said.

"And you, Henry." Rutherford pointed to a tall man with cheeks stretched cadaverously over a bony face. "Are you going to stand for Kentucky bounty hunters roaming our mountains, kidnapping and shooting our citizens?"

"Don't like it at all." Henry Ragland's voice squeaked as it always did when he got excited. "Floyd, you've got to get the state militia down here right away, that's all there is to it. This is the kind of job we elected you to do. Get enough troops along the Tug so Phillips won't dare come raiding into our state."

It was a relief to hear a sentiment being raised for militia to go after Kentucky posses instead of the Hatfields. Cap was beginning to feel more confident that Floyd was improving their situation.

"Let's show the Hatfields how much we appreciate that they've guarded our border all these years. And their sacrifices." Floyd pointed to the blanketed corpse. Then he raised his hat and yelled, "Hip, hip, hoorah!"

Some men in the crowd raised their hats and shouted, too. But not Nighbert and not Ragland.

"I'll set out for Charleston first thing in the morning to speak to Governor Wilson on behalf of the city of Logan," Floyd said. "We need the militia down here now."

"Soldiers? In Logan?" Mrs. Nighbert-to-be was speaking up. Short, dark-eyed and plump-cheeked, Vicie Fowler radiated a strength of will, whose lack she had not been able to tolerate in her first husband. "We don't need soldiers here. We need a church, not a war." She drew her buxom self up as tall as she could as if to show what everybody already knew—she was a force to be reckoned with.

"War is already here," Floyd retorted. "Follow me, Mrs. Fowler, and any of you others who are interested. I'll introduce you to three Kentucky raiders caught in Logan County just the other day."

"We heard they were being held in our jail," Vicie Fowler said. "And frankly, it worries me that Phillips and his men might come to rescue them."

"Please follow me, Mrs. Fowler." John Floyd smiled and waved his derby hat toward the courthouse. "And tell me, after seeing these scum, whether you want them let loose in Logan's streets." He clapped the hat back on his head and led Nighbert, Mrs. Fowler, Doc Rutherford, Henry Ragland, and a few others into the jailhouse.

Cap and Pappy exchanged uneasy glances. Strong sentiments were being stirred up here. Cap reckoned that only Pappy's trust in John Floyd was persuading him to wait in the street for everyone to return.

Cap strained to hear Floyd ask the jailer to exhibit the prisoners. "Leave me alone, you jackasses." He didn't have to strain himself to know that was Cunningham.

In a few minutes everyone who'd entered the cell block came trooping out, looking shocked and upset. "You dungscabs better let us go," a voice bellowed after them. "Or else Frank Phillips'll come over here and kill everybody in Logan County."

"All right, James." Vicie Fowler was standing under the street lamp with her husband-to-be again. "Just what are we going to do about this? Floyd, I know you'll talk to the Governor. But it'll be days, maybe weeks, before he can get troops down here, if indeed he ever does. In the meantime nobody in Logan will be safe from the likes of such unholy heathens."

"Well!" Nighbert drew himself up tall. "We'll deputize a posse of our own to guard our borders. I personally will pay to outfit these men, with a little help from you, Ragland, and a few other of Logan's finest."

He looked to Vicie as if to see what impression his words had made on her. He didn't want her tossing him out as she had the spineless Fowler, Cap would bet. But he certainly wasn't volunteering to arm himself and personally join the posse.

Cap feared that if a band of untrained town folks tried to take over hunting down Phillips's posse there would be more men killed, more prisoners taken, and more rewards collected by bounty hunters. Town men weren't up to the job. The Logan sheriff's main duty was to collect taxes and pull together road-building crews. He'd never been known to venture across the mountains to the Tug. And the constable had never done anything more dangerous than breaking up drunken fights in the streets and taverns. If one drunk shot another in a Logan brawl, fatal or not, the shooter was never arrested or prosecuted because nobody thought such a killing was premeditated or even intentional. Neither the sheriff nor the constable had ever arrested a killer or tracked a man down in the mountains. Very few men from Logan would be of any help hunting down Phillips's men.

Cap scrutinized his father's face to see if they shared the same concerns, but Pappy remained silent and expressionless.

Floyd dropped back from the edge of the crowd to stand by Cap's horse.

"Mr. Cunningham put on a capital performance," he whispered. "All Logan's on your side now." Floyd's eyes were glittering with excitement. Cap had always liked and admired Floyd for his ability and enthusiasm for controlling his listeners' emotions. He was far more than a dandy in fancy clothes.

"We got a problem here, Floyd," Cap whispered. "Looks like Nighbert, or maybe I should say Vicie Fowler, is gonna be in charge of this here posse."

"Just like in the army," Pappy said. "My Logan Wildcats served alongside other regiments under one colonel. Now the Hatfield regiment will serve alongside the Logan regiment."

"They'll need an old hand to be the colonel." Floyd winked at Cap.

Cap wondered where Pappy would be without John Floyd or where Floyd would be without Pappy.

Chapter 17

This time they'd finish off the Kentucky raiders. As soon as Pappy and Cap had moved their belongings to Logan, they and three of Cap's kin caught up with the posse that had been hastily formed in Logan. Armed and paid by Nighbert and Ragland and their business allies, Logan's Constable Thompson and ten deputies were still on the Logan side of the mountains, on their way to the Tug Valley. Thompson was carrying a warrant for the arrest of Jim Vance's murderers, which amounted to a warrant for Frank Phillips and any men riding with him.

As he approached, Cap studied Thompson's men, recognizing all of them. Some would be of help, some would only get in the way. To begin with, he was uneasy about Thompson himself, a town man in his early forties. He'd never hunted another man. One of his deputies, Bill Dempsey, was only a teenaged boy. Five others were Hatfield friends or kin, but four were not known supporters, maybe even against the Hatfields, and were probably only hiring themselves out to make a little money.

"We're hot on their trail," Thompson announced. "Hoofprints, fifteen or twenty horses." He pointed to the trampled mud and snow around him. "Not very old."

"That's gotta be Phillips and his gang," Pappy said. "Snow's blowed in those tracks, so it's been a day or two since they was here."

Cap saw Thompson was surprised at how cold his "hot" trail was.

"Then they might be back in Kentucky by now." Thompson sighed in disappointment or relief, Cap couldn't tell which.

"Naw." Pappy spit on the ground. "They aint gonna leave here till they've caught themselves somebody that'll get em some reward money."

"Well, we know which way they went." Thompson pointed toward the mountains. "If we don't catch up with em tonight, we can stay in a loggin cabin one of my men knows about up there."

"Naw." Pappy shook his head. "We aint sleepin in no cabin. Too easy to get trapped in a cabin. We'll sleep in the woods."

Thompson slumped in his saddle. "It's cold and wet out here."

"Right you are," Pappy said.

It was clear to Cap that in a few short minutes Pappy had assumed control of the posse.

"Let's ride out, men." Pappy pointed in the direction Phillips had gone.

"Quiet. No need to let them fellers know we're comin."

Near sundown, when they reached the top of a ridge overlooking the gleaming ice-covered Tug, Pappy announced they'd set up camp.

"We can see in every direction from here," he said.

Pappy, Cap, his cousins, and four or five of Thompson's men had blanket rolls that kept them off the snow and ice. But poor Dempsey and the rest of them had none and shivered so bad all night that they looked forward to sentinel duty when they could get off the ground and walk around. Cap did his turn with young Bill Dempsey who showed him the two dollars and fifty cents Thompson had already paid him.

"I can buy me an accordion," Dempsey said. "If I get enough money I'll buy a fine suit from Charleston to wear when I play it."

At dawn, January nineteenth, eighteen days after the New Year's raid, they had a breakfast of cold biscuits and hot coffee made over the tiny fire Pappy permitted to be lit behind a large boulder. "There's a road down there." Pappy pointed down toward the river.

Cap peered in that direction and glimpsed a skinny, rutted farm road.

"Phillips and his men probably went that way," Cap said. "Easier ridin than these trails."

Pappy nodded. "That's what I figure. If we get goin right away, we might catch up with em before they break camp."

"Let's saddle up and ride," Pappy called out. There was some grumbling, but every man soon had himself, his gear, and his rifle on his horse.

They'd ridden the mile or so to the road when a woman, coatless and hatless in the cold, ran out of the woods, waving her hands for them to stop. As they reined in their horses, she began to shriek, "They's a bunch of them Kentucky fellers back behind the barn! And they's armed." She pointed up ahead to Jim Ferrell's place, then scurried back into the trees. Cap had never seen the woman before, which was a surprise since his own home was little more than two miles away.

He'd barely had time to consider the situation when the crack of rifle shots from the direction of the barn, followed by the ping of bullets off nearby trees, sent him and Pappy and the others ducking into the woods. They waited on their horses, watching and listening. There was no sight or sound until they spotted the woman dashing through Ferrell's apple orchard beyond the barn and farmhouse.

"Looks like a ambush," Pappy said. "That woman's part of it. She tells us the posse's over to Ferrell's. They fire a couple of shots from that direction, but the main body's up ahead waitin for us to get sidetracked."

Pappy got down from his horse and everyone else followed. "Thompson, you fellers keep your eyes on Ferrell's place. Cap and me'll scout out the road up ahead."

Keeping to the woods, far back from the road, Cap and Pappy slipped quietly through the trees. One snap of a twig or crunch of snow under a boot and their position might be given away. Occasionally they glimpsed the orchard across the road, barren and leafless, walled in behind a low stone fence. When they were opposite the end of the wall, he and Pappy cautiously approached the road, from which they spotted a group of tethered horses.

"Looks like they're all over to Ferrell's," Cap whispered.

Pappy nodded. "Don't believe there's a ambush."

Cap agreed, but it was better to check and discover an ambush early, than to be caught by one later. They ducked back into the woods and hurried to rejoin Thompson and his men.

"We spotted their horses behind Ferrell's," Cap reported. "Eighteen of em."

Thompson thought a minute before he spoke. "I think we ought to sneak across the road, come up behind that stone wall and spread out along it. We might get a shot at em from there."

"Good a plan as any," Pappy approved.

They tied up their horses and trudged through the trees until they reached the roadside. There was no cover for about fifty feet between the woods on the two sides of the road. Cap volunteered to go first. He got down on his belly and wriggled onto the rough road, dragging his Winchester at his side. Once across, he rose to a crouch and dashed into the woods. One by one, they all made it across without drawing gunfire. When they reached the wall, they crawled on hands and knees to spread out behind it. Cap cautiously peered over.

Bud McCoy's face, topped by a thatch of brown hair, protruded above a chicken coop on the other side of the orchard. Cap drew a bead on the space between the eyes and fired. Bud staggered, then fell from sight. That left seventeen in the Kentucky posse and one less McCoy in the world if his shot had hit where he'd aimed. Bud was so ornery that Cap believed not even his kin would miss him. Cap crawled over to a new position as shots came back from Ferrell's.

Up the road, Cousin French Ellis poked his head over the wall.

"Can't see nothin for them dang apple trees," he said.

"Get down!" Cap yelled.

A rifle barked and Ellis rolled to the ground, clutching his shoulder. Thompson crawled over to help the writhing man.

As Cap turned from Ellis back to the action, he caught sight of Bill Dempsey dashing through the orchard and watched the boy in fear and admiration. Bill was just a kid who'd hired himself out. He shouldn't risk his life out in the open like that.

Another of Thompson's deputies got a leg over the wall, on his way to joining Dempsey when a shot rang out. The man fell back, screaming in pain. A bullet had entered his thigh, which began gushing blood. Cap crawled over, ripped off the groaning man's shirt, pressed it on the wound until the bleeding stopped, then bandaged his thigh. Leaving the deputy lying in the snow, he crawled to a new position.

Down the road, he spied Pappy, poking his rifle out over the wall. When a man dashed pell-mell out from behind the barn toward the orchard, Pappy picked him off. Without a cry, the injured man fell, draped over a tree stump. Sixteen of the enemy left now, fourteen of the Hatfield and Logan posse.

From behind a shucking pen about a hundred yards from the barn, Dempsey picked off two men who'd run out to rescue the fallen man. The boy looked back in Cap's direction, grinned proudly, then started running for the barn. But he'd taken only two steps when he went down with a bullet in the leg. Dragging himself as far as the open side of the shucking pen, he left a trail of blood across the snow.

"Help me!" he called out.

"Why should we?" a voice answered from behind the barn.

"I'm hurt bad," Dempsey managed to say between groans.

Guffaws came from behind the barn.

"Water. Please!" Dempsey began sobbing.

"Tell your men to hold their fire," a voice called out from behind the barn.

"We're holding," Thompson shouted.

Pappy crawled to where Thompson was hunched behind the wall.

Four men, including Randall McCoy's oldest son Jim, stepped out from behind the barn. When one of them swaggered out into the open, Cap took a deep breath. That had to be Bad Frank Phillips. He was young, about the same age as Cap, and "pretty" the way women went for, with a big black mustache.

"I don't trust Phillips," Pappy said.

"We got to trust him," Thompson answered. "We got no other choice."

The Hatfields and the Logan men lowered their rifles.

The four men strode over to where Dempsey lay. "I aint no Hatfield. I only come out here 'cause the sheriff told me to. A drink of water. Please!"

Phillips handed him a canteen and motioned the others away. As Dempsey touched the canteen to his lips, Phillips drew his pistol, pressed it to the back of Dempsey's head and pulled the trigger. The boy sprawled to the ground with blood and gore spurting from his forehead onto the snow.

Cap shot as fast as he could get his rifle up. Rifles were firing all around him. But Phillips had ducked behind the shucking pen and the other three had disappeared.

"They're movin out," Pappy called out, just as Cap caught the sounds of horses' hooves and snapping branches coming from in back of Ferrell's place. They blanketed that part of the woods with rifle fire, but the horses were soon out of earshot.

Thompson stood up. Everyone who could followed his lead. Rifles at the ready, careful to cover every direction, they made their way through the snow-covered orchard to where Dempsey lay.

"Poor Billy." Thompson shook his head. "He didn't have no stake in this war. Just a boy needin a little cash."

"It makes me sick to think of that boy dyin to protect Nighbert's and Ragland's money," Cap said.

Face bright red, Thompson turned to him. "Maybe it would of been all right if he'd died for you Hatfields?"

"You had no business bringin him with us to fight." Cap held back his impulse to slug Thompson. "He didn't know nothin about fightin and a shootin war. Didn't understand the danger of it."

"You Hatfields aint nothin but trouble," Thompson said. "Nobody would be dead or hurt if you hadn't started all this on New Year's. I'll say that right to your face."

"You don't know what it's like, livin out here on the border." Cap felt the weight of the New Year's killings settle on his back again. "If them fellers from Kentucky would leave us alone, the feuds'd be over and done."

They lifted Dempsey and carried him gently across the orchard. Pappy and Thompson agreed it was better to take their dead and wounded back to Logan than to pursue Phillips. With one dead, three injured and three needed to look after the wounded, they didn't have enough men. They rode in silence, winding among the tree trunks lined up like tall, lifeless soldiers frozen in place. The woods were silent, too—birds, squirrels, raccoons all, as if in horror at what they'd just witnessed.

"We aint winnin this fight, Cap," Pappy said. "That Phillips is a evil man, shootin a bleedin boy."

"And he's still over here in our territory." As Cap had feared, the Logan men weren't up to the job of eliminating Phillips's posses. The next time he and Pappy should bring only experienced trackers and gun fighters.

The next time? Today they'd lost as many men as Phillips had. The Hatfields probably couldn't raise more than thirty-five or forty men altogether and not all of them on any one day, while the Kentucky Governor's offer of two thousand seven hundred dollars per head for Hatfields could raise who knew how many bounty hunters and posse members.

Cap stared at Dempsey's body lying across a saddle and at the bleeding, groaning French Ellis riding ahead.

Chapter 18

Death on his mind, Cap walked into Uncle Elias's totally unprepared for the red-tasseled gold cloth spread over Aunt Betty's little round sewing table, crowned by a similarly tasseled red glass dome atop a kerosene lantern. None of that had been in this house three days ago when they'd left. It seemed to him that every day since New Year's, the world he'd grown up in had lost another piece, and today it had lost several.

"What the frig is that?" Pappy blurted out to Aunt Betty and Mama, seated on either side of the forest of fringes.

"I knew you'd say that." Aunt Betty gave Mama a knowing look.

"We just finished returnin a dead boy to his parents and now, when we've come for the comfort of home, there's this." Pappy stood over the fringed frippery, fist clenched, as if he was considering smashing it.

"Dead?" Mama said. "Who's dead, Anse?"

"Bill Dempsey. Does anyone in this house care? Or am I amongst a bunch of stone-hearted folks that don't take no notice of nothin outside of what's bein sold in Logan's stores?"

"Bill Dempsey! Tell me it aint true." Aunt Betty started to cry. She'd known Bill since he was born.

As Pappy began the sad story of their battle, Cap slid in next to Nancy on the kitchen bench and tried, unsuccessfully, to shut out the day's disasters. Uncle Elias stepped over to the fire, poked a piece of kindling into it to light his corncob pipe, and eyed Pappy through the smoke.

Pappy left out no details of the deaths and injuries they'd suffered. "Bill was layin in the snow beggin for water. Phillips gave him a drink, put a pistol to his head and shot his brains out," Pappy finished. "Cold-blooded whoreson!"

Nancy held tightly to Cap's arm. He wished she wouldn't do that, he felt so weak and worthless. Today, once more, he'd failed to be the man she needed, a man who could protect his family.

Uncle Elias sucked on his pipe, then shook his head. "Whole business of men in packs like wolves, huntin down other men is cold-blooded."

"Elias, you're gettin to be like everybody else down here in Logan." Pappy flipped a couple of tassels on the kerosene lantern. "Sittin in your town man's house, jawin about other fellers when they're off doin the fightin for you."

Elias pointed his pipe at Pappy like an accusing finger. "You aint got no good excuse to fight no more. You got a chance to move out by Main Island Creek and you aint takin it."

Pappy grabbed Elias by the front of his shirt. Before Cap could jump up and pull them apart, Aunt Betty got to her husband's side.

"Now you two just remember you're brothers." She pulled on Elias's sleeve and drew him to a seat on the other side of the hearth.

Nancy folded her arms across her belly. "I swear I don't want to hear no more tales like this for the rest of my life."

"We don't have the money to keep this up and we've lost too many good men." Cap had never felt so defeated, so incapable of struggling on.

Pappy paced the floor, staying clear of Elias. "I'm just as sick of these wars as anybody. I can't let Phillips get any more of my men. And I've got to think about timberin. Spring's comin in a few weeks."

Cap stood and blocked Pappy's path.

"Let's get Wilson to send the state militia down here and patrol the Tug. They can put a lot more men on Phillips's tail than we got. Let the militia do the fightin for us."

"Amen!" Elias pointed his pipe at Cap. "John Floyd's gone back to Charleston. Let's get a message off to him right away."

"Tell him, and tell him to tell Wilson about Bill Dempsey's murder," Pappy added. "And about the Mahon brothers and Selkirk McCoy and my brother Wall, kidnapped and a prisoner in Kentucky." His voice trailed off, his head drooped, and his eyes fixed vacantly on the stone hearth.

"You can add Cotton Top to the kidnappin list," Nancy said. "Bounty hunters got him up on his mama's farm."

"Poor old Cotton Top." Pappy's head hung down further. "He just wasn't borned with his fair amount of sense."

"Poor old Cotton Top!" Cap was infuriated. "He made up his mind to kill Allifair McCoy and then he done it. Poor Allifair, and poor all of us, I say."

"Over here, Cap." Uncle Elias had laid paper, pen, ink and a blotter on the kitchen table.

Cap sat down and pulled a sheet of paper towards him. He addressed the letter to "The Honorable John B. Floyd" and began listing the murders and kidnappings committed by Frank Phillips and his men in West Virginia. The more he wrote of these crimes, the angrier he got, and the faster he wrote.

Pappy stood behind him the whole time. Cap would bet he wished he could read right now.

"Cap's readin and writin's comin in handy, aint it?" Uncle Elias chided Pappy.

Pappy ignored the remark.

Within a few minutes, the letter was finished. Elias handed it to his oldest boy, along with three dollars. It would take a day and a half to ride to Charleston with an overnight stopover at a cousin's on the way.

"Bring back a answer from Floyd," Pappy called out as Elias and his son headed to the barn.

After they left, no one spoke. These days Cap hated silences. Left to his own thoughts, a terrible melancholy would creep over him.

"Over in Pikeville, they don't know they got Allifair's killer," he said.

"They think you done it," Pappy answered. "But we don't have to leave it that way."

Cap stared down, through the red glass, into lantern smoke, blood-colored and swirling, smelling of burning kerosene.

"I can still see Allifair's blood runnin out over the snow." He looked around. Nobody had a word to say on Cotton Top's behalf. But nobody wanted to rat on a cousin either.

A loud bang on the front door made Cap jump. Elias, back from the barn, strode over and opened it.

Johnse lunged into the room, out of breath, his eyes agleam. "My wife's terrible mad," he said, waving his arms like a crazy man. "She's hotter'n a poker in the fire. 'You was there on New Year's,' she says to me. 'I know you was.' She's been carryin on like that for days."

For once, Cap and his family were too stunned to say anything.

"She kept after me," Johnse went on, his eyes darting wildly. "Till I told her. 'Sure I was there. Why wouldn't I be?' And she knowed I shot first. I want to know how she knowed that."

"Maybe we got a spy in our midst," Pappy said.

"Stop right there!" Uncle Elias sliced the air with his pipe. "Next thing you know we'll be after some feller's head because somebody's took a notion he's a spy."

"I'll tell you how she knows." Cap saw it plain as day. "They're holdin Cotton Top in the Pikeville jail and he's talkin. It aint that he means to tell secrets, it's just that once his mouth gets started he can't turn it off."

"Sit down, son," Mama said to Johnse. She stood up. "You're a terrible sight for a mama to see, all worked up like you are." She eased him into the rocking chair she'd been occupying.

"That chair's for you, Mama." Cap came close to dragging Johnse out of the chair. "Johnse don't need it." He turned to his brother. "Get out of there."

But Mama stood behind her oldest son, stroking his hair while Johnse looked up at Cap with eat-your-heart-out-I-deserve-this eyes. "She says me and Pappy and Cap and Bobby Lee's all killers." His voice shook with anger and sorrow.

"Oh, son, I hate to hear this." Mama took the comb from the back of her hair bun and began running it through his matted, dirty hair, pulling gently at the tangles. Johnse closed his eyes and relaxed. "I told her she aint got nothin to complain about. I always treated her good."

Cap and all the family had known from the start that Johnse's marriage to Nancy McCoy was a big mistake. If his brother was looking for another Roseanne, he surely hadn't gotten it in her sharp-tongued, hatchet-faced cousin Nancy.

"I promised her I aint gonna do no more fightin." Johnse leaned back to peer up at Mama. "I'm sick and tired of it."

"Don't talk to none of us about fightin." His whining disgusted Cap. Johnse hadn't been out by the Tug when Uncle Jim had died and he hadn't been in today's battle. "You aint doin none of it, you aint never stuck your neck out for nobody."

"That way you're talkin. I got to get away from that." Johnse brought his fists down on the arms of the rocking chair. "I'm movin out. All the way to Washington Territory by the Pacific Ocean. They got lots of good timber there. Biggest trees anybody's ever saw."

Mama stopped, comb in midair. "You got no family out there at all."

"No, I aint. But my wife's gonna come out soon as I get settled."

"I thought you was tired of fightin." Cap sneered at Johnse.

"Who wants to buy my place?" Johnse looked around the room. "All I want for it's a bit of travel money. I was thinkin maybe Bobby Lee. He aint got much of a cabin. No barn. He can have mine."

Cap bet that Bobby Lee would snap up the offer if he could scrape up money. Bobby Lee and his wife were lying low at a cousin's place right now.

"I aint said yes or no to this." Pappy stood over Johnse.

"He aint no help when we have shootin to do." Cap wanted to remind Pappy that he had only one son he could count on when it came to defending the family. "You know that." He glanced at Mama, hoping she wouldn't be mad at him for talking against Johnse.

"Washington's so far away." Mama's thoughts were apparently concerned only with losing her oldest son. Cap doubted she had any idea how far away Washington Territory was and wondered if Johnse himself knew. When he'd once tried to show both of them maps of the United States and North America, they'd had no interest.

"Not that I wouldn't be happy to see you get away from this fightin, son." Mama had stopped combing and was addressing Pappy as much as Johnse. "I spent many a year worryin about your Pappy and your brothers. Still do."

"You can all come with me, Mama." Johnse reached out and began fingering the tassels on the table cloth beside him. "This is mighty pretty, Aunt Betty."

Nose hooked downward, disgust in his eyes, Pappy watched Johnse stroking the tassels. "Go ahead. Go to Washington. I aint gonna stand in your way."

Johnse stood and clapped a hand on Cap's shoulder. "Want to buy my land?"

Cap couldn't believe Johnse could be so quick to leave his family. "Go talk to John Sergeant. Nancy says he's ready to make an offer for all our property." Saying the words, he nearly choked with emotion. It would be better for Johnse if he settled somewhere else for the time being, far from the Tug and far from Logan. But all his life he'd been Johnse's brother.

Nancy gave her brother-in-law the details of Sergeant's offer and told him where to find the speculator's office. When Johnse had left and the women had gotten busy cleaning up after supper, Elias went to the barn to look after his horses, while Cap sat in front of the fireplace, silently sipping whiskey with Pappy.

Finally Pappy spoke up. "You're my number one son, Cappie. Always have been, always will be."

Cap nodded. For so long he'd sought and hoped for Pappy to say that. It was the best thing that had happened to him today, a day when "best" didn't have to meet a very high standard.

Chapter 19

That night Cap and Nancy were snuggled up in a bed so small that, in order to roll over they had to move at exactly the same time. Straw from the mattress poked Cap's arm and his butt hung low in the mattress supported by ropes that had gone slack. Pumpkin had crowded his way into the space between him and Nancy and was purring loudly.

"What wouldn't I give to be back in our own place!" he said.

"Sssh, you'll wake everybody," she whispered.

"No, I won't. They're all upstairs." Uncle Elias and Aunt Betty had one room to themselves and Mama and Pappy another. It didn't make sense to divide the upper floor so that you couldn't squeeze in as many beds or bunks as when there were no walls. But that was the way they made houses in Logan nowadays.

"I'm jealous of Johnse in a way," Nancy said. "He's gettin shed of all these troubles."

"We can't just up and leave like him. I got to take care of the family when Pappy gets older."

"I know. But Cap, that land out on Main Island Creek would be just right for us. You wouldn't have to leave the family and I'd feel safe out there when the baby comes. Do you realize that's only a few more weeks?"

"If it's a girl, what do you think of namin her Allifair?"

"No!" Nancy pulled away from him and tried unsuccessfully to sit up, dumping a complaining Pumpkin halfway down Cap's legs. "That's a terrible idea. We aint bringin Allifair McCoy back. We're havin our own baby."

Cap sighed. No matter how he tried it seemed he'd never find a way to undo what had been done. "I'm wanted for murderin that girl. We been run out of our home, Phillips is on our tail all the time, and half our men's in jail." He pounded his fist into the straw tick and the mattress sank lower on its ropes. "Even Pappy says we're losin the war."

"Things would be better if we moved out on Main Island Creek." Nancy hugged him.

"We gotta start cuttin timber right away. We need money to keep ourselves armed, buy grub, pay lawyers, pay a timber crew. If Phillips and his posses keep us from loggin, we'll lose everything we have. Then what'll I do, Nancy? Sharecrop like a McCoy?"

"Maybe you could scout up timber and land for speculators like John

Sergeant. There must be somethin you can do. You don't see Nighbert and Ragland workin for other folks, and you're as smart as them."

"Nancy, I'm a farmer and a timber man. I'm tough and I'm a crack shot. I don't take no crap off nobody. That's the kind of man I was brung up to be and that's who I am. I aint no other kind of feller. I don't want to be no other kind."

"You mean you can't figure out how to beat Nighbert and Ragland at their own game? You aint smart enough?"

Cap felt trapped. "Leave me alone. I got enough troubles." He wished he could roll over, but instead clenched his teeth and chewed on his rising anger.

Nancy soon fell asleep. She slept a lot when she was pregnant. Cap lay staring at the lights and shadows from the flickering fire, unable to sleep and unable to toss and turn on the narrow bed.

Finally, he got up and pulled on his clothes and boots. As he stepped outside, the cold night air shocked him even wider awake. Striding out onto Logan's main street, he started when his feet crunched loudly on the snow-dusted cinder walk in the quiet night. Soon he was clattering along the downtown boardwalk, passing the jail side of the courthouse building. The barred windows of the cells holding Cunningham and his men were dark.

He came to Nighbert's house, looming high above him, its smooth white-painted boards glowing dimly in the light of a street lamp. Of course, the street lamp had been erected directly in front of Nighbert's house. The huge front veranda had a roof held up by a row of round white posts. Below the roof, he could make out glass windows, each one three or four times the size of those Uncle Elias had. Each of the upstairs windows had its own fancy little roof. A round tower ran up one side of the house with windows so far above the street that Cap guessed the place must have at least three floors.

He wondered what all was in this great house, but knew Nighbert would never invite him and Nancy inside to see. Rumors had it there was a dining room on the second floor to which trays of food were pulled by ropes up through a hole in the ceiling of the kitchen on the first floor. He sneaked up to the porch railing and tried to peer in the windows, but they were covered with frilly white curtains.

Dead quiet, the house was dark. No smoke rose from the chimney. Nighbert slept while he, Cap, walked the streets.

It used to be that to look after himself and his family a man had to carry a gun and be prepared to use it. There were few sheriffs or constables in Logan and Pikeville and hardly any of them ever set foot in the Tug Valley. If Cap's family hadn't been armed and ready to fight at all times, Hatfield timber would have been stolen by Cline and his henchmen, Hatfield men would have fallen prey to McCoys, and fear would have ruled their lives.

But now, stealing up on everybody like a fog, a change had crept into the mountains. Now Hatfield men were being captured and killed, while the likes of Nighbert and Cline, who'd never shot at a man or been shot at, thrived. Things had changed so gradually he hadn't realized until now that greedy businessmen had begun using Hatfields and McCoys to fight for them.

This was no longer a personal war between two families, or even an action to protect timber from thieves like Perry Cline. This was a war between men of money in Kentucky and West Virginia hankering for real estate near the railroad, rich men who could pay armies to fight for them. They were in tight with their states' governors who could offer bounty hunters large rewards and call up state militia to kill or capture men from the other state. Governor Wilson wasn't entirely on the Hatfield side, as John Floyd kept insisting. He was taking up their cause partly, or mostly, to enhance his reputation as a strong governor among the voters of West Virginia and to please the Nighberts of the state. This was verging on another war between states.

Cap's head was clear in the chill night. This battle was too big, its armies too large, for either the Hatfields or McCoys to win. Let the hired guns fight it out while Cap and his family settled where they could farm and timber in peace, somewhere far from the Tug.

And who'd been pushing him to do just that? And hadn't he stubbornly ignored her? Nancy had never accepted Pappy's ways without question the way he had. All his life it had been Pappy's standards he'd aimed to live up to. He'd always tried to be a top marksman, a fearless fighter, crafty in stalking the enemy, and above all a fierce, well-armed defender of his family. He'd been so deaf to any other way of thinking that his wife had just about had to hit him over the head with a two-by-four to get him to listen to her.

Chapter 20

Cap first got to know Nancy in the fall of 1882 at the Mate Creek store she and her murdered husband had run. The little store appeared to be every bit as well stocked as it had been before his death. Floor-to-ceiling shelves were stacked with dishes, bolts of cloth, oil lamps, and kerosene lanterns. Small boxes and glass cases on the counter held needles, thread, scissors, and patent medicines. A kerosene barrel sat near the door where, if it leaked, the kerosene wouldn't get into the flour and sugar barrels at the end of the counter.

Tall, with lots of dark wavy hair and rosy cheeks, Nancy really was the prettiest woman Cap had seen in the settlements. And she acted like she knew it, lifting her gaze from the store ledger and tossing her head in a sassy way. He eyed her and she looked him over before either said a word.

He leaned against the counter top, trying not to show she made him nervous. "I heard the bad news about your husband."

"He left me with a baby son to remember him by."

He was surprised she didn't look forlorn or get tears in her eyes. Maybe the rumors were true—that Nancy's husband, ten years older than she, had always been on the road, leaving her at home alone to take care of the house and store. Not much of a life for a young woman who wanted a man around.

"I was most sorry to hear about his passin," Cap said. "By the way, me and Pappy had some business we was doin with your husband."

"You can do business with me. I'm gonna keep the store open."

"You're very young to take on a store and a baby."

"You don't think I can do it."

"I didn't say that."

"Everybody tells me that." She let disgust show in her sigh. "I'm only seventeen, I'm a girl, and my folks aint in much of a position to help."

"Well, I aint everybody." Cap stood up from where he was leaning on the counter, stretched his arms out in front of him with fingers intertwined and cracked his knuckles while Nancy stared at his chest and the blue homespun shirt sleeves tightening over his muscles. "And you aint neither," he added.

"No, I aint. I'll keep this store open, I'll dig ginseng, I'll trap beavers and sell their skins, whatever I got to do."

He grinned. "You remind me of Mama when you set your mouth like that."

"I hear your Mama runs a good house in spite of all—" She stopped short.

He wondered if she was thinking in spite of all the feuding. It was just a month since the three McCoy boys had been executed.

"In spite of all what?" He put his elbows back on the counter and laid his hand close to hers, resisting the temptation to touch her. He wanted her to see there was no reason to be afraid of him.

"In spite of all the children she has to raise." Nancy looked down at the floor before looking back at him.

She might be trying not to show how much she was attracted to him.

"I'd like one of them big galvanized wash tubs," he said. "For Mama's wash. And I'd been talkin to your husband about some other things he was gonna get for me."

"Some other things?" Nancy cocked her head to one side.

"We ordered a right smart number of other things from your husband."

"Silly Cap Hatfield! You think I don't know you want that tub for your still? And your 'other things' is jugs? You're the first thing's struck me funny in two weeks!"

Funny! She had no call to laugh at him.

"I aint no ornery boy runnin a still so I can be drinkin and drammin. I'm nineteen years old. I come to your store to do some business."

"Your jugs has come in, Mr. Hatfield, sir. Come look, Mr. Hatfield, sir." The skirt of her calico dress swinging with every step, she led him across the room.

"I didn't mean to sound that way," he stammered. She was taking everything he said the wrong way.

"Them jugs come in big crates." She showed him the stack of crates in the back of the store, twelve pottery jugs per crate. "I can't lift em and neither can my hired boy."

"I got a cart hitched up to my mule out front." He picked up a crate and lifted it waist high, then hoisted it over his head before putting it down again. "I'll load it up myself."

Her admiring look told him she was impressed.

"How much for the jugs and the tub?"

Nancy took a pad of paper and a pencil out of a drawer and added it all up. "Nine dollars and twenty cents."

She could keep track of money. That had always been a problem when he and Pappy tried to figure out how much money they owed or were owed. They had to guess or rely on the people they were doing business with, most of whom couldn't write numbers or do figures either.

He pulled out a little leather pouch he carried in the pocket of his overalls and counted out nine dollars and some coins. At least he could do that. And he could show her he didn't have to buy on credit or carry a store truck account the way a lot of folks did.

The following week when Cap returned to the store, Hence, the hired boy, was calling out the items he was unpacking, and Nancy was writing the list in a book with a blue cardboard cover.

"Six ladies' bonnets, three skinning knives, two hand pumps with handles. . ." She looked up. "What can I do for you, Cap?"

"Coffee and sugar. For Mama." He peered down at the ledger, but couldn't read a thing. "You can write," he said, feeling jealous.

"I learnt from a school teacher. It aint hard. Comes in handy when I keep the store books and write letters. I got some books I like to read, too."

"You don't carry no books in your store."

"Who'd buy em? I keep mine upstairs." She pointed at the ceiling. "I live up there."

He leaned close to her, but couldn't see down the front of her blouse buttoned to a few inches below her neck.

"If I help you out around the store today, will you let me come up and see them books when you got some time? Maybe you could show me how to read one."

She touched his shoulder. "We'll have a little while after I close before Mama Glenn brings Joey over."

Once they were upstairs, Cap peered around to satisfy his curiosity about how she lived. There was a big feather bed in one corner with a baby cradle beside it, a small wooden table covered with blue oilcloth, two wicker chairs and a wooden rocker with an embroidered cushion on the seat. Clothes were hung neatly on poles, and dishes, pots, and about twenty books were stacked on shelves.

"This aint like a regular house. Fireplace is downstairs in the storeroom. Have to cook down there. Have to bring water from the well all the way up them stairs." Nancy sat down at the table and motioned him to sit, too.

"You got it hard." He reached out and gently squeezed her hand, then let it go, his skin tingling.

She smiled. "Would you like a sip of somethin nicer than that old whiskey you boys make out at the still? I got some blackberry cordial me and Mama made last summer."

In his opinion, cordial was sickeningly sweet, but he answered yes as if he liked cordial better than anything. She poured it from a glass pitcher etched with flowers into matching etched glasses, instead of the tin cups most people used. He took a slow sip, no noisy gulping in front of her.

"Fancy glasses." His stomach and gullet felt the fire of the cordial, then the heat flowed into the rest of him.

She smiled. The sun shone through the windows onto the cut glass and into her eyes, sending sparkling messages to him. "Nice thing about ownin a store, you can get yourself some pretty things once in a while."

He had another sip, settling into a warm, tingly feeling.

"Do you want to try an easy book, Cap?"

"Whatever you want to learn me. How about his one?" He reached over and pulled out a worn, brown one with pictures of blue and white flowers on its cover.

"That's McGuffey's Sixth. It's the hardest."

"Then you better do a good job learnin me." He dragged his chair over to her side of the table, set the book in front of her, and sat so close that his arm lightly touched hers.

After glancing sidewise at him—she liked looking at him, he could tell it—she opened the book.

"Do you know your letters, Cap?"

"I know H is for Hatfield." He pictured the *H* he burned into the ends of logs ready to float down river to the mills.

"What's this?" She pointed to something that wasn't an *H*.

"You tell me." He pressed slightly closer to her to see the details of the letter.

"It's an *A*, Cap. When you see it in a word, you can say *a* like in cat or *a* like in gate. Look here." She pointed to strings of letters. "There's big *A*s and little *a*s. That word starts with *a* and it says *anecdote*." She stressed the *a* sound.

"Anecdote?"

"An anecdote's a yarn. A short one with a point to it."

He traced a finger under the word. "How do you know which end it starts on?"

Nancy squinted at him. "You sure you want to learn how to read? Seems like you aint never tried it before."

He sipped his cordial and smiled what he hoped was the sweetest smile she'd ever seen.

"I aint never had no one to learn me." Then he dropped the smile. "Pappy never wanted us to read."

"Big as you are, Cap Hatfield! You let your Pappy tell you what you can do and what you can't?"

It was humiliating to have her looking at him that way, as though she was a grownup and he was a small child. "There's one *a* and another one here and another one here." He pointed them out.

She laughed. "You missed one." She reached over took his finger and pointed it to another *a*.

She laughed at him! If it weren't for the warmth of the cordial, the tingle of her hand on his, and the softness of her skin he would have told her a thing or two. Instead, he sat there and grinned like an idiot.

She giggled. "Want to know what this says?"

"'Course I do." Still grinning, he didn't care that he was beginning to feel foolish.

She took his finger and moved it across the page as she read. "A laughable story was circulated during the administration of the old Duke of Newcastle, and retailed to the public in many forms. This nobleman, with many good points, was known for being profuse of his promises on all occasions." She read on about the adventures of the duke.

This was unbelievable.

"Why that's just a yarn!" Cap peered at her.

"What'd you expect?"

"I don't know, but Pappy's always sayin books is mostly lies made up by folks tryin to pull the wool over your eyes."

"How's your Pappy gonna know what's in books if he can't read?"

"Read me some more. But first, what's *profuse of his promises*?"

"I don't exactly know, but I read the story before and the duke makes a lot of promises he can't keep."

"*Profuse of his promises.*" He liked the sound of those words. "Read me some more."

As she read on about the duke and a place called London and a dying king, he asked her a lot of questions. It was a very strange story about some very strange people.

At one point Nancy said. "Cap, this part's supposed to be funny." But he never once felt like laughing.

When she finished the story, Nancy leaned closer to him. "Do you like me to read to you?"

And that was how he'd begun to read in spite of Pappy. And how he'd fallen in love with Nancy. She'd shown him a thing or two that lay beyond Pappy's ken.

Now here was Nancy wanting him to turn his back on Pappy's ways again—stop fighting, sell their Tug Valley land, and move to Main Island Creek on the Logan side of the mountains. Seeing the world through Pappy's eyes, which was how he'd always seen almost everything, he'd been dead set against such a move. But now, when he thought about the deaths of Allifair McCoy, Uncle Jim, and Bill Dempsey, the family's increasingly desperate need for money, and the posses and bounty hunters swarming over the border, he was beginning to agree with her. He decided to take a look at John Sergeant's Main Island Creek property.

Chapter 21

Henry Smith was raising his rate to ten dollars a day for keeping Cap's and Pappy's ten pigs, two mares, three mules, and Pappy's big old ox in his livery stable.

"Nothin else I could do but pay him." Pappy shook his head repeatedly as he and Cap headed down the boardwalk past some stores. "But this can't go on."

"We need some money comin in." Cap slowed down to match Pappy's foot-dragging pace. They paused in front of the tannery and leather goods shop to look at the boots in the window. *One year garrantee*, he read.

"Can't afford em no matter how good their garrantee is."

"We could buy anything in that winder if we could work." Cap liked the shine of the boots in the window. His homemade ones couldn't take a shine.

"There you go iffin me again."

"Plenty of timber out by Main Island Creek just waitin for somebody to cut it."

"Now how would you know?" Pappy sneered. "John Sergeant told Nancy and your Mama there was timber out there and they believed him. Don't know that I do."

"Yesterday I went to see for myself." Without making any promises, Cap had allowed Sergeant to show him what he had. He'd been so impressed by the stands of timber, the isolation, and creeks where they could float logs to market, that he could hardly keep from running off at the mouth about it. But he forced himself to slow down and play his cards carefully.

"You did what?" Pappy thundered.

"I figured you'd want to know what was out there so's you could make a good decision."

"I already made my decision."

"I told him I was only scoutin the place out for you so you'd know what he had." Cap wasn't going to make the mistake of sounding like he wanted to take over the family's affairs as he had on New Year's. "Where Sergeant took me to—hardly anybody else ever goes there. There aint nothin you'd call a road or a trail in most places. Our horses had to go up and down the steepest hills and around the biggest boulders you ever seen. Half the time the trail was just a stream bed full of sharp rocks. Many places tree branches was hangin so low we had to look out for our heads. After we was two or three miles out of Logan, there was no more houses and no riders, no sign there'd been anyone through there for some time."

"You tryin to tell me no posses nor reward hunters would come after us if we was to move out there?" Pappy stopped in front of the courthouse yard. "Is that what you're up to?"

"It's a long, hard trail. And out by Main Island Creek that trail's way down in a skinny holler. You'd only need one or two men as lookouts."

"How about timber? I aint interested in no place that's got no timber." Pappy picked up a few stones and began flinging them at jail windows where they clattered off the bars.

In this respect, Cap had really good news. "About four thousand acres of beech, poplar, red and white oak. Never been worked by a timber crew, far as I could tell."

Pappy's eyes opened wide. "Not timbered? Why not? No way to get nothin out to a mill?"

A man's face appeared at one of the jail windows, but Cap couldn't see who it was.

"I was thinkin the same thing till Sergeant showed me Beech Creek on the back side of the property. It floods in the spring and we could float logs down to the Tug. Of course, that would mean we'd have to ride em past the McCoys and the posses along the border."

"I reckon they couldn't watch our loggin camps like they can now, so they might not know when we was comin. If we had to, we'd sneak our timber down the river at night. That you, Cunningham?" Pappy yelled at the window.

The face ducked out of sight and Pappy ambled on down the street chuckling to himself.

Cap was beginning to detect some interest on Pappy's part in the land's prospects. "Timber's not the whole story neither. He's got about four hundred acres of good bottom farm land."

"How much poplar's out there?" Pappy asked. High grade poplar brought the best price.

"Thick stands all over them mountains. Big trees—two to eight feet acrost." Cap thought over his next words, with the aim of provoking the reaction he wanted. "But I guess we'll have to forget about Main Island Creek." He sighed. "We have to live out by the Tug if we're gonna guard the border. Can't see no other way."

"Well, I don't know about that border." Pappy peered down a side street that ended at the Logan Mercantile, harrumphed and moved on. "Hardly anyone's left out there. My brother Ellison is dead, Jim Vance is dead, Johnse is movin away, my brothers Elias and Smith and Patterson have settled in Logan, and my brother Wall's in prison in Kentucky. Only you and me and Bobby Lee's left. We got a good fort, and we can round up enough men to hold it, but not enough to hang onto our homes, too."

Cap had been pretty sure that as soon as he said "we'll have to" and "can't see no other way," Pappy would argue with him. His instincts had been right. Where the boardwalk ended, they stopped talking and slowed down to hear what strong talk Vicie Fowler was dishing out to John Buskirk.

"You don't need that little patch of land as bad as Logan needs a church," Vicie was saying.

"That's where I grow my corn and tomatoes in the summer." In brown jacket and dungarees, Buskirk the hotel owner was not a fancy dresser like some Logan businessmen.

"What's more important?" Vicie smiled triumphantly, showing she thought she'd got him where she wanted him. "God or your tomato plants?"

"God can put His church anywhere He pleases, but I need my tomatoes where I can watch out for worms first thing every morning and last thing every evening before I go to bed." He peered at her over his spectacles, obviously unshaken by her argument.

"There's no church for James and I to marry in." Vicie wasn't giving up. "But wouldn't it be nice if there was one when your daughters are old enough to wed?"

"Yes, I agree with you on that. We got just about ten years to find another place," Buskirk answered.

"A church," Pappy muttered when they were out of Vicie Fowler's earshot. "One more reason not to live in Logan."

"Aint no church out on Main Island Creek." Cap, hoping he wasn't pushing too hard, couldn't resist speaking his mind one more time.

Pappy glared at him. "Get off my back."

Cap determined to keep his mouth shut the rest of the day, let matters simmer in Pappy's head for a while. But it was going to be hard. Keeping quiet had always been hard for him.

Chapter 22

Cap and Pappy walked from Uncle Elias's to the courthouse. Even though it was late January and cold, there was only patchy snow left on the ground. Farmers and timber men from all over the county, along with many town folk, were gathered in the courthouse yard and in the half frozen mud of the street. Logan court days came only once a month and were a time for visiting, more than the usual drinking, horse trading and street races to show off the horses. One galloped wildly by, out of its rider's control.

With so many strangers in town, Cap and Pappy would normally have brought their Winchesters along. But because Judge "Law and Order" Harvey had strict rules about what he would and wouldn't allow in his courtroom, they were carrying revolvers holstered out of sight under their coats.

A stranger in a brown coat down to his knees, with matching hat and gloves, was pestering three mountain men. "Land speculator, doin his best to talk folks out of their property," Cap said. "Do you suppose he's heard about the railroad goin in?"

"They's all heard about that." Pappy pointed out two more such strangers—it certainly was easy to spot them—eyeing local men hanging around the courthouse. "Except for John Sergeant they's buyin for furriners. Sergeant's buyin for hisself." Pappy called anyone outside of West Virginia, Virginia, or Kentucky a "furriner."

"Sergeant's the only one you can trust," Cap agreed. In the *Louisville Courier-Journal* he'd read about speculators buying coal and timber property, hoping to make big profits reselling it to east coast syndicates. He didn't exactly know what east coast syndicates were, but he was pretty sure they were in America. Not some foreign country.

Cap followed Pappy up the ice-covered steps and entered a dark hallway with the jailer's office and cells opening off one side and the courtroom off the other. They almost ran into Judge Harvey, in a black robe, emerging from hallway shadows.

"Judge." Pappy pulled a letter from his coat pocket and thrust it into Harvey's hand. "This here's from Governor E. Willis Wilson hisself. He's gettin two companies of militia ready to march down here." Cap had gotten an answer to his letter to his own Governor, but none from the Governor of Kentucky about the prisoner exchange.

Harvey peered at the letter over tiny spectacles perched on the end of his nose. "Am I to infer from this that you finally took my advice and learned to read?"

Pappy ducked the question and launched into a speech about how Wilson had two hundred militia ready to send to support the citizens of Logan if Kentucky didn't restrain posses from raiding in West Virginia. Cap doubted Harvey was going to be impressed by the letter, even if it was from the Governor. And besides it had nothing to do with their court business today and might be seen as an attempt to influence the judge in Pappy's favor, which in fact it was. The judge scowled and handed the letter back to Pappy.

"If another war between the states breaks out down here, you and your Kentucky counterpart good-for-nothings will be to blame." Harvey stuck his chin in the air and, robes swishing, headed into his chamber.

Before Pappy could get himself into more trouble, Cap yanked on his arm. "Come on. We gotta talk to our lawyer."

"What kind of a idiot is that Harvey?" Pappy sputtered as Cap opened the courtroom door. "Don't he understand nothin I'm tellin him?"

The courtroom was grander looking than when Cap had been here five years ago for a sawmill permit. The door he'd come in opened on an aisle between rows of benches leading up to a long, highly polished table that had replaced the former rough-hewn plank one in front of the judge's seat. The judge's bench was now on a platform high above everyone else in the room. Portraits of Governor Wilson and John Floyd had joined those of Robert E. Lee and Jefferson Davis on the walls. Dark green velvet drapes had been hung beside all four floor-to-ceiling windows.

Pappy fingered a drape. "Place looks like a goldarned whorehouse."

"Or the inside of Nighbert's house," Cap said, eyeing Nighbert, who was sitting at the long, shiny table. It didn't look good for the Hatfields that Nighbert was up front where he could lord it over the rest of the courtroom.

Pappy's creditors, or phonies persuaded to pose as creditors, occupied the front bench on the right—the owner of a store where the Hatfields often bought food and cooking gear for the logging crews, a man who sold axes and saws and chains, the tanner, a farmer who'd sold them an ox, two lumbermen, and even the county surveyor. Perched on the end next to the aisle was George Lawson, lawyer for the creditors, in a freshly pressed black suit and shiny black shoes.

On the left, the Hatfield bench was empty except for their lawyer, Charlie Blair. Charlie's red hair had faded almost completely white and his rumpled, faded suit had become too tight.

In the last two rows sat a few men and women who had nothing to do with the case as far as Cap knew.

"That's him!" one man said, pointing as Cap and Pappy walked by. "That's old Devil Anse hisself."

Danged busy bodies, minding other people's business. They were here to gawk at him and Pappy, maybe hoping to see them lose today's lawsuit. Cap slid in beside Blair on the Hatfield bench, but Pappy stomped to the other side. He let his eyes wander over the men sitting there.

"Aint I always been square with you? Aint I always paid what I owe?"

Not one man would look up.

"Too ashamed to look me in the eye, are you?" Pappy strode the length of the bench, pausing in front of each man. "I brung you fellers a lot of business. You figure you can get along without old Devil Anse now?" Pappy stopped in front of the man who owned the timber supply store, reached over and flipped the man's shiny blue tie. "Purty tie. Take good care of it. You aint gonna have the money for another one like it when I take my business someplace else." He stomped over and plopped himself down next to Cap.

Jim Chafin the jailer appeared at the front of the courtroom. "Hear ye! Hear ye! The January Logan County Circuit Court will now come to order. The Honorable John Harvey presiding. All rise."

Judge Harvey, his long black robe cutting the silence with a swoosh, marched up the aisle and, smoothing the robe deftly under him, settled into his chair. He peered out over his spectacles at the courtroom. "You may be seated."

Before sitting, Pappy called out. "Get the frig out of here, Nighbert. You aint the judge or nothin. You aint got no business squattin up there."

To Cap's terrible embarassment Nighbert didn't budge and Harvey dealt with Pappy by saying, "Sit down and remain silent, Mr. Hatfield." There was a murmur from the spectators. None of them, nor anyone they knew, would dare talk back to Devil Anse Hatfield like that.

Judge Harvey summoned the plaintiff's attorney, George Lawson, to stand before him. Lawson, puffy pink face sprouting from a stiff white collar, began droning a long list of debts Pappy allegedly owed. As Lawson read on in his high whiny voice, Cap began thumbing through some papers Lawson had handed to Charlie Blair a few minutes earlier.

Suddenly, his eyes fastened on one sentence. He went back to the beginning, now reading more carefully. The document said that instead of paying his debts in cash, Pappy was to sign over five hundred acres of his Tug land to his creditors and one hundred acres to Nighbert, who was listed as a business partner of one of the plaintiffs. There was a place for Pappy's name on the last page.

This trumped-up lawsuit could be a land grab in disguise. Cap wouldn't be surprised if Harvey, sitting up there so smart and righteous, was in on it, too.

In front of the courtroom, Lawson was still reading ". . . and to Mr. Stollings three hundred thirteen dollars and twelve cents."

Cap leaned his head back and stared at what had formerly been a ceiling of rough-hewn planks and now was an elegant display of smooth-planed, varnished wood. There seemed to be more money than people knew what to do with floating around Logan these days. If these jackasses got richer from his and Pappy's land, they'd have even more power to mess with the Hatfields.

Cap stood up, catching stares from Pappy and Judge Harvey, and made his way to the back of the courtroom and out the door. In the street, he ran down the boardwalk until he came to a glass window spanned by black letters advertising "John Sergeant, Land Purchases and Sales." Inside, a small fire smelling pungently of coal dust burned in a grate. Sergeant, looking like a queen bee in his yellow and brown checkered jacket and sticky-looking black hair parted in the middle, had a smile for Cap.

"Thought you'd be interested in this." Cap held out the document. "Looks like Nighbert's tryin to get his hands on a good-sized piece of our land that we was thinkin about signin over to you. You might not of knowed this. I sure didn't know about it till now."

Sergeant read the document slowly, much more slowly, Cap thought, than he had.

"These law suit settlement papers?" Sergeant said softly.

Cap nodded.

Sergeant frowned. "These folks are planning on getting six hundred acres of your property. If your family does decide to go ahead on my proposition, I want all your Tug land. I don't want to be messing with Nighbert and his gang."

"Nighbert looks like a fat hen sittin on a nest egg up there in front of the court. He thinks he's got a done deal."

Sergeant smiled. "Nighbert doesn't know this is only the first inning of the game."

Cap caught Sergeant's drift without knowing exactly what he meant. An inning was part of the new ball game Sergeant was always trying to get everyone to play in a neighbor's cow pasture.

"I don't know about you," Cap said. "But I don't like any part of payin em off in land instead of money."

"Would you rather your family sold the land to me?"

"You bet."

"We need a few minutes with your father here in my office. Why don't you run back and tell the judge you were surprised and shocked by what you read and need an hour's recess to consider it. That's such a short time my guess is he'll grant it."

Cap ran back to the courthouse and barged into the courtroom, banging the doors against the wall. He strode to the front of the room and plopped the document in front of Nighbert.

"What's the meaning of this disruption?" Harvey asked.

"Hornswogglin. I found hornswogglin in these here papers."

"Hornswogggling?" Harvey's nose wrinkled.

"No one told us our land was gonna be handed over to these fellers if we lose this suit. Wouldn't you call that hornswogglin?"

"You were unacquainted with that provision?"

"Never heard of it before."

Harvey stared down at his hands for a minute. Nighbert pulled nervously on his symbol of power, a gold watch chain stretched across his vest.

"We want a hour recess to think this over," Cap said.

Harvey sighed. "All right. Court will recess for one hour."

"You gonna tell me what's goin on here?" Pappy asked on the way out of the courtoom.

"We're goin to see John Sergeant," Cap said.

"What in heck for?" Lightning flashed in Pappy's eyes.

Inside his office, Sergeant motioned them to heavy, padded chairs, while he sat across a big oak desk from them. Cap remembered when most of Logan had turned out at the landing to watch the big desk and chairs arrive on a push boat poled up the Guyandotte from the Ohio. The furniture had taken up almost the whole deck and had strained the backs of the polers who'd brought it upstream.

"Your son made an important discovery," Sergeant began. "As things stand, if you lose this suit today, the court will award several hundred acres of your land to your creditors. Nighbert is counting himself as a partner of your creditors, by the way. So he'll get some, too."

"They aint gettin my land." Pappy's nose hooked down sharply.

Cap started to interrupt, but Sergeant held up a hand. "They probably will. You could propose a change to the settlement document, but I don't know if that change will get the creditors' or the court's approval."

"I'll shoot anyone sets foot on my land," Pappy declared.

Cap rubbed his forehead in anguish. When Pappy got riled up, there was no telling what he'd do.

"You and I know, Anse, that would only add to your troubles." Sergeant leaned forward and rested his elbows on the desk. "But you have a way out."

"This had better be good," Pappy replied. "I'm listenin, but not for long."

He was listening. Cap held his breath.

"Convey your family's Tug Valley land to me right now, today. It's worth about two to two-fifty an acre now and I'll offer you two-fifty. The Main Island Creek property's got no navigable river and no prospects for a railroad. It's going for about a dollar fifty an acre. So I'm willing to trade you four thousand acres of my Main Island Creek property plus four thousand dollars cash for your four thousand acres by the Tug."

Cap fastened his gaze on Pappy's face. The big moment had arrived with a bang. This was far more money and property than Pappy could have imagined. But to get this deal, he'd have to make his decision today, right now.

"Four thousand dollars," Pappy muttered. "I can build me a new cabin and I won't be needin to cut and sell no timber for at least another year."

"If you consummate the deal now, before you go back into the courtroom, you can tell the court no one can claim your Tug land because you don't own it anymore. There'd be nothing anybody could do about that. If your creditors win their case, they'll have to accept cash."

"I aint even seen that land yet."

"But your son has." Sergeant nodded in Cap's direction. "And you know he liked what he saw. Isn't that good enough?"

Pappy's mouth hung open. He rubbed his forehead, then licked his lips. He tapped his fingers on Sergeant's desk. "All right. Let's do it."

Cap felt light as a feather, as though he could waft to the ceiling and float around there. All the arguing, persuading, fretting, and worrying he'd gone through for the last month had now born fruit in less than five minutes. The Hatfields were going to Main Island Creek. He wanted to shout with joy, but didn't.

Sergeant pulled out printed property conveyance forms from a cabinet, filled in the places that needed filling out, including references he had on hand to the proper deeds on file in the courthouse. He agreed to trade Cap six hundred acres of Main Island Creek property plus six hundred cash for his six hundred acres by the Tug. Pappy told him Johnse had six hundred acres, too, but probably would want his all in cash.

"You gonna sell my land to Nighbert?" Pappy signed his "H" on the document and Cap signed his name. "I hope you charge him a heck of a big price."

"Think I'll just sit on that land for a while." Sergeant's smile was as broad as it could get. "Until that railroad comes in. I'll be takin a chance it could go up the Kentucky side. If it does, I'll make a little money at three dollars an acre. But if those railroad tracks end up in West Virginia—Whooee! I'm a rich man!"

Cap wondered what Sergeant's vision of himself as a rich man included. A fine suit bought in Charleston or Cincinnati, a big house with hired girls to cook and clean and hired men to take care of the house and horses, the best baseballs in the Sears Roebuck catalog?

Once he'd reconvened the court, Judge Harvey got right to the business at hand. "I have considered the issue of requiring forfeiture of Mr. Hatfield's Tug Valley property to pay his debts and have determined its legality in the event he loses this suit."

Cap stood up. "Beg your pardon, your honor. But it aint legal." He started to grin. He was about to have a good, hand-clapping, foot-stomping time.

Harvey shook his head vigorously. "I determine what is legal and what is not in this court."

"Is it legal to force my father give up a tract of land he doesn't own?"

"Of course not." Harvey peered over his tiny spectacles at Cap. "But I don't know what you're driving at. It's well known the defendant owns the land at issue." Harvey glanced at Nighbert, who nodded.

Harvey thought Nighbert knew the score. Cap got a laugh out of these two. He could hardly wait to see their faces when they heard the news.

"That aint so." Cap's voice grew louder and echoed off the walls. Everyone else in the courtroom had hushed. "John Sergeant owns that land."

"What?" Harvey turned to Nighbert. "I was given to understand Anse Hatfield owns thousands of acres by the Tug."

Nighbert frantically fingered his gold watch chain.

Cap slapped his thigh and chuckled. "My Pappy don't own nothin out by the Tug and neither do I."

"You can prove this?" Harvey's voice was hoarsening.

"Ask John Sergeant. He'll show you his deed."

"This is true?" Harvey turned to Pappy.

"Bein a peaceful man by nature, I have decided to move away from the Tug where I must always be defendin myself and my family against armed men from Kentucky. Out there, I was never left alone to enjoy my children and my little babies."

Pappy spoke so seriously and sincerely that Cap no longer felt like laughing. He, Pappy, Nancy, Mama, and Johnse—they were all sick of the feud and the posses.

Chapter 23

Cap and Pappy were barely inside the Floyd family cabin when Pappy screwed up his face and sniffed the air. "What's that stink?"

"Books." Cap set a jug of Johnse's whiskey on the table and, with pleasure, breathed in the aroma of old paper and leather. John Floyd was staying with his ailing father, George Rogers Clark Floyd, who now lived here alone in two rooms—one for eating and sleeping and one for his library. Cap sometimes envied Floyd, being raised with books by a father who'd sent his sons and daughters to college, something no one else in Logan County had ever done.

Pappy ran his gaze around the room, over the floor-to-ceiling and wall-to-wall shelves of books of all shapes and sizes. "It aint a purty smell."

Cap chuckled to himself. From books, he and Floyd had picked up ideas beyond Pappy's control, and Pappy was finding it hard to put up with that.

"My dad doesn't keep them for their smell." Floyd grinned. "Sit down and have a drink, Anse." Floyd pointed to the jug and glasses on the table. "Brewed by your son Johnse, I believe."

"He run off to Washington Territory and left his whiskey behind." Easing into a chair, Pappy peered warily around at the looming bookshelves. "Said he's fed up with fightin."

Floyd let out a low whistle. "That's as far as you can go from West Virginia and still be in America."

"He's been gone a week." Cap was surprised at how much he already missed his brother. "Sold his land to John Sergeant, took the money and cleared out. Goin to get hisself a new life, he said."

Three thousand miles to get a life of his own. For his part, Cap was proud to have had a hand in getting Pappy to move away from the Tug and proud to have moved with him. He'd always been stronger and more loyal to the family than Johnse. And he had a good wife, while Johnse had married another McCoy, one of the worst of the lot. Cap was once more convinced he'd head the Hatfield family—not right away, but eventually.

Floyd poured whiskey from the jug into each of their glasses and added ginger ale to his.

"You're drinkin like a Charleston dandy, John Floyd!" Pappy declared. "You aint lookin much like a Logan man these days."

"I asked you here because I have news," Floyd replied. "Governor Wilson sent his representative to Kentucky to look into the welfare of your relatives in the Pikeville jail. His man reported back that your brother Wall plans to mortgage his property out by the Tug to pay for his legal defense."

"No need for him to do that," Pappy said. "I got money now. I can pay his lawyer."

Floyd tapped his fingers on the table. "You might not want to pay the lawyer he's picked."

"Sure I will. Wall's a bit peculiar, but he's my brother."

"Wall's hired Perry Cline as his attorney, Anse. You'd be paying Perry Cline."

Cap searched Floyd's face, hoping he'd see a wink and a grin. But Floyd's demeanor remained grim.

Pappy's nose hooked down and his beard jutted out. "Maybe I ought to take some men to Pikeville and get Wall out of there."

Floyd shook his head. "We were told the sheriff lets your brother roam without supervision because Wall gave his word he wouldn't escape. He could run away if he wanted to, but he's been spending a lot of time with Sally McCoy. She lost all her furniture in the fire, and he's making her a new bedstead."

"Why the man's gone plum crazy!" Pappy roared.

"Wall's saying he never harmed any man. He says you, Cap, Johnse, and Bobby Lee are to blame for the New Year's raid and the killings in '82."

"Wall said that?" Pappy's voice was only a whisper.

"What have they been doin to Uncle Wall over in Kentucky to get him to tell such a lie?" Cap had never known a Hatfield to talk against another. "No one saw what happened in '82. Certainly not him. And none of us kilt no one on New Year's. Not him, not me, not Pappy, not Bobby Lee." All the Hatfields knew that Wall had refused to have anything to do with the executions, did not witness them, and had been nowhere near the McCoy place on New Year's. "Wall's talkin crazy."

"He seems to see himself as a model citizen," Floyd said. "An innocent victim of the feuds, wrongly imprisoned, certain to have his name cleared in court."

Cap held his head in his hands. "The law aint about to stand behind him. He's in Kentucky and they're gonna twist Wall's law to where he won't recognize it. Don't he remember how Abner Vance paid with his life for trustin the law when it was in the hands of his enemies?"

"Wall got all them crazy notions of his from readin." Pappy glared at the books around him. "Before this, nobody in our family's ever turned against his own kin. We aint that kind of people."

"I doubt it's the books," Floyd said. "I think it's his pride. It was his idea of heaven when he was Justice of the Peace, calling himself a man of the law. Now that he's accused of murder he's an angel fallen from heaven."

"Wall can be a Justice of the Peace, call himself a man of the law or a judge, anything he wants right here in West Virginia." Pappy, steely gray eyes softened in puzzlement, stared at Cap.

Cap doubted Wall had ever found it easy to be a Hatfield and at the same time anything he wanted to be. And now, when he was trying to make his own way of life, putting the law above everything, Wall was making a big mistake. Kentucky "law" was going to destroy him.

When Cap thought about it, he knew any man living out by the Tug needed to think a long time before he took a different path than Pappy. Pappy had kept the family safe and doing well for many years in spite of there being no law to speak of out there.

"How about this son of yours, Anse?" Floyd asked. "What if Cap wanted to be a justice of the peace? Or a judge, like Harvey?"

"We could use a judge in this family." Cap winked at Floyd. He felt the warmth of Johnse's whiskey begin to spread over his body.

"You got just about as much chance of growin feathers and bein a bird as you got bein a judge," Pappy snapped.

"Anyhow, Wall aint betrayed us any more'n he's betrayed hisself," Cap said, reluctant to get crosswise with Pappy at this delicate time. "Cline aint gonna get him off. He's gonna grab Uncle Wall's land and put him away where he can't never get it back."

"There's reason to believe you're right, Cap." Floyd replied. "The Mc-Coys are telling folks Cline's promised them Wall will be sent up for good."

"I sold Wall that land," Pappy said. "It was part of what I got from Cline back in '72."

Floyd grimaced. "That explains a lot."

"We got somethin to tell you," Pappy said. "We're gonna tell everybody Cap went to Washington with Johnse so them posses'll quit lookin for him."

"I need some breathin room to help set up our new place." Cap helped himself to more whiskey, hoping to take the sting out of the news about Wall.

Floyd smiled. "I'd never believe it if I heard you'd left. You're the heir apparent, the future head of the Hatfield family."

Pappy's beak of a nose hooked dangerously above his beard. "The future aint here yet, John."

Floyd raised both hands in surprise. "Cap's a first rate choice to follow in your footsteps. And he can read, write, and do his figures. He's prepared to deal with the modern world."

Pappy's face turned red. "I learnt him all he needs to know."

Floyd raised his glass to Pappy. "You made him the man he is."

"The acorn don't fall far from the oak tree, John." Pappy cackled like a crow, the way he usually reserved for his own jokes.

"A lucky son to have such a wise father."

Cap gripped his glass. That was Floyd, first playing up to him and then to Pappy. No wonder they called him "The Nuthatch" after the little bird that could peck going up a tree or down, it didn't matter which.

"Want me to do anything in your behalf for Wall?" Floyd asked.

"Nothin." Pappy stood up and shook hands with John.

Floyd turned to Cap. "You're welcome to borrow any of these books you'd like." He waved a hand at the shelves.

"This one." Cap pulled a book by Merriweather Lewis from the shelf. "It's a true story about Lewis and Clark," he explained to Pappy. "Eighty years ago they went all the way from Tennessee to Washington Territory."

"Where Johnse is headed? You'd best read me that one."

"You may want Cap to read you a lot of my books some day," Floyd said

After Pappy was outside, Floyd lowered his voice. "I'm serious about you going into law, Cap. Think about it."

Chapter 24

"You don't have to shutter em," Cap told Mama. Along with the children, they'd crowded around the windows as March winds rat-tat-tatted the glass with bullets of rain. "They'll hold against most any storm."

Mama had wanted glass windows like Elias's and Betty's in her new home. So he'd put them in her cabin and his. It had taken a month to round up friends for raisings so far up the holler from town, often a nigh impossible ride over the mountains by the Tug. But once folks had gathered, they raised each cabin inside a week.

"You aint gonna listen to this, are you, Levicy?" Pappy said from where he sat in front of his great new stone fireplace. "Better shutter em up like we done in our old place. Always worked good."

"Now, Captain Anderson," Mama said. "Have some faith in your son."

Lightning flashed and a moment later thunder rattled the windows. Cap's sister Elizabeth screamed and put her hands over her ears.

"There go your winders!" Pappy shouted.

But the windows held.

The lightning flashed again, and thunder crashed even louder right after it. The children laughed and shrieked.

Cap wondered if his baby son was sleeping through the thunder and lightning. Coleman was only three weeks old, too little to expose to the cold rain for the half-mile walk to Pappy's. But someday he'd take his son out in a storm like this, let him feel the drops pelting his skin and the fierce winds tugging at him. Let him hear the winds howl—come on out, it's time to float logs, time for the thrills of riding huge log rafts down the Tug, wildly swollen with spring rains. His son was going to love it. Last spring he'd ridden with Johnse. But this year Johnse was gone and no timber had been cut.

On the way back to his cabin, Cap splashed hatless and soggy through the driving rain. No use hunching down and pulling up his collar—he'd be soaked by the time he got home anyway. He slapped his hands against his cheeks, enjoying the sting of the cold.

Slogging through the clearing by Pappy's house, he passed stumps of trees felled by the timber crew to build the cabins and barns. Not surprisingly, there was a lot more work needed to clear the fields for spring planting. In less than four months since buying this land, they'd built two cabins, a fort and a drawbridge, leaving stumps to be pulled out, root houses and smoke houses and barns to be built. And Mama and Nancy needed wash sheds. And on and on and on.

He passed the 32-foot drawbridge he'd designed, a towering structure of long poles with cross planks laid on it, raised and tied high over the tumbling muddy creek. When it was down, it was strong enough for loaded wagons to be pulled across, and when it was up anyone they wanted to keep out would find it hard to go down the steep bank, cross the deep and fast-moving creek, and climb up the other side.

During lightning flashes, he caught glimpses of the fort they'd built high on the ridge, from which you could almost see Kentucky. One of Floyd's books had given him the idea for the palisades slanting out below the fort, and the roof formed from shingles on hinges that could be lifted from inside to spot and shoot at enemies trying to get past the palisades. Many times Pappy had made him feel good by bragging about this fort to friends.

Cap told himself he had a right to feel good. He'd seen to it that the family was solidly protected out here on Main Island Creek.

For his part, Governor Wilson, after whom Pappy and Mama had named their new son E. Willis Wilson in appreciation for his efforts in behalf of the family, was doing his best to rid Logan County of the threat of Kentucky invaders. Wilson had sent a writ of extradition for murder to Governor Buckner of Kentucky for Frank Phillips and all the men known to be riding with him when Jim Vance and Bill Dempsey were killed. But tempers were still running high in Kentucky even though the New Year's raid was nearly four months ago, and Buckner was stalling. So Wilson had also charged Phillips with kidnapping in federal court. And Wilson was pressuring Buckner to rescind his offer of rewards for capturing Hatfields and their men, arguing that the rewards provided incentive for criminal invasions into West Virginia.

Cap believed Wilson had some interest in the Hatfields' welfare. But Wilson was outraged at Kentucky's total disregard of West Virginia's sovereignty and aimed, for political reasons, to show the citizens of West Virginia how he was standing up for their state. Cap was grateful anyhow.

Cap noticed, however, that none of Wilson's efforts included denying the murder charges against him or Pappy or Johnse or any other Hatfield or Hatfield cohort for either the New Year's raid or the executions five years ago right after the election in '82. Pappy had always said the executions were just and legal, but Uncle Wall had never agreed, and Cap was beginning to suspect the governors of West Virginia and Kentucky didn't either. No matter how many times he turned it over in his head, Cap couldn't decide the issue to suit himself.

* * *

Election Day in August of '82 had promised to be trouble-free. To prevent fights and arguments with the McCoys, Pappy had stayed home and forbidden Cap, Johnse, and Bobby Lee to go to the polling place in Kentucky. The family had gone to bed that night, falling asleep to the drumming of rain on the roof and closed shutters, when they woke to the sound of a man yelling and pounding at the door.

"It's me, Plyant. Let me in. Something awful's happened."

It took a while for Cap's exhausted, rain-soaked cousin to catch his breath enough to say that Pappy's brother, Uncle Ellison, had been stabbed and shot at the polling place.

"He aint dead," Plyant said. "But he's full of cuts and blood's foamin from his mouth."

Pappy sat in his chair, doubled up like he had a terrible stomach ache, his head in his hands. "His wounds are wounds to my own flesh."

The way Plyant told it, Tolbert McCoy had gotten into a drunken argument with Bad Dan about whether Dan had paid Tolbert for the fiddle he was playing. Tolbert had kept worrying Dan about the money until somebody had started yelling for a fight. When the racket woke Ellison from sleeping off his whiskey in the peach orchard, he came over to see what was going on.

Seeing the argument didn't amount to much, Ellison decided to break the tension by joking. "I don't know why you're arguin about who's the best man. I'm the best goldarned man on earth!" He laughed.

That didn't strike Tolbert right and he stomped over to Ellison and said, "Well, I'm the devil on earth," then spit on Ellison. Ellison, nearly a foot taller than Tolbert, grabbed Tolbert's neck in the crook of one arm and held on. Before anyone knew what was happening, Tolbert pulled a knife from a sheath on his belt and stabbed Ellison in the chest. Ellison never let go his grip on Tolbert and down they went, Tolbert knifing Ellison over and over. Ellison still managed to get his hands on a big stone and was fixing to dash in Tolbert's brains when Phamer and Randall Junior joined their brother in stabbing Ellison. Blood pouring from his mouth, Ellison never let go the stone until Phamer took out a pistol and shot him in the back. The bullet plowed all the way through his chest.

"What was the rest of you doin? Just standin there lettin my brother get kilt?" Pappy yelled at Plyant.

Plyant answered that Uncle Elias had snatched the pistol from Phamer and fired at him. But Phamer ducked and only got creased. Just as Ira McCoy pulled his knife to threaten Elias, Matt Ferguson, the Kentucky constable stationed at the polling place, came over with his pistol drawn and made Ira back off. Ellison raised his head and tried to speak, but all that came from his mouth was blood.

To carry Ellison to a safe place out of the McCoys' reach, Jerry Hatfield brought out a blanket and some Hatfield men cut down saplings and made a litter. The nearest place they judged to be safe was Ferrell's cabin almost ten miles away on the West Virginia side of the Tug, which they reached about seven o'clock in the evening. Soon afterwards, Plyant's brother Dock set out across the mountains to get Doc Rutherford from Logan and Plyant went to fetch Pappy.

Pappy and Cap grabbed rifles and coats, getting ready to leave, when Pappy thought to ask what, if anything, Ferguson had done with the McCoy boys.

"Matt deputized four fellers on the spot and headed down the road for the Pikeville jail with Tolbert, Phamer, and Randall Junior," Plyant answered. "Said he'd put em behind bars where they'd be safe."

"To keep em safe!" Cap headed for the barn with Pappy. "They aint gonna do nothin to em in Kentucky. What are we gonna do when we get our hands on em?"

It was so dark, between the nighttime and the storm clouds, that Pappy's voice came to him out of a black void. "Nothin. Not so long as Elllison lives."

They stopped at Uncle Jim's place and persuaded him to round up more men to meet at Ferrell's. Then they picked up Johnse at his cabin. As they left, his wife Nancy began screaming and carrying on. "Don't you dare join up with your Pappy against my kin, Johnse! Don't you dare do nothin to those boys! They're my cousins and that makes em your cousins, too."

"They aint my son's blood cousins," Pappy sneered.

As he closed the cabin door and shut off his wife's torrent of words, Johnse muttered: "I wish I'd been borned some place else, some other time."

Cap shook his head. Whatever Johnse had hoped for, any fool could see his marriage to Nancy McCoy would never bring peace between the families. His marriage was a misery that everyone but him had seen coming.

When they got to Ferrell's cabin, Uncle Wall told them Ellison was bad off. "He's lost a lot of blood and he's ravin and mumblin. Don't know if he'll know who you are."

"Where's Doc Rutherford?" Pappy wanted to know.

"He aint got here yet," Uncle Elias said. "It's nigh impossible to get through them trails in some places, what with the rain and floods and mudslides."

Inside, Ellison lay stretched out on a bed put up near the fireplace. A bloody blanket lay over him, blood had soaked his blond beard and his bloody clothes were piled on the floor. His face glistened with a light sweat, and his skin was pale. Each labored breath brought a red froth to his lips. His eyes were open and staring.

Cap shuddered in horror. Uncle Ellison was the tallest and strongest of all the Hatfields, a man he'd always thought was indestructible.

"Ellison," Pappy said. "It's me, Anse."

Ellison nodded his head a little.

"You're gonna get well," Pappy said. "You aint gonna die on me."

"Loggin." Ellison smiled weakly. "That's what you want me alive for."

"Dang right. You can't leave us, Ellison. You're the best logger I got and the most decent man of all us six boys."

"I'm a dead man, Anse."

"Just say the word and the McCoys'll pay for what they done."

Cap couldn't tell whether Ellison heard or not.

"Did you hear me?" Pappy bent down close to his brother's lips.

Uncle Ellison whispered words into Pappy's ear that Cap couldn't hear.

"I'm goin after them McCoy boys," Pappy told his brothers. "If Ellison pulls through, they aint got nothin to worry about from me. But I can't let Ferguson put em in the Pikeville jail where we got no chance of getting our hands on em."

That seemed more than fair to Cap. At dawn he, Johnse, Pappy, Uncle Wall, Uncle Jim, and about twenty others rode off in a light rain. Elias and the Ferrells stayed to care for Ellison and wait for Doc Rutherford.

Early in the morning they caught up with Constable Ferguson, his deputies and the McCoys only just leaving Ferguson's cabin where they'd evidently spent the night, warm and dry. Lawmen and prisoners alike looked fresh and rested. Confirming Cap's suspicions about Ferguson's intentions, the McCoy boys weren't tied up, didn't look like they had a care in the world and were joking around with the deputies.

Uncle Wall spoke to Ferguson on behalf of the Hatfields. "You ought not to take them boys to Pikeville. They oughta be tried in the district where the crimes were committed, and that would be the Tug Valley."

"I got to take my prisoners to Pikeville," Ferguson replied. "I aint got no jail out here to keep em in."

"Ellison wasn't stabbed and shot nowhere near to Pikeville," Uncle Wall countered.

Ferguson frowned. "How is Ellison?"

"Bad," Wall replied. "Lost a lot of blood. Why don't you just bring them McCoys down by the river. When we see how it goes with my brother, and we should know today I'd guess, we can charge em and try em right near where they done it."

"Seems reasonable to me," Ferguson said. "I agree it's a good idea if we're all near your brother at this time. But we'll need a place to get in out of the rain if we have to wait a while."

"I know just the place," Pappy said as they headed out.

When Ferguson motioned to his deputies and told them they were heading back toward the Tug, Tolbert yelled "Hey, Matt, where you takin us?"

"Back near the Tug. Your trial's gonna be out here. You better hope Ellison lives or it'll be for murder."

"You said we was goin to Pikeville."

"Well, I changed my mind." Ferguson scrunched up his nose. "I got a right to do that."

While Pappy and about half his men rode ahead of the deputies and prisoners, Cap and the rest of the men covered the rear where he had to listen to Tolbert complaining about being dragged away from Pikeville. Tolbert shook his big fists and tossed his head of red hair like a ball of fire. He began kicking and yelling and his brothers followed his lead until the prisoners' horses were all over the road, bucking and snorting.

"We can't get nowhere this way," Ferguson said. They stopped at a farmer's cabin, borrowed a corn hauling sled, forced the McCoys into it in a standing position and tied their wrists and ankles to the wooden poles that formed the sides of the sled. Tolbert's shoulders, thick neck and head stood high and defiant, while his younger and smaller brother Randall's tow head hung in despondency. Phamer, dark eyes ablaze, lips pulled back from his teeth, yanked and tugged ferociously at the ropes around his wrists.

When the sled started to move, pulled by the McCoys' own horses, young Randall began to cry.

Uncle Wall rode to the sled and spoke to Randall. "Stop that. We aint gonna hurt you none."

Randall continued to whimper, tears running down his cheeks. Cap couldn't look at him. That was no way for a man, even a young one, to behave.

When they got to the Tug, Ferguson approached Pappy. "Where's this place you got for us to get out of the rain?"

"Over there." Pappy pointed across the river.

"But that's in West Virginia!"

"I expect you'll want to stay over here."

Nobody had yet made a move when the sound of galloping horses came from down the road. Pappy and his men readied their rifles as Randall McCoy and his oldest son Jim rode up and reined in their horses.

"Leave my boys be, Devil Anse!" Randall shouted.

"They'll be all right if Ellison lives," Pappy replied. "But if he dies, they got to pay for what they done."

"You got no right! You aint the law!" McCoy started to lift his rifle, but changed his mind when thirty Hatfields raised theirs.

"Don't be stupid," Pappy said. "You're way outnumbered."

"I'm goin to Pikeville and get me a sheriff and some real deputies." Randall's face was red with rage. "Then we'll see who's givin the orders around here. You stay here and keep a eye on things." He nodded to his son Jim.

Cap liked Jim who, unlike his father and brothers, usually looked for a way to settle things peacefully. He hoped Jim wouldn't get in the way and get himself hurt.

"Don't you worry none," Randall said to his boys, then rode off toward Pikeville.

"Pa!", young Randall called out and began to cry again.

"McCoy," Pappy said to Jim. "I reckon you oughta go back with your Pa."

Jim turned to Ferguson. "This aint right, Matt."

"I expect Matt and his deputies better go with you" Pappy said. "You fellers done a good job holdin onto these boys till we got here. But you aint needed now and you got no business goin over to West Virginia, you bein Kentucky law."

Ferguson looked over the crowd of armed Hatfields as though he was counting men and rifles.

"There's a old schoolhouse right over there." Pappy pointed across the river. "Where we can get out of the rain."

Ferguson thought a minute. "Give me your word they'll be on this side of the river when the time comes for the trial. I know you're a man of your word."

"My word." Pappy's face was solemn.

"No!" Cap rode over to his father. "You don't have to give your word to nobody here."

"My word!" Pappy's beak of a nose hooked dangerously down.

"It's the law, Cap," Uncle Wall said. "They hurt Ellison in Kentucky, they got to be tried in Kentucky."

"I give my word," Pappy said again to Ferguson.

Ferguson tipped his hat in salute. Then he and his deputies and Jim McCoy headed back toward Pikeville.

* * *

A nearby flash of lightning was followed instantly by a bang of thunder and the cracking sound of a tree split asunder. Cap smelled the after burn of the lightning, happy it wasn't one of the cabins or the fort that had been struck.

Even today he could find nothing illegal or evil about what the Hatfields had done in taking the McCoys to the West Virginia border. The McCoy boys had done an evil and illegal act when they attacked Uncle Ellison, a fair man who never looked for trouble, so large and tough he could thrash anyone foolish enough to pick a fight with him. And the Hatfields had had to consider Sheriff Ferguson's statement that he'd put the McCoys behind bars where they'd be safe. If left in Ferguson's hands, the McCoy boys weren't going to be prosecuted. They were going to be protected.

Cap remembered Uncle Wall's words on the issue clearly. As a man who valued the law and knew a thing or two about it, Wall's opinion was in high regard on both sides of the Tug and he'd said the prisoners should be tried in the Valley. So Cap had always believed the law decreed they should be tried there. Right and good as that opinion seemed then, he wasn't sure now what the law really was, only what he'd always thought it was.

Furthermore, both sides of the law, West Virginia and Kentucky, had agreed that the McCoys could be held in West Virginia as long as they were brought back to Kentucky for their trial. No one could deny that taking the prisoners across the river had been a perfectly legal act.

Chapter 25

At the river bank, Pappy pulled an old skiff out from under some bushes into the water and told Johnse and Cap to untie the boys. They led the prisoners to the skiff, which Uncle Wall and Charlie Carpenter poled to the other side. Pappy and his men rode across, leading the McCoy horses. In minutes everybody was in West Virginia.

Pappy turned to Uncle Wall. "We can't all go look in on Ellison. Some of us got to guard them boys."

"I'll guard em," Cap volunteered.

"Don't think that's a good idea," Wall said. "You and your Pappy go on over to Ferrell's. Send a messenger over to me soon as you know how he is."

Wall wasn't being fair. Cap was eighteen years old now and had become a lot less of a hothead than he'd been at sixteen and seventeen, yet Wall wasn't going to trust him to guard the McCoys. It was Wall who shouldn't be left alone with the prisoners. By himself, Wall might begin to ponder on the law and who knew what he might do then.

Nevertheless, Cap, with Pappy and Johnse, headed for Ferrell's. As they came over the top of a hill, dark blue and purple clouds blotted out the sun as it set. Pappy reined in his horse.

"A sunset like that means a life is comin to an end," Pappy said.

The omen frightened Cap and Johnse.

When they got to Ferrell's barn, Uncle Elias came down with a lantern.

"It's startin to rain again," Elias said. "August, and I'm shiverin like it's winter."

"He's worse, aint he?" Pappy unsaddled his horse.

"He's feverish. Can't sit up or raise his head."

"Doc Rutherford here yet?"

"Yup. But he says there aint nothin much he can do besides bandage him up and try to cool off the fever by wipin him down with cold water."

They went inside the cabin, where Ellison lay with nothing on him but a light sheet from the waist down. Doc Rutherford, his suit coat tossed aside, shirt sleeves rolled up, was wiping him with a damp cloth where he could, there were so many bandages. Dried blood was on Ellison's lips and in his beard. His eyes were closed and his breathing was shallow and raspy.

"Ellison," Pappy said.

There was no answer.

"Not sure he hears you," Rutherford said.

"What do you think, Doc?" Pappy asked.

"He aint got long." Rutherford shoved his spectacles back up the bridge of his nose. "Nothin I can do. The gunshot went through his back and took out a lung. And he's cut in too many places, lost too much blood."

Cap couldn't accept that answer. "But he's strong. He's a fighter."

"Every fighter comes to his last battle sooner or later, Cap."

"I'll go tell Uncle Wall what's goin on." Cap couldn't bear to stay and watch Ellison die.

Pappy nodded.

Cap went out on the trail in the dark and the rain, taking it slow over the slimy, muddy trails. The rain blew under the floppy brim of his hat, making little rivers that ran under his coat collar and found their way under his shirt and into his underwear. He shivered and ached, glad to be wretched, wishing he could carry all of Uncle Ellison's misery for him.

Cap found Wall under the roof of the schoolhouse porch. "Doc Rutherford thinks his life is leavin him. He's feverish and he's lost a lot of blood."

"When's your Pappy comin over here? I want him to take over so's I can see my brother before it's too late."

"Go ahead. I'll watch over things whilst you're gone."

Wall stared hard at Cap, and Cap returned his gaze. "Don't do nothin to them McCoys without your Pappy and me," Wall warned. "And don't let that crazy Cotton Top do nothin neither." Cap nodded.

Aunt Sally, the boys' mother, suddenly appeared on the schoolhouse porch, clothes dripping and the sunshade of her wet bonnet drooping half over her face. "Wall, you got children yourself. Let me see my boys."

"You can stay on the porch out of the rain if you want," Wall said. "I don't want you to catch your death of pneumony out here. But you can't go inside and start makin trouble."

"Let my boys go," Aunt Sally begged. "If you do, my husband won't come into West Virginia after you, I promise." Tears ran down her face.

"Keep her out here, Cap." Wall rode off to Ferrell's.

Leaving the guards to watch Aunt Sally, Cap went inside, picked up someone's coat and took it along with a lantern out to the porch. He put the coat around her shoulders and hung the lantern by the door. Aunt Sally grunted her thanks.

Back inside, Cap lit another lantern. A small blue flame flickered about the wick, then flared up bright orange, casting light on rows of dusty, cobweb-infested little school desks and on the three McCoys sitting on the floor against a wall, their hands tied behind them. The lantern soon made the damp room smell like burnt carbon and kerosene. To pass the time some way other than just staring at their prisoners, Cap and the others began to share a jug of Johnse's whiskey.

After a while, Charlie said, "Let's sing a little song for these boys."

"Swift to its close ebbs out life's little day," he began.

Not having been exposed to hymn singing like the others had, Cap could only listen.

"Earth's joys grow dim, its glories pass away," Tom Chambers joined in.

"Change and decay in all around I see," Cotton Top howled.

All the men joined together: "O Thou changest not, abide with me! Hold Thou Thy cross before my closing eyes."

As they finished the hymn, young Randall began to whimper and Tolbert's face looked drawn.

Tolbert was afraid! Cap saw it in his face and eyes. The Hatfields couldn't scare Tolbert, but religion could. Cap knelt in front of Tolbert.

"Swift to its close ebbs out life's day." He repeated what he'd just heard.

Tolbert began to sweat.

"Earth's joys grow dim," Cap sang softly staring into Tolbert's averted face.

Like Pappy always said, when folks took up religion, they only replaced worldly fears with fear of God and the Devil. If he was alive and could think, Ellison was thinking about death. Was Ellison afraid?

"You scared of dyin?" he asked Tolbert.

Tolbert kicked out at Cap. "Why would I be? Your Pappy promised Matt Ferguson he'd bring us back to Kentucky. And your Pappy's a man of his word, aint he?"

Cap hunkered down on his haunches. "You knowed what you was doin when you stabbed my uncle. You got to be ready to pay the price."

"He started it. Me and Bad Dan was arguin. Your uncle butted in."

"He didn't hurt you none."

"Leave my boys alone, Cap Hatfield!" Aunt Sally leaned her head through the doorway.

Cap went out on the porch as three figures on horseback appeared out of the rain—Pappy, Uncle Wall, and Johnse. They tied their horses to the rail in back of the schoolhouse before coming around to the porch.

"How is he?" Cap asked.

"He come to a while," Pappy said. "And told me about the whole fight, how it started with just him and Tolbert. Then all three of them McCoy boys jumped him at once. He don't remember no gunshot. Didn't even know he was hit."

"He's better then?" Cap thought he must be better if he was talking so much.

"Might be," Pappy said. "He talked to me for nearly half an hour. Then went back to sleep."

Aunt Sally hurried over when she heard all this. "You're lookin after your folks, Anse. Now let me look after mine. Let me go see my children."

Pappy shook his head. "Can't do that, Sally."

Aunt Sally began to wail. She got down on her knees and threw her arms around Pappy's knees. "Please, for the love of God," she begged, tears streaming down her face.

Cap couldn't stand her tears and begging and went inside.

"Ma's carryin on aint helpin none." Tolbert nodded towards young Randall who sat dejected, his head hanging, tears running down his face.

Cap thought he would have felt the same way if he were Tolbert. During the War, mothers weren't on the battlefields or with prisoners of war, pleading for their sons' lives. The end of life was the soldier's last and greatest opportunity to show his bravery.

"Shut up, woman!" Charlie Carpenter yelled. "We aint gonna have no more of this!"

Aunt Sally kept sobbing and wailing. Suddenly Pappy, his long-legged stoop-shouldered form silhouetted against the light of the porch lantern, waved Sally inside. Cap reckoned he was thinking of how he and Mama would feel if their boys were in the fix Aunt Sally's boys were in.

"Go away!" Sally shouted to the men in the room when she got inside. "Get out of here and leave me with my boys!" Cap grabbed his rifle and headed for the porch, but Chambers and the others stayed behind, which Cap thought was disrespectful of the old woman. Loud arguing broke out between Aunt Sally and Cotton Top.

"Cotton Top! Get out here and leave them folks alone," Pappy yelled.

Cotton Top came out with a sulky face and stomped up and down on the porch. "Don't do this, Cotton Top. Get out here, Cotton Top." He sat down on the porch steps with his head between his hands. "I got a right to settle things with them McCoys. They hurt my Pa."

Cotton Top's real name was Ellison Mounts and he'd always claimed he was Uncle Ellison's out-of-marriage son. His mama had told him, he said, and she ought to know. Cap had once asked Pappy if that was true. "Good chance he's Ellison's woods-colt," Pappy had replied.

About noon Cap saw a man, hunched under a broad-brimmed hat against the rain, riding across the clearing toward the schoolhouse.

"It's Uncle Elias," Cap called out. "He wouldn't be here if Uncle Ellison needed him. He must be better."

Elias tied up his horse and got up on the porch. "He never come to again. Just passed on peacefully." Tears fell on Uncle Elias's already rain-wet cheeks.

Cap felt his own throat tighten and his knees grew weak. He went to stand beside Pappy, put his arm around him and tried to comfort him.

"There's news!" Tolbert called from inside. "I heard a horse comin and they're talkin out on the porch."

Aunt Sally grew quiet.

"He was a big man, my brother." To Cap's surprise, Pappy leaned head-first onto his shoulder. "He'll need a big coffin." His father had never leaned on him, had always been tough as stone. Cap trembled. He'd never thought, never wanted to think, of him any other way.

"What are we gonna do with them boys?" Cap whispered.

"Take em back to Kentucky."

"Take em back to Kentucky!" Cap almost shouted the words. "You said the McCoys'd pay the price if Uncle Ellison died."

"They're gonna take us back to Kentucky," young Randall shouted with joy. "I heard Cap say it."

"'Course them boys is guilty of murder," Pappy said, keeping his voice low.

"Everybody seen the killin," Wall agreed.

"I asked Plyant," Pappy said. "Did you see young Randall stab my brother? Did you see him with your own eyes? He said 'I seen him.' And he said he seen Phamer shoot Ellison, and we all know what Tolbert done. Then Ellison, when he was awake, told me the same thing, except he didn't remember getting shot."

Elias nodded in agreement. "I seen it all, too, just the way Plyant said."

"Then that's it. All three of em's guilty. Agreed?" He turned his gaze to his two brothers.

"Hold on just a minute," Uncle Wall said. "You gave your word you'd return them boys to Kentucky for trial. Somebody oughta ride over there for the Justice of the Peace."

"They're goin back to Kentucky," Pappy said. "But we don't need no Justice of the Peace. We know they're guilty."

Wall looked indignant. "That's no way to think. The law's about makin sure a jury of peers with no involvement in the case agrees and decides on guilt. Takes the personal grudge and hysterical carryin on out of things. It gives the community a settlement of the case they can believe in. We got to get a Kentucky Deacon, Anse, and a jury."

"Let's get these boys movin," Pappy said.

Wall went inside and spoke to Aunt Sally. "You'll have to go now."

"You don't reckon they'll kill us, do you?" young Randall cried out. "I heard em say we was goin to Kentucky."

"Naw, aint nobody gonna hurt you none, boy," Tolbert answered.

Wall took Aunt Sally gently by the elbow.

"I don't want to go nowhere," Sally pleaded. "I want to be near my boys."

"We want to make sure your husband don't come lookin for you," Wall said. "Makin trouble for us. You go on up the hill to your sister's."

Cap, Cotton Top, and Uncle Wall went inside and got the boys to their feet.

"Where you takin us?" Tolbert asked Uncle Wall.

"Seein as my brother promised you'd be returned to Kentucky, that is what we're gonna do."

Young Randall smiled and looked relieved. "It's gonna be all right, Tolbert. Nobody in Kentucky's gonna do nothin to us."

"We aint there yet," Tolbert said.

Outside, the rain had stopped, but the hot, steamy August air soaked every man's clothes. Along with Cap and Pappy, Cotton Top, Johnse, Uncle Elias, Uncle Wall, Charlie Carpenter, and Tom Chambers trudged with their prisoners across the schoolhouse meadow where wet trees and grass sparkled and goldenrods blazed like little suns. They took a trail through woods that were hushed as they always were during summer afternoons when birds and animals rested in the shade.

"I'm sorry it come to this," Tolbert said. "I never meant to hurt Ellison so bad."

Pappy glowered at him. "You meant it, you didn't mean it. Either way Ellison's just as dead."

"Well, I didn't mean it. He was a good man."

They arrived at the Tug near dusk, when the trees cast long shadows across the river. Gnats, mosquitoes, and river bugs hummed their mournful dirges above the water. Low clouds, blood red as the sun in their midst, hung over Kentucky.

"River's down enough to where we don't need the skiff," Pappy said. "We'll wade across the ford."

Wall peered across the river. "You go ahead. I'm goin back to the school-house for my horse and ride to Logan for an affidavit."

"A what?" Cap asked.

"A affidavit sayin we brung our prisoners back alive to Kentucky," Wall said. "We'll all take an oath and sign it." He headed back up the path toward the schoolhouse.

"Are we gonna do right by Uncle Ellison?" Cap turned to Pappy.

"I promised him I would."

They waded into the river, Charlie Carpenter and Cotton Top leading the McCoys by ropes tied to bonds about their wrists. The warm, sticky, muddy water came up to their knees, then their hips, before they got to the Kentucky side.

"We're almost home," Randall said.

After struggling up the slippery river bank, Pappy had them veer to the right and proceed on in the direction of an increasingly awful stench.

"This aint the way to Matt Ferguson's," Tolbert said. "And it aint the way to Pikeville. Where you takin us?" No one answered.

They kept on until they came to a sinkhole, a low wet place in the ground with a spring seeping into the bottom of it. The carcasses of two dogs, mouths open as though in agony and foamy spittle on their lips, lay there. Probably mad dogs their owners were afraid to touch. People often threw dead animals they didn't want to bury into the sinkhole.

In here it was so cold that Cap shivered in his soaking wet blue jeans. Only the trail they'd come in on broke the line of tall trees brooding over the sink hole. Their thick foliage allowed almost no light into the area, causing years' accumulation of fallen leaves to rot in seeping water. Fungus of every kind—from huge dark, shaggy mushrooms to poisonous bright yellow toad-stools—sprouted from fallen trees and dead stumps. A calf's half-eaten rotting carcass lay at the bottom of one tree where two turkey buzzards perched on upper limbs were waiting for everyone to go away so they could resume their meal.

"Not here!" Cap pleaded with Pappy. The sinkhole was a devilpit with its tentacles grasping at Hatfields and McCoys alike.

"Best place I could think of," Pappy muttered. "Aint no one gonna see what we do. Untie them boys."

"You gonna let us go here?" Phamer asked. "It's a place that's good for nothin except gettin away from," he snickered.

Cap, Cotton Top, and Charlie Carpenter untied the McCoys.

"Now tie em up to them trees." Pappy pointed to three pawpaw trees growing from the muck of the sinkhole.

"Tie us up?" Tolbert bellowed.

"Let's get out of here." Phamer lunged out of Charlie Carpenter's grasp and tried to run. Charlie grabbed him around the neck and dragged him kicking and yelling to one of the trees.

"What are we gonna do with em?" Cotton Top asked.

He and Tom Chambers and Charlie Carpenter tied Phamer and Randall to the trees, but needed Cap's help holding Tolbert still enough to tie him.

"I hope I die in a better place than this," Cap whispered to Johnse. Johnse looked at him from drunken eyes. "My wife's sure gonna raise Cain with me when she hears about this."

"She aint gonna know you was here if you keep your trap shut."

"What about our trial?" Tolbert hollered. "What about a Deacon and a jury?"

"We know you're guilty," Pappy said. "Plyant, my brothers Elias and Wall—they all seen you do it. Ellison himself, on his deathbed, told me you knifed him and Phamer and Randall joined in to finish him off. Now we're ready to carry out the sentence."

"You're gonna shoot us, unarmed, tied up?" Tolbert's voice rang out. "What kind of men are you?"

"Ellison wasn't armed when you kilt him," Pappy replied.

"You must of come out of the bowels of the earth through this sink hole, Devil Anse." Tolbert howled like a catamount. "This is where your kind gets borned."

"Help! Pa! Come save us!" young Randall yelled out.

They all stopped and listened for an answer, but none came.

Pappy turned to Cotton Top. "Cotton Top, my brother said you are his first born son and you have the right to put the first bullet into the man that kilt him. Do you want that right?"

Cotton Top stood proud and tall. "I'll shoot em all."

"You're gonna let a idiot do your dirty work," Phamer sneered.

"Every man here has a right to shoot," Pappy said. "Ellison was somebody to all of us—brother, uncle, friend. But Phamer McCoy fired the bullet that finished off your pappy, Cotton Top. He's yours."

"Do you fellers want your eyes covered?" Cotton Top said, parading up and down before the three boys, Tolbert and Phamer struggling against their ropes, young Randall hanging limply from his.

"I want to look the man in the eye that shoots me," Tolbert said.

Randall stared blankly as if he didn't hear or see a thing.

Cotton Top stood back and raised his rifle.

"Wait!" Cap said. "Seems like this is happenin too fast."

Pappy's beard jutted out with determination. "Let's get on with it."

Pappy was so sure of himself, Cap didn't exactly know why he wanted to wait. He knew they had to punish the McCoys and avenge Uncle Ellison. He sighed.

"Let's do what we got to do," Cap said.

"All right, Phamer first," Pappy called out. "Ready, Cotton Top?"

Cotton Top raised his rifle and shot Phamer in the chest. Then Pappy's, Charlie Carpenter's, and Tom Chamber's guns roared at once. But Johnse didn't shoot and neither did Cap. He stared at Phamer's limp and bleeding body hanging from the ropes tied around his chest.

"You're dead." Cotton Top strutted before Phamer's corpse. "You're dead, you dungscab."

To Cap, it looked like Cotton Top wasn't as saddened by his father's death as he was proud of executing his killers.

Still sobbing, young Randall called out for his Pa and Ma.

"Let him go," Johnse said. "Let the boy go."

"No!" Charlie Carpenter said. "We don't want no survivin witnesses to what we're doin here."

Randall turned his tear-stained face towards Charlie. "You'll burn in hell."

Charlie raised his rifle and shot Randall point blank. Cotton Top shot him, too—one, two, three times. Randall's blood and flesh splattered into the pawpaw tree. Cap felt he was going to be sick.

Cotton Top grinned at Pappy. "I done it."

Finally, what Cap had hoped wouldn't happen did. Pappy nodded to him. Tolbert didn't flinch. Cap's throat went dry.

"Do it now, son," Pappy ordered.

From only ten feet away, Cap raised his rifle and pointed it at the center of Tolbert's forehead. Long ago, from the time he'd killed terrapins on Pappy's orders, he'd learned to keep his mind on taking care of his family. He couldn't worry about how much Tolbert wanted to live and how much Aunt Sally would miss him.

"Goodbye, Tolbert," he said and fired.

Tolbert's body slumped to its knees, then slid sideways, hanging by the ropes that bound his chest to the pawpaw tree. He put his hand over the bullet hole in his head as his last gesture in life.

Pappy nodded his approval. Cap stared at the lifeless body, at the blood oozing down its face. He felt light-headed and powerful. Light-headed and sick to his stomach. He wanted to cry and throw up.

"Let's get out of here," Pappy said. He didn't look happy either.

* * *

Cap was soaked through by the time his cabin came into view. This was 1888, the executions had been carried out in 1882, and he was still unsure how legal they had been.

When they'd done what had to be done at the sink hole is when the legal waters had gotten muddy. Pappy had certainly been right about everyone knowing what Tolbert, Phamer, and Randall Junior had done. Guilty was guilty. No jury was needed to decide that. But there was this pesky question of the law and who should pronounce guilt.

If twelve jurors, none from his family and none from Randall McCoy's, had pronounced the boys guilty and sentenced them, there would be no accusation of murder hanging over himself, Pappy, Johnse, Cotton Top, Uncle Wall, Uncle Elias, or anyone else. The hitch in this idea, and it was a heck of a hitch, was that in Kentucky the boys would probably have been set free without a trial, or not found guilty of murder if there was a trial, and even with a guilty verdict almost certainly not executed for what they'd done. No one from the north part of Kentucky had ever been punished for attacks on or murder of an outsider. It just wasn't done. Not in Kentucky.

What did the law have to say about murder in a lawless land?

This close-up image of Cap Hatfield, armed and dangerous, was taken in 1888. – from the West Virginia Archives

In one of the earliest known photographs taken at the most violent period of the feud era, Cap and Nan (Nancy Elizabeth Hatfield) pose solemnly with their children. – from the West Virginia Archives

The Hatfield family. Cap is shown extreme right with his rifle in the second row. Nancy "Nan" Smith Hatfield sits beside him. Anderson "Devil Anse," also with his rifle, and Louvicey are positioned second and third from the left in the second row. — from the West Virginia Archives

Devil Anse Hatfield, the "Boogerman," on his horse, Fred. — from the West Virginia Archives

Closeup: Anderson "Devil Anse" and Louvicey Hatfield.

Johnse Hatfield — from the
West Virginia Archives

Heavily armed, Cap was living at Beech
Fork when this photo was taken.
— from the West Virginia Archives

172

Anderson "Devil Anse" Hatfield
— from the West Virginia Archives

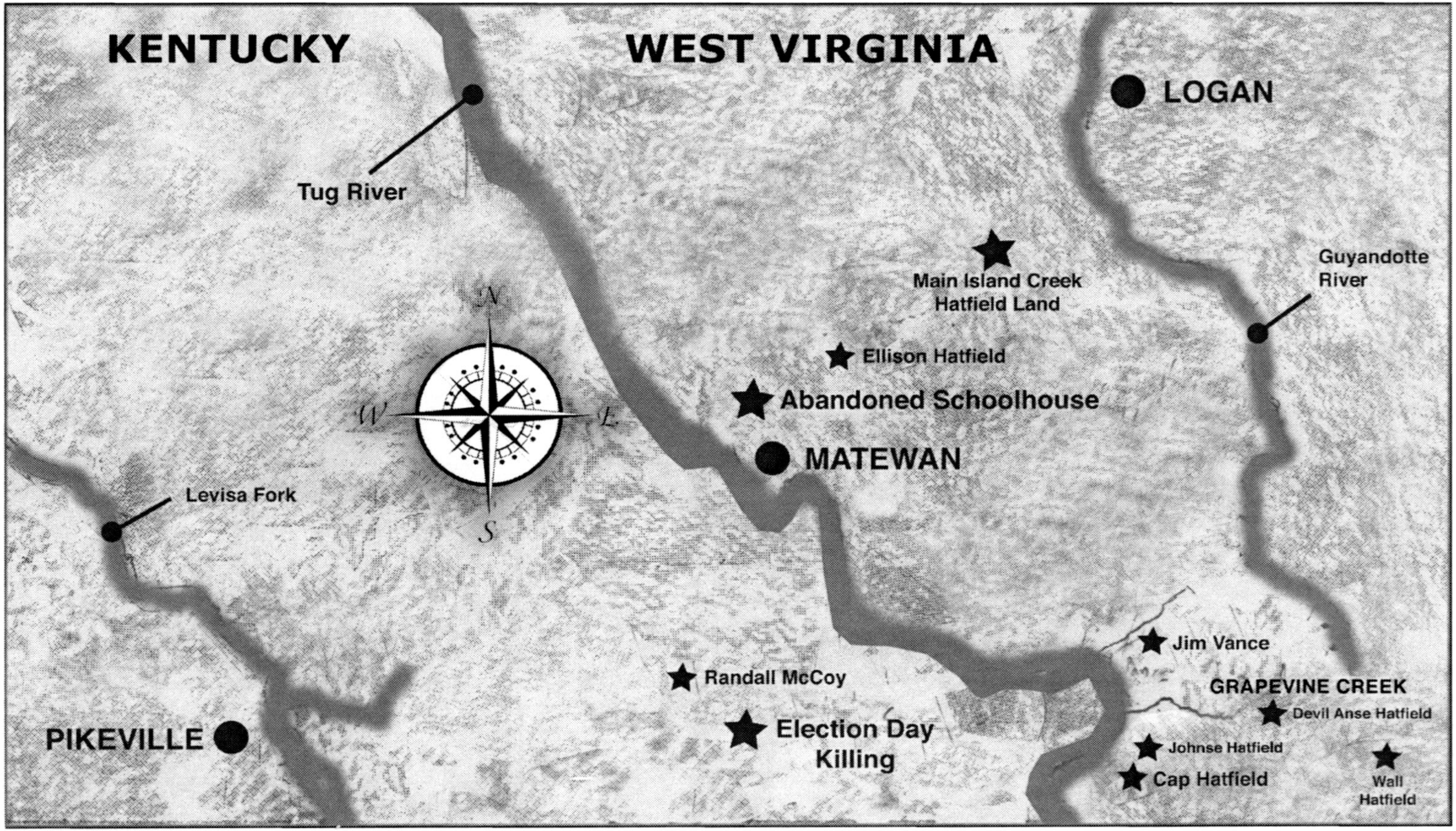

KENTUCKY

WEST VIRGINIA

PIKEVILLE

Levisa Fork

Tug River

LOGAN

Guyandotte River

Randall McCoy

Election Day Killing

MATEWAN

Abandoned Schoolhouse

Ellison Hatfield

Main Island Creek Hatfield Land

Jim Vance

GRAPEVINE CREEK

Johnse Hatfield

Cap Hatfield

Devil Anse Hatfield

Wall Hatfield

Scale: One inch to ten miles.

174

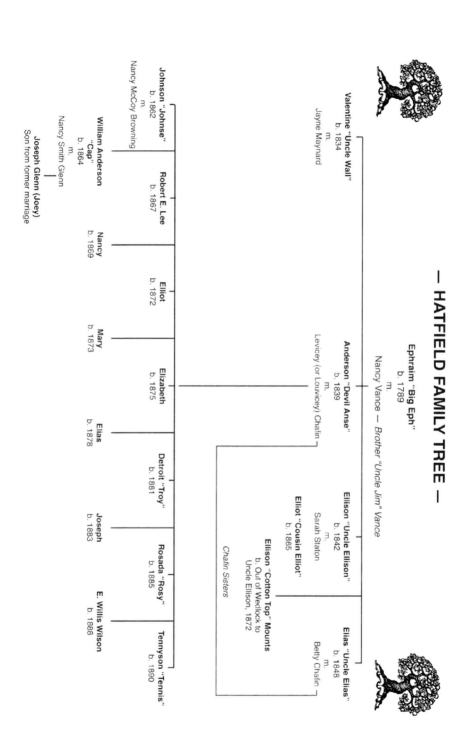

— HATFIELD FAMILY TREE —

Ephraim "Big Eph"
b. 1789
m.
Nancy Vance — *Brother "Uncle Jim" Vance*

Valentine "Uncle Wall"
b. 1834
m.
Jayne Maynard

Anderson "Devil Anse"
b. 1839
m.
Levicey (or Lowicey) Chafin

Ellison "Uncle Ellison"
b. 1842
m.
Sarah Staton

Elias "Uncle Elias"
b. 1848
m.
Betty Chafin

Chafin Sisters

Johnson "Johnse"
b. 1862
m.
Nancy McCoy Browning

Robert E. Lee
b. 1867

Nancy
b. 1869

Elliot
b. 1872

Mary
b. 1873

Elizabeth
b. 1875

Elias
b. 1878

Detroit "Troy"
b. 1881

Joseph
b. 1883

Rosada "Rosy"
b. 1885

E. Willis Wilson
b. 1888

Tennyson "Tennis"
b. 1890

William Anderson "Cap"
b. 1864
m.
Nancy Smith Glenn

Joseph Glenn (Joey)
Son from former marriage

Elliot "Cousin Elliot"
b. 1865

Ellison "Cotton Top" Mounts
b. Out of Wedlock to
Uncle Ellison, 1872

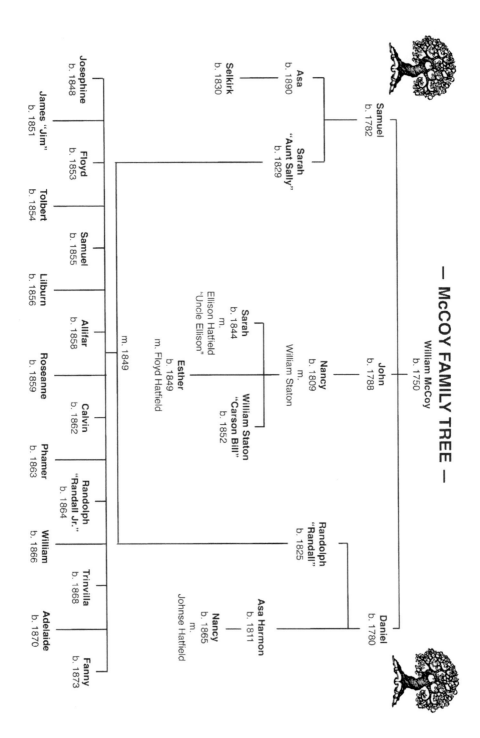

— McCOY FAMILY TREE —

William McCoy
b. 1750

John
b. 1788

Daniel
b. 1780

Samuel
b. 1782

Nancy
b. 1809
m.
William Staton

**Randolph
"Randall"**
b. 1825

Asa Harmon
b. 1811

Asa
b. 1890

**Sarah
"Aunt Sally"**
b. 1829

Sarah
b. 1844
m.
Ellison Hatfield
"Uncle Ellison"

**William Staton
"Carson Bill"**
b. 1852

Nancy
b. 1865
m.
Johnse Hatfield

Selkirk
b. 1830

Esther
b. 1849
m. Floyd Hatfield

m. 1849

Josephine
b. 1848

Floyd
b. 1853

Samuel
b. 1855

Allifar
b. 1858

Calvin
b. 1862

**Randolph
"Randall Jr."**
b. 1864

William
b. 1866

Trinvilla
b. 1868

Asa Harmon
b. 1811

James "Jim"
b. 1851

Tolbert
b. 1854

Lilburn
b. 1856

Roseanne
b. 1859

Phamer
b. 1863

Adelaide
b. 1870

Fanny
b. 1873

176

Chapter 26

Cap sloshed across the clearing surrounding his house. It was a good-looking cabin, every log laid straight, the chinks thoroughly filled in, a huge stone chimney rising up one side. There'd been lots of good, flat chimney stones down by the creek. He felt warm in spite of the cold rain. His brain was on fire, fueled by an idea that had been been waiting to be ignited since John Floyd first put the idea there. He was going to find out what was required to clear himself and the others of all charges they'd murdered the McCoys because he was going to become a lawyer, the sharpest one in the mountains, feared in the courts of both West Virginia and Kentucky, turning the tables on Nighbert and his pals, bringing lawsuits against them for a change. Every permit the Hatfields sought, like the one they needed to build a sawmill on Main Island Creek, would be flawlessly written so that any judge would grant it. Even John Floyd and Governor Wilson would turn to him for help in extraditing the murderous Kentucky posse members to West Virginia and hauling them to federal court. Floyd himself had said so when he'd first suggested that Cap study law.

That is, he'd do all these things if he could persuade Pappy to approve of what he planned to do. Becoming the family's only lawyer should raise him far above any other candidates to succeed Pappy, but he'd never been able to predict, let alone control, Pappy's reaction to any idea of his.

He knocked on the door and called out "It's me." Since New Year's they always latched their door from the inside. So did Pappy.

Nancy, holding a fussy baby Coleman on her shoulder, opened the door. "I was hopin the rain would let up before you come home."

She settled into the rocker and offered her breast to the baby, who stopped fussing and went to work. Already, Coleman had a personality—demanding attention, but content and placid when he got it. Cap reveled in watching his son become a human being.

He began to take off his wet clothes and spread them on the hearthstones in front of the fireplace. "I've made my decision," he said as he pulled on dry blue jeans. "I'm gonna go to law school."

"You'll be doin a wonderful thing." Nancy smiled. He kissed the dimple at the edge of the smile, then pulled up a chair beside Nancy's rocker and gently stroked the baby's back. "'Course I'll have to persuade Pappy first."

Nancy rocked back and forth, back and forth, a little faster each time.

"I have to," Cap said.

"I'll wager if you just did it—went off to school, then come back and passed the bar exam—you'd still be the number one son. Who else could he pick?"

"None as good as me. That's why I got to talk him into it, why I think I can talk him into it."

Chapter 27

Cap paced up and down the floor of Pappy's cabin, carrying four-month-old Coleman, who could now hold his head up and shout baby babble about the curious things he was seeing. Both he and Coleman were sweating where their bodies were pressed together. In his favorite cane-bottom chair, Pappy was using one foot to rock Cap's youngest brother Willis, asleep in a wooden cradle. Contrary to Pappy's boasts that he never sweated from heat or shivered from cold, moisture had formed on his forehead and the underarms of his shirt were wet.

"It aint much more'n a month since the Supreme Court went against Wilson and us, and already Phillips and his men is back on our side of the Tug." Pappy surreptitiously wiped his forehead with his sleeve.

Standing at the open window to catch the breeze, Cap grunted. The Supreme Court had ordered Phillips and his men released from federal prison in Kentucky, ruling they had not violated federal kidnapping laws, but had committed state crimes in West Virginia and must be tried there. Yet the Governor of Kentucky continued to deny their extradition. To top everything off, the danged Supreme Court had decided that Kentucky could keep the kidnapped Hatfield men it was holding in the Pikeville jail and try them for murder. To Cap's way of thinking, neither of these decisions was fair to the Hatfields. The Supreme Court must be in Kentucky hands.

Cap blew on Coleman's neck to dry off the sweat and got a dimpled smile in return. "I heard they got fed up with Phillips over in Kentucky, and he aint a deputy no more. But with rewards out for us, that won't matter none to him."

"Long as we stay out here we're safe," Pappy said. "None of em's gonna come on this side of the mountains or they might end up lyin dead in the brush or locked up in the Logan jail."

"Holin up out here solves some of our troubles." Cap fidgeted with Coleman's shirt. Time to quit stalling and tell Pappy what was on his mind. "But the way things are, we can't make any money without floatin logs down the Tug past Kentucky. We got to come up with somethin that'll make better sense for our future."

"I left one home behind." Pappy spit tobacco into the fireplace. "I aint leavin here."

"Aint no place else I'd want to live," Cap agreed. "I mean there isn't any place else." Nancy had been busy teaching him grammar from a school book ever since he'd made the decision to become a lawyer. John Floyd had strongly advised it.

"How long you and Nancy gonna keep on talkin peculiar? It's gettin tiresome."

"It's how Nighbert and Judge Harvey and John Floyd talk. No reason we can't learn it, too." Cap winced as Coleman's strong little hand twisted his earlobe.

Pappy giggled. "That boy's more'n you can handle, son. You aint a old hand at this baby business like me."

"You're not doin all that much, pushin that cradle with your toes." Cap smirked. "Here, you hold Coleman and I'll rock Willis." He handed the boy to Pappy. Coleman dug his fingers into Pappy's beard and pulled. Both men laughed and Coleman squealed.

"I got somethin to tell you," Cap said, feeling like he was jumping out over a ravine without a grapevine to hold him up. He sat down at the other end of the cradle, put his toe on the rocker and pushed down when Pappy did, countering Pappy's push. "The reason Wilson can go to the Supreme Court is he's a lawyer."

Pappy nuzzled Coleman and jabbered baby talk, as if to show Cap he was close to ignoring him. Cap raised his voice above the jabber.

"We gotta get ourselves into law and business."

"We got a timber business." Pappy had trouble talking with Coleman's little fingers wound into his beard. "What the heck are you talkin about?"

"But we'll be riskin our lives at it. A lawyer doesn't have to go out in the woods, and a sawmill owner doesn't have to go down by the river where a rifleman can pick him off. You don't see John Floyd or Perry Cline out there."

"What kind of wild ideas you got now?" Pappy rolled his eyes.

"Doin what we always done isn't good enough anymore, Pappy."

Nancy and Mama, carrying two buckets of blackberries, came in from the outside with all the children big enough to walk—Nancy Belle, Mary, Elizabeth, Elliot, Troy, Elias, Joe, Cap's stepson Joey, and little Rosie struggling to keep up.

"Blackberry pie." Nancy smiled and put her hand on Cap's shoulder. "Looks like you just sat yourself down and left all the babies to your Pappy, you lazy man."

"No, I didn't. I'm rockin Willis." Cap kept on rocking in opposition to

Pappy, pushing down on his end each time Pappy pushed on the other.

"I can handle these babies myself." Pappy patted Coleman's back while he fought Cap for control of the cradle.

Cap looked up at Nancy and took a deep breath. Their eyes met and she nodded.

"I'm thinkin of goin away for a while, Pappy."

Pappy jammed his foot under a rocker and stopped the cradle.

Mama looked frightened for an instant, then smiled. "You goin out West to look after your brother, son, like you always done? I think about him all the time out there all by his lorn self."

Cap nudged the cradle off Pappy's foot and resumed rocking. "Johnse can look after himself. I'm not goin out West."

"You fixin to take Nancy and Coleman with you?" Mama looked anxious, but Cap was sure she'd be happy when she heard his plans.

"We have good news, Mama Levicy." Nancy smiled to assure her.

Mama went to stand behind her husband and put her hands on his shoulders. "You'd best tell your Pappy what this is all about, son. Spit it out."

"What's he gone and done, Levicy?" Pappy shook his head back and forth.

"I want to go to school." Too excited to control his voice, Cap shouted the words. "Law school."

"What!" Pappy kicked Cap's foot aside and dragged Willis's cradle close to himself. "What kind of nonsense is this?"

"Now, Anse." Mama rubbed Pappy's neck and patted his chest below the thick, wiry beard. "Let's hear Cappie out."

"Look what an education in law did for John Floyd," Cap said. "Got him to the state legislature and now he's Secretary of State."

"Look what the law done to your Uncle Wall. He's in jail! Best law I know of is right over there." Pappy pointed to the gun rack full of Winchesters.

This was more than Cap could bear. "I don't ever want any more killins on my mind. I can't get shed of Allifair McCoy no matter what I do. She's with me when I'm out huntin, she's there when I come home to supper and when I go to bed, she's in the barn and she's in the smoke house. Seems like she came unstuck from her time to be with me all the rest of my life. Her and Uncle Jim. I think of him dyin out there all alone, too." And, in spite of his belief in the justice of the McCoy boys' executions, he often saw Tolbert's taloned eyes tearing at him just before the shot.

Pappy shook his head. "And now you think you oughta be a lawyer."

"I want to go to the University of Tennessee in Knoxville." Cap had to get up and walk his nerves off. "John Floyd told me about a law school there. It's the only law school in this part of the country that'll take you without a college degree first. And nobody knows me in Knoxville, nobody will be huntin for me there."

"I don't want to listen to this," Pappy said.

Cap pressed on. "Floyd thinks I can read and write good enough to do the schoolwork. Then I'll come back and take the West Virginia bar exam. You gotta do that to be a lawyer in this state. When I'm done with that, this family's gonna start winnin in court. I'll be there when there's a debt suit against you, I'll represent any of us that's hauled off to jail, I'll make deals with Nighbert and maybe even Perry Cline. I'll get our men out of the Pikeville jail and put Phillips and his kind in jail. And I'll get us a sawmill permit."

Pappy bounced Coleman on his lap. "Cocka-doodle-do! Listen to your pappy crowin. Thinks he's gonna be a lawyer."

Little Rosie put her hands on Pappy's knees and tried to pull herself into his lap. "Cocka-doodle me," she said. Pappy put Coleman back onto his shoulder and allowed his darling little curly-headed Rosie to climb onto his lap.

Cap stopped pacing and smiled to think how the yellow rag newspaper writers would never have believed the sight in front of him. The most ferocious feuder, the Devil himself, with one baby on his shoulder, a toddler on his lap, and a cradled infant at his feet.

"I bet Cap could take on Nighbert's lawyer and that mean old Judge Harvey." Nancy Belle stepped in front of Pappy, while the other children stood back in wide-eyed silence.

"What do you know? You're just a girl." Elliot often said how tired he was of his older sister's opinions. She had a lot of opinions.

"You could take em on in a fist fight or a gunfight," Pappy said. "But in court!" He put his lips together, snorted like a horse, and was immediately imitated by Rosie.

"The time for fists and guns has come and gone."

"Phillips and his posses got another opinion." Pappy gave Cap a look of disgust.

"If I was a lawyer Phillips might still be in jail. And there's one thing I know for sure. He isn't out in the woods lookin for lawyers."

"It was me that made you what you are," Pappy shouted. "What you are and who you are—a timber man, a family man. I don't want to hear no more about this lawyer foolishness."

Rosie, upset by loud voices, pulled on Pappy's thumb to get his attention.

"I'll tell you somethin, Pappy." In her calico print dress and bare feet, Nancy Belle planted herself in front of Willis's cradle. "The way things are I aint got no chance of knowin a young feller and keepin company. No one with half a ounce of sense wants to come out here and court a girl from a family that's always shootin and fightin. Mary and Elizabeth and me's gonna be spinsters our whole lives if things don't change. I want Cap to be a lawyer."

Pappy's eyes bulged out, but not with anger. He'd been hit where it hurt. "Them posses and bounty hunters aint none of my doin," he sputtered. "I'm sittin out here tryin to mind my own business."

"I know it aint your fault," Nancy Belle answered. "But they're out there shootin at folks and spiritin em off to Kentucky all the same."

"Of course, we both want you girls to marry some day," Mama said. "We'll do our best to see that happens, won't we Anse?"

"That's the truth," Pappy answered.

"Captain Anderson." Mama spoke from behind her husband, her hands still on his shoulders. "I think Cap's learned a lot from books. Him and his books was a big help to you buildin the cabins and the fort and the drawbridge."

Pappy stared out the window. "City fellers aint gonna respect you as a lawyer, son. They respect you and me for bein timber men, for payin our debts, and for standin up for ourselves—fellers they better not mess with. They won't think much of a Hatfield callin hisself a lawyer."

"Right now that's so. But I'd be a fool to keep on bein bullet bait, fightin men that's just as foolish while other folks is grabbin our land and our timber and our money. Nighbert and his pals aren't shootin or hidin. They're sittin in town winnin. When I'm a lawyer, we'll win our share, too. And I'll get us a legal permit for a sawmill so we won't ever have to float timber down the Tug again. We'll make lumber for all of Logan County right here on Main Island Creek."

"I don't know how you got such notions in your head." Pappy began rocking little Willis again. "Sure didn't come from me."

Cap felt like he wasn't even getting close to persuading Pappy.

"'Course it come from you, Anse." Mama laid the sleeping Coleman in the cradle with Willis. "You taught Cappie to take care of hisself and his family, to stand up for hisself and for us."

"I always said he'd learn everything he needed from me. This aint from me."

"You raised Cap smart," Mama said.

"Dang right!" Pappy's nose hooked down. "But it don't look like he's stayin smart."

"I think you learned a lot from your Pappy, didn't you, son?" Mama's steady gaze insisted Cap agree.

"I surely did." Cap played Mama's game.

Pappy twirled his bushy mustache and smiled. Cap couldn't help grinning. He didn't entirely like saying he was smart because of Pappy, but he got a kick out of seeing the old man so pleased with himself.

"You made Cappie so smart," Mama continued, "he's goin to law school. Not like them McCoys. None of them's smart enough to go to law school." Pappy gasped. Nancy Belle giggled. Cap almost cried trying not to laugh. He looked out the window where he wouldn't have to meet anyone's eyes.

Pappy leaned back in his chair and looked out the window, too. "It's a peculiar thing, but I've taken a fancy to them winders. You can see a lot with them things." Cap knew better than to use this opportunity to say he'd told him so and so had Mama.

Pappy took hold of Mama's hand that rested on his shoulder. No one said anything for several minutes. Finally, Pappy cleared his throat.

"You and me's a couple of real smart fellers," he said to Cap. "If we keep workin at it, maybe someday we'll be smart as your Mama."

Everybody relaxed and laughed.

"John Floyd says law school will cost money," Cap said.

"You been talkin to John before you talked to me?"

"Had to. I didn't know where to go or how much it'd cost."

"We can't tell anybody where Cap's going," Nancy said. "We don't want a bounty hunter to find him. Tennessee isn't that far away."

"How will you get to Tennessee, son?" Mama asked. "How far is it?"

"I'll take a pushboat down the Guyandotte to Catlettsburg, catch a steamboat down the Ohio to Paducah, then up the Tennessee River to Knoxville where the University is."

"You been plannin this for a while." Pappy scowled.

"Yup. I know about how much it'll cost me for the boat trips, the school, and a roomin house to stay in. The money Sergeant paid me will just about cover my expenses for two years. I figure I'll be ready to take the bar exam by then, maybe earlier."

Pappy whistled. "Whooee! All your money to go to some school you aint never seen!"

"You're comin back home here, to the mountains, to Pappy and me when you're finished with school, aint you, Cappie?" Mama pleaded. "You and Nancy and the children's gonna live close by?"

"'Course we will. This is our home. You're my Mama. And I'm Pappy's number one son, aint I?" He winked at Pappy.

Chapter 28

Eight three-story brick buildings—he counted them—crowned the hill where Cap stood, staring up at the clock on the highest tower he'd ever seen. Without even considering the rest of Knoxville, the University of Tennessee had more brick buildings than he'd ever seen in his life.

Around the buildings the earth had been treated peculiarly. A few trees and bushes were scattered about, but there were no crops or tree stumps. Only grass grew on what looked as if it could be decent farm land if given a chance. Not until his gaze moved down the hill toward the Tennessee River did he see the earth put to good use. Rows of fruit trees and a well-tended vegetable garden ran along the hill's contours. A gravel road leading down to a swampy area by the river looked to be in good repair and was lined with large, leafy trees. But at the bottom of the hill, he spotted a rusty old cannon, its wheel spokes mostly broken, and the crumbling ramparts of what looked like a small fort overlooking the river and was offended by the sight. Old junk shouldn't be left sitting around this grand school.

Below the hill, the river was wide but shallow, muddy and dotted with small tree-covered islands. On low hills on the other side were more structures that could have been fortifications. With forts on both sides, an army could easily control river travel and shipping. Cap wondered if the forts had been used that way in the War.

He turned to face the clock tower again, then called out to a young man dressed in a suit, shirt and tie. "I'm lookin for the law school."

"South College." The fellow pointed to a building behind the clock tower, all the while scanning Cap from head to foot. What this fellow was gawking at? He was clean and wearing a suit, tie, and hard shoes as John Floyd had advised. They were brand new from Sears Roebuck. All the same, he felt as strange to this place as the young man must have sensed he was.

Cap took a paved path, not a dirt or cinder one, until he came to South College, identified by a metal plaque beside its massive wooden door. He paused to study the building where he would soon become a lawyer. Three stories of windows, each sheltered by a green and tan striped canvas awning, were arranged in rows and columns across the face of the building. Here and there, chunks were strangely missing from the brick wall and from the concrete window ledges, as though an attacker had smashed the building with a heavy hammer.

He took a deep breath, then resolutely pushed open the door to see polished wood floors and richly glowing wall paneling. The floor seemed to have been smooth once, but was now gouged and rough in spots. The long, narrow room he'd entered, or maybe it was a wide hallway, was empty. Pictures of men in dark suits stared down from above, spaced between doors with black lettering on them. The biggest, most prominent picture showed the upper half of a man about thirty-five years old with immaculately cut and combed black hair that John Floyd would have admired. He had a heavy face and jowls and a bushy mustache. His double chin pushed into a stiff white shirt collar. "Dr. Charles Dabney, President" a brass plate under the picture proclaimed. A determined mouth and steady gaze told the world he understood his own strength and importance.

Dabney was so young. Maybe he hadn't been forced to wait for an older man's approval before he could be president, as Cap was waiting for Pappy. Cap pondered the source of Dabney's importance—knowledge of the law, wealth, the respect of other important men? Was Dabney feared? Some day he intended to have a look of confidence and success like that man's.

The lettering on one door said "Justice Thomas I. Freeman, Dean of Law." Pushing it open, he saw a young man sitting behind a desk cluttered with papers.

"How do you do, Mr. Freeman." Cap reached out his hand.

"I'm Pickens, his clerk." The man snickered. "That's the dean's office." He motioned to a closed door.

Cap strode over and reached for the knob.

"Hey! You can't just barge in there." The clerk jumped to his feet. "You need an appointment."

"I got business with him." Cap pushed the door open and went in.

From behind a desk, a white-haired old man looked up from a book to peer over his spectacles at Cap.

"Good morning." Cap reached out his hand. "My name's William Anderson and I'm rarin to get started in your law school." Knowing that the Hatfields, and he in particular, had been called brutal killers in newspapers he wasn't going to use his last name and risk being arrested and extradited to Kentucky.

"I don't recall an appointment with you on my calendar, Mr. Anderson."

"I'll get one the next time I drop by, if that's the way you like to do things."

"It's the way I insist on doing things."

"In the future I'll do that. But now that I'm here, I want to pay my tuition so I can start studyin."

"Are you seeking to enter the school next fall? In 1889? If you are, pick up the application forms from my clerk, fill them out and return them any time in the next six months."

"Heck, no! I want to start now."

"This is September and next week the fall semester begins, Mr. Anderson. All our young men are already enrolled. They applied and were accepted earlier this year. That's what you must do, too."

"I don't have time for all that." This foot dragging was driving Cap crazy. "I got money for tuition right here. I'll pay you and you'll accept me. Right?"

"Not so right. I certainly can't accept you without knowing anything about you. Where are you from?"

"Virginia." He'd keep where he was from to himself. He pulled his leather money pouch from a suit pocket. "Here's ninety-three dollars for the tuition." He counted out the bills and spread them on the desk. "The money's right here. Count it."

"Mr. Anderson, I know nothing about you. I need to know about your schooling up to now, your preparation for studying law."

"I've hardly ever been inside a school, Mr. Freeman." A vision of the empty, dusty schoolhouse where the McCoy boys had been held before they were executed in '82 flashed through his mind. "My Pappy always said he'd teach us everything we needed to know. But I can read and write and do figures. My wife taught me how."

"It's true not all our young men have graduated from college," Freeman said. "President Dabney still permits that when we're presented with a candidate of unusual merit. But all of them have spent many years at school."

"That tells me where their behinds were. But it doesn't tell me much about what's gone into the other end of em."

"I suspect you're right." Freeman laughed, and Cap thought maybe they were going to get along all right after all. He shoved the money closer to the dean.

"You have to realize that law school is hard work. Impossible if you aren't properly prepared. Can you read legal material and understand it?"

"Let me borrow your book for a minute and I'll read it." Cap reached out his hand.

"I happen to be looking at a congressional resolution introduced in 1850 by Senator Henry Clay of Kentucky. Would you like to read this first page and tell me what it means to you?"

"There's nary a body in Kentucky can write better'n I can read."

"You certainly have a lot of confidence in yourself. How old are you?"

"Twenty-four. It's time I got settled down to my law work." He began reading aloud.

"'One—Resolved, that California, with suitable boundaries ought upon her application to be admitted as one of the states of this Union, without the imposition by Congress of any restriction in respects to the exclusion or intro-duction of slavery within these boundaries.

'Two—Resolved, that as slavery does not exist by law, and is not likely to be introduced into any of the territory acquired by the United States from the Republic of Mexico, it is inexpedient for Congress to provide by law either for its introduction into or exclusion from any part of said territory; and that appropriate territorial governments ought to be established by Congress in all of the said territory not assigned as the boundaries of the proposed state of California, without the adoption of any restriction or condition on the subject of slavery.'"

Cap read it over again to himself silently.

"Well, sir, it's like this. This resolution was spoken about by Mr. Clay in 1850, which was before the time of the War, when slavery was still legal in some parts of the United States, and California and these Mexican territories was wantin to join this country. Mr. Clay said, and rightly so, that the United States government should mind its own business and not try to force its will on California and the territories about slavery."

"Well said, Mr. Anderson! And you never attended school? Amazing. I take it that you don't care much for the federal government meddling with states' rights?"

"No, I don't. Laws made by fellers that don't know a thing about the people and the countryside they're makin the laws for are just plain no-account."

"You realize that Mr. Clay was leaving the door open for California to adopt slavery? Do you believe one man should ever own another?"

"My Pappy saw slaves when he was in the War. He said no man should have to live that way."

"Then how can we justify states' rights in the case of slavery?"

"We don't have to justify anything now that slavery's illegal everywhere in this country." Danged if he knew how to resolve this dilemma.

"Would you obey a federal law if you felt it conflicted with your local interests?"

"Yes. I go by the law. 'Course, it's up to the local folks to figure out how to deal with it."

"What do you mean?"

"Well, take my Pappy's timberin business. Some fellers back East workin for the Singer Machine Company took a hankerin after Pappy's land and decided the way to get it was to fine him so much money for cuttin timber on their property that Pappy'd have to deed over his land to pay the fine. They paid a varmint by name of Clawson a lot of money to say he'd seen us cuttin Singer's timber, and then they took Pappy to court.

"Now everybody in town knew what was goin on, that Pappy pretty much stuck to loggin his own land, and if on occasion he was mistaken a little bit about where the property boundaries were and got a few trees that belonged to somebody else, he'd pay for the trees if they asked him to. People in town don't like the Singer Company or Cole and Crane Timber or any of those outsiders comin into the neighborhood. So when Pappy talked to folks about what was goin on, they understood and were pretty much on his side."

"But did your father obey the law? Did he answer the summons to appear in court as directed or did he get people behind him and mutiny?"

"He went to court and lost. The jury said he'd cut trees on Singer land and owed em money."

"What did you mean, then, by saying it's up to local folks to learn to use the law properly? I was afraid you were talking about some kind of rebellion."

"The folks back home knew how to handle this. When it came time for the jury to make a decision, they agreed with the prosecutor that Pappy had strayed onto Singer land and owed them money for fifteen, maybe twenty trees. But Singer hadn't come to Pappy in a peaceful way and hadn't asked him to settle. Instead they forced him to pay for a lawyer and take time away from his business. So the jury told Pappy he had to pay exactly one penny in damages. And he did."

"I think I see." Freeman grinned. "You're saying a community cannot be forced to accept legal decisions that don't meet with their idea of fairness. Nor can laws be effectively forced upon them that are an affront to their way of life, which was Mr. Clay's position also. The logical extension of this argument is that we don't need the federal government telling us what we can and can't do in Tennessee and you don't need it in Virginia. Am I right?"

"You bet your britches." Cap answered with a wholehearted genuineness he hoped pleased the dean. They were getting along pretty well now.

Freeman looked over his glasses at Cap. "Are you a man of good moral character? No criminal record? That would automatically bar you from law school, of course."

"My character's as good as any man's."

"Could you get me a letter of reference?"

"Not before school starts next week." John Floyd had thought of writing him one, but Floyd was Secretary of State of West Virginia and Cap wasn't going to own up to being from the state of the Hatfield and McCoy feuds, which had been written about in newspapers all around the country.

"President Dabney is simply not accepting any more wayward farm boys whose fathers want to straighten them out. Unfortunately, that's how this university was used before the War."

Cap scowled. "My Pappy never called me a wayward boy."

"Anderson, I'm willing to give you a chance, however slim. Your case is so unusual I'll need to consult with President Dabney. He's setting high standards for this university and is reluctant to admit students to the law school who have not finished college, let alone not been to school at all."

"But you're the boss here." Every time he thought he had Freeman in his pocket, the deal started slipping away from him.

"I'm a dean, not a dictator. President Dabney, the faculty, and I must all become convinced that there would be merit in teaching law to a young man with limited schooling, however burning his desire to study with us. Understand?"

"I understand you're not gonna let me in your school today."

"That's right. But come back tomorrow at two o'clock. We'll see where we are then."

Cap was beginning to sweat. Not to get into this school meant he and his family would have to go on timbering and dodging bullets at the same time. He leaned forward and clenched his fist, then decided he'd better not pound on Freeman's desk. Freeman had the upper hand here.

"I want into this school real bad," Cap said. "I want to be like you and that fellow Dabney out there with his picture on the wall. I want to hold my own with the law against fellows out to get the best of me. I want educated folks to show me respect. And I don't want anybody pullin the wool over my eyes, tellin me a piece of paper means one thing when it really says another."

"You certainly have a strong desire to study law. You might even have the ability. Come back tomorrow. I'll have my faculty, perhaps even President Dabney, here so you can argue your case."

"Will you tell that fellow out there that I have an appointment?"

"Two o'clock."

Outside on the sidewalk, Cap wondered what to do with himself. He didn't want to go sit in his little room in the boarding house the rest of the afternoon and worry about whether he'd be admitted. Walking up and down the streets, he came across what he needed—a tavern.

Two young men dressed in suits and ties sat at the bar, drinking. Cap sat down on a barstool beside one of them.

"Got a drop of whiskey for a thirsty man?"

"Jack Daniels or Wild Turkey?" the bartender asked.

Cap had never heard of either one. "I'll try em both."

The two young men watched him gulp down the two whiskeys.

"It's a pleasure to see a man who likes his liquor the way you do," said the taller of the two who had a blond mustache something like Johnse's.

Cap wondered what was worth noticing about the way he drank.

"Why didn't I think of that?" said the second one, who was shorter and more muscular. "If you can't make up your mind what bourbon to drink, drink em all."

"Don't favor neither very much. Hardly got any taste to it."

"Know anything better?" the taller one said.

"Sure do. Say, who are you boys? My name's Anderson, Will Anderson."

"Carl Browning here," the tall one answered. "And this ugly fellow is Charlie Wheeler. We're upperclassmen, juniors. How about you? Are you University?"

"I'm headed for law school. What's this about upperclassmen and juniors?"

"You don't believe we're juniors?" Carl looked surprised.

"Don't know anything about juniors."

"Why, where did you do your undergraduate studies, man? I thought all colleges were the same—freshman, sophomore, junior, senior."

It took a couple of more Jack Daniels and Wild Turkeys all around, Carl and Charlie now imitating Cap's two-fisted drinking style, before the boys understood Cap had never gone to school and knew nothing about college life. They wanted to know how the heck he'd ever gotten into law school, an issue that Cap managed to dodge. They told him about the four undergraduate years, the campus fraternities, and the courses they'd studied. They complained that Dabney was making school harder for everybody by stressing classics, literature, logic, mathematics, and science.

"But I'm glad to be rid of uniforms and six AM reveille with breakfast and prayers at quarter till seven," Charlie said.

Carl grinned and elbowed Charlie in his meaty ribs. "Your old man liked it better the old way. He thinks you need straightening out."

Cap floated back to the boarding house on a cloud of whiskey. He entered without attracting anyone's attention and climbed unsteadily up bare wooden stairs. Too late for supper, he'd have to go hungry.

He opened the door to his little room furnished with a narrow bed, a desk, a chair, a cabinet holding a wash basin, and a hanging gaslight. Yesterday evening he'd spent a long time investigating that wonder, following the gas pipe through the floorboard, asking his landlady Mrs. Chapman where the pipe went, where the gas came from. She hadn't known.

After removing his revolver and shoulder holster, he put his pocket watch on the desk, threw his clothes over the chair, and lay down on the bed. Good thing he'd had all that whiskey. Before last night he'd never slept in a room alone and the emptiness got on his nerves so bad he'd tossed and turned all night.

Chapter 29

Next morning, Cap took a bath in the boarders' bathtub, which wasn't a tin laundry tub, but a large white basin with black feet. You could sit back in it and get hot or cold water just by turning a handle. As he soaked, he reflected on the Henry Clay resolution. He liked the sound of the words and turned them over and over in his head.

He shaved his face close, watching himself in the mirror over the bathroom sink. He didn't have a mustache anymore, so no need to trim that. Mustaches were for dandies like Johnse. Or like Johnse used to be. He combed his stubborn, straight black hair back from his face, hoping it would stay there today and not fall across his forehead.

At the noontime dinner, Mrs. Chapman introduced him to the other boarders—two university boys about twenty years old who were studying mechanical engineering and a pale, thirtyish, unhealthy looking man who worked downtown at the tobacconist's. Cap told everyone to call him Will.

Except for the boarders, there was no other man in the house—Mrs. Chapman was a widow. She'd spent her morning preparing fried chicken, mashed potatoes, green beans with salt pork, corn bread, and apple pie, and Cap knew right away he was going to enjoy eating at her table. She'd done all the cooking herself, her only help being a young girl who came after school to tidy up and do the dishes and laundry. For an extra fifty cents a week, the girl would do a boarder's laundry, too.

The students occupied themselves by discussing a piece of engineering equipment at school, while Cap made a deal with Ambrose the tobacconist for some Johnny Reb. Mrs. Chapman, whose conversation centered on the food, served the meal herself and ate with them. Cap missed the company of his family at home. But no matter, he'd soon be too busy to worry about the life he'd left behind.

After eating, he headed for the University, allowing himself more than enough time to arrive at Dean Freeman's meeting. The day was sunny, the air cool and brisk. Tall shady trees lined streets paved with brick or stone, giving Knoxville the orderly appearance of a place arranged and controlled by unseen hands.

It shouldn't be hard to convince Freeman and the rest of the faculty to admit him. He'd learned at the feet of a master how to deal with a gathering of both friends and opponents and come away with no enemies, only allies.

Even when they seemed to have contradictory aims, John Floyd always found something to suit each side in a controversy, and he would, too.

This time he made sure to tell the clerk he had an appointment before entering the dean's office.

Inside, two men looking very serious stood talking to Freeman. Cap drew a deep breath.

"Gentlemen, our candidate, Mr. William Anderson." Freeman shook Cap's hand energetically. "Mr. Anderson, this is Mr. Charles Turner, Professor of Law. And Professor Beese, also a member of our faculty."

Cap shook hands with each in turn. Turner was as tall as Cap. His skin hung loosely from high cheek bones to a wide mouth and a long jaw, his expression shifting from scorn to amusement and back. Beese was short and slight with thin black hair. His teeth protruded badly over his lower lip and his spectacles were held on by a black velvet ribbon tied at the back of his head. He gave Cap a friendly smile.

Turner stuck his thumbs into his vest pockets and leaned back on his heels. "Dean Freeman may have called you a candidate, but as far as I'm concerned we can't go around admitting anybody just because he *wants* to get into this school." He spoke with an air of snickering superiority that riled Cap instantly. Turner squinted at him. "We have rules about when to apply, and we insist on proper references. We don't absolutely require an applicant to have finished college, but he must have had enough schooling to cope with our curriculum. I've heard you have little or no schooling."

"Professor Turner!" Beese said. "Rules are made to show the path, not block the road. If the rules don't do that, then I say throw them out."

"Horrors!" Turner threw up his hands in mock shock. "Heresy! Mocking President Dabney's rules."

"I'm more concerned about Anderson's ability to complete the courses of study than I am about rules," Freeman said.

"How's he going to complete courses if he's never been to school?" Turner snapped.

Cap quelled his temper and went to work on Turner with John Floyd in mind. "My wish was to study in a school as fine as those you have in Knoxville, but I couldn't because I had to work in my family's timber business. However, at night and in winter time I did my best to read many of the books your students use in their classes. Religion, for example, taught in the sophomore year. I've read the Bible, and I can recite a great deal of it from memory."

He'd read much of it several times and discussed its stories with Nancy because it was one of the few books besides the McGuffey's Readers and Ray's Arithmetic she'd owned before they were married.

Dean Freeman smiled and nodded. "Show them, Anderson. Give us a verse appropriate for the day."

Cap thought a minute before he began. He wanted a cheerful quote, no dire threats of hellfire and brimstone. "'He causeth the grass to grow for the cattle, and the herb for the service of man: that he may bring forth food out of the earth and wine that maketh glad the heart of man.' God wants us to enjoy the fruits of our labor."

"Hear that, Turner?" Beese said. "God wants us to enjoy our time on earth. Why don't you dispose yourself to relax and enjoy life a little?"

Cap had seen men like these before, each looking to get himself a piece of ground a little higher than the other's.

"What else have you studied?" Turner asked.

"Charles Dickens, who your boys read in their sophomore year, the Americans Poe and Hawthorne and Washington Irving, who are studied in the junior year. I'm good enough at mathematics to design a drawbridge and a mill." He told them how he'd figured out how to dig for a dam that would accommodate a twenty-foot mill wheel and how the wheel should be built and installed. He told them nothing about his biggest achievement, designing and building the new fort.

Beese looked at Freeman. "He knows what our undergraduate curriculum is and appears to have undertaken to duplicate it on his own."

Cap felt he was inching closer to closing the deal, but still needed to work on Turner. "And history and biographies. I've read many biographies, and they are my favorite."

"Whose?" Beese asked. "Whose did you particularly like and why?"

"Daniel Webster, for one. A great lawyer and a man who followed talkin."

"Followed talking?" Beese asked.

"Yes, it was his profession. He could recite from many books when he was but a boy. As a grown man, he spoke at the U.S. Congress and before the Supreme Court of our land. He understood that the governments of the states have a solemn duty to stand between their citizens and the terrible power of the federal government. Webster was Mr. Clay's friend and ally in Congress."

Freeman winked at Beese. "He knew I'd like that."

Cap understood the pleasure John Floyd took from his political successes.

"I suppose you can quote from Mr. Webster, too?" Turner screwed up his face as though in thought, rather than in a sneer.

Cap hoped his most stubborn adversary in the room was beginning to soften. This was the perfect opportunity to show off his ability to recall whole pieces of writing. "Mr. Webster once said this of Alexander Hamilton. 'He smote the rock of the national resources and abundant streams of revenue gushed forth. He touched the dead corpse of public credit, and it sprung upon its feet.' Webster always found the most fittin of words."

"What did I tell you?" Freeman said. "Yesterday he read from a congressional resolution of Clay's couched in rather legalistic terms and analyzed it instantly and cogently."

Cap recited the portion of the resolution he'd read in Freeman's office.

"Word for word!" Freeman said. "What a memory!"

"Bravo, Anderson," Beese said.

"I believe you have the capability to learn anything you want." Freeman beamed on Cap. "Amazing!" The dean looked as proud of him as Pappy sometimes did.

"It's not only a matter of soaking up what he's read," Turner said. "Can he write a paper, take an examination?"

Cap was determined to hold his temper and deal with this obstacle lying between him and law school.

"I can write," he said.

"But have you ever written a paper?" Freeman peered over his eyeglasses. "An exposition on a topic complete with a thesis, the evidence to support that thesis, and a body of conclusions correctly deduced from that evidence?"

"Careful, son." Turner made a mock scowl. "You're talking to the Honorable Thomas Freeman, Justice Emeritus of the Supreme Court of Tennessee. Watch your words."

Cap didn't give Turner the satisfaction of reacting to this jab. "I've never written a paper, but I've read many. I know I can write one if I apply myself to the job."

"This is hopeless," Turner said. "He'll be eaten alive when it's time to turn in a paper or take an examination."

"We have only eleven new students enrolled in law this fall," Freeman said. "It wouldn't hurt to try him. If he doesn't work out, we'll be back to eleven, that's all."

"I'll help him," Beese volunteered. "I won't write his papers or take his examinations, but I'll coach him on how to write and what to expect."

"You're really caught up in this, aren't you, Beese?" Turner said. "The eternal optimist. The sophomoric enthusiast."

"How you do keep me on my toes, Profeessor Turner." Beese smiled. "I wouldn't be nearly as sharp as I am if I didn't have you to joust with every day."

"Well, what do you say, Turner?" Freeman asked.

Turner pursed his lips into a pout. "What's Dabney have to say? Does he know about Anderson?"

"Certainly! I spoke with him." Freeman was indignant. "If we conclude Anderson should be admitted, we have his permission."

"Then go ahead, if that's what you're determined to do. Anderson's admission can't do more than destroy our entire system of rules and order, and drive Dabney into an apoplectic rage. Of course, my assent comes with the proviso that he works with Beese, as proposed."

"Well, do you still have that money, young man?" Freeman asked. "I think we're ready to accept it now."

Cap whipped out his leather money pouch. "I've never paid for anything I wanted so much." He laid out his money and counted out ninety-three dollars.

"Hand it to Professor Turner," Freeman said. "He takes care of financial matters around here. Congratulations, Anderson." He pumped Cap's hand.

"You understand," Turner growled. "If you fail, you'll get none of your money back."

"I won't fail."

"Let me tell you where my office is," Beese said. "Come around tomorrow at nine. I'll tell you what books you'll need and where to get them. Maybe we'll even get started on expository writing."

Cap wiped the sweat off his palms inside his pants pockets before shaking hands with Beese and thanking him. Once outside, he turned to look again at the front of the ivy-covered brick building. It was a fine-looking building.

Chapter 30

Humming and whistling as he put on his tie and combed his hair, Cap winked at his reflection. What a good-looking face, what intelligent eyes, what manly vigor! He sniffed the heady aroma of soap on his freshly washed body. His tie was yellow with brown diagonal stripes that matched the color of his new brown suit. His snowy white shirt collar was high and starched stiff, an uncomfortable thing, but every bit as impressive as Nighbert's or Dabney's.

Strapping on his leather shoulder holster, he cinched it tight. He took his shiny Colt revolver from where it lay on the bed and gently slipped it into the holster, then put on his suit coat. John Floyd had advised him to keep his revolver and rifle out of sight in Knoxville. The rifle stood in a corner in a cardboard carton.

He'd start his first day at school with Professor Beese. Back home Pappy would never have thought the small man wearing overlarge spectacles tied with a black velvet ribbon to be a worthy friend or ally. But here in Tennessee, neither he nor anyone else had to worry about what Pappy thought. The idea made him feel free and unfettered, but at the same time kind of uneasy.

He thump-clomped down the wooden steps to the breakfast table. The sight and smell of griddle cakes, sausages, and coffee made up in part for the fact he'd once more had trouble sleeping without Nancy in his bed, a bed with lumps and springs that poked him, unlike the soft feathers in theirs at home.

He joined Mrs. Chapman and the other three boarders, downing griddle cakes drenched in maple syrup without saying much. His mind was back home. Some day he'd show Pappy he could win battles using just his wit and the law. Nothing aroused Pappy's admiration more than a battle cleverly fought and won. He pictured himself laying waste to Nighbert's cowering lawyers in front of Pappy and an amazed Judge Harvey.

"I've laid out your first term's course of study." Beese smiled warmly from behind his desk. "History of Law in England and America, American Constitutional Law, Contract Law, and the Law of Torts. Does that sound adventurous enough for you?"

Cap fidgeted uncomfortably in his seat. He was in trouble already. He had no idea what torts were. "Contract Law, that's for me. When those business fellers come to us with their 'Sign this contract—we'll explain what it means later'—I want to be ready for em."

"Have you had much occasion for signing contracts?"

"The way Pappy sells timber, you see, is he enters into a contract binding over a certain number of logs in return for credit at a store for supplies for his crew. He backs up his credit by putting up land in trust. If he doesn't deliver the amount of logs needed to cover the supplies, he loses some land."

"More sophisticated than I would expect out in the backwoods."

Beese might be thinking of him and Pappy as stupid hillbillies just as Judge Harvey did. That would all change once he was a lawyer.

"Trouble is, we used to make a talkin deal in good faith and that was it, but nowadays, the court holds everyone to the exact letter of a contract on a piece of paper. My Pappy once signed a contract that didn't name a price markup above the cost of the supplies he bought, even though there'd been an agreement on ten per cent in the talkin stage. So the judge ruled that whatever the store owner wanted to charge was what Pappy owed."

"Knowledge of contract law will certainly help, as will the course in torts."

That word again. "I don't know what a tort is," Cap finally muttered.

"The law of torts governs compensation for personal injury and damage to property, income, or reputation."

"They got laws about damage to personal reputation?" If this were true, he could prosecute most of the McCoys under tort law.

"Why didn't you tell me right away you didn't know what a tort is? I want you to ask questions when you don't know something. There's no shame in that. I don't like passiveness in my students—it keeps me from knowing what I need to teach. Sitting there hiding your little secrets will only make a poor student of you and a poor teacher of me."

"I'm ashamed of what I don't know." Cap could scarcely believe he'd said this. Pappy always said not to let anybody know your weaknesses and get an advantage over you.

"A wise man knows that it's no shame to live and learn. A fool lets his pride keep him from knowledge."

Cap sat back and gripped the arms of his chair. "I don't like bein called a fool."

"I didn't call you a fool. I was telling you how not to behave like one."

Cap wasn't sure he liked that answer any better.

Beese was no longer smiling and relaxed either. "I think you're a man from a culture very different from anyone here at the school—students or faculty. You must be very strongly motivated to come to a place so far from your home in so many ways."

Cap was glad Beese didn't know how different his life had been. But he resented needing to hide his past, as though it somehow made him less of a man than the others here.

"Something has begun to concern me," Beese said.

Cap's heart sank. He didn't want any bad news.

"It's your eye. I noticed your left eye turns out. Doesn't it make reading difficult for you?"

"I read with my good eye." Cap felt a little nervous, remembering that the handbills offering a reward for his capture mentioned the walleye he'd gotten from a stray bullet while fighting Phillips and his gang at Grapevine Creek.

"Good. Now let's get started." Beese drew Cap a little map showing him where his classes would be and where the bookstore was. He gave Cap a list of the books he needed to buy. "Now I need to explain the classroom process to you so as to prevent you from suffering confusion and embarrassment. We're going to go through the motions as though we were in an actual class-room." Beese picked up some papers, stood before Cap, and explained that he would lecture; Cap would be allowed to ask questions at some points and would be questioned at others.

Cap nodded as he stood up and began pacing around the room, looking out the window, and reading the titles of the worn leather-bound books on Beese's shelves.

"No, no, Anderson. You must sit while I lecture."

"Like we're in a courtroom?"

"Same deportment. There will be eleven other students in your classes. If all of you tromped about, you'd set up a clatter, you'd distract me, and no one could concentrate on my message."

Cap sighed and sat down. When he was excited, he wanted to be on the move.

"Today's lecture is on the first amendment of the Constitution. You'll need to take accurate notes." Beese brought out a pad of paper, a pen, and an inkwell and put them on the desk in front of Cap. "Write down the most im-portant points I make. It will help if you develop a sort of shorthand of your own."

"How will I know what's most important?"

Beese sighed and scratched the top of his head. "You probably won't at first, but you'll learn in time." He took a deep breath. "I didn't realize until now how difficult this would be."

Beese didn't need to worry. John Floyd had told Cap he was confident he could learn law. And John, being a lawyer himself and knowing Cap just about all his life, was in a position to know what he was talking about.

After the mock session, Cap strolled around the University, locating the buildings Beese had drawn on the map. From in front of West College, he looked down the hill and, spotting the old cannon and fortifications, decided to explore. When he got to the crumbling stone and mortar structure, he saw it was a small fort with a rotting plank roof and gun ports overlooking the river. Gouges in the walls were similar to those in the buildings at the top of the hill. Yankee cannons must have blasted the fort and the University.

Inside, he found a dirt-encrusted skillet and a few rusty tools. Crumbling yellow newspapers proclaiming Confederate Army successes were still posted on the walls. This was an exciting discovery, very likely the site of actual battles in the War Between the States.

Outside he found a dilapidated wagon, meant to be pulled by horses. Maybe an ammunition wagon. He ran his hand over the rusty cannon barrel, remembering the roar Pappy said cannons made. Looking out over the river, he imagined he was commander of the fort and the enemy was approaching.

He shook his head, annoyed with himself. He needed to replace his dreams of being a great soldier with dreams of becoming a great lawyer.

Hearing the crunch of approaching footsteps, Cap whirled to see who was there. The bearing of the stout man in the black suit, the cut of his hair and mustache, were those of the president's portrait at school.

"Dr. Dabney here." The man reached out to shake hands with Cap. "Are you one of my students?"

"Yes." Cap stood tall to get the most advantage he could out of the two inches he had over Dabney. "I'm William Anderson, here to study in your law school."

"Ah, the young man with the keen mind but no schooling?"

"I had no chance to go to school. My Pappy never sent me."

Dabney shook his head. "A serious handicap. You must strive to overcome your background." He waved his hand expansively in the direction of the fort and cannon. "Just as this University must surmount its past. Look at this place—it was used to train Confederate soldiers. During the War, first the

Confederacy, then the Union, used it as a fortress. When I came here three years ago, the students were still required to dress as soldiers, drill as soldiers, and were disciplined by a military court."

"Looks like the school was hit by cannon fire," Cap said.

"Oh, yes! A great deal of damage was done to the exterior. And the interior floors were gouged out when Union soldiers occupying this site pulled their cannons inside. The scoundrels! I've petitioned the state legislature for money for repairs. I'll not have any more reminders that encourage clinging to the past. In order for this to be a modern university, we'll have to get rid of these fortifications, too, just as we've ended military dress and regimen."

"The War's over now." Cap slapped his hand on the cannon barrel, making it ring. "It's time for the old soldiers to change their way of thinkin."

"You understand, I see. You know, my father was chaplain to Stonewall Jackson during the War. I grew up hearing old Army stories."

Cap felt a great kinship to Dabney. "My Pappy was a Confederate captain. He still wears his captain's pin all the time. When my Mama wants his attention, she calls him Captain."

Dabney laughed. "Our fathers—will they ever free themselves from the War?"

Cap ran his fingers over the cannon barrel. "Pappy used to tell me how the cannons would roar."

Dabney's gaze wandered down the hill. "My father spoke of the courage of his men when the enemy charged them on a hill much like this."

"Pappy said he was never scared. He always told us to get fear on your side, use it against your enemies."

Dabney paused. "The problem is that once you use fear you become a person who uses fear, once you use a gun you become a person who uses a gun. The men who served us well in the War acquired identities as soldiers, identitites not easily relinquished."

"It's hard for Pappy. Identity is like a suit of clothes. Before he gives up the old one, he needs to find a new one that fits."

"It's up to our generation to change things." Dabney began walking up the hill, Cap accompanying him. At the top they shook hands and parted.

Cap hustled off to the book store. On the shelves he found the four textbooks he needed. Next he picked out notebooks, pens, a bottle of ink, and a satchel to carry everything. He fingered the beautiful clothbound books with their brilliant lettering in red or gold or blue. Beese's worn books must once have looked like these.

"If you want to keep them nice, you ought to get book covers," the young woman clerk said.

Cap bought covers and stood at the counter putting on the stiff paper jackets. These books must always be as perfect as they were today.

"I'm glad to see you treasure your books," she said. "Many of the students are very careless."

He realized she was trying to prod words from him, looking him up and down, sizing him up in a way that reminded him of Nancy when he'd first met her. But this girl must feel like a stone statue in a man's arms. From her neck to just below her waist her body was so tightly bound underneath a long-sleeved, high-button dress that Cap couldn't see any wiggle or jiggle like he was used to in the women back home. And her hair was rolled into a tight wheel on top of her head, not like Nancy's that fell in loose black waves.

Then he smelled her sachet. Being without Nancy for a long time was going to be hard.

Chapter 31

The next day, Cap left for school with his legal history textbook, notebook, pen, and bottle of ink packed in his new satchel. Children carrying writing tablets and readers shared the sidewalk, but not his mood. He would change that.

"Be happy, little puppies! Wag your tails, prance your feet, and be happy. We're goin to school!" The children, startled at first, began to laugh and smile, following Cap in a zany zigzag back and forth across the sidewalk, in and out between the other pedestrians, just as his younger brothers and sisters had often followed him in and out among the trees near the cabin. But his brothers and sisters had never had a chance to go to school.

Waving goodbye to his young friends, he entered Morris Hall and found his classroom. Dark wood like that he'd seen in Dean Freeman's building paneled the classroom walls. Four rows of wooden desks filled most of the room, each with its own bench. In front of a slate board and behind a desk on a raised platform, sat Freeman, head down in a book, showing the part in the middle of his white hair. He looked up when Cap came in, nodded briefly, and went back to his reading.

Cap remembered Beese had told him Freeman was a perfectionist and laughed to himself. Freeman didn't worry him. No college professor could demand more of him than Pappy.

He took a seat in the back. Pappy had taught him never to let any man get behind you where you couldn't see what he was up to.

Other young men were sauntering in. Soon a dozen seats were filled. Cap took his notebook, pen, and ink bottle from his satchel and opened the notebook to the first page.

Dean Freeman stood up, introduced himself, and began calling out names. By the time he read "William Anderson," Cap knew to answer "Present."

"Legal history is an essential part of any lawyer's education," Freeman began. "Unless a lawyer understands the development of the corpus of law in England and in our own country over time, he can make little sense of modern law as it's now written and interpreted."

Cap couldn't possibly write down all of Freeman's words. "Is this important enough for me to write in my notebook?" he asked. Everyone turned to gape at him. A few smirked and laughed. Cap clenched his jaws. If they knew what was good for them, these boys had better stop laughing at him.

"If my words weren't important," Freeman replied after a pause, "I wouldn't bother to say them. The study of history, in conjunction with preparation for the law, is in consonance with Dr. Dabney's designs for this university. He is very insistent that graduates of our professional schools understand the foundation of their discipline, as well as its place in modern society. However, you will not be tested on my philosophies, advice, and generalities, but only on the facts and theory of the law. I suggest you discuss techniques of note-taking with Professor Beese, Mr. Anderson."

Cap decided not to write anything down yet. A couple of the students kept staring at him.

"We will first study the differences and similarities between English and American law. One of the earliest differences was a declaration that on death intestate in America all children inherit land and property equally, not just the oldest son as in England. This reflects the fairness of the American people as compared to the English, who still adhere to some of the old aristocratic ways."

Cap had to set Freeman straight on this matter. "That can't be right. My pappy didn't inherit a speck of land or timber from his pappy."

Freeman looked pained. "Did your grandsire die intestate?"

Cap wished he'd kept his mouth shut. He didn't know what intestate meant. It sounded kind of like Grandpa's manhood was in doubt. "Grandpa was a regular man. He just didn't cotton to my Pappy." He shrugged.

Some of the class began to snicker and a few guffawed loudly.

"Mr. Anderson," Freeman peered over his spectacles at Cap, "I appreciate your interest in this subject matter, but we have certain standards of courtroom—I beg your pardon, I meant to say *classroom* conduct here at the University. You are not to interrupt me every time a thought enters your mind. I'll never finish my lecture if you do. And what of the other students? I cannot let their studies be sacrificed to your insatiable curiosity."

"I do apologize. You see, I don't know your ways here in Tennessee. But I'll learn em."

More laughter rippled over the classroom. Freeman's face grew increasingly red and his hand shook.

"In my day, I ran a good, disciplined courtroom—no swearing, no outbursts, no tardiness. I shall maintain that standard in this classroom, and anyone who thinks otherwise will suffer the consequences."

One look at Freeman and at the faces around him registering embarrassment and scorn told Cap he'd better talk to Beese before speaking up in class again. But no harm done. By tomorrow he'd have the lay of the land.

After the lecture was over, he consulted his map and schedule. Beese's class was in twenty minutes, and he might get a chance to talk to him beforehand. As he ambled along, enjoying the warm Indian summer sunshine and noticing that the leaves on the trees were beginning to turn orange and red, he felt a thump on his shoulder and another in the middle of his back. He whirled around in time to see three of his classmates hurl prickly buckeye balls at him.

"Hey, country boy!" one yelled. The young man was stocky, muscular, and not quite as tall as Cap.

Cap caught the next two buckeye balls, one in one hand and one in the other, as he strode up to the student who'd yelled.

"I just might make you eat these things." He held the buckeyes up to the student's face.

"Try and make me, you dumb hick." Laughing loudly, the boy looked at his two friends for approval.

Cap slammed both buckeyes into the taunter's face. His would-be tormentor staggered backwards, blood trickling from his nose and mouth.

"Now you've done it," the bloodied young man snarled. "I'm going to beat the crap out of you." He took off his suit coat, handed it to a friend, and started to roll up his shirt sleeves.

Cap put down his satchel, removed his coat, and laid it over a tree branch.

"Look out!" his challenger shouted. "He's got a gun."

"I don't need a gun to lick you." Cap reached for his revolver in order to remove it from its holster and put it in his coat pocket. His tormentors disappeared behind two trees and a bush.

"Holy crap," one yelled. "Our hillbilly is a maniac."

"I'm gonna start shootin if you're not out here on the sidewalk by the time I count three." Cap was going to have some fun with these boys. They'd think twice about bothering him again. "One! Come out from behind those trees."

They leaped onto the sidewalk.

"Two! Now get movin!" He waved his revolver wildly in their general direction. They started down the sidewalk, increasing their speed at each step.

"On your hands and knees. On all fours like the jackasses you are." One student, eyes wide with fear, dropped to his hands and knees. The other two flopped down beside him.

"Now get!" Cap fired into the air. "Get movin, you jackasses!"

Down the sidewalk, the three scrambled on their hands and knees as fast as they could. Onlookers who'd heard the gun go off stared at them, pointing and laughing. Cap fired a couple of more times and watched the three crawl around the corner, out of sight behind high shrubbery. He holstered his revolver and put his coat back on. They wouldn't bother him again.

The next class was "Torts," taught by Beese, who glanced around the room with a puzzled look when three of his students failed to answer the role call.

This class went better for Cap. Beese carefully defined several kinds of torts, and Cap managed to write down all the definitions by leaving out some words and letters that could be filled in from memory when he got back to his room. He asked no questions, but listened carefully when others addressed Beese. Nobody tried to contradict Beese or asked about taking notes. When the class ended, Cap wrote down the reading assignment and headed out the door.

Dean Freeman, Professor Turner, a sheriff, and the three students who'd thrown the buckeyes were standing just outside. Freeman stepped forward and confronted Cap.

"These young men have been in my office and have made some serious charges against you." His eyes were glittering like Pappy's when he was mad.

"What did I do?"

"Did you or did you not chase these young men down the street while shooting at them?" Freeman's angry eyes searched Cap's clothing, looking for his gun, Cap suspected.

"Shoot *at* them? I shot over em in fun. If I'd shot *at* them, they'd be full of holes." *Why are these people het up over a little sporting around?*

"Shoot over them, shoot at them." Turner glowered at him, his large mouth turned far down at the corners. "A gun is not a toy, Anderson, and shooting at a human being is not a game. It's a crime."

"A jailable offense," the sheriff said.

"Well, if they leave me alone, I'll leave them alone," Cap said.

"Did they shoot at you?" Freeman asked.

"No," the students and Cap said simultaneoulsly.

"Did they endanger you, threaten you?" Freeman continued.

"They laughed at me and bounced a few buckeyes off my back, then that one tried to pick a fight." He pointed to the boy with scratches on his face.

"And for that you pulled out a gun and shot at them?"

"Shot over em," Cap corrected Freeman. "Way above. Here's what happens when I shoot *at* something." He drew his revolver with his right hand, threw a buckeye about thirty feet into the air with his left and shot it dead center, shattering it into fragments that rained down on them.

"That's a heck of a shot," the sheriff muttered.

"I told you it was a mistake to admit him," Turner shouted from where he'd ducked behind a hedge. "He's uncivilized—a backwoods troglodyte."

"I hate to admit it, but it appears you were right." Freeman shook his head. "At least we've learned his true nature early."

"This officer will escort you to jail, Anderson, where you can't endanger anyone else," Freeman continued. "He will bring you to my office at ten o'-clock tomorrow morning. I am going to assemble the University disciplinary committee, including President Dabney. You will undoubtedly be expelled. You are intelligent and I had hopes your talents would flower here, but I see now that you are one of the hopelessly lawless sort who still roam remote regions of our nation."

Cap was stunned at the turn of events. He was so flustered he could hardly stammer out a reply.

"If— If I was hopelessly lawless, I wouldn't be here to study law. I know I have to learn new ways and I will. Just give me a little time."

"If we give you more time, you may kill somebody," Freeman said.

The sheriff drew his revolver, backed up a few feet from Cap, and pointed it at him. "With one hand, real slow, lay that pistol down at your feet."

Cap thought fleetingly of trying to escape, but judged he wasn't close enough to kick the sheriff's gun out of his hand. He laid his revolver on the ground. Nobody had ever taken a gun from him.

The sheriff led him off to a two-story brick jail, where he was searched, then locked in a cell with a cot in the corner and iron bars over the window, just like a criminal.

He perched uneasily on the edge of the cot. Not even one entire day at law school and he'd been thrown in jail. He'd been given a chance, but he wasn't going to be given a second even though he'd hurt no one. If only he hadn't been raised with guns instead of books, he wouldn't be in this fix. He wouldn't be in this cell instead of a classroom. Pappy's advice to never be without a gun had doomed him to failure in Nashville.

He pounded his fists into the cot, striking the mattress, forcing the prickly horsehair stuffing up through the coarse cover and into his skin. His mind raced furiously with ideas for escaping. Maybe he could overpower the jailer or steal the cell key when he wasn't looking. But if he broke out of jail, his chances of staying in law school would go from almost none to none, along with his plans for himself and his family.

His chances were probably zero anyway. Dabney, Freeman, Turner, and now even Beese believed he was lawless, uncivilized, and a liar. And none of them knew he was wanted for murder. He was hunted and hated in the mountains and despised here in Nashville. The only men in the whole world who saw any promise in him were Pappy and John Floyd.

Finally drifting into a troubled sleep, he dreamed of raising his rifle and shooting Tolbert McCoy. The three McCoy brothers hung limply, where they were tied to paw-paw trees, then came alive again. Over and over Cap shot them, then saw them come to life again.

Chapter 32

Cap woke in a sweat, leaped to his feet and peered between the bars of his cell window. It was night time and there was no moon, no stars. A lone gaslight in the distance lit his cell just enough for his mind to create a ghostly vision of Allifair McCoy in the corner, a vision he was able to banish only by approaching and reaching out with the fingers of one hand as if to touch it, knowing full well his heart would have stopped and he would have died if he'd actually encountered her flesh with his.

Opposite the window, the bars on the cell door stood out even in the dark. In one swift stride he reached the bars, seized two adjacent ones and tried to pull them apart. Although he strained with all his might, they didn't bend.

From down the hall, he heard the clang of a metal door opening. The scrape-clunk of a man's boots approaching made his heart leap. But when the owner of the boots came into sight, Cap saw it was no rescuer, only a jailer with a lantern in his hand and a ring of keys hanging from his belt.

"Evenin." The jailer grinned, showing brown-stained teeth with gaps between them. Dull watery gray eyes stared out from under a thatch of white blond hair.

Not much, but at least he was someone to talk to.

The man held the lantern close to the bars and squinted at Cap.

Cap loosened his grip on the bars so as not to give the impression he was trying to get out. His fingers ached.

"You must be in charge here. My name's Anderson. What's yours?"

"Higgins." Higgins puffed out his chest. "I'm in charge of this whole jail all by myself every night."

"Aw, now. You don't expect me to believe that! The whole jail by yourself? A big place like this?"

"By myself."

"That's amazing! This jail must hold a lot of men and you in charge of the whole lot! How many would that be?" Cap had seen the two-story brick jail from the outside and guessed it had four to six cells per floor.

"About a thousand, I reckon." Higgins rolled his eyes and grinned.

"A thousand!" Cap rolled his eyes in return. "How many in here now?"

"Three besides you, I guess." Higgins shrugged. "They're asleep. Been puttin in sewer pipe all day."

"Well, you got to catch yourself a few more prisoners. Just four of us aint hardly worth the talents of a man like you." Cap tried to match his grammar and speech to Higgins's. Getting on the good side of this jailer might be useful.

Higgins grinned and ran his fingers coyly along the bars. "You like me, don't you?"

"I'd admire to have a drink with you, sir. You wouldn't have a drop of whiskey on you, would you?" If he could get this man drinking, there was no telling what doors might be opened.

Higgins's smile vanished. "They said if they catched me drinkin on the job again, they'd bust my butt."

"That wasn't very friendly of em."

"I like my job. Got me a room in a boardin house. Don't have to live in no shanty town."

It wouldn't do to frighten Higgins by pushing for whiskey. Cap was trying to think of another distraction when Higgins spoke up.

"They said you was shootin at some of them college boys."

"I didn't hurt em none. Shot over their heads. They was makin fun of my ways, them college students. Makin fun of folks like you an' me. They was laughin at us, Higgins."

"They aint got no call to do that. I wish I'd of seen you shootin at em." Higgins wiped his mouth and giggled.

He wants me to talk to him some more, Cap thought. "What are them other fellers in here for?"

"Forgin checks, fightin. One feller stabbed somebody. I got to go look at em."

Cap listened as Higgins's footsteps scraped down the hall, a door clanked open and the boots clomped up some stairs. Darkness closed in again. Cap sat on the cot and put his head in his hands. Higgins was gone now. He was going to have to sit here alone until morning when they would drag him out and throw him out of school.

In a while, he was glad to hear Higgins's footsteps return. His lantern lit up the cell.

"All your prisoners accounted for?" Cap asked.

"Yup. They's all wore out from workin. 'Cept the killer. He never sleeps."

"They let him out to work, too?"

"Naw. They don't let him out, only the mist'meanors. On account of they

212

don't have no handcuffs on when they work."

"You reckon they'll work me?" Cap pictured himself outdoors with no handcuffs and a guard he could watch till he got a chance to disarm him. He had no intention of staying in this jail for long. If he couldn't go to school, he'd go home to timber and try to survive long enough to save the money and get a permit for a sawmill.

Higgins peered at him and licked his lips. "You a mist'meanor?"

"I reckon so."

"Then they'll put you to work. I got to go now and sweep out the sheriff's office and take the trash to the incinerator out back and wash the winders."

"Why don't you have me help you? I'd like to be busy. My nerves is all bad."

Higgins's face lit up. "You could work for me like them other fellers is workin for the sheriff."

"'Course I could. No sense in you workin so hard when you got me here."

As Higgins unlocked the cell, Cap noted which key he used. He followed Higgins down the stairway to the sheriff's office.

In a closet Higgins got a broom, pail, and scrub rag for cleaning the windows. As Cap swept dust into a pile, he peered around the room. A straight-backed chair was shoved up to a worn wooden desk with a scratched top, bare except for a pipe in a stand. Beside the desk was a coat tree where a man's mackintosh hung. Near the front door two shotguns were locked into a gun rack fastened to the wall. A cabinet with four drawers stood along a wall beneath a ticking clock.

While Higgins was filling the pail with water from a spigot outside the door, Cap pulled open a desk drawer. There was nothing but chewing tobacco inside. He shut it as Higgins returned.

"Floor's done," Cap said. "Where'll I put the sweepins?"

Higgins motioned to the back door. Cap swept the little pile out into the dark.

"Now you got to do the winders." Higgins stood tall and puffed out his chest.

It took Cap only a few minutes to wash and wipe the two windows. While he wiped, he thought.

"What about them boots?" Cap pointed to a pair of grubby, worn leather boots by the gun rack. "Whose are they?"

"Sheriff's."

"What do you say I polish em up for him? You could tell him you done it."

"Yeah!" Higgins grinned. "I know where he keeps the polish, but he don't hardly ever use it." Higgins took out a little tin of polish and a rag from a desk drawer that Cap saw had nothing else in it. Sitting in the sheriff's chair, he went to work on the boots.

Higgins picked up the trash. "I got to go out back now to the incinerator." He looked at Cap uncertainly.

"Don't worry yourself none about me. I'll just keep on shinin these here boots."

As soon as the back door closed behind Higgins, Cap opened a third desk drawer and found a treasure—three pairs of handcuffs and three keys. He tried the keys in the handcuffs. Each cuff had its own key that fit no other. He shoved two of the cuffs to the back of the drawer, left one in front and pocketed its key, leaving the other two keys in the drawer, one by the cuff in front, the other by the two in back.

Opening a drawer on the other side of the desk, he found his Colt, checked to see that it was loaded, and put it in his pants pocket. Now he could pull his gun on Higgins and escape. When he heard Higgins outside the door singing "Dixie," he shut the drawer and picked up a boot and the polishing rag.

Higgins smiled when he saw Cap hard at work.

"I'll be just another couple of minutes," Cap said as he rubbed the boot. If he broke out of jail now, that would be the end of law school for sure. Soon he held the boot up. "Look purty good?"

"Purty enough to be in a store winder," Higgins replied, his eyes wide.

Cap began polishing the other boot. "I bet the sheriff'll have some good things to say to you when he sees them boots." He winked at Higgins. His chances of getting back into law school were next to zero anyway.

Higgins grinned.

"How about your boots?" Cap pointed to Higgins's worn, dirty ones. "I'll shine em for you." But he had a slim chance. If he arranged things right, he could still escape tomorrow after the come-to-judgment meeting if it went against him.

Higgins grinned again and nodded.

Cap walked over and helped him remove one boot. Crossing behind Higgins, he slipped his revolver into a pocket of the mackintosh, then helped Higgins remove the other boot. Now, if the sheriff searched him in the morning, he wouldn't find the gun, but it was in a place where he could get to it. After he finished polishing, he held the boots out to Higgins.

"You'll look just as fancy as the sheriff."

"I will, I will!" Higgins strode back and forth, staring at his boots and laughing. "You're a nice feller, Anderson. I hope they goes easy on you."

Cap thought Higgins was a nice fellow, too. "You better put me back in my cell and look in on the other prisoners."

Higgins stared at his boots the whole way back to Cap's cell.

Cap lay back on his cot to consider what he could possibly say to Freeman and the rest of the faculty to convince them not to throw him out.

Chapter 33

In the morning, the sheriff opened Cap's cell, patted him down and found no weapon. He had Cap precede him to his office, where he took a pair of handcuffs from the front of a drawer and snapped the cuffs onto Cap's wrists behind his back as Higgins stood nearby and watched.

Cap, in a silent moment of triumph, saw these were the cuffs for which he had the key.

"Look at them boots!" He grinned at Higgins. "My they're shiny."

"I shined em and I shined these, too." Higgins handed the sheriff his boots.

"That was real nice of you, Higgins. You didn't have to do that." While the sheriff sat at his desk, took off his brogans, and put on the gleaming boots, Cap backed up to the coatrack, removed his revolver from the pocket of the mackintosh, and slid it into his suit coat pocket. He could escape right now if he wanted.

"They never looked so good since they was new," the sheriff said.

Higgins beamed from ear to ear.

Outside, strolling with the sheriff into the bright, crisp coolness of the autumn day, Cap's mind grew sharp despite his lack of sleep. He needed to be as sharp as he'd ever been to convince them to let him stay in school and to be ready to escape if he didn't succeed. He was nervous about appearing in a rumpled, slept-in suit, uncombed hair, and unshaven face.

They soon arrived at South College, where Cap found Dabney and the three faculty members.

"You!" Dabney pointed a meaty finger at him. "You are anathema to this University!"

Cap had no idea what anathema was, but had a suspicion that Dabney was referring to the shooting episode.

"Hold on," the sheriff interrupted. "I got to go take care of some matters. It'll be all right. There's four of you and he's handcuffed. When do you want me to come back for him?"

"No more than ten minutes," Turner said.

"I, too, am inclined to dismiss him posthaste," Dabney said. "However, every dog should have its day." He turned to the sheriff. "Give us an hour."

The sheriff left, pulling the door shut behind him.

Cap took a deep breath and eyed Dabney and the others. Right now he had an opportunity to throw off the handcuffs, pull out his revolver and escape. But if he wanted any chance to study law here, he'd have to face these men and do everything he could to convince them he should stay.

Dabney, feet planted wide apart, had stationed himself before Freeman's desk, his expression reminding Cap of a Primitive Baptist preacher about to bring God's judgment down on the sinners in his congregation. Freeman, red-faced and trembling, was slouched behind his desk. Across from Dabney stood Turner with a triumphant I-told-you-so look on his face. Beese was pacing up and down the room, biting nervously at his lip.

"I don't understand this, Anderson," Beese began. "Everything was going so well when you left my office yesterday. What went wrong?"

"Nothin. These fellows from Dean Freeman's class were prankin me, and I shot over their heads to scare em away. I didn't hurt em none."

"You discharged your gun on my University's campus." Dabney spread his arms wide as though to say Cap's guilt was a burden to the entire world. "You hot-headed, gun-toting hillbilly!"

Hot-headed. Pappy's words for him. He hadn't deserved to be called that since he'd grown up and didn't deserve it now.

"The only reason you didn't hurt those young men is they ducked and ran," Freeman sniffed. "You might have killed them!"

"Ducked and ran?" Turner snorted. "They crawled. And, frankly, they deserved to crawl for instigating this whole mess." He turned to Cap. "Don't believe for a minute I think their misbehavior excuses yours."

"As long as we're going to hear you out, Anderson, I guess we should take this step by step," Dabney growled. "Why were you carrying a gun in the first place? It's incomprehensible to me in view of the conversation you and I had yesterday."

"Where I come from every man carries a gun. I had one since I was twelve. My Pappy wouldn't send me out in the woods without protection."

"And you mistook the University campus for the woods?" Turner sneered.

Cap paused. He had to hang onto his temper. "You have to understand my Pappy to understand me. Our family was always in danger from catamounts, bears, rattlesnakes, and thieves and robbers roamin the hills. There's no law enforcement to speak of in the mountains where I grew up. And then came the War, Union soldiers trampin into our country, burnin the county courthouse."

Dean Freeman nodded, as Cap had hoped he would.

"So snakes and Union soldiers made you do it." Turner scowled at Cap. "Sometimes I think I've heard all the excuses in the world, but you have imagination, Anderson. You came up with a new one."

It was hard to keep from lashing out, hard to keep his head clear. "So my Pappy and all the men I knew had to carry guns and be ready to use em. Pappy taught me it's a man's duty to keep his gun at his side at all times to protect himself and his family."

"You were probably carrying a gun when I met you yesterday!" A red-faced, enraged Dabney looked ready to chew him up and spit him out on the floorboards. "How you cajoled me about the evils of war that pervade our lives. Dispose of that cannon, the old people cannot rid themselves of their wartime ways, we must do it for them, you said. And here you stand, guilty as they. No—guiltier! They, at least, are honest, if mistaken, about their views while you are a miserable deceiver."

This turd was calling him a liar! Cap pictured, could almost feel, himself slamming a fist into that fat, insolent face. He could break Dabney's nose, he could. . .

He had to get hold of himself and think. Slowly, he slipped the key to the handcuffs from his pocket.

"I wasn't bein deceitful. You think I shot at those boys, but I didn't."

"You came close to it," Beese said. "And you certainly behaved in a reckless, negligent manner. This is a civilized place. Knoxville citizens may own shotguns or rifles for hunting, but no one carries a pistol, particularly a concealed one, within the city."

Cap's mind went numb. How did they protect themselves?

"So you were brought up to carry a gun," Freeman said. "Now let's hear why you think you had the right to shoot it."

Cap inserted the key into the handcuffs behind his back. The cuffs opened and he slipped the key out of them. "I only meant to teach those ornery boys a lesson, put some fear into em. People where I come from don't mind that sort of fun. I didn't know anyone would get het up about it."

The cuffs nearly fell off, and he had to jerk his arms up to keep them on. Nobody said anything. They probably thought he had a case of nerves.

Dabney scowled. "You have the wrong philosophy for this University."

Cap feigned total concentration on their argument while he considered whether or not he should make his escape now.

"You said you want to change your school," Cap said, staring right into Dabney's eyes, "give it a new identity, not based on the War. How can I make you see that I want to make that very change for myself? And for my Pappy. But it's hard for a man to think of a different way of life from that of his parents if he's never seen and never heard of any other way. How could I say to myself 'I want to live like the people of Knoxville' if I'd never seen Knoxville or known how its people live? I've never been to a place where a man didn't consider it his duty to carry a gun. Before this week I'd never seen a college or a library or a bookstore."

Dabney's angry expression softened to an attentive one.

"Pappy is a good man, and he did what he had to do to take care of us when there were animals and robbers and Union soldiers and other kinds of varmints about with nobody around to look after us but him. But now the soldiers and many of the animals are gone and the mountains are full of another kind of robber—men dealing in land, money, coal, and timber. They tell us we're backwards, uneducated, uncivilized hillbillies. And they're right to say we don't know the things they do. But do they help us to understand? Do they teach us? Do they invite us into their society so that we may learn?"

Freeman and Turner exchanged knowing looks, while Dabney's face took on a more thoughtful look.

"No, they do not," Cap continued. "They take advantage of our lack of education. They cheat us in business, they trick us in the courts, they treat us so bad we can't hold up our heads in our own mountains. That is why I came to Knoxville, to your school—to become educated and civilized, to learn to be nobody's fool.

"I want to see how men like you live and think, to mold myself after you. I want to learn from you. I want to bring back what I learn to help my people. I want to earn my entries on the credit side of The Great Ledger."

"Haven't we had enough of this?" Turner looked around at the others.

"He's making some good points," Beese countered. "If you were suddenly set down in the backwoods, far from civilization as you know it, would you know what to do?"

"For Christ's sake," Turner snarled. "We gave Anderson a chance and look what he did with it."

"You've spoken surprisingly eloquently on your behalf," Dabney said. "It's an appealing notion that we might influence your life and thereby help civilize a backward people. But I think I can speak for the others, as well as myself, when I say we have doubts that you are motivated by anything more than a desire to stay out of jail and perhaps to save yourself further humiliation. You've deceived us once. Why on earth should we, all of us lawyers who have heard a lot of pettifoggery over the years, believe you?"

In desperation, Cap swung the handcuffs out in front of him and threw them onto Freeman's desk. Then he reached into his pocket and brought out his revolver.

Everyone gasped. Turner edged toward the door.

Cap glared at Dabney. He was in charge now. He could do anything he wanted—escape, shoot up the room, terrorize these men, his tormentors. But he wanted something from them so badly that he gently laid his revolver, handle first, in Dabney's hand.

"I could have shot the lot of you and escaped anytime this morning. What more proof could you ask that I want to stay here?"

"You are full of surprises!" Dabney turned the gun over in his hands, shaking his head at every turn.

"Surprises?" Turner shouted. "The devil's full of tricks. How on earth did he get out of those handcuffs?"

"I've learned to live by my wits as well as by my gun," Cap retorted.

"You're uncivilized!" Turner was red in the face and still shouting. "Imagine pulling a pistol on the president of the University."

"Hold on," Beese said. "This man could have easily escaped if he'd wanted to. Instead he risked being returned to jail. He has put his desire to remain in school beyond dispute."

"Who gives a darn about his desire?" Turner slammed his hand on Freeman's desk.

"The question is," Freeman said, "Has he honestly told us his reasons for wanting to stay? Would he comport himself appropriately?"

"Are you proposing to allow an armed and dangerous man to have the run of this University?" Turner sputtered. "You, the dean of a law school?"

"What about that 'armed and dangerous' part, Anderson?" Dabney demanded. "If you were allowed to stay, would you not only surrender this gun, but give up the use of arms in our city?"

With bounty hunters and McCoys looking for him, Cap didn't want to be without his revolver. But he still had his rifle back at the boarding house and as far as he knew nobody but his family and John Floyd knew where he was.

"Take it," he said to Dabney. "Keep it till I graduate. I want it back when I leave because my Pappy gave it to me."

"Six bullets." Dabney emptied the gun's chamber. "He could have killed us all with two to spare."

"Well, now what?" Freeman scowled. "Yesterday we were planning to expel this man."

"Perhaps we created a tempest in our own little teapot yesterday," Beese said. "Overreacted to an act we thought threatening when it was merely reckless."

Freeman nodded. "From the start I favored putting a man with his strength, wit, and intelligence back into the mountains with his head full of law and civilization."

"Here we go again." Turner threw his hands in the air. "Letting him stay on this campus would be like letting another Jesse James loose among us on his word that he wouldn't rob and steal anymore."

"You have my gun," Cap said.

"You could get another one."

Cap squirmed. He didn't want to make his ultimate offer unless he was forced to. "You know I'm not gonna do that. If you found another gun on me, you'd throw me out of your school."

"What will others say about *us* if he takes up a weapon again?" Turner turned to Dabney.

"Letting him stay is appealing in some ways, but it entails risk, and the stakes are high. Perhaps too high." Dabney frowned and pondered the floor.

With sentiment growing against him once more, Cap had no choice but to play his last card.

"What would you call my offense? A felony or a misdemeanor?"

Beese looked at him curiously. "A misdemeanor. Discharging a firearm in a negligent manner. You didn't actually shoot anybody or threaten to shoot them."

"Let me tell you about the men in jail here for misdemeanors," Cap said. "They leave jail every morning, no handcuffs, to work in your city the whole day long. When they go out in the morning and when they come back at night, they're searched for weapons."

"Yes, yes, I know," Freeman said. "I've heard this described many times in my courtroom."

Cap clenched his jaws and prepared to make the most humiliating offer of his life. "I have committed a misdemeanor and I'm willing to serve my sentence. But I deserve to be treated the same as others who've committed such an offense. Lock me in jail every night, release me to work here at the school every morning, search me for weapons every day."

"Bravo!" For the first time this morning, Beese looked pleased.

"Every night in jail." Freeman nodded. "That ought to keep him out of trouble."

"I think that would satisfy me," Dabney said. "What about the rest of you?"

"Quiet place to study." Beese smiled.

"A jailbird!" Turner slapped his forehead. "If you think your fellow students teased you before, what do you think will happen when they hear about this?"

"What about that, Anderson?" Freeman asked. "Can you hold your temper if they give you trouble again?"

"Why I forgive em already. They were just havin a little fun. We're all new to each other and strangers always take gettin used to. We'll be friends before you know it."

"Well?" Dabney looked at the others.

"In jail every night." Freeman pursed his lips and stuck his thumbs into his waistcoat pockets. "And they'll search you every morning and every evening. I like it."

"What about you?" Dabney inquired of Turner.

"Looking after Anderson will give the sheriff something to do to earn the money we pay him. And it will be his responsibility, not mine, if this doesn't work."

"And you, Beese, I assume you concur?"

"Certainly."

"Looks as if you've won yourself a second chance, Anderson," Dabney declared. "I'll tell the sheriff of our agreement. I wonder what he'll have to say about the pistol and these handcuffs."

"We'll say the cuffs slipped off and he doesn't need to know about the gun," Beese said.

"So sly and sneaky." Turner shook his head and tsk-tsked. "I would never have thought you had it in you."

But Cap knew that was the only way to protect Higgins from being fired and who knows what restrictions being put on himself. Beese's idea was as cunning as any of Pappy's.

"Thank you, gentlemen." Cap solemnly shook hands with each man. He was a law student again.

Chapter 34

A week after the hearing, Cap was settling into a routine of going to classes during the day. None of the students knew where he spent his nights. The faculty told them, if asked, that he was on probation and his revolver had been confiscated. He'd kept his room at Mrs. Chapman's where he continued to have all his meals except breakfast, explaining to her that he had a night job downtown. Now it was Sunday and he'd been let out for church, which he avoided, and for meals at the boarding house.

"Judge Bond gives all the misdemeanors thirty days," the sheriff had told him after the hearing. "'Less I say I need more workers, then he stretches their sentence out some." Cap wondered what his professors would think of this brand of justice.

He was relieved to be serving only thirty days and did his best to learn what misdemeanors led to jail terms in Knoxville so he could avoid them in the future. Everyone in this town knew how to keep out of trouble, but he had to learn.

He was busy raking leaves for Mrs. Chapman and burning them in a pile beside the street, the smoke with its acrid autumn smell wafting over the neighborhood. At home, this time of year, the air was filled with the scents of trees and green things preparing for winter, of farm animals freed from summer's sweat, and of fresh-hewn logs stacked for burning during the cold months. The autumn odors in Knoxville filled only half the air. The aromas were leeched from the other half by bricks, stone, iron, and pavement. The air felt empty to Cap.

From where he stood he could see a row of frame houses with wooden porches like Mrs. Chapman's on both sides of the street, lined up one after the other, a sight he wondered if he'd ever become accustomed to. Now and then a horse-drawn buggy passed by, clattering along a street paved with bricks, rather than slopping through mud and manure. No matter how much he scrutinized the men driving or strolling by, he could not find tell-tale firearm bulges. It seemed to him he'd left the real world.

He tried picturing Pappy and Mama living on this street. Picturing wild bears living there would have been no harder, no more incongruous. Pappy wouldn't stand for being cooped up in a city house squeezed in next to others, denied the right to carry or shoot a gun. He was dead set against any situation that demanded adaptability from him. He closed his mind to everything new

that came his way, especially what he had no control over.

Back home, Joey might be kicking up piles of red, orange, and yellow leaves to see the colors splash around him and taking in the smells of fall as only a little child whose head was not far above the earth could do, as Cap himself had done as a boy. Coleman would be only eight months old now, too young to play in the leaves, but he could see and smell them.

Eight months old. He hadn't seen the boy for two months and wouldn't see him for at least eight more. These were almost the same months over which Pappy, away during the War, had lost Johnse to Mama. Cap would hate to lose Coleman.

And how was Nancy doing? It was time for hog slaughter. By now Pappy must have sent over ham and pork sides for their smokehouse. If someone had been lucky enough to find game in the vicinity of the cabins and fort, there might be venison and bear meat, too.

At home they had to provide for themselves. They grew fruits and vegetables; raised pigs and chickens; hunted bear, deer, foxes, raccoons and squirrels; smoked hams and churned butter. But here in Knoxville, Mrs. Chapman bought nearly everything she needed at a grocer's with wooden bins full of goods. Cap had gone there for her once. You could buy chickens, sausages, apples, eggs, canned beans, white potatoes and sweet potatoes, soap, molds of butter with pictures of flowers pressed into them, and coffee with fifteen cents a pound printed in red letters on the side of the tin. Knoxville had definite advantages over Main Island Creek when it came to vittles.

Cap used a rake to stir the dwindling pile of smoldering leaves. Despite the strangeness of the place and his constant anxiety over whether he was living in a way acceptable to the University, he'd done well this week. He hadn't gotten into trouble in any of his classes and nobody teased him anymore. Best of all, he liked studying the law, the careful thinking that went into it, and the importance of precise wording that could make so much difference when applied to people's lives. He wished Nancy were here to talk to about the things he'd learned.

Spending nights in jail hadn't been as bad as Cap had feared either. He was up late every night studying in his cell until he was too dog tired to stay awake thinking about being lonely and humiliated.

Feeding the fire with more leaves, he turned his mind to the paper he'd been assigned to write by the end of the coming week for Turner's course—a plan including the important points for a contract to be written later in the term. Cap had chosen a contract between a store owner supplying a logging crew and a timberman delivering logs in payment for supplies.

He knew enough to write down how much above cost the store owner could charge for supplies and how much the timberman could expect to be paid for his logs. Unless you wrote prices down, according to Judge Harvey, a merchant could charge anything he wanted for axes, log chains, nails, all the things a timber crew needed. One greedy owner had taken Pappy to court when he'd made that mistake and no Hatfield would make it again. That is, no Hatfield who could read and write.

One of the most worrisome problems Pappy had was putting up the deed to his land in trust in case he failed to deliver the promised logs. It didn't seem fair, but all the land-hungry merchants were beginning to insist on it as part of the deal.

That evening, Cap set his plan for the contract on paper. When he stopped in for an early morning appointment with Beese, he showed him what he'd written.

"A good beginning, Anderson." Beese leaned back and stared at the ceiling. "I have to decide where to draw the line. If I tell you how to improve this, I don't know if it would be fair to the other students."

"Improve it?" Cap felt his face grow hot. This plan deserved nothing but praise.

"You've got the right general idea. But like any beginner, you've not thought of everything."

Cap felt his arm and fist muscles tighten. Beese had better have some darned good reasons why this plan wasn't perfect.

"I think teaching is the important criterion." Beese squirmed in his chair. "I think it's more important for me to help you learn than to concern myself with giving you a minor competitive edge over your classmates."

"What's wrong with my plan?!"

"Let's start with organization. You should first say how you're going to lay out the contract. How do you propose to begin it?"

Cap tried to recall contracts he'd seen. "With the names of the store owner and timberman, where they live and the date. Don't need law school to know that."

"Bear with me. What's next?"

"The part about agreeing on a price and no unfair mark-ups, I guess."

"You want the next section to spell out the merchant's obligations in the agreement. How do you want to describe the loggers' supplies? Do you want to include anything the merchant carries or only specific items?"

"He doesn't carry anything we don't need at one time or other."

"Then what constitutes a valid timberman's order?"

Cap didn't know how to answer.

"Can anyone who works on the crew come in and place an order your father would be expected to pay for?"

"No, can't do that. Wouldn't do to let my cousin Cotton Top order anything."

"Then you need to give the merchant a list of names of those who may legitimately place orders. Must the order be written or can it be oral?"

"Better be oral. Hardly any timbermen can read or write." Including Pappy.

"Then your contract should require the merchant to write down what he will supply in response to the orally delivered order and what its price is. A logging crew member will then sign that he has received what was written."

"Hardly any timbermen can sign their names."

"Yours is a different world from what I'm used to." Beese rubbed his chin.

"No stranger to you than your world is to me."

"I have an idea. Why don't you write in your contract that the merchant must get the crewman's signature or mark on the invoice? When it comes time to settle—logs for supplies—you'll at least have invoices to review. Maybe some of your crew will even get motivated to learn to read and write."

They went on to define the merchant's costs and mark-up.

Lastly, Cap and Beese got to the timberman's part. They decided the amount of timber would be expressed in feet of logs within a certain range of diameters. Then they considered where and how the logs were to be delivered—at a specified dam on a particular creek during April of the year the supplies were charged. The logs were to be of a good hardwood—poplar, maple, oak and not rotted from lying on the ground. The merchant could either float the logs he now owned to a downriver mill or pay the timberman a specified amount to do that for him.

"This is a dad-burned lot of bother," Cap said. "I'm plum wore out thinkin about it."

"We could make it simpler, but then it wouldn't be adequate. Write it all up in your plan. See what you can do with the issue of putting up land in trust as collateral for credit. I'll give you a hint. Deal with it as you dealt with the logs and supplies—on an equity basis. The merchant should not be entitled to all the land if the supply invoices are partly paid off in logs."

When Professor Turner handed back the graded contract plans, Cap's had EX-CELLENT written across the top in well formed fine-lined letters. To his surprise, Turner had Cap read his plan aloud to the class as an example of good, well thought-out work. This time no one made fun of him. But the empty seats on either side, in front and in back of him, spoke for his classmates. They still wanted nothing to do with him.

He was so proud of himself that he wanted someone to tell the good news to. He was on his way to tell Beese about his success when, passing the bookstore, he noticed the young woman who'd once waited on him watching him through the store window.

He went inside.

"Do you have some legal paper? Mine's used up." He laid the plan on the counter between them face-up where she couldn't help seeing it.

Turning to a shelf behind her, she took down a sheaf of white legal paper with blue lines and laid it next to Cap's plan.

"Oh my!" she exclaimed, seeing the word EXCELLENT written across the top. "You must be a very good student. I thought you were from the way you care about books."

"I wrote the best paper in the class," Cap said. "I spelled out the terms of a contract so well it'll stand up in any court. No lawyer could have done better."

"You ought to be proud of yourself. I'd be proud of you if you were my brother or my beau." She eyed him and pouted her lips in a flirting way he found appealing.

"Lady, you sure know how to please a man." He winked at her.

Chapter 35

"Why, Will, you'll be late for work." Mrs. Chapman smiled up at him from where she sat crocheting the latest in a long line of afghan bedcovers with which she furnished her rooms. Mrs. Chapman smiled all the time. He'd never known anyone who smiled so much.

"They don't need me downtown anymore." Cap was happy to be at the boarding house in the evening now that he'd finished serving his thirty days. But he got lonesome studying in his room alone at night, listening to the winter winds as they moaned and howled, blowing in off the river. Wind at night was the most lonesome sound in the world.

He lowered himself onto a fancy divan draped with yet another afghan. Mrs. Chapman, who liked company, encouraged her boarders to visit with her at the kitchen table or here in the parlor, a cozy room lit by embers glowing in a small fireplace and by a three-light gas chandelier hanging from the ceiling. The divan and Mrs. Chapman's Morris rocker were especially cozy—upholstered in soft, deep red material. "Brocaded Roman velour," she'd proudly called it. If Aunt Betty could see this room, Cap knew she'd want to duplicate every bit of it in her house in Logan.

"Nice room you have here, ma'am," Cap said. "It's a wonder the other fellers aren't down here." He picked up her copy of *The Knoxville Journal*, which was delivered daily, as usual scanning the front page for Hatfield and McCoy stories like those that had often appeared in *The Louisville Courier*. Today the paper had mainly local issues, with a lot of space given to the rumor that the University might be admitting women in the near future. That, he was sure, would never happen.

"Jim and Chester's trying to fix my pump organ at the school's mechanical shop. I should never have bought that contraption. It cost me seven dollars and sixty cents, and it only worked a week." Mrs. Chapman shook her head and tittered.

"Where's that tobacco shop feller?"

"In his room." Mrs. Chapman leaned forward. "When he's here, Ambrose is always in his room. But I think many times he goes out alone in the middle of the night." She peered over her glasses and waited, as if expecting Cap to explain the mysterious lodger. "I don't like that mustache on his top lip, with hairs growing every which away. Do you?"

"I haven't gotten to know him yet." Cap could think of two types of men who might stay to themselves so much and only go out at night when they wouldn't be seen—hunted ones like himself and their hunters.

"You'd like some company your own age instead of an old lady like me." This time Mrs. Chapman's smile was sympathetic and understanding.

"I'm kind of restless, but that's not on account of you. Been studyin for hours." He was sick of being alone upstairs in his room.

Mrs. Chapman smiled approvingly. "Think how glad you'll be you studied so hard when you're a lawyer."

It was nice having an older woman smile at him approvingly like Mama always did, so Cap went on talking.

"I admire your home, Mrs. Chapman—indoor plumbing, hot water whenever you want it, an ice box, gas lights, good-looking furniture. You've made this room as pretty as could be. And I've taken a real fancy to your boiler in the basement hooked up to the steam radiators in all the rooms. What a fine place." He'd spent a fascinating afternoon studying the boiler with its fire pot, flues, water and steam gauges, and valves. "At home all we got is a big fireplace in our kitchen. The sleepin room and the loft get cold at night."

"Lots of folks move to the city for its comforts," Mrs. Chapman said. "I wouldn't trade my nice, easy life for a hard one on a farm. Maybe when you finish school, you'll get married and settle down here."

"Knoxville's a fine city."

Mrs. Chapman was assuming he was single. Well, let her. The less he resembled the Cap Hatfield wanted for murder the safer he felt. Not sure how sturdy the soft velour was, he leaned gently back on the divan and stared into the orange and blue flames dancing among the fireplace embers. A lot of men in his place would think seriously about setting up a law practice in a place where life was comfortable and no one needed to fear being hunted down and shot at or hauled off to a Kentucky jail. But he wasn't looking around for something to do or somewhere to live like a lot of young men. Years ago he'd known his future. He was to head his family, protecting them from dangers and keeping them from enduring poverty, disgrace, and humiliation at the hands of the better educated, wealthier citizens of Logan. Once he finished law school, that's how he'd spend the rest of his life.

However, there was nothing to keep him from importing a few city comforts to the mountains. Running water, gas lights, and a grocery store any closer than Logan were out of the question. But the furniture, the ice box, and a kitchen stove like Mrs. Chapman's were possibilities.

That stove was an iron wonder standing on four heavy legs. At the top was a heat closet with a hinged door where you could keep food warm. Below the warmer were two stands where a tea kettle and coffee pot could be kept hot. Below them were six cooking circles, up as high as Nancy's waist, that would free her from having to bend and lift heavy skillets and pots from the hearth. A broiler with a hinged door hung out on the left side of the stove, directly exposed to the fire. Under the cooking surface were the firebox on the left and a large oven with twin racks on the right. Attached to the right side was a heat reservoir with its tank of hot water. Somehow he'd find a way to get a stove just like that lugged out to Main Island Creek.

"You seem very happy here, Mrs. Chapman."

She smiled. "This is my world. I don't want any other."

Here was this woman, a widow living alone, yet secure and happy. Back home widows were afraid to live alone because of the hard work needed just to survive and the dangerous men and beasts that had to be dealt with.

Things were harder than usual in West Virginia this year. He'd just received a letter from Nancy, routed by way of a cousin in Virginia so that no one at the Logan mail post would know she was sending it to Knoxville. Because the family hadn't been able to round up many hogs to bring with them when they moved to Main Island Creek, she hadn't received much from Pappy in the way of hams or pork sides to smoke. Hunting hadn't been good either because, to avoid crossing paths with raiders from Kentucky, Pappy and his men didn't range far from their houses and the fort. And hardly anyone rode into Logan or out to their place from Logan to bring in flour, coffee, sugar, or anything else from the stores because they feared the raiders might wait for them along the trail. With Uncle Jim and Uncle Ellison dead, Cap and Johnse away, and Uncle Wall and Cotton Top and seven others in the Pikeville jail, Pappy was having a hard time rounding up a crew for spring logging. He'd need enough men for guard duty and to do the work. The trial for the Hatfield prisoners in Pikeville had been set for August of the coming year. That meant that Pappy would soon have to hire lawyers for all except Uncle Wall.

"You fellers sometimes think about buyin yourselves a gun?" Cap asked as he sat in the kitchen one night playing Rook with Jim, Chester, and Ambrose who they'd dragged into the game because they needed four. "To protect yourself and your family?" He never detected the bulge of a hidden weapon on any man he saw on the streets of Knoxville, a fact that still fascinated him.

"Protect ourselves from what?" asked Jim, the vigorous-looking farm boy turned university student sitting across from him.

"From the bad sorts, the kind that's always makin trouble."

"Oh, there's a shooting down by the saloons once in a while." Chester pulled on his black mustache to make it curl up. Chester was always trying to look dashing, which he believed appealed to women. "There was a man stabbed last summer in a fight over a woman. But none of that has anything to do with us."

He picked up the four cards he'd won in a trick and slapped them triumphantly onto his growing pile of tricks and point cards.

"You thinking about getting a gun, Will?" Ambrose had just tried to cheat by peeking into Cap's hand.

"Nope." Cap had sized up many men over his life, and he'd known from the start this one was not honest.

Jim snorted. "What would Will do with a gun? Hold up Mrs. Chapman? Demand all her afghans?"

"Shoot holes in her blasted pump organ?" Chester pointed a finger like a gun and shouted. "Take that you ugly monster!"

Cap laughed. The daily fear he'd first experienced when going without his revolver had begun to ease. Sometimes hours would go by before he'd even think of it. But he was still trying to understand why no one in Knoxville was armed. On the one hand, those he asked often said they believed in law and order, but on the other hand how could a man trust that absolutely everyone he encountered shared his beliefs? It seemed that in their very depths the people of Knoxville trusted each other to behave in a civilized way. He didn't believe they were born different from folks in West Virginia and Kentucky. But he knew people here grew up believing guns had no place on their streets. How different his life would have been if he'd grown up in Knoxville. It would have been different for Allifair McCoy, too.

One morning, in Beese's office, he brought up the subject of getting permits for a dam and sawmill. Beese suggested he and Pappy enter into a contract with their neighbors, where if Pappy occasionally would have to hold water in reserve behind his dam for operating the mill, the downstream farmers would share in the profits that year to compensate them for losses to their farms. And Pappy could offer farmers the right to water their livestock behind the dam and provide them some flood control in the spring. These measures, Beese thought, might make the neighbors feel like part owners of a mill, water, and flood control system.

Cap was amazed at what lawyers like Beese could come up with. No one back home had ever had an idea like this. John Floyd would be proud of such a contract. And the trust this type of agreement might build with their neighbors could be useful in many ways. A neighbor you were in business with would be unlikely to point your home out to a bounty hunter.

Cap also had some thoughts about carrying weapons he wanted Beese to hear.

"People in this town don't carry guns. But suppose you lived in a place that wasn't like Knoxville at all, where most fellers were totin pistols and rifles and musket loaders. And suppose some of em threatened to shoot you on sight. What would you do then?"

"I'd get the heck out of there. But I understand what you're saying. Where you live, leaving your gun at home could mean your life."

"You bet. Some fellers'd be tickled to death to catch me gun naked."

"Then you don't only have a family to change." Beese spread his hands in the air. "You'll have to bring a law-abiding spirit to your whole community."

To his whole community! It was hard enough to convince and change Pappy, let alone change how things were done all over Logan County and parts of Kentucky. He'd have to chew on this idea a little piece at a time.

Someone knocked loudly on Beese's door.

"Come in," Beese called out.

President Dabney strode in.

"Good morning, Beese," Dabney boomed. "And Mr. Anderson." He looked Cap up and down, as if he was checking for a weapon. "How are you doing?"

"Been studyin hard."

"He's able to keep up with his work?" Dabney turned to Beese.

"He's doing well enough to be proud of himself."

"Good, good." Dabney seemed to be in a hurry. "Please excuse us, Anderson. I have a problem to discuss with Professor Beese. I intend to recruit women into this university and I'll need allies. The board of trustees and the legislature are both fighting me."

Women in the university. So the rumors were true. But why was Dabney doing this? Women didn't need to be educated and most of them would never be able to cope with college. Then he thought of Nancy. With her love of reading, Nancy would have been a good student if she'd ever had the chance. She was a good teacher. She'd taught him to read. But she couldn't cope with schoolwork now that she had a home and children to care for. Any woman admitted to the University would have to be unmarried. What a difference between this place and Logan County where almost no man or woman thought about going to college.

Back at the boarding house, he picked up the newspaper from Mrs. Chapman's porch where the newsboy had put it. The front page headline was about the financial collapse of an effort to improve the navigability of the Tennessee River. The left-hand column was titled "Supreme Court Decision Leads to Mass Invasion of West Virginia to Capture Hatfield Feuders."

Chapter 36

He couldn't keep his hands from shaking. This was a story he'd been on the lookout for, a story that, as time passed, he'd begun to believe would never appear in the Knoxville paper. He sat on the porch steps to read where others wouldn't see how upset he was.

He read about the Supreme Court's May decision that there was no process of law requiring that a person unlawfully abducted from West Virginia to Kentucky and held in Kentucky for an offense committed there must be returned to West Virginia, reading with the same disbelief and outrage as when he'd first read of it. Bounty hunters, posses, detectives, and all sorts of raiders, knowing their captives could not be returned to West Virginia and cause them to forfeit the reward of two thousand seven hundred dollars the governor of Kentucky was offering for each were again scouring southern West Virginia with the aim of snatching up Hatfields and their associates and hauling them off to Kentucky. The paper said posses had already brought in nine Hatfield men and expected to catch more. Interspersed within the text, right on the front page, were drawings of desperate-looking characters carrying rifles, with captions under the pictures reading "Devil Anse, Leader of the Hatfield Clan," "Johnse, Oldest Son of Devil Anse Hatfield," and "Cap Hatfield, Brutal Child Killer."

Child killer! He wanted to bellow like a bear beset by dogs. Scrutinizing the drawing of himself in a rough jacket and dungarees tucked into knee-high mountain boots, a bandoleer of bullets across his chest, a rifle cradled in his arms, hair drooping onto his forehead, and a mustache on his upper lip, he knew that today, in his suit, white shirt, store-bought hard shoes, and clean-shaven face, this picture couldn't be used to identify him. But because he couldn't identify himself, he had no way to refute those child killer charges. The only thing any reader of this newspaper would remember about Cap Hatfield was that he'd murdered children.

He considered pitching the paper into the incinerator out back, but anyone seeing him would notice the act. Attention would be called to him when attention wasn't wanted. He must do exactly what he and the other boarders always did when they picked up the paper. He brought it inside, carefully refolded it, and laid it on the sewing cabinet beside Mrs. Chapman's chair in the parlor, then went to his room to study until supper.

At the supper table he kept his ears open. He complimented Mrs. Chapman on her beef stew and her white cake with brown sugar frosting. Jim and Chet said they were ready to give up on Mrs. Chapman's pump organ. Ambrose warned that if anyone wanted pipe or chewing tobacco, they'd better get it now because prices were about to go up. No one mentioned any story in the newspaper.

The reaction of the law school faculty was totally different. When Cap reached Beese's office the next morning, the three of them were involved in an intense debate.

"I don't see how you can argue against the Court's decision," Freeman was saying. "There's no provision in the Constitution for requiring the return of a captured prisoner held in the state where he committed a crime to the state from which he was abducted. And I, for one, insist that the federal government take no action not specifically granted to it in the Constitution."

Cap tried to behave as though he were uninterested in their conversation, merely waiting for his morning appointment with Beese. He sat down and let his head droop a bit to hide his anxiety.

"Anarchy!" Turner was already shouting. "That's what this type of judicial reasoning results in. Invaders who can grab citizens of a neighboring state and abscond with them across the border do so with impunity. That's what I call anarchy."

"Remember that the rights of individual states must always be weighed against the prevention of conflict between states." Beese was, as usual, attempting to mediate between extremes. "The Supreme Court, even though not granted the specific power to demand the return of West Virginians to their home state, is charged in the Constitution with the more general power to resolve issues between states."

Turner asserted that Congress should enact a law to ensure the return of the abducted. Freeman countered that individuals could get a trial by jury, whereas states could not and, therefore, required stronger protection. And Beese maintained that the Supreme Court should have come down strongly against invading another state and abducting its citizens by ordering the federal arrest of the abductors and perhaps even of Governor Buckner who'd instigated and supported the invasions by offering rewards.

Cap needn't have worried about their suspicions. Each of these men was focused on displaying his academic expertise and overcoming the others' arguments. If he'd walked in brandishing a rifle and wearing a bandoleer of ammunition, no one would have noticed.

When he got back to the boarding house, he saw Mrs. Chapman bending, somewhat impeded by a long skirt and layers of petticoats, to pick up the newspaper from the porch. Normally, she waited for one of her boarders to bring it inside.

As he came up the steps, she was already scanning the front page.

"Nothing new," she muttered. "I was hoping for more pictures of those feuders." She moved closer to him, then looked about her. "One of those men looked very familiar to me."

Cap's mind reeled, he was speecless.

"Come inside." She crooked her finger for him to follow her into the parlor, where she picked up yesterday's paper and pointed to the drawing captioned "Cap Hatfield, Brutal Child Killer."

"Take a good look at this picture."

Her hushed and conspiratorial voice sent chills through his body. Searching her blue eyes nearly a foot below his, he saw excitement, but no anger or hostility. Was she sympathetic to him, wanting to help him? Like him, did she too have a secret?

"Jim, Chet," Mrs. Chapman called out to the students, who had just come in and were about to go upstairs. "I was just showing this to Will." She pointed to the drawing of Cap. "Tell him what you think, what we all think."

Feeling his forehead breaking into a sweat and starting to drip, Cap wiped his face with his jacket sleeve.

"It's just a suspicion, Mrs. Chapman." Jim's gaze fixed on Cap. "We're not dead sure it's him."

How could they have identified him from those drawings! Cap gripped a stair post to steady himself. Should he run? What did they plan to do, now that they knew, or at least guessed, who he was?

"Jim and Chet and I think that's Ambrose," she whispered. "But, naturally, we didn't want to mention it at supper last night. What do you think?"

"I don't know." Cap's mind was as empty as a gun out of ammunition.

"There's a big reward out for him. Two thousand seven hundred dollars!" Mrs. Chapman's eyes widened. "That's a lot of money."

Cap tried to think. Although his mind was barely functioning, he realized this was an opportunity to focus attention on Ambrose and away from himself.

"Their hair's kind of alike," he said.

"It's the eyes, those criminal eyes." Mrs. Chapman held the paper right up to Cap's face. "Ambrose has those terrible eyes. And I don't think he can read and write. The paper says all those Hatfields are illiterate."

Cap didn't like hiding behind this lie, but it helped relieve his mind. "He was cheating at Rook the other night."

"I know. Jim and Chet told me." She peered at Cap as if trying to size him up. "Do you think you boys could turn him over to the authorities in Kentucky? We'd all split the reward."

Cap stood back as though aghast. "Us? Why, Mrs. Chapman, that Hatfield feller's armed and dangerous. We'd be riskin our lives."

"Of course, of course. I don't know what I was thinking." Mrs. Chapman frowned, the first frown Cap had seen darkening her face. "Or I do know. It was personal greed. I confess I wanted to get that reward." She sighed. "But if we're not going to turn him in ourselves, we must tell someone."

Cap knew better than to suggest the sheriff. He didn't want to bring Mrs. Chapman and the sheriff together where they might talk about the shooting at school and the jail term, conceivably stumbling close to identifying him. He had to come up with someone else.

"How about the feller he works for at the tobacco shop?" Cap had suspected Ambrose of something that wasn't on the up and up, involving frequent nighttime trips. If the tobacconist was in cahoots with Ambrose, or even if he wasn't, he might warn his employee of Mrs. Chapman's suspicions. If Ambrose then hightailed it out of town, everybody's thoughts would turn to something other than Cap Hatfield, child killer.

"I'm going over there right now." Mrs. Chapman clutched yesterday's newspaper to her bosom. "Supper will be late tonight."

This would be the first time Cap had known supper to be late. Mrs. Chapman had an important mission to carry out.

He headed upstairs to the bathroom mirror to assure himself that his eyes were not evil, he was not brutal, he was not a child killer. He'd made a big mistake leading the raid that ended in Allifair's and Calvin's deaths. But a mistake was foolish and unwise, not evil and brutal. He'd executed Tolbert McCoy for the crime of murder and he'd taken down men at the battle on Grapevine Creek and up on Thacker Mountain trying to save Uncle Jim, ugly necessities of warfare. But a man who'd eliminated enemies during war and who'd ended the life of a murderer commonly received the gratitude of his fellow human beings. In a world that had right and wrong straight, his caption should have read "Protector of His Family" or "War Hero."

He inspected his eyes in the mirror—first wide open, then squinted, from the side, from the front. No sign of evil here. This was no devil.

Chapter 37

Because the manhunt for him was still on, Cap didn't go home when the University closed for the Christmas holidays. And Nancy couldn't come to Knoxville for fear that some smart bounty hunter might follow her to him. Beese and his wife had him over for Christmas dinner, Mrs. Chapman went to her niece's, and Chet and Jim went home. Ambrose was gone.

The night Mrs. Chapman had gone to speak to the tobacconist of her suspicions, Cap had lain awake listening to feet running up the steps, scrambling around in Ambrose's room, then dashing down the stairs and out the front door. By the next morning it was plain to Mrs. Chapman and her boarders that their suspicions had been confirmed. She told everyone she met they'd discovered the identity of that horrible killer and he'd fled. Cap was glad Ambrose was gone, taking Cap's identity with him, but he hated hearing the lurid descriptions of Cap Hatfield, savage killer. He felt particularly sad and angry because, in some ways, Mrs. Chapman resembled his mother.

The day after New Year's, Cap headed back to school, picking his way around slushy spots on the snow-dusted sidewalks to spare his store-bought hard shoes. A bright red cardinal on a branch of a barren tangle of honeysuckle vine cocked his head and eyed him as if to ask what a roughneck mountain man like him was doing on civilized streets. Cap believed birds and animals saw beyond the clothes and shoes a man was wearing and how he cut and combed his hair to sense his true nature. Only human beings could be fooled by a man's outward appearance.

At their morning meeting, Beese told Cap he must prepare for the coming semester final examinations. He brought out old exams so Cap could see what was expected.

After spending all his waking hours for two weeks studying, Cap was disappointed to find the exams he took were too easy to show the extent of his understanding of the law, the true/false and multiple choice questions being especially trivial. Only the essay questions in contract law and torts gave him an opportunity to shine. His grades were at or near the top of his class in every course.

The letter he received from Nancy just after exam week was worrisome. The logging crews weren't able to cut much timber because they'd had to spend too much time holed up in the fort or down at Pappy's house. Nearly every time they tried to go into the mountains to work, they were warned by lookouts who'd spotted strangers they suspected were posses and bounty hunters. She and the children were doing fine, but eating more shucky beans and corn grits than pork chops or venison.

He sat down and wrote how much he missed her and the children and promised to come home as soon as school let out for the summer. Realizing that Pappy would soon have to make deals with the merchants who supplied his logging crews, Cap wrote a short sample contract for Nancy to copy as needed. He told her how good his exam grades were. She could count on him to become a good lawyer.

The second semester began where the first had left off, except that Real Property took the place of Contracts. Having learned of his good grades, the other students were now more willing to sit near him and discuss issues brought up after class. One even invited him to join his study group, but Cap didn't believe the arrangement would be to his advantage, since he'd already outshone the others by studying alone.

He also learned from faculty conversations Beese let him sit in on. Often there were discussions about constitutional law and Supreme Court cases.

"The question is, does the Constitution give the Negro the same right to vote as we have?" Turner was pacing the floor and addressing Freeman and Beese as though he were in a classroom. "The Negro man, I should say. Not the woman, of course."

"Unfortunately, all this recent right-to-vote activity has roused the Ku Kluxers from their abode in Hell." Freeman described atrocities of the Klan in Tennessee—beatings, killings, lynchings—and how the authorities were condoning, or at best mildly critical, of them.

How unfair could life be? Cap wished he could tell them the violence done in the Hatfield/McCoy feud was nothing compared to the Klan's war against Negroes. Yet the Hatfields were described as savages in the newspapers and hunted by posses encouraged by the governor of a state, while Klan activities were condoned or overlooked.

Beese spoke up. "We all know what the moral thing to do is—recognize the Negro man's right to vote and jail anyone, Ku Kluxer or not, who assaults any of our citizens, Negro or not. We should register Negroes to vote here in Knoxville and be done with it."

Cap was amazed at how the power of this man's intellect and morality overcame his small size and puny appearance. Back home, a man like this would have been at best ignored, at worst bullied. He was beginning to view Beese as a heroic figure.

"Can't do that." Freeman wagged a finger at Beese. "The power to vote is given, or not given as the case may be, by the federal Constitution, as in the case of women, for instance. Individual states can sometimes deny rights. Some states prohibit people without property or convicted felons from voting."

Turner's large expressive mouth turned down. "States can withhold a right from you, but it takes the federal government to grant it."

Cap wouldn't mind if Negroes voted as long as they supported Floyd and Wilson.

Sometimes the three professors discussed economic theory and financial matters, a lot of which, Cap learned, involved lawyers.

"They're going to dredge out the shallows in the upper Tennessee and build a canal around the shoals." Freeman waved his hand through the air in imitation of flowing water in a river. "There will be coal and cotton barges going all the way from the Ohio to Knoxville and back. I don't know where to start investing first."

"We'll all be rich, won't we Freeman?" Turner laughed out loud. "No more lazy students and university politics for us!"

"My money's going into river barges," Beese said. "Coal seams can run out and cotton crops can fail. But barges will be needed to haul whatever's at hand."

Turner shook his head in disagreement. "Coal may be more risky, but that's where the big money will be."

John Floyd had informed Cap that coal and timber businesses and railroad companies had complained to Governor Wilson that tracks couldn't be built on the West Virginia side of the Tug, let alone into Logan County, until the area's lawlessness was ended. And without railroads, West Virginia coal could not be gotten to market, and timber would have to be floated down the rivers as it always had. Some businessmen were backing Kentucky's efforts to round up Hatfields to eliminate the violence, some wanted Buckner to withdraw his reward offer and forbid bounty hunters' raids, and some were requesting that federal troops be sent in to restore order. Cap had the feeling Turner, Freeman, and maybe even Beese would see an equivalence between dredging the Tennessee River in Tennessee and running the Hatfields and bounty hunters out of Logan County.

Being in the way of big business, Cap was beginning to see, was as dangerous as standing on the tracks in the way of a steam locomotive. To thrive, the Hatfields needed to ally themselves with coal, timber, and railroad interests instead of taking them on as enemies. When he got home, he needed to do whatever he could to see that it was safe for the planned railroad to be built on the West Virginia side of the Tug, all the way up close to the backside of Pappy's Main Island Creek land, near where the sawmill was going to be built and where coal could be dug right out of the ground by a man with a shovel.

One morning Beese gave Cap his recommendation for the subject of a paper for Turner's constitutional law class. "Why don't you tackle that recent Supreme Court decision against the state of West Virginia? That's become a popular issue around here, and I'd welcome the chance to read a well thought-out opinion on the subject."

Cap already had an opinion—the Supreme Court's decision was flat out wrong. The Court knew that members of the Hatfield family and their associates had been illegally kidnapped from West Virginia and jailed in Kentucky. That should have been the end of the matter, and the Hatfields should have been returned to West Virginia.

"Don't make up your mind so fast," Turner advised when Cap mentioned he thought the Supreme Court order was a pile of crap. "I want you to go back and review what the Constitution has to say about jurisdiction and extradition."

Cap found three copies of the Constitution in the one-room law library, currently consisting of Beese's, Freeman's, and Turner's personal collections. Seated at the only reading table, he started with Article III, Section 2, concerning the judicial power of the federal government. He read that its power extended to controversies between two or more states, between a state and citizens of another state, and between citizens of different states. It seemed clear that, according to this part of the Constitution, the Supreme Court had the power to decide controversies between the Hatfields and the state of Kentucky and between West Virginia and Kentucky.

He read Article III, Section 3: "The Trial of all Crimes, except in Cases of Impeachment shall be by Jury; and such trial shall be held in the State where said Crimes shall have been committed." This was pretty clear, too. Because the 1882 executions, which Cap still doubted were criminal acts, and the New

Year's raid both occurred in Kentucky, the Constitution required the murder trials to be held in Kentucky. And it also required that Frank Phillips be brought to West Virginia to stand trial for the murders of Uncle Jim and Bill Dempsey, as West Virginia had requested.

He went on to Article IV, Section 2: "A Person charged in any State with Treason, Felony, or other Crime, who shall flee from Justice, and be found in another State, shall on Demand of the Executive Authority of the State from which he fled, be delivered up to be removed to the State having Jurisdiction of the Crime."

He had to think about that one. The Constitution didn't say who or what was supposed to do the delivering up. He'd always heard that the only legal method was for the governor of a state to grant extradition rights. That is, if the Hatfields hadn't been abducted, Kentucky's governor could have requested extradition of an indicted Hatfield from West Virginia's governor and if extradition was granted, a Kentucky law officer could come and arrest that man. But what if the man was kidnapped and spirited off to Kentucky before extradition was granted? Would it be legal for a Kentucky sheriff or McCoys and bounty hunters to come into West Virginia and "deliver up" Hatfields to a Kentucky jail? That the Constitution didn't make that possibility illegal seemed to be a huge oversight. What if the abducters took an innocent man? What if they injured, or even killed, their captive in the process of "delivering him up"?

For help with these issues, he went to Turner, who seemed willing and almost eager to discuss law with him these days. Cap got right to the point. "I'll be burned if I can figure out what's meant by 'delivering up' in Article IV, Section 2."

"'Delivering up' is made more clear in a later Article." Turner showed no sign of scorn or condescension. "The governor of Kentucky can request that the governor of West Virginia grant extradition of an indicted man. If extradition is granted, Kentucky officers may come to West Virginia to arrest him. Or the governor of West Virginia can issue a warrant for the arrest of the indicted man, cause him to be taken and detained, then extradite him to Kentucky. These are two peaceful ways to settle the issue. What is neither legal nor peaceful under the Constitution is the invasion of one state by another. That is, the governor of Kentucky may not authorize anyone to violate West Virginia's territory by invading in order to capture one of its citizens and haul him to Kentucky. As I understand it, Governor Buckner did not authorize invasion. Allegedly on his own, the Pikeville sheriff undertook the kidnappings. In this case, Buckner's action, no matter how slyly done, is probably legal, but the sheriff's is not."

Cap went to Beese with his concerns about the Supreme Court decision.

"I've come across some things that don't seem right." Cap read from the decision that the Constitution "provided no mode by which a person, unlawfully abducted from one State to another and held in the latter State upon process of law for an offence against the State, can be restored to the State from which he was abducted."

"But," Cap pointed out, "the Constitution says the Supreme Court's supposed to settle disputes between states."

Beese frowned. "It doesn't seem probable that the law would have provided for no redress in a case like this. The Constitution provides a peaceable remedy for someone who's committed a crime in another state and then fled back to his own—extradition. I'd argue this provision has two purposes—to secure the return of the accused to stand trial and to prevent problems between states. After all, states are not sovereign nations with treaties or the ability to make war on each other."

That didn't square with Cap's understanding of the Court's decision. "But the Supreme Court decided abducting a prisoner from one state to another's one crime and committing murder's another. And someone illegally kidnapped from one state to another to stand trial for murder can't use it as a defense in his trial."

"He can't use his own kidnapping as a defense for murder," Beese agreed. "Only as a reason he should be returned to his own state."

Cap now understood that there were strong legal reasons for the Supreme Court's decision to leave the Hatfields in custody in Kentucky, and strong reasons against the decision. It was clear to him that the Court's opinion wasn't made because its members were bribed or beholden to men in Kentucky as he'd once believed. He was still mulling over the discussion, marveling at how the faculty, unlike Pappy, seemed to enjoy arguments for and against all sides of an issue, when he arrived at Mrs. Chapman's. Upstairs, he found a letter slipped under his room door. It was from Nancy.

"Your father sent a lot of money, two hundred fifty dollars, to Perry Cline because Cline had promised, or at least suggested, if the cost of taking our men prisoner and keeping them was paid, he'd see that they were let go to keep peace between the states. The money was sent, but there's no sign our men will be released. So your Pappy has decided to invade Kentucky and rescue them. He figures to save them from jail sentences or worse, and to add the men he rescues to his timber crews. I tried to talk him out of this because I think he'll only lose more men in the attempt. Even if he succeeds, the governor of Kentucky will probably raise the reward he's offering and over here there'll be more varmints, as your Pappy calls them, looking to make money from kidnapping our men, and the governor of West Virginia will find it hard to refuse to arrest your Pappy and his army for invasion of another state."

How could Pappy do this? A lot of men could be killed or injured. Yellow dog newspapers all over the nation would splash the tale of a criminal invasion by criminal Hatfields across their front pages, spreading his own infamy as a child killer. Governor Wilson might be forced by his constituency and by federal demands to arrest Pappy and his men. Businesses would shy away from the West Virginia side of the Tug. What Cap had learned in law school about setting up a sawmill and about settling issues in courts would be useless. No one would come to court his sisters. Pappy was about to throw the family's future away.

Cap couldn't sit by and let this happen. He headed downstairs and out the front door toward the Knoxville landing to arrange his departure on the first steamboat to Paducah he could get. It would take almost two weeks to get home, and he could only hope Pappy wouldn't act that fast.

Chapter 38

Catlettsburg! He was almost home. Cap steadied himself on the deck of the steamboat tossing on choppy water, the river's slosh and the soggy air bringing back memeories of riding log rafts in springtime down the flooded Tug to the Catlettsburg timber yards. While his wild brother Johnse had manned the rudder to thrust their raft into the fastest rapids, Cap had poled frantically to avoid banks, boulders, and shoals. He'd always looked after his crazy brother. Where was Johnse and who was looking after him now?

Two young men jumped from the deck to a wharf, then tied the steamboat to large mooring posts. Cap waited in the shadow of the bridge as the cargo was being unloaded and deck hands rolled large barrels down planks stretched over the water to a muddy landing area. There were no fancy wharves here.

On the way up the Ohio from Paducah, he'd avoided the other passengers, even though they were all strangers. Dressed in a suit, shirt and hard shoes, and clean shaven, he could only be recognized by someone who knew him well. But he tried not to let anyone get a good look at him anyway. Once he stepped off this boat into Catlettsburg things would change. He was bound to run into people who'd recognize him.

Adding to his nervousness was the fact that he had no pistol. As far as he knew, Dabney still had it. With barely enough time to throw his clothes into a couple of duffle bags, his law books into a box, and to tie the cardboard box holding his rifle with strong yellow cord, he'd rushed off without speaking to anyone at law school or even Mrs. Chapman. He'd put a note under the office door of each of his professors and on Mrs. Chapman's sewing cabinet, explaining he must go home to help his family through an emergency, but that he'd be back to finish his schooling. That's when he'd get his gun back. Meanwhile, he'd have to find someone who'd loan or sell him one.

When the last of the male passengers had helped his long-skirted lady pick her way over the planks laid across the mud, Cap stepped from the shadows and motioned to one of the teenaged boys who hung around the docks looking to make a little money.

"Give you two bits if you help me get my gear over to Sutphen's mill." Cap pointed to the two duffles holding his clothes.

The boy grinned and tipped his cap, probably pleased to get so much money. With a box of books hanging from a strap over Cap's shoulders, the rifle box in his hands, and the boy lugging the duffles, they made their way through muddy streets past warehouses, furniture factories, iron works, and fenced-in heaps of coal. Cap's heart beat faster at seeing again the town where he and Pappy and Johnse and Uncle Jim had sold timber and bought supplies so many times.

When they arrived at the huge weatherworn, unpainted Sutphen Mill and Lumber Yard building, Cap paid the boy, then poked his nose inside and scouted out the cavernous interior. Just about anyone with timber to sell might be here. Light from a single kerosene lantern struggled through a dense haze of sawdust to illuminate crates, cane bottom chairs, file cabinets, and a large wooden table piled with drawings. Under the same roof, screeching bandsaws were ripping into wood and planks were zinging off the saws and crashing to the floor. Workmen were shouting to overcome the racket. The pungent smell of newly cut wood filled the air. Cap sneezed as sawdust got up his nose.

Through the haze, Cap managed to locate Phineas Sutphen hunched over a desk in one corner. Keeping a wary eye out for other men, he lugged his duffels and boxes over to where Sutphen was working, his long, bony fingers gliding over a page of the ledger he was writing in. The mill owner peered over the spectacles on the end of his nose and stared up at Cap. His mouth flew open.

"Why, if it aint Cap Hatfield," he began.

Cap stopped him with a finger to his lips. It was unlikely anyone had overheard his name, but taking an unnecessary chance could be fatal.

"What brings you here?" Sutphen lowered his voice until Cap could hardly hear him over the mill racket. "I aint seen you for over a year."

"Been away awhile. You appear to be mighty busy, Phineas. Doin well, are you?"

"Fair to middlin. But this aint nothin compared to the business I'll have if they build that railroad through here."

"A railroad!"

"If they ever start the danged thing, I'll be makin crossties."

"What are they waitin for?" Cap was afraid he knew the reason.

"They aint decided what to do about them posses and bounty hunters roamin around the Tug shootin at folks. I hear they're hirin guards for the surveyors."

Cap appreciated Phineas's tact in not mentioning his family's part in the violence. "Any of my family been down here lately?"

Sutphen took Cap's elbow and led him outside to where a man sat smoking a corncob pipe, then went back inside. When the man turned to face Cap, gray eyes like Pappy's looked up over a hooked nose a lot like Pappy's.

"Uncle Elias!"

Elias startled, then jumped to his feet and, grabbing Cap's hand with both of his, shook it hard. "Mighty good to see you back, Cap."

"I thought somebody'd be bringin in our timber about now."

"They was the most pitiful small bunch of logs you ever seen." Elias sighed. "Your Pappy and me'll be lucky to clear five hundred dollars. Gettin em here weren't no pleasure neither. We floated em out at night, no lanterns, no moon, nothin. Ran into all kinds of boulders and little islands. Had men on horseback ridin on our side of the river to help with any that run aground. Even so, we lost a few at the ford near the old fort. We just left em and kept goin. Sutphen's upset—he's always counted on us for plenty of top grade oak and poplar."

Cap shook his head. "Times are hard and they're gettin worse."

"You know what your Pappy wants to do? He wants to raid the Pikeville jail and get our men out."

"Nancy wrote me about it. That's a bad idea."

Elias touched Cap's suit coat and eyed his now muddied store-bought shoes. "Law school do you any good?"

"I think I can take care of us in court on even terms with Nighbert and Judge Harvey now."

"That's good to hear!" Uncle Elias grinned his approval. "Hope you can talk some sense into your Pappy."

"He'd cut both his ears off before he'd listen to me."

"Hey, I got somethin to show you. Look over there. What do you see?" Cap looked where Elias was pointing, between two huge stacks of lumber, to a wooden building with a fresh coat of yellowish brown paint, four large windows, and a fancy sign in black and gold letters that read "Norfolk and Western Railroad." A slightly stooped, bearded man in a frock coat and stove-pipe hat was pacing up and down before two men in dark suits and derby hats. The man pacing was alternating between gesturing wildly and clasping his hands behind his back, all the while talking a blue streak.

"If I didn't know better, I'd swear that was Abe Lincoln over there," Cap said.

Elias chuckled. "That's Perry Cline. My guess is he's tryin to talk them railroad fellers into buildin their railroad on his side of the river."

"Perry Cline! I never would have believed it." Cap had only glimpsed Cline a few times several years ago. "Why in tarnation would he want to play like he's Lincoln?"

"It's Cline, all right. Phineas told me and everybody that works around here knows it. Seems them fellers standin over there come all the way from London, England, with money to build a railroad. Folks say they're hog rich and great admirers of Lincoln. Cline wants them to think he's a big Republican politician, too."

"They must be gettin a big laugh out of Abraham Cline." Cap started to laugh, then stopped. "I could shoot that son of a bitch from here."

"We don't need no more trouble of that sort."

"Don't worry. I'm peaceful as a kitten." This would not be a good time to ask Uncle Elias to loan him a pistol. "But if some feller was to strike Cline dead, I wouldn't hold it against him."

"I'm takin home a wagonload of supplies," Elias said. "I'm hirin a boy to drive it so you and me can ride in the back and keep out of sight."

"Thanks." Cap was grateful, but furious that he was back to hiding, worrying about being kidnapped or shot, while Cline was running about Catlettsburg openly and freely.

A thought cut cleanly through his rage. A man dressed like an imitation Lincoln had to have a serious weakness.

Chapter 39

The minute Cap heard the clatter of the horse's hooves on the drawbridge, he shoved aside the tarp he'd hidden under during the ride from Catlettsburg. He waited until they stopped to stand up, then staggered, stiff-kneed and giddy from lying in the bottom of the wagon for most of three days, riding over narrow roads, creek beds, and rock piles never meant for a horse and wagon. The only comfortable part of the ride had been over the streets of Logan where Uncle Elias had gotten out and gone home while he'd stayed hidden, not for fear of being shot at, but because he didn't want word to get out that he wasn't out west with Johnse.

The first person he saw as he stood up was Pappy. Such a broad grin spread over Pappy's face that Cap felt like leaping off the wagon into his arms as he had many times as a little boy.

"Got a few things in the back for you," the driver called out to Pappy.

Cap knew these "few things" intimately by now—bags of flour, sugar, coffee and apples, rifles and ammunition. When he'd asked Uncle Elias why he was helping Pappy arm, he'd replied he was dead set against the raid, but wanted it to go well if Pappy decided to go through with it.

Pappy nodded to the driver and told a couple of men to unload the wagon. Then he yanked on Cap's sleeve. "Get down from there, son. I'm sure glad to see you. Come surprise your Mama."

Realizing how wobbly he was, Cap leaned on Pappy's shoulder with one hand and put his other in Pappy's to steady himself and to ease his way down. As he touched Pappy's rough, warm hand and strong shoulder, Cap turned his face aside, embarrassed that tears had filled his eyes.

At the cabin door Cap called out to Mama, then asked where Nancy and their children were.

"At your place," Pappy said. "Probably readin. Nancy's bound and determined her and Joey's gonna read every book you brung her from George Floyd's."

Cap grinned. "Good for her! Pretty soon Coleman'll be readin, too. Those boys'll be like John Floyd, growin up with books, goin off to college."

"You aint changed a bit." Pappy shook his head sorrowfully.

Cap didn't say, "Neither have you," but it was on the tip of his tongue.

"Thought I heard Cappie's voice." Mama stepped through the cabin door. Beautiful little Mama, with her blue calico frock and white apron, her graying hair held by a comb in a neat bun at the back of her head, her brown eyes welcoming him. Under the collar of her frock, she wore the gold breast pin Pappy had given her years ago. "I'm gonna wear this pin every day of the rest of my life," she'd declared.

She reached up and gave him a big hug and Cap hugged back. Mama was both strong and soft. "Not a day went by in Tennessee I didn't think of you, Mama."

Mama wiped her eyes with a corner of her apron and looked him over. "Well, I guess you're still my Cappie. With your hair combed slick back and your mustache gone. Kind of pale lookin, but you're a sight for these sore eyes."

"You should have seen me a couple days ago, all dandied up in my suit and white shirt and store-bought shoes." Before getting into the wagon, he'd changed to blue jeans, jacket, and mountain boots, hoping he hadn't already ruined his hard shoes and pants in Catlettsburg mud.

"Prodigal son come home," Pappy said.

"Captain Anderson! That aint no way to speak of Cappie. He's been a good son, and he's gonna be a good lawyer."

"He's got more important things to do."

Mama's happy face faded, and she began twisting the corner of her apron.

"Anse, why don't you get some pork chops out of the smoke house. I'll fix Cappie a good meal." Mama gave Cap another, longer hug and went inside. Cap wondered if that hug was meant to carry a message, like a warning, she didn't want to say in front of Pappy.

The message he heard loud and clear was about pork chops. Since leaving Catlettsburg, he hadn't eaten anything but stale biscuits and a few apples. Uncle Elias hadn't wanted to shoot any game they'd come across for fear of attracting attention from bounty hunters.

"I need to talk to you." Pappy took his rifle and motioned to Cap up a path along the creek.

Cap wanted to go see Nancy and the boys right away, but he was obliged to stay for Mama's dinner. And with the afternoon sun warming his back and a feather bed of rain clouds floating over the mountaintops, he could almost forget why he'd come home. Redbud trees and white service berry flowers peeked out from among the trees. Dogwood blossoms winked at him. Cardinals and robins were singing. Nothing in Knoxville had pleased him like the beauty of these mountains.

He followed Pappy into the woods, walking beside a feeder creek until they came to a place where water splashed and sprayed from far above over the steep rock-strewn mountainside to a quiet pool at their feet.

Cap took off his blue jeans and shirt to splash water over himself and scrub his skin. He hadn't washed in over a week. "Good place for a dam and sawmill," he said through chattering teeth. The creek water was cold. He missed Mrs. Chapman's bathtub with its hot and cold running water.

Pappy frowned. "No need of a dam or mill when you aint got no logs."

"We got to change all that."

"First order of business is gettin our men out of the Pikeville jail."

"Cline and Phillips must have it guarded pretty tight." Cap fought to keep his voice down and not shout his objections at Pappy. Having nothing to dry with, he shook himself off like a dog.

"They got no more'n twenty men at one time at the jail and usually a lot less."

"We're apt to lose some lives if we try to break our men out of jail, Pappy. I'm wearied of death. I always think of Uncle Ellison and Uncle Jim and Bill Dempsey." And all the dead children of Randall and Sally McCoy.

"We'll pick our time so's not to run into too many guards. But we got to bust our men out. The Pikeville court's liable to hang em if somebody don't get up a lynchin party first."

"Maybe there's another way of savin em." Cap hadn't thought about lynching, but that could happen if the townspeople over there were whipped up enough. Beese had said it wouldn't be enough to change Pappy's mind, he'd have to change the way things were done all around him.

Pappy's nose hooked down sharply. He patted his rifle. "This is the only savior that's any good."

"I chanced to see Perry Cline in Catlettsburg. All dressed up like Abraham Lincoln."

Pappy chuckled. "I hear he takes a picture of Lincoln to the barber's so he can get his hair and beard cut the same way. He's makin a dang fool of hisself."

"Cap! Pappy!" Nancy Belle was calling them.

Cap pulled on his shirt and blue jeans.

As soon as he sat down at the table, the children were all over him. Four-year-old Rosie climbed onto his lap and made a triumphant face at her six-year-old brother Joe who sat next to Cap. Troy squeezed in on Cap's other side between him and Elias. Only little Willis, using chairs to hang onto while he walked, eyed Cap suspiciously.

"He doesn't remember me," Cap said. "He was just six months old when I went away." With a pang he realized Coleman probably wouldn't know him either.

When Nancy Belle brought a bowl of corn pone to the table, Cap noticed her faded calico dress and the worn mocassins on her feet, as he'd never noticed them before. Knoxville women had money and access to stores and seamstresses, dressed fashionably in clothes, either new or in perfect repair, and would have thought Hatfield women looked like paupers.

"I'll give you some of this, Cap," Nancy Belle taunted him. "But first you have to promise to tell us everything you done and everywhere you been."

"If you don't set that grub down, I'm gonna die of hunger. Then I won't be able to tell you anything."

Nancy Belle set the bowl before him. Everyone watched as Cap sniffed deeply, enjoying the aromas of pork chops, corn pone, and hot biscuits with gravy. Mrs. Chapman's food had filled his stomach, but had never smelled this good.

"Now take hold and eat." Thirteen-year-old Elizabeth sounded a lot like Mama. "I don't know about you, but we aint had nothin but grits and shucky beans for almost a week."

Grits and beans. Because no one dared go out and hunt for meat. And they hadn't had time for a potato or root crop last summer when they'd been busy moving, so there were no potatoes or turnips. Cap looked around the table.

"Bobby Lee and Johnse still out West?"

Pappy nodded. "We got a letter from Canada. Some feller writ it for em. They're on a timber crew near a place called Vancouver."

Cap had never heard of Vancouver. He started on his second pork chop. Nothing tasted as good as pork chops from pigs fed on acorns from the oaks around home.

"Tell us about Tennessee, Cappie." Mama's eyes were full of love and admiration.

"It's hard for you to imagine what Knoxville is like till you've been there." Cap waved his fork with a piece of meat waggling on it. Rosie shrieked, giggled, and tried to grab it, but Cap popped it into his mouth before she could, then cut her a little piece. He laughed as he played with his curly-headed baby sister, the cutest little girl he'd ever seen. "All the streets are paved with cobblestones or brick, smooth as the glass in your winders, Mama. And the houses! I wish you could see the bathroom in my boarding house. There's a bathtub with little black feet on the floor. You turn on the faucets and hot and cold water comes gushin straight into the tub. You don't have to fetch it or heat it at all."

"Feet!" Nancy Belle shrieked. "Does that bathtub run around on them feet?"

"All around the bathroom and up and down the stairs." Cap laughed.

"Bathtubs aint alive like us," Elliot sneered. "They can't run nowhere. You're makin that up."

"Oh, come on, Elliot," Nancy Belle shouted. "Let Cap tell it his way. It's his story."

"He should tell it right," Elliot huffed. "Or not tell it at all."

"Oh, shut up, Elliot," Nancy Belle said.

"Shut up, Elliot," little Rosie and Joe echoed.

"There's one thing you'd like about Knoxville, Mama." Cap buttered a biscuit for Rosie and gave it to her. "And it's for certain true." He pretended to glare at Elliot. "Nobody in Knoxville carries a gun except the sheriff and his deputies. You never have to worry about who's behind you. You never have to be thinkin about what an argument's comin to, gettin ready to reach for your pistol. From September to March, I never saw, never even heard of one man shootin another."

"Oh, Cappie, that sounds like heaven!" Mama exclaimed.

Pappy scowled. "How's a man gonna look after hisself and his family without no gun?"

"No one needs a gun in Knoxville. It's peaceful."

"I want to go to Knoxville," Joe said. "And live in a house with a bathtub that's got little black feet."

"I want to go to Knoxville and go to the university where the law school is," Elliot said. "Doc Rutherford and George Floyd say I'm smart and I ought to go to college."

Cap was so jealous he almost choked on his biscuit. At Elliot's age, nobody had ever loaned him books to read and told him he was smart and ought to go to college. He wished he could live his life over.

"Look what you started, Levicy," Pappy said. "Our children's wantin to leave their fine home here for Tennessee that's full of nothin but strangers."

"I don't want to move to Knoxville, and I don't believe any of us really do." Cap looked around the table. No one contradicted him. "We'd never be happy anywhere else. We wouldn't have a business like timber to build on anywhere else. We have to stay and we have to learn new ways, make a place for ourselves in 1889."

"New ways?" Pappy snorted. "You forgettin you're a hunted man? Half of Logan'd be glad to see you hauled away to jail and half of Kentucky's over here tryin to do that very thing."

"Anse, give Cap a chance," Mama said.

"Listen to Cap for a change," Nancy Belle said.

After dinner, Mama and the girls took the pots and pans and dishes to the washing shed, and the children ran outside, leaving Pappy and Cap at the table.

"So far, I got sixteen men lined up to ride to Pikeville with us." Pappy lit his pipe. "You and me makes eighteen."

Cap shook his head. "You try breakin into that jail and you'll most likely get some of our men killed or hurt. And then what? Suppose we got all nine out and brought em back here. Kentucky'd double the rewards, and everybody in Logan would be after Wilson to send the militia after us."

"Now listen!" Pappy smacked his open hand on the table. "We aint got much time to get in and get out before anybody starts talkin about lynchin and before Wilson's out of office. He'll look after us long as he's the governor, but the recount can't last forever and Fleming might get in."

"What're you talkin about? What recount? Who's Fleming?"

"Fleming run against Wilson in November. Floyd done what he could for Wilson, but the way things are I couldn't help much. And there's northerners in this state wantin Fleming in. The vote was so close they're havin a recount."

"How long'll that take?"

"Long as Floyd and his friends can drag it out." Pappy grinned, his eyes twinkling in the glow of his pipe. "Some of them ballot papers got theirselves lost, some's goin real slow over them bad roads to Charleston. Floyd got Judge Jackson in Charleston to say some of em aint legal."

"How'd he do that? Those northern Republicans got Jackson in their pocket. Heck, they send him a whole carload of coal every year."

"You know, Jackson aint fussy. The Republicans give him coal, Floyd finds him some cash, I slip him some whiskey—it all pleasures him."

Cap was glad the law school faculty wasn't hearing this. "If we lose Wilson, Floyd'll go out with him. Then we'll have no more influence in Charleston. But invadin Pikeville's not the answer to our problems."

"We aint gonna let them men die!" Pappy shouted. "Wall's still my brother, even if he is actin plum crazy. My nieces is cryin their hearts out for their husbands Luke and Andy. Selkirk McCoy stuck by us, fought for us, worked on my loggin crew. Sam, Plyant, and Doc is all family, too. I aint about to let any of em die."

Cap noticed Pappy hadn't mentioned Cotton Top. "I don't propose we let em hang either. I'm thinkin of persuadin a few big investors to put some pressure on Kentucky's governor and on Cline and Phillips."

"Now how you gonna do that! You're just gonna waste time. We got to ride to Pikeville before it's too late."

"Suppose investors from the Norfolk and Western Railroad were to think we were doin our best to settle these troubles peacefully and that Cline and Phillips are the ones stirrin up trouble."

Pappy frowned. "You got things wrong end to. Them railroad fellers think we're the problem, and Cline and Phillips is what's needed to fix us."

"Suppose I write a letter to Governor Buckner sayin I'm ready to surrender if that'd bring peace? Suppose I write the newspapers and say we're through with makin war? Let em print a peace proposal from us instead of all those lies Cline gets printed about us?"

"What if you was a bird, then you could fly?" Pappy sneered. "Besides you aint gonna surrender."

Cap grit his teeth at hearing one of Pappy's old what ifs. "I might talk for awhile like I was gonna give myself up." He gave Pappy time to consider the idea. "And I could fetch some of those newspapers—the ones that wrote about Cline buyin rifles and ammo for Phillips and the McCoys to go after us—to Catlettsburg and show em to those railroad men from England. Show em the trouble old Abe Cline is stirrin up."

Pappy pulled on his beard. "You aint tryin to say any of this is gonna make the Pikeville jailer open his doors and let our men go? You aint sayin that, are you, Cap?"

"Not right away, I suppose."

"Then there's nothin more to talk about. You can go after givin Cline a black eye if you've a mind to. But it won't open them jail doors. We're gonna go get our men soon's we can."

Cap felt like giving up. It was as useless to argue with Pappy as it always had been. But he wasn't going on a stupid raid no matter what Pappy said.

Chapter 40

Carrying his Winchester and the only duffle bag he could manage along with the sacks of flour and apples Mama had insisted he take home with him, Cap hurried through the woods to Nancy. He had a lot to say to her about school and Pappy's pig-headed attitude toward the raid. But those weren't the first things she'd want to hear. He felt uncomfortable thinking about the things they used to say to each other—he hadn't seen her in more than eight months.

She'd always thought him handsome. What would she think of him now, with his mustache shaved off, his hair combed back with no part? Had he gotten soft from sitting, reading, studying all the time? He flexed his arm muscles. Weak. He'd have to start cutting and hauling timber again.

About halfway home, he heard hoofbeats. To be safe, he ducked into the woods until Nancy came into view holding onto a little boy riding in front of her, with Joey trailing behind on his mule.

Coleman! This wasn't a chubby baby propped in a wad of blankets. This was a boy with a firm chin, his little legs sticking out over the horse's back, looking around and noticing things. Their baby had become a person while he was gone.

"Nancy," Cap said softly.

She was wearing a pale blue calico dress with blue flowers and a blue bonnet. She'd always looked to Cap for a smile when she dressed in blue. He smiled now. But as they came closer, he began to see all was not well with Nancy. Her face was thin and her once thick, wavy hair hung limply.

"Nancy!" He shouted this time. "Coleman! Joey!"

Nancy reined in her horse and Joey stopped his mule. Coleman stared at Cap, startled.

"Cap!" Nancy's smile was as big and bright as the sun that shone through the treetops.

Cap strode over and lifted Coleman down from Nancy's arms. "How's my big boy?" He searched his son's face for a sign of recognition. Coleman squirmed sideways and tried to dive for the ground.

"Down!" he shrieked. "Get down!"

"He's as hard to hold onto as a wild pig!" Cap yelled.

Nancy jumped down from her horse and grabbed Coleman. "Here." She sat on a mat of dry leaves with her son and patted the ground for Cap to sit with them. When he was beside her, hugging her close, he felt that her body had grown thin.

Joey scrambled off the mule and pushed his way into Cap's arms beside Nancy, hugging him around the neck and giggling. Cap grasped the skinny young body in his arms, and the smooth young cheek pressed to his. Such a little boy! Joey needed a father to watch over him.

"Let's look at you." Cap held Joey at arm's length. "You're a fine lookin young feller." He winked at Nancy.

"I'm glad you're back, Cap," she said.

Cap winced inwardly. She sounded like she was talking to someone she hadn't seen in a long time and no longer knew well. "Pappy said you been readin old man Floyd's books."

"Yes." She nodded. "What do you think of your son?" She set the boy on his feet beside Cap. He held out his hands, but Coleman toddled past him to touch the barrel of the Winchester.

Cap grabbed the rifle and put it beyond Coleman's reach, leaning it against a tree. "I don't want a rifle to be his first memory of me." He sat again, holding his knees with his hands. "Haven't been home a day and already I been havin a hard time with Pappy."

"You're very young to be takin on a ferocious man like him."

He smiled as he caught onto her game. "You don't think I can do it."

She raised her chin and looked at him in mock seriousness. "I didn't say that."

"Everybody tells me that. They tell me no one can go up against Pappy and live to tell about it."

She laughed. "Well, I'm not everybody." She caressed his face with her cool, gentle hand. "And you're not everybody." She slowly traced his upper lip with her finger.

"Do you like me without my mustache?"

"Let's see how it feels." She leaned over and gave him a long, lingering kiss.

Cap was beginning to feel the kiss all over his body when Coleman squirmed his way between them and held onto his mother. He put his head down next to Coleman's and nuzzled an ear, making the boy squeal.

"Come on, let's go home," he said.

The next morning Cap hummed to himself as he shaved, leaving untouched the beginnings of a mustache and beard. Nancy winked at him from across the kitchen where she was fixing eggs, ham, red-eye gravy, and biscuits made with the flour he'd brought.

"Nine months from now." Cap half sang the words. They were both sure they'd have another child in nine months. "How'd you like to have a little sister, Joey?"

"A sister'd be okay." Joey was working on a pile of alphabet blocks at one end of the table, trying to get Coleman to put one block squarely on top of another. "It's a fort. You have to make the walls straight, Coleman."

A fort! Cap felt a mixture of pride and annoyance. Joey had built a fort like Cap had built up on the ridge, the Hatfield war ethos passing to the new generation. One more aspect of family life Cap must change.

Coleman set a block very carefully on top of Joey's neat wall.

"He's a fast learner," Cap said. "Let's try something." He picked up a block with an "A" on it.

He pointed to the letter. "A," he said to Coleman.

"A," repeated Coleman.

"Good boy." Cap grinned and looked at Nancy. He hadn't known what an "A" was until he was nineteen years old.

"A! A! A!" Coleman shrieked, and Cap laughed aloud.

Leaning over to lift heavy skillets from the fire, Nancy grunted with the effort and brought breakfast to the table. Cap decided right then to find a way to get a stove like Mrs. Chapman's up to Main Island Creek for her. Nancy was so thin and pale from trying, with the off and on help of a couple of Pappy's men, to care for the horses, a few cows, chickens and pigs, not to mention Coleman and Joey, that he had to do everything he could to help her. And she needed better food for herself and the boys. There was little in the way of ham, bacon, or pork chops in the smokehouse, no venison or bear meat and nothing in the root cellar. Like Pappy's family, they were mainly living on grits, shucky beans, eggs, milk, and butter.

"I wish I could be there and see his face when you tell him," Nancy said.

Joey looked up. "Tell who what? What's goin on?"

"Your Papa's goin over to Grandpa Anse's," Nancy said. "To talk about makin some money. Wouldn't that be nice?"

Last night they'd agreed Cap should let the railroad company know what the Hatfields had to offer in the way of timber and a sawmill for making railroad ties. He hoped to bring John Floyd along to Catlettsburg to help persuade the railroad men to deal with him. But first he'd have to get Pappy's approval.

After breakfast, Nancy brought him more coffee, and he sat down to write letters to the governor of Kentucky and West Virginia newspapers—the *Wayne County News, Charleston Gazette,* and *Wheeling Intelligencer.* And Kentucky's *Louisville Courier.* He worked for over an hour on the first letter until every word said what he wanted.

Editor, Wayne News:

I ask space in your valuable paper for these few lines. I wish to declare a general amnesty in the Hatfield and McCoy feud. I do not wish to keep the feud alive and I suppose that everybody, like myself, is tired of the names of Hatfield and McCoy and the Border Warfare. The war spirit in me has now abated, and I sincerely rejoice at the prospect of peace. We have devoted our lives to arms. We have all undergone a fearful loss of lives and valuable property in the struggle. We being not the only transgressors, now I propose to rest in a spirit of peace.

Yours respectfully,
CAP HATFIELD

Then he began another to the governor of Kentucky. "His Honor Governor Simon Bolivar Buckner: My life is no satisfaction without peace. . ." he wrote.

He closed the letter with an offer to surrender to the Kentucky authorities if such an act would bring peace to the West Virginia-Kentucky border area. When she saw them, Nancy wanted to rip the letters up, until he managed to convince her he'd never actually surrender.

When Cap went to Pappy's, looking for approval of his plan, Pappy insisted that the two of them talk while working on Mama's new battling trough. She'd had to leave the old one behind when they'd moved and was tired of making do with big rocks and logs down by the creek. They split a poplar log about eight feet long and turned it flat side up. Next came the hard part, hollowing out one end. The job was tedious, back-breaking work. It would take hours to gouge out a trough four feet long and nearly two feet deep where Mama and the girls could soap and rinse and rub the clothes. The other half of the log they'd leave flat for beating dirt out with a battler.

They both started out hacking with adzes, Pappy in one spot and Cap at another.

"Got to cut a lot more timber this year," Pappy grunted as he tugged at a kindling-sized splinter of wood he'd gouged loose. "Good thing we got all that cash from Sergeant because what we sent down to Catlettsburg this spring weren't enough to keep us in guns and grub, let alone pay our taxes and loggin expenses."

Cap hacked half-heartedly at what must have been the hardest piece of wood in West Virginia. "Norfolk and Western's got a building in Catlettsburg. They're gettin ready to build a railroad."

Pappy kept working as he eyed Cap rubbing his back. "Look at you. Young man like you and you can't keep up with your old Pappy."

Cap felt ashamed of his performance. It was just like Pappy to pit himself against Cap in a contest Cap had no chance of winning. But Cap wasn't going to get sidetracked. "There's a lot of money to be made from the railroads."

Pappy stood and chopped savagely at the small bowl-shaped hole he'd made. "Not for us!"

Cap tried to put more energy into working his end, where he'd made only a few scratches and gouges. "Why do you say that?"

"We aint got nothin down by the Tug no more and that's where the railroad's goin."

"We got a lot of timber." Cap stood and stretched, trying to loosen his cramped shoulder muscles. "You know how they make a railroad? They smooth out the ground like they're gonna build a road. Then they lay out timbers across the roadway, one after another, about a foot apart—crossties, they call em. Then they lay the track on top of the crossties and nail it down. All we need is a chance to timber, make it into crossties and get em to where they'll be layin em, and we got ourselves a lot of business. Sutphen's gonna supply the crossties down by Catlettsburg, but there's no one up along the Tug with a sawmill."

Pappy laid down his adze and stared at Cap. "That's kind of interestin, son."

"We can build a mill, fetch our own timber to it, cut crossties and sell em to Norfolk and Western to use all the way up the Tug, maybe all the way into Virginia. That'd be a lot of crossties."

"Sounds like a smart idea. But how we gonna build a mill and make crossties when I got to use men to guard our crews and watch for the enemy every day? Soon as somebody spots a stranger close by, we gotta hole up at our cabin or the fort. Most days we end up getting' no work a-tall done."

Cap jabbed his adze into the wood. How could Pappy do more work at fifty than he could at twenty-five? He'd have to try harder. "I want to go down to Catlettsburg and work a deal with the railroad just like Sutphen did. All we need to do to solve our problem is persuade them to tell Cline and Buckner to cancel the rewards, call off the posses, and stop buyin rifles for Phillips and the McCoys." He shoved his adze under a big splinter and tried with all his might to break it out, with no luck.

Pappy scowled. "You aint got much chance of doin that. And I don't want you gettin in my way. When the time comes, I'll need all the men I can get to bust open the Pikeville jail."

Exhausted, Cap hacked more slowly. "We'd have to get the mill up and runnin real soon, maybe this summer." He intended to write a dam and mill permit and get the help of downstream neighbors, the way Beese had suggested. "When's the trial?"

"August."

Cap was relieved. "It's only April. We got lots of time."

"That blasted Randall's tryin to get up a lynchin party. And Phillips wants to join in on the fun."

"Nobody's gonna listen to Randall."

"Could be you're right." Pappy kept right on chopping, his hole a foot deep now. "Phillips is busy tryin to catch more of us and you say Cline's busy tryin to work a deal with the railroad fellers. But I aint bettin my men's lives on any of that."

"Why not get started on the dam? What's it gonna hurt? I'm bettin the Norfolk and Western fellers can take care of Cline and Phillips."

"I aint countin on no railroad men I don't know nothin about. We're goin to Pikeville soon's we get the men and guns together—about the middle of May, I reckon."

"The middle of May!" Then he'd have little more than a month to fix things so Pappy would have to forget about raiding. "We've already had a fearful loss of men, and if you go over there we're apt to lose more. We could end up with no timber, no money, no land, nothin to eat but grits and shucky beans. Is that what you want?" And, of course, he'd never get to be a lawyer.

"I want them men out of that jail." Pappy's eyes bulged.

Cap stifled a curse. "You can't rule this part of the country with your men and your guns like when you came out of the War. Times are different. You got to learn that."

"I got to learn somethin from you?" Pappy hacked away as energetically as he had at the start, while Cap could barely lift his adze anymore.

Mama was watching them from the garden where she was planting flower seeds. Cap wished she'd come over and talk some sense into Pappy.

"Wait till I go to Catlettsburg and see if I can interest the railroad in a crosstie deal. Then we'll talk about Pikeville."

"You forgettin who's in charge of things around here, son?" Pappy glared at him. "I'm the head of this family. I am the Captain of my armies. You been to a fancy law school, but around here you aint nothin!"

He'd made a big mistake. Much as it would pain him to do it, he had to learn the fine distinction between making suggestions as Pappy's underling and giving orders like an officer.

"What I meant was, the sooner we get the dam and mill built, the sooner we can start makin money. Where do you think the mill should go?"

"We aint gonna build no mill."

Cap's mouth went dry. "Maybe there's no call to start on it until we got a deal with the railroad. I'll go to Catlettsburg real quick and see what I can do. They'll be needin those crossties by the end of summer. We'll have to order a band saw pretty quick."

"Catlettsburg." Pappy stared into the hole he'd made in the battling trough. "Down there you're liable to run into some folks that'll take a shot at you, might even try to kidnap you for Judas money."

"I'm gonna disguise myself. All those newspapers have been writin that Hatfields are illiterate and antireligion. So I'm gonna go as a fat preacher, with a beard on my face and a Bible in my pocket."

"You, a preacher?" Pappy let out a big hee-haw, loud as a mule.

"Whole thing won't take me much more'n a week. Couple days to get there, a few days to make the deal, a couple days to get back."

"Well, preacher, I want you to buy some rifles and cartridges while you're there. And some dynamite. Enough to blow a big hole in the side of that jail."

Cap jabbed his adze into the trough. Now he had one more problem to deal with.

Chapter 41

Two days later Cap met John Floyd in Logan, ready to ride with him to Catlettsburg. Floyd doubled over laughing at Cap in a black suit and black brimmed hat, the short beginnings of a beard, rags stuffed under his shirt and pants to make a fat belly, and a Bible protruding from his suit jacket pocket.

"You ride behind me," he said. "I'm liable to fall off my horse laughing if I have to keep looking at you."

On the two-day trip to Catlettsburg they met only three men bound for Logan, none of whom took any special notice of them.

"Enemy territory," Cap muttered as they entered the Kentucky town. He hoped his disguise was good enough. He was bound to run into someone who knew him.

"No one will recognize you, believe me." Floyd didn't seem concerned. "All the same, let's get ourselves a room and get off the streets."

After a hot meal at the hotel, Cap went down the hall to a room with a bathtub and a flush toilet. He put the plug in the bottom of the tub, ran himself some nice warm water, and soaked in comfort. He missed Mrs. Chapman's bathroom.

Once dry, he put the entire disguise back on. Although he was going to the railroad office as a businessman, not a preacher, he felt he had to be extra cautious since lots of men who knew him came to Catlettsburg. He didn't expect those railroad men would be bothered by his outlandish getup. He wasn't half as peculiar looking as Abraham Lincoln Cline, and they were already talking to him.

Cap and Floyd exited their room into a dark, narrow hallway with creaking, uneven floor boards and went downstairs. As they were passing through the lobby, Cap noticed a bar, a few leather chairs, some wicker-bottoms, and plenty of spittoons. Nice and comfortable.

A whiny, nasal voice rose from one of the leather chairs facing away from them: "I'll be down here to check up on things every now and then. I'll want to know who's willing to sell land and who's buying and where."

Cap couldn't hear the reply, but he knew that irritating voice from somewhere. Putting his finger to his lips, he motioned Floyd to be quiet. They stood, listening.

"If you come up with information I can use, I'll pay you good money, Witten."

A shock went through Cap. "That's Nighbert's pal, Henry Ragland," he whispered.

"I know." Floyd whispered back.

"I want that land near Mate Creek," the voice went on. "So keep your ears open."

Muffled words came from the other man—excuses, they sounded like.

"And what about the gun shops? Anyone been buying large amounts of rifles, revolvers, ammunition? I want to know who's arming themselves."

"I been watchin," the answer came. "They aint nobody buyin nothin but a rifle or two."

Ragland's voice rose like the pitch of a band saw. "You haven't been partaking of alcoholic beverages, have you Witten?"

"'Course not."

"Ragland's dead set against whiskey," Floyd whispered in Cap's ear.

Cap pointed to a rear exit from the lobby. "Let's get out of here. Can't let him see me."

"We'll have to watch each time we go in and out of our hotel." Floyd spoke normally once they were outside. "And in the streets, too. Ragland would be delighted to point you out to a sheriff."

They walked briskly along boardwalks past the blind tigers where Cap and the boys on the logging crew used to have a drink or two. Cap thirsted for whiskey, but fought the impulse to go in. Nighbert and Ragland didn't like dealing with men who smelled of liquor and for all he knew, English businessmen shared that attitude.

"I'll watch my step," Cap said. "But listen, John, we got a big problem with Pappy. He's determined to bust our men out of Pikeville next month. He told me to buy rifles, cartridges, and dynamite to blow a hole in the jail while I'm here."

"My God! We've got to stop him!" For the first time Cap could remember, Floyd looked flustered. "That would ruin everything we're trying to do. And if you buy an appreciable amount of arms here, Ragland's cohort will know immediately."

"Pappy's dead set on a raid. He's afraid our men are gonna be hanged by the law or lynched by a mob, one or the other. I got to turn up with some way to see that nobody hangs."

Floyd threw his head back, nearly losing his brown hat with the little feather in its crown. "Cap, don't be a fool. Don't buy guns and cartridges. And, for heaven's sake, no dynamite!"

"Then help me think of somethin to tell Pappy."

They walked in silence towards the river, past stores and warehouses crowded with men buying and selling, until they arrived at Sutphen's mill. Cap located Phineas and introduced Floyd to him. Sutphen, once he'd gotten over the shock of Cap's disguise, didn't need much persuasion to leave the deafening noise of the sawmill and go to a local hash house where they could talk.

Floyd went inside first, looked around, then signaled them to enter. After they'd all ordered coffee and apple pie, Sutphen peered at Cap over his spectacles.

"Well."

"Cap has a business proposition for you," Floyd said. "He has an idea that will help you and his folks at the same time."

"Always did like doin business with the Hatfields." Sutphen picked up his coffee cup, his long agile fingers curving through the handle. "When your Pappy says he'll deliver timber at a price we've agreed on, he does it. Don't care what folks say. Anse Hatfield's an honest man."

Some day Cap wanted to hear somebody say they liked dealing with *him*, that he was an honest and capable man. He'd begun to crave a reputation for something other than a child killer.

"What I want to do, Phineas, is set up a sawmill to cut crossties like you do," Cap said. "Only up by the Tug. Right now no one has a mill up there."

"I see." Sutphen leaned back in his chair and stared out the window. "How far down the river you aimin to supply these crossties?"

"That's part of what we want to talk to you about. I'd like to work things out with you so's we're both comfortable."

"I can ship my ties up river by barge as far as the fork of the Tug and the Big Sandy," Sutphen said. "That's about it. Gets too shallow after that and the only alternative is to use wagons, a lot of wagons."

"How about if you take the Big Sandy all the way to the Tug, and Pappy and I'll take things from there?"

That amounted to seventy-five or eighty miles of crossties for the Hatfields. Cap held his breath.

"Have you talked to the Norfolk and Western people?"

"No. I wanted to talk to you first, Phineas."

Sutphen sipped on his coffee. "They realize I'd have a hard time gettin my ties all the way upriver. They been talkin to Kanawha Lumber and Cole and Crane Timber about the rest."

Of course! A big outfit like Norfolk and Western wouldn't wait until the last minute to figure out where their crossties would come from. Cap's mind reeled as he tried to think how he'd get around the big timber companies.

"They haven't closed a deal yet, have they?"

"Not that I know of. It'll take at least three months to get track laid as far up the Big Sandy as I can go and we aint started. They still got time."

"You're already doing business with them," Floyd said. "Would you put in a good word for Cap? They know your reputation and would value your opinion."

Sutphen laid his fork down. "You're wanted for murder in this state, Cap. And the way things are, with bounty hunters after you Hatfields, Frank Phillips roamin the mountains lookin for trouble, and all them shootins goin on, a lot of investors don't even want to set foot in West Virginia, let alone have anything to do with your family. They want to stay clear of trouble like yours."

"I'm through makin war. And so's Pappy. We've lost too many men and too much property."

From his brief case, Floyd drew out a copy of the letter to Governor Buckner where Cap had offered to surrender and the one to the newspapers where Cap had proposed peace. He laid them in front of Sutphen.

"You wouldn't surrender." Sutphen looked Cap in the eye.

"Don't think I'll have to. But I am through with feudin."

"We'll convince Norfolk and Western they can work unmolested," Floyd said. "Leave that to me."

"I'd like to have you help me set up the sawmill, Phineas," Cap said. "I need your advice, and I'd be happy to pay you well. How's two percent of our take sound?"

Sutphen slapped his thigh. "Deal! Let's go over to Norfolk and Western and see what we can do."

The Norfolk and Western building had been built in Kentucky and showed it—rough, painted plank walls and wooden floor with nail heads showing. But inside, the desks and chairs were large and made from richly dark wood. Waist-high bookcases were crammed with ledgers and catalogs. The tray of a large silver tea set covered the top of one bookcase.

After they'd met the Englishmen, Holmby and Byrnes, Floyd stood and began speaking.

"As Secretary of the State of West Virginia, I hope to soon welcome your railroad to our great state." Floyd waved his arm in a grand flourish. "Governor Wilson and I would be delighted to have you choose us for your historic enterprise, and I am proud to represent one of our finest citizens, Mr. William Hatfield, in his efforts to assist you."

"What firm's he with?" Holmby, a black-haired, smartly dressed Englishman, seemed to outrank the older Mr. Byrnes.

"His family's," Floyd answered.

"Our policy is to deal only with large firms. Isn't that so, Byrnes?" Holmby turned to his partner.

"Quite so." The tips of Byrnes's bushy gray mustache twitched as he rubbed his chin. "Established firms. As we're accustomed." He tilted his chair backwards, his belly stretching his vest and straining its buttons.

"The Hatfield firm is large enough, and certainly highly experienced." Floyd fairly purred his assurances. "Look at these." From his brief case, Floyd produced pictures Cap had brought to him from home that had been taken by a travelling photographer two years earlier. Floyd laid them on Holmby's desk. One showed a crew of twenty men standing near a pile of poplar logs ten men high. In another a team of oxen was dragging felled timber. A third showed men poling huge log rafts on the Tug.

Holmby leaned forward and closely studied them. "That's a great deal of timber."

"The Hatfields have been deliverin timber to me for years," Sutphen said. "Always been fair and reliable."

Cap felt that Floyd and Sutphen were his two best friends in the world.

"I'll be candid with you gentlemen," Holmby said after sniffing a pinch of snuff from a silver box on his desk. "We demand the lowest price, the highest quality timber, and a guaranteed speedy delivery. Price, quality, schedule. What can you offer us?"

Cap's heart skipped a beat. At least they were talking. "Let's take one thing at a time. I can get you any kind of timber you want—poplar, beech, ash, oak, maple. Price depends on your choice."

"Red oak and white oak. We've had our best luck with oak." Holmby pressed the fingers of his two hands together, matching their tips precisely.

Cap grinned. "I got a mountainside of oak up on Beech Creek. Bet I could turn out enough crossties to get your railroad from the Tug fork of the Big Sandy all the way to the East Coast."

"What evidence of your capabilities do you have beyond your personal assurance and these three photographs?" Holmby raised his eyebrows and looked at his partner.

Byrnes studied the pictures. "Even if the quality and quantity of the raw timber meets our standards, what of the crossties? Can you cut them to our specifications and deliver them when and where we need them?"

"We have a timber crew of about thirty men, a team of oxen, several mules, and all the cross-cut saws and axes we'd need. We've already picked a place to build a dam up on Beech Creek. That's where we'll put the sawmill and that's where we'll start the ties floatin down to the Tug."

"Then you don't actually have a mill in operation?" Holmby frowned.

"Not yet. But Mr. Sutphen here's going to help us set it up."

Sutphen nodded. "I've known Cap and his family for more'n twenty years. Be pleased to work with them settin up a mill. Soon as you give the word, I'll order a couple of band saws from a firm I do business with in Pittsburgh. Take about six weeks to get em to Cap's place."

Byrnes tipped his chair forward till it sat firmly on the floor again. "I say, Holmby. Neither Kanawha Lumber nor Cole and Crane Timber has either a sawmill or a dam to power it as yet. And you know how very slow and bureaucratic large companies can be."

"Quite." Holmby inhaled another pinch of snuff. "And they're the very dickens to pin down on cost and schedule. Here's what I suggest, Mr. Hatfield. Furnish us with a price and delivery schedule by the end of the first week in May, and your firm will be considered along with the others."

Cap struggled to keep a poker face. That was very close to when Pappy was planning to storm the Pikeville jail.

"I'll get you a price and schedule by tomorrow," Cap managed to say evenly.

"Tomorrow?" Holmby raised an eyebrow.

Cap leaned forward on Holmby's desk. "It looks like your railroad can start any day now with Mr. Sutphen's help. Then you'll need the first crossties from us three or four months later. Let's say by the first of August, the rest spread out over the coming year. If we start cutting trees now and have the mill up and running two months from now, you fellows can meet that schedule. But if we're going to do this, I need to order those band saws right away, then go home and start my crew working on the dam and mill."

"Kanawha Lumber says they can turn out crossties for the Tug regions six weeks after we give them the go-ahead," Holmby snapped.

Cap rolled his eyes and shook his head. "What they probably mean is they can't get started for at least six weeks. I bet they don't even know where their timber's going to come from or where they're going to put a mill."

"We will not be pressured." Holmby glowered at Cap. "We always deliberate carefully before making a decision. But you are welcome to proceed. Bring your price and schedule in tomorrow if you can. Let me caution, however, your numbers must be realistic and supported by evidence. We do not propose to buy a pig in a poke, as you people call it."

Cap grinned. "Agreed. Now let's talk particulars." He reached for a pen and a pad of legal-size paper Floyd had laid on the desk. "Red oak and white. Does it matter which? Any beech or poplar?"

Holmby leaned forward. "Oak only. No matter, red or white."

Cap was very glad he could write. Imagine if he'd had to ask Floyd or Sutphen to write for him. "The ties. How many? How long? What cross section?"

Chapter 42

Bleary-eyed, Cap faced the equally bleary-eyed Floyd and Sutphen. After spending all night at this table in Sutphen's favorite hash house, which had catered to him by staying open, they'd pulled together costs and schedules to present to Byrnes and Holmby.

They'd gone over Sutphen's records, figuring the time and labor needed to cut four hundred thousand crossties. They'd searched sawmill equipment catalogs for prices. Cap had reckoned the timber crew's pay and the cost of food and supplies. Carefully and methodically, they checked their numbers one last time, then gathered up the papers and headed outside. Although they'd not slept, they were wide awake.

Floyd breathed deeply of the cool, crisp morning air. Cap, watching him flex his fingers, could almost see him flexing his mind. Getting the Englishmen to go along with everything wasn't going to be easy, but the harder the challenge, the more Floyd had always enjoyed his part.

When they reached the Norfolk and Western office, Holmby and Byrnes said they were pleased and somewhat surprised to see them. A small fire in a grate scarcely warmed the chilly riverfront office.

"Would you gentlemen care for tea?" Byrnes asked when everyone was seated. "This beastly river climate reminds me of London. I must have my tea to become tolerably warm."

"Why, thank you." On their side of the desk, Floyd nudged Cap with his toe.

"Yes, thank you," Cap echoed. He soon held a cup of steaming tea, milk and sugar like the one he'd once tried at Mrs. Chapman's and had ended up pitching down the sink.

"Before you begin, I have an item to show you," Floyd said. "An indication of southern West Virginia's enthusiasm for your railroad." He reached into his brief case and pulled out a newspaper. "The first issue of the *Logan Banner*."

"A Logan paper! Let's see it." Cap was surprised and proud that Logan was now part of the same world as cities like Knoxville.

"A man named Ragland publishes it," Floyd began. "Hopes to educate the citizens on the advantages of encouraging investors to come into Logan County."

Ragland. Cap glared bullets at Floyd.

"Listen to this." Floyd began reading aloud. "'Prosperity on Logan's Doorstep.' That's the headline. 'Ere we can realize it we will hear the snort of the Iron Horse, and see wealth and prosperity staring us in the face. Soon the extension of the Norfolk and Western Railroad from the Ohio will be an accomplished deed.' The whole state of West Virginia welcomes the Norfolk and Western to its shores."

Cap guessed he didn't mind quoting Ragland if it helped his cause. He spread several sheets of paper covered with figures across Holmby's desk. "Cost of logging, cost of mill equipment, cost of milling the crossties, cost of everything, it's all right here. All itemized."

By mid-morning, the Englishmen were becoming convinced that the Hatfields owned a dam site, timber stands, and all the necessary logging equipment, and could get a skilled crew for reasonable wages and, with Sutphen's help on the mill, manage the operation themselves. Bringing in the timber, cutting and delivering the crossties, would cost the Hatfields about ninety thousand dollars. At twelve percent profit, the total bill to the railroad company would come to one hundred thousand dollars, or about twenty-five cents per crosstie.

"Yes, yes." Byrnes smacked his lips. "Most interesting."

Holmby's face relaxed from its usual guarded demeanor into a half-smile. "Mmm," he murmured. "You do save money owning the property and running the business yourselves, don't you?"

Byrnes tilted his chair back and looked pleased.

"I have a proposal to make to you gentlemen," Floyd said. "We're not asking you to take Mr. Hatfield's word on things. You've told us you need evidence. Why don't you get someone to watch over things here for a few days. Come back with us to Main Island Creek and see for yourselves the Hatfield oak trees, inspect the mill site, meet the timber crew. It's beautiful country in the springtime."

Cap stiffened all over at the shock of Floyd's words. How would he carry rifles, cartridges. and dynamite back if Holmby and Byrnes came with them? "The roads are in pretty bad shape, John," he blurted.

"They're drying out," Floyd said cheerfully. "It hasn't rained for days."

Cap didn't know what else to say. Floyd must have completely forgotten he had to buy supplies for Pappy's dang raid. He'd have to derail this plan somehow.

"How would we get there?" Byrnes looked apprehensive.

Holmby's face brightened. "On horseback, of course! We've not been more than five miles from this little river town for six months. I'd relish an adventure such as you've suggested, Mr. Floyd."

Byrnes sighed and settled more deeply into his leather chair.

"You'll never have a better opportunity to explore these mountains." Floyd beamed at the two men. "Mr. Hatfield and I look forward to escorting you."

"The idea is most appealing." Holmby was beginning to look downright eager.

Cap appreciated Floyd's quick thinking and politician's instinct for people. But what were they going to do about Pappy's raid supplies?

Floyd cleared his throat. "There's one more matter I wish to discuss."

Cap's stomach tightened into a knot.

"Yes?" Holmby, now beaming broadly, raised an eyebrow.

"Do you know a man named Cline? Perry Cline?"

"We most certainly do," Byrnes replied. "He's been here many times trying to persuade us to build the railroad in Kentucky, to buy our supplies from him, to let him represent us in court. One scheme after another to line his pockets."

"All got up like Abe Lincoln—beard, hat, everything?" As Cap chuckled, he wondered what the Englishmen thought of his own absurd get-up.

"The man's obsessive about Lincoln," Holmby said. "To the finest detail. He has a carriage he transported here from Pikeville on a riverboat and has hired a local coachman to drive him around. He claims the carriage was purchased from the same merchant as Lincoln's."

Floyd frowned. "This pretender is somewhat of a problem in West Virginia, particularly to the Hatfields."

"Why?" Holmby asked. "What's he done?"

"I don't think I need spend much time explaining Mr. Cline's motives to you gentlemen," Floyd responded. "Buying land near the railroad and getting business from your company is his game. Land to build stores on, land to build homes on, land with timber easily accessible by railroad. Men in West Virginia and Kentucky are going to make money when the railroad comes in, but Cline only has holdings in Kentucky, almost none of it along the Big Sandy or the Tug. The race to buy land is on and Perry Cline is running well behind the pack."

"He's desperate, do you think?" Byrnes asked.

"You probably don't know how low this bogus Abe Lincoln has stooped in his desperation." Floyd paused, hung his head, let his shoulders droop, then looked up again, his face solemn. "Relatives of Mr. Hatfield's own land down by the Tug—valuable timber land. Cline had these men kidnapped and imprisoned in Pikeville by a wretch named Frank Phillips. Mr. Hatfield's dear Uncle Wall is one of them, along with several of his cousins and timber crew members."

"Kidnapped!" Holmby blinked as if to clear his eyesight. "My word! I never would have thought Cline capable of kidnapping. Is he under warrant for arrest? He's been so open and flamboyant I should hardly think so."

"Not Cline himself." Floyd reached into his brief case. "But Phillips and his entire so-called posse, which consists mainly of a family named McCoy and some hired gunmen, are wanted for murders and kidnappings committed in West Virginia." Floyd brought out West Virginia warrants, signed by Governor Wilson, and laid them before Holmby. "Cline never does the manhunting and kidnapping himself."

"I see Phillips and his men are wanted in your state," Holmby said after carefully reading the warrants. "But there is no evidence in these documents of their association with Cline."

Floyd reached into his brief case again. "Look at this." He held up a copy of the *Louisville Courier-Journal* with an article quoting Cline's boasts that he'd supported the governor and some state legislators in the 1884 and 1886 elections because they were running on anti-Hatfield platforms.

"Listen to this," Floyd read. "'No man could make me darken the doors of the Pike County Jail with any man for the mere killing of one or all of the Hatfield men. Killling a Hatfield is no crime.'"

When Holmby had finished reading the article, Floyd handed him a letter from Wilson to Governor Buckner of Kentucky, protesting the kidnappings by the Phillips gang, laying out the Cline and McCoy involvements and praising the Hatfields as fine citizens defending West Virginia's borders. Holmby read this carefully, too, and then handed it to Byrnes.

After reading the articles and letter, Byrnes looked shaken. "Shocking! These are serious criminal acts."

"We in Kentucky are shocked, too," Sutphen said. "We're embarrassed at the bad reputation these hooligans are givin our state. I've already lost a great deal of business because of them."

"Yet Cline and Phillips appear to believe they have some legal status."

Holmby pressed his fingertips together. "I note that Cline refers to Phillips as 'Deputy Phillips' and alleges the Hatfields have committed 'dreadful crimes' and deserve to be hunted down. I take it these claims have no merit in your estimation?"

Cap was happy to leave the answers to these questions to Floyd. He'd feared from the first that bringing all this up would do more harm than good.

"Phillips was a deputy sheriff for a while," Floyd replied. "But he was relieved of that office after being arrested by a federal marshal for kidnapping."

"They never should of given him a sheriff's badge in the first place," Sutphen grumbled. "Everyone knowed he was a hot-head and a bully just lookin to make a name for himself. Likes to get drunk and shoot at men's feet, make em dance. Can you imagine that?"

"Is Phillips still in jail?" Byrnes asked.

Floyd shook his head. "He was out in a few months. The federal court ruled the case is outside its jurisdiction because he can be arrested and tried only in West Virginia where the crimes were committed. The federal prison where he was being held just happened to be in Kentucky."

"Don't you have extradition laws in this country?" Holmby asked.

"Yes," Floyd replied. "But Govenor Buckner is beholden to Cline and his associates for rounding up votes for him. Cline even served as a legislator in Buckner's party at one time. And Buckner is making political hay in Kentucky by loudly standing up for its citizens. He's not about to extradite anybody."

"A young country like yours!" Byrnes clucked his tongue. "And you're already mired in the mud of politics as we are in England. Only America is wilder and more dangerous."

"What about these 'dreadful Hatfield crimes' Cline speaks about?" Holmby looked hard at Cap.

"I'll explain that." Cap went through the story of how three McCoys killed Uncle Ellison in 1882, someone executed the murderers, and the McCoys accused the Hatfields. "They had no proof and after a while everybody calmed down and the matter was forgotten. There was no more trouble between our families for many years until 1887 when word got around the railroad was coming. Then Perry Cline starts thinking about my family's land out by the Tug. He gets warrants out for the arrest of some of us for that old 1882 row. He gets Randall McCoy all riled up again, buys him and his boys rifles, and talks Buckner into offering a reward for us. Next thing we know Cline's recruiting and outfitting Phillips and his gang and they're all over the mountains killing and kidnapping my people."

"Have you not tried to have them arrested?" Holmby asked.

Floyd sighed and said yes, but that things had only gotten worse. He told them of the Logan posse sent after the kidnappers. With energetic moves and gestures to indicate battle actions, he told how Phillips and his men had been confronted in a West Virginia orchard, but had refused to surrender to the law. Out of revenge, Phillips had personally shot and killed an injured Logan boy who was begging for water. Then Phllips and his men had escaped back into Kentucky where they couldn't be legally pursued by our West Virginia lawmen.

"Governor Wilson and I considered sending militia along our southern border, but deemed it too dangerous and provocative." He laid a hand on his forehead. "That could have started a war between West Virginia and Kentucky. Instead, we took the matter to the Supreme Court in Washington, which ruled the kidnappings were crimes committed in West Virginia and, therefore, fall under the jurisdiction of West Virginia and not the federal government. So we're back to trying to catch Phillips and his marauders in West Virginia."

"Good Lord!" Byrnes exclaimed. "How can you conduct your lives and businesses with all this going on?"

"How?" Cap jumped into the conversation. "My father and I sold our lands near the border and moved away from Kentucky. We're timbering up on Beech Creek now, but we've had to arm ourselves and run for home if our scouts spot men that don't belong out there. It's a hard way to live and work."

"This is what I particularly want to talk to you gentlemen about," Floyd said. "We need your help in persuading Cline to call off the McCoys and Phillips and his gangs so the Hatfields can work in peace to provide your crossties."

"We'll concede him the Tug land owned by my Uncle Wall and Cousin Plyant," Cap said. "If he'll leave us alone and see to it no more of my family's kidnapped and none of them are hanged."

"That appears to be a more generous offer than he has a right to expect," Holmby replied. "I don't know if I'd let him extort land from me if I were you."

"I don't think we should get involved in any of this, Holmby." Byrnes glanced uneasily at his partner.

"No involvement for us, really." Holmby helped himself to more tea and sugar. "We shall simply tell Cline that if he wants a contract to supply our construction crews, he must leave the Hatfields alone. If we hear of any further trouble from his quarters, he's out. Of course, you must keep the peace also." Holmby eyed Cap.

"Of course." Cap nodded in agreement.

"Mr. Hatfield badly wants peace for his family." Floyd took out copies of the letter Cap had written to Governor Buckner and those he had written to newspapers in pursuit of peace.

"I wish you success in your efforts," Holmby said after reading them. "But I fear this trouble could affect our trip to your place near Logan. Cline must call off his men before we go." He turned to Byrnes. "Get Cline in here as soon as you can."

When they'd left the office, Cap turned to Floyd. "We got em hooked, John. I think we got em." He could hardly wait to tell Nancy of their success.

"The battle's engaged, and we've captured a hill. Now we have to prepare for another battle after they've seen Cline."

"You got me in some trouble back there, John." Cap glanced up and down the street to see who might overhear them. "How'm I gonna get all those rifles, cartridges, and dynamite to Pappy with Holmby and Byrnes along?"

Floyd grinned. "You're not."

"What do you mean I'm not? We can't get cross-wise to Pappy. He'll just tell you and me and everybody else to get on down."

"That man over there's going to provide us an alibi for your father." Floyd pointed to Henry Ragland, who was entering the newspaper office across the street from their hotel. "Go up to the room and wait for me."

Cap ducked into a doorway and peered out to watch and wonder as Floyd followed Ragland into the office.

Chapter 43

"Cline had some interesting things to say about you, Hatfield." Holmby was presiding over a meeting in his office with Cap, Sutphen, and Floyd, while Byrnes was offering tea and squishy little cakes. "He claims you and your family refuse to let your neighbors live and work in peace, that you are a pack of scoundrels and murderers, that Byrnes and I should turn you over to the authorities if we see you. I did not inform him you were in Catlettsburg, of course."

Cap gripped the arms of his chair. What if the Englishmen intended to, or already had, informed on him, in spite of what Holmby had just said? Unless a man's finiancial, political, or his very physical survival depended on you, he couldn't be counted on to have your interest at heart. For all he knew, Holmby was going to turn him in for the reward.

"Floyd explained all that to you." Sutphen drummed his fingers on the table. "Cline's doin this to get the Hatfield land and timber."

Holmby never took his eyes off Cap, peering at him through the steam from his porcelain teacup. "Cline says he can provide all the timber we require."

Cap was close to heading for the door. Was Holmby expecting the arrival of a sheriff at any moment?

"Not a chance!" Sutphen scoffed. "He hasn't been near a timber operation for twenty years. You can't count on him to deliver anything."

"Cline says you people are criminals, you say he is," Byrnes said. "Frankly, I don't like the sound of any of this. I think we'd be safer going with Kanawha Lumber or Cole and Crane Timber."

Holmby smiled fleetingly. "Unfortunately, neither company can meet the Hatfield schedule or come close to their price."

Byrnes set his cup down with a thud. "How can these people meet a schedule and simultaneously fight a war? For all we know the Cline and Hatfield factions will kill each other off, and we'll have neither crossties nor supplies for our crews. What happens to our schedule then?"

"We want to make a deal with Cline." Cap said. "He stops hunting us, calls off his dogs. We let him have land by the Tug. You get your railroad built in a timely way. Cline and I make money and live in peace." If Holmby had any sense, which he obviously did, he'd see a much greater business advantage to getting his railroad built than in collecting a measly 2700 dollars for capturing a Hatfield.

Holmby pursed his lips and thrust out his chin. "Here is what I propose. If you and Cline come in here arm in arm, in peace and harmony, then we will seriously consider your proposition. Only then will we be willing to go with you to Main Island Creek to inspect your operation."

Come in arm in arm with Cline? Cap almost laughed out loud.

"I had hoped you would persuade him," Floyd said quickly. "He might be more willing to talk to you first."

"That would only show that Cline wants very badly to deal with us," Holmby replied. "We already know that. We also know you want to manufacture crossties. What I want to see is him wanting to deal with you and you with him."

The situation had turned bad in a way Cap would never have predicted. How could he persuade Cline to cooperate when what Cline wanted was to put him in jail? Cline would never deal with him unless he was forced to.

Cap paced slowly back and forth in the dark outside the Catlettsburg Livery. Cline's carriage had to be here. This was the only place in town where a visitor could keep a carriage and horses. He fidgeted under a gaslight that scarcely illuminated the street through the river fog. Cool, damp river air mixed with the hot smell of horses and manure. He took a watch from his pocket, not the preacher's suit pocket, but his own jacket pocket. His disguise would only attract attention down here. Seven thirty. The stableman had said Cline went out nearly every evening when he was in town. If he was going out tonight, he'd have to leave soon. Cap replaced the watch, then reached nervously under his suit coat to finger his revolver. He hadn't done a fast draw in quite a while.

He wondered what a man like Cline did every night. Have supper with friends? Meet a lady of the evening? Play poker? Attend Bible meetings? He flexed the fingers of his right hand. Floyd was probably wondering where he was by now. Well, let him wonder.

A dust-covered buggy came in from the road. A big carriage with two kerosene lanterns mounted in front lurched out of the livery onto the rutted roadway. Inside, a family—husband, wife, children—chattered.

Then Cap saw another coach leaving—one with carved wood trim and a driver dressed in dungarees and mountain boots. By the gaslight, Cap could see that the passenger was a bearded man with a stovepipe hat.

As the coach pulled into the road, Cap quickened his step to keep pace.

Peering in at the bearded man who was staring straight ahead, he thought he could make out the same features he'd glimpsed across the sawmill yard a week ago. He hadn't seen Cline up close then and couldn't see well inside the darkened coach now. He put his hand on the door latch by the empty passenger seat. The man continued to look straight ahead.

Pulling down on the latch and yanking, Cap leaped inside and pulled the door shut behind him.

"What?" The man gasped and turned to see Cap's pistol pointing at his head.

"Perry Cline!" Cap whispered hoarsely.

"Who are you? What do you want?" Cline squeaked out the words.

Cap gripped Cline's arm with one hand and pressed the revolver to his temple with the other, feeling sick with the desire to choke the life out of the whoreson, beat his head against the carriage door.

Instead he said, "Don't make a sound."

Cline began to tremble.

"I'm Cap Hatfield."

"You better leave me be," Cline whimpered.

"Tell the driver to go over to the railroad yard." Norfolk and Western had begun to store heavy machinery and iron rails on a tract of land they'd leased.

"What are you going to do to me?" Cline was still whimpering.

"Tell him." Cap jabbed the revolver into Cline's temple. "Now."

Cline choked as though beginning to sob. "Driver, take me to the railroad yard." His voice cracked and quavered.

"What'd you say?" the driver called out.

"Railroad yard, down by the river," Cline squeaked.

The horses turned a corner. Peering out a cloudy window that distorted the view, Cap could make out the dark shapes of stores closed for the day and the open doors of well-lit saloons.

"What do you want?" Cline muttered. "If you kill me, they'll know you did it. You or some other Hatfield."

"I don't want to kill you," Cap whispered into his ear. "So don't do anything to make me do it."

Past the last saloon, Cap saw endless blackness. He could barely make out the shapes of some large pieces of equipment.

"This where you want to go, Mr. Cline?" the driver called out.

"Tell him you're getting out," Cap whispered. "You want to look over the railroad with your friend—that's me. You'll walk back later."

"It's dark," Cline whined. "Anything could be out there."

"Don't worry." Cap giggled and elbowed Cline in the ribs. "You're with me, so you'll be safe." He burst out laughing. "Tell the driver to stop."

"Drop me off here, driver," Cline called out.

"Now get out," Cap said. "Don't try anything. I'm puttin my pistol in my coat pocket where the driver won't see it, but it's still pointin at you."

As Cline opened the carriage door and stepped to the ground, Cap was right behind him.

"Sure is dark." The driver peered down from his seat at Cap. "Muddy. Holes everywhere. Don't like to bring the horses out here."

Cap turned to Cline. "Let's take one of the lanterns with us. Don't want to fall into a ditch. A lantern for Mr. Cline, driver."

Leaning down, the driver passed one of the two carriage lanterns to Cline, who was trembling as he grasped the handle. The driver kept looking at Cap who, after all, hadn't been in the carriage when they'd left the livery.

"Take my carriage back to the livery," Cline said. "I'll walk back."

"I want my two bits." The driver reached down from his seat.

Clearly this driver cared nothing for his passenger and only wanted his money.

"Give it to him," Cap directed.

Cline got a quarter from a little pouch and handed it up. The driver inspected it, grunted, and drove off.

"Hold that light up high," Cap ordered. "Look around."

Cline did as he was told. The lantern lit up piles of gleaming rails and two great cranes squatting on wheeled platforms.

"Pretty sight, isn't it?" Cap kept his revolver trained on Cline.

"I don't like it out here," Cline grumbled. "River air's cold and damp, I could catch my death."

"Wouldn't want you to get sick." Cap was enjoying toying with Cline, but he needed to get on with what he'd brought him here for.

"What do you want with me? I've done nothing to you. I've been representing your Uncle Wall, tryin to get him off." Cline's hand trembled where he was holding the lantern handle.

Cap pushed the revolver against Cline's temple. "You know what I want?"

Cline whimpered and shook.

"I want to be your friend." Cap whispered the words right into Cline's ear.

"My friend? Cap Hatfield my friend?"

"Look around you." Cap stepped back from the shivering man. "Rails piled by the thousands, maybe tens of thousands to build miles and miles of railroad going up beside the Big Sandy and the Tug. Crews will have to be fed and supplied with tools and boots and shirts. Stores and banks and barbershops, hotels and rooming houses will be built. Timber and coal will be taken from the mountains and brought to the railroad. Enough to make a lot of men rich, enough to bring schools and doctors and paved streets and gaslights to the Tug Valley."

Cap paused. Slack-jawed, Cline gawked at him.

"You know what's needed for you and me to partake of this opportunity? Do you know?" Was Cline going to listen and think? Cap realized he was taking a big risk trying to deal with a man he didn't know, who he'd heard could be stubborn and full of hate beyond reason. But he had to try to work with him. "As human beings, and I trust you count yourself as one of our number, we're natured to fight over the past, lettin our pasts become our futures. But I propose we put aside the old and attend to the new. It's in our own best interests.

"I say we cease our scrimmaging, Cline. Then Norfolk and Western'll give me a crosstie contract, and they'll give you a contract for the construction crew supplies. We'll all live in peace and prosperity."

"How do you know this?" Cline had stopped shaking and was looking hard at Cap. "How do you know we'll get those contracts?"

"The Norfolk and Western fellers told me. Unless we're at peace, they don't want anything to do with either one of us. I tell you, Cline, we've got the world by the tail—all the money we could want, peace and safety for our families, a good name among the big investors and our neighbors. All we have to do is be friendly and cooperate with each other."

"I'm a peace-loving man." Cline held the lantern where it lit up Cap's face. "You're the Devil carrying a pistol. If you want peace, why are you pointing that thing at me?"

"Never would have gotten a chance to work with you, never would have gotten you out here without it. But you'll never see me with it again if you listen to what I say and come to a settlement with me."

"You're not the kind of man I'd trust."

"Let me tell you what else I want. Nine of my people are in jail. You get em off with nothing worse than a little more time and you'll get the deed to Wall's and Plyant's land down by the Tug."

"All of it? All of Wall's and all of Plyant's land?" Eagerness and greed replaced the last traces of fear in Cline's face.

"Yes. I want you to call off your dogs. No more rewards out for me or anyone else in my family, no more posses, no more riling up the McCoys."

"I can't do all that. Phillips is out of control. He does what he pleases. And Randall McCoy's crazy for revenge. How can I get your relatives off with jail sentences? Lots of folks in Kentucky are looking forward to hanging them."

"You just tell everybody, including Norfolk and Western, you've decided to help our men so you can bring peace and prosperity to the border region between our two states. You'll be a hero."

Cline tugged at his beard and smiled.

"Think of it, Cline. If we act together, help each other, we stand to gain everything we both want. If we keep up the war, we lose it all—money, peace, safety, the respect of our communities. Even if we hate each other's guts, it has to be worth it for us to help each other."

"What's come over you? You get religion? Have you come to our Savior Lord Jesus Christ? Does your father know what you're up to?"

Cap resisted the temptation to spit on Cline. "Pappy sees things pretty much my way. I don't know what Jesus Christ's view is. Come on now. How about those jail sentences and those posses?"

"Maybe I can get Buckner to withdraw the reward offers. He's sometimes inclined to do that anyway. Then Phillips and his men would lose interest in you. Especially if we offer him another job that pays good money."

Cap put his arm around Cline's shoulder. "See what we can do if we just cooperate? We can save my relatives and get you land by the Tug and railroad contract money to develop it."

Cline slid out from under Cap's arm. "I don't know about saving all your relatives. Someone has to pay for Allifair McCoy's death. That's the one that's really got folks angry. The McCoy boys—well, you could say they asked for what they got. But Allifair never caused anybody any trouble."

In his mind Cap saw Allifair's body lying in the snow, blood spreading from the gunshot wound in her chest. If only he could reverse the forward rush of time and put this treaty with Cline before that awful New Year's. A minute or two passed before he realized Cline was staring at him, waiting for a reply.

"Do the best you can. Only one man you're holdin is guilty of murder." If one man eventually had to pay the price in Pikeville, it should be Cotton Top.

"Sally McCoy says you did it."

"Well, I didn't. I want you to save em all, get em off with short prison sentences, but if one has to go, talk to me and I'll tell you which one. Agreed?"

"Why should I trust you?"

"Do you believe I want Phillips off my tail, that I want to save the men of my family from hanging?"

"Yes, I suppose I do. That's the only thing anybody admires about you Hatfields. You take care of your own."

"Then that's the basis of our trust. That and the land deeds we'll put up along with a written agreement to sign them over to you after the men are sentenced. Now how do I know I can trust you?"

Cline threw out his chest. "I am a man of honor. My word is as good as gold."

Cap snorted.

"You know you can trust me the same way I know I can trust you, Hatfield." Cline's eyes darted around, and he took a deep breath. "You know I want that railroad supply contract and that land by the Tug. We'll trust each other because we understand each other's desires. I've wanted Tug land ever since your father took mine in '72. I figure I'll be even if I get Wall's and Plyant's."

"Then I can count on you? I'll see you tomorrow morning at the Norfolk and Western office?"

"You aren't planning on leaving me out here, are you, Hatfield?"

Cap groaned. Cline was a crafty businessman one minute and a frightened rabbit the next.

"Don't fret yourself. I'll walk you back to your hotel. Remember, if you yell 'Help!' you're a dead man, and you'll ruin the whole deal for both of us."

"I understand."

"By the way," Cap said as they left the railroad yard and headed up a muddy street. "I despise you."

"I hate you, too."

Chapter 44

"This is not a road," Byrnes complained as he, Cap, Floyd, and Holmby rode along a rocky creek bed running through a narrow hollow. "This place is so isolated we might as well be journeying into darkest Africa."

Holmby laughed. "That shall be our next venture, Byrnes. Building a railroad in darkest Africa."

"With posses and bounty hunters coming over from Kentucky all the time, we couldn't live in a place that's easy to get to," Cap said. "These mountains aren't like it was in Knoxville where I went to law school."

"You're a lawyer!" Holmby said. "Why didn't you tell us that before? But I should have guessed when you drew up our contracts yourself."

Cap decided to keep his mouth shut about not quite being a lawyer.

"We've scarcely passed any homes," Holmby said. "Even though I believe we've ridden about fifteen miles today. Where does your timber crew live, and how do they get to this place?"

"They'll be coming from all over these mountains when they hear there's money to be made. We're gettin close to my place now. You'll meet some of the fellows there."

Rounding a bend in the road, they came upon Uncle Elias with a heavy bag over one shoulder and a Winchester in the other hand. Cap's little cousin Edna, in a faded calico frock, walked barefooted beside him, gaping up at them with big frightened eyes. Yesterday, in Logan, Cap had spoken to Elias and told him the English he was bringing with him were Norfolk and Western men looking for a supplier of crossties. He hadn't had time to spell out any details.

"Are they the ones gettin the feather bed in the loft?" Edna asked. "Daddy told Grampa Anse two men was comin, and he had to let em sleep in the loft all by theirselves or there wasn't gonna be no deal."

"Shush!" Elias said. "Mind your tongue."

"Yes, that's us." Byrnes laughed. "How I long for a room with only one or two in it after that Logan hotel. I could not bear another night in that place. They have no concept of privacy there. All night long, people came and went as they pleased. They slept on the beds, on the floor, any place they chose, sometimes five or six at a time. Not once did they knock or make any excuse for their presence."

The desire for privacy was a peculiarity Cap had seen only in Knoxville citizens and these two men. Until he'd gone to law school, he'd always been surrounded by family day and night and liked it that way. Nights and evenings spent by himself in his room at the boarding house had been lonely.

He spied Pappy across a field. If Uncle Elias hadn't already told him, he'd soon see they had no guns, ammunition, and dynamite with them, unless he mistook as his supplies the personal belongings piled high on two mules Holmes and Byrnes had in tow.

"Hullo, Anse!" Floyd called out.

"How-do, John Floyd." Accompanied by one of his bear dogs, Pappy strode across the field, old black hat flopping, boots squish-sucking in the mud, a Winchester under his arm.

"This is Mr. Roger Holmby, and this is Mr. Reginald Byrnes," Floyd said. "From the Norfolk and Western Railroad." Pappy's dog began barking.

"Rattler!" Pappy spoke sharply. "Leave them fellers be!" The dog retreated behind Pappy, where it continued to growl.

Winchesters and a mean dog named Rattler. Cap could only imagine what the Englishmen were thinking about his family's suitability as business partners.

"How-do!" Pappy reached out his free hand, first to Holmby and then Byrnes. "Come on over to my place and rest your bones. Elliot, Elias, get these men's horses and mules, unsaddle and feed em. And take this here dog with you." Pappy motioned to Cap's younger brothers, then looked up at Cap. "Hee, hee!" he giggled, knocking the stock of his rifle on the roadway with each guffaw. "You're a ridiculous lookin sight in that get-up. How much of that belly is yourn?"

"Take this stuff and put it in the house." Cap yanked the rags from under his shirt and handed them to Elliot along with the black hat and coat. He rotated his shoulders and flexed his arms, glad to be free of all that material.

Holmby and Byrnes were staring at his revolver in its shoulder holster. "You look quite a different man now," Holmby said. "Not pudgy at all, but trim and fit. And you're armed. Everyone around here appears to be armed."

"The hat, the coat, the stomach was a disguise. Folks around here think I went out West with my brother. I don't want them to think any different until the warfare's over." Cline had said he'd get with Governor Buckner and Frank Phillips right away, but right away could take a few days or weeks, depending on how hard these people were to reach and persuade.

"Everybody's armed but us," Byrnes muttered. "We're defenseless."

"You aint defenseless when you got us with you." Pappy clapped a hand on Byrnes's shoulder. "Aint that right, John Floyd?"

"You couldn't ask for better protection."

At least Pappy was in a cheerful, hospitable mood. He had to be pleased at the prospect of doing business with the railroad. But how would he react to the truce with Cline and Cap's failure to bring home rifles and dynamite?

After they'd crossed the drawbridge, Cap helped Pappy winch the great log structure up to tower over them.

"Amazing!" Holmby looked up and down the swollen spring creek. "That's the only reasonable way to cross this creek for as far as can be seen. And you've closed it off."

"Cappie's idea, that bridge." Pappy looked proud. "And the fort up yonder." He pointed to the ridge above. "Aint nobody can catch us unawares."

Holmby stared up at the fort. "Look at the size of those logs! Are there more like that in your forest, Mr. Hatfield?"

"Four thousand acres." Cap answered.

Inside the cabin, cane-bottomed chairs had been lined up in front of the fireplace, where embers were smouldering. *Just right to sit around and talk business*, Cap thought.

Nancy came through the door from the back of the house and kissed him.

"How'd it go?" she whispered in his ear.

"Near perfect," he said before she disappeared again to help Mama and Nancy Belle with the cooking.

Pappy put a huge log on the fire, obviously cut from a very large tree, and pulled up three chairs in front of the fireplace.

"Set right here where the fire's best," he said to the Englishmen. "And, John, you set next to em." Pappy positioned himself all the way to the right of the fireplace, and Cap took a chair all the way to the left, a place of almost equal importance. A half dozen guards took the other chairs. Children sat on the floor in front of the men and on the beds behind them. Everyone wanted a look at the visitors.

Things had changed since Cap had left a week ago. Four beds littered with Winchesters were now crowded into this room where there'd been only a table and chairs. Pappy must have ordered several of the guards to sleep at the house, too many to fit into the sleeping room along with the nine children. Cap began to worry that Pappy might be getting his men ready to go to Pikeville earlier than the middle of May.

"Your son has brought us a proposition we find most interesting." Holmby pressed his fingertips together as Cap had seen him do repeatedly in the railroad office when he was organizing his thoughts.

"You fellers must be kind of dry after that long haul from Logan." Pappy went to the shelf where the whiskey and tin cups were kept. "Let's have ourselves a touch of whiskey before we get to talkin."

Cap wasn't sure the Englishmen weren't like Nighbert and Ragland who disliked doing business with drinking men.

"Maybe these gentlemen would like to talk first," he said.

Pappy made no reply, but filled two tin cups with whiskey and handed one to each of the Englishmen, then filled three more for himself, Cap, and Floyd.

"It's our custom to have tea in the late afternoon." Byrnes stared morosely into his cup.

"Well now, you'll get 'customed to this here whiskey real quick." Pappy slapped his thigh and hee-hawed.

"I brought along some ginger ale, Anse." Floyd got up and walked over to where he'd hung his saddle pockets from a wall peg and drew out a brown glass bottle with a stopper. "Perhaps it would be better if these gentlemen cut their whiskey a bit. It's pretty strong stuff if you're not used to it. I like the taste of ginger ale in whiskey myself."

Floyd reached for Holmby's cup, but Holmby waved him away. "I'll have my whiskey as served, thank you."

Pappy nodded approvingly. "It's got a right tasty flavor. Sweet as molasses, warm as a winter fire, feisty as a she-ba'r with cubs."

"Be careful," Floyd cautioned. "Anse's whiskey can render a man senseless before he knows what's happened to him."

Holmby raised his cup. "To our host. And to our mutual good fortune." He swallowed about half the cupful in one gulp, sighed and smiled.

Byrnes sipped his diluted with ginger ale, holding the tin cup by its handle as if it were a teacup.

"These gentlemen came out here all the way from England to oversee the railroad construction," Cap explained. He felt things might as well get started, although he could tell it wasn't going to be easy to steer Pappy the way he wanted to go.

"That so?" Pappy cocked one of his great hairy eyebrows. "My foreparents come from England and brung my great-granddaddy with em when he was just a boy. I hear it's purty country over there."

"England is pretty country." Holmby nodded in agreement. "But no more so than your lovely mountains, Mr. Hatfield. Your trees are magnificent."

"Wait till you see the oaks out by Beech Creek," Cap said. "Thousands of them, all over the mountains. Every one at least six feet across. We'll go out and look at them tomorrow."

"I wonder, Mr. Hatfield." Holmby held out his cup for more whiskey. "Might we have the opportunity to do some hunting in your woods?"

"That'd be a easy thing to do," Pappy said. "Except we got to send scouts out first, make sure there's no enemies around."

"I suppose that situation could not have changed this soon," Holmby said.

Pappy looked puzzled.

"We got a baby b'ar out back." Cap's brother Elias was sitting on a bed among some rifles. "Someone kilt its mother."

"A bear?" Byrnes jerked himself upright. "My word. I've never seen a bear close at hand."

"Come on outside, and I'll show you." Pappy led the way out, ambling over to a shed. He came out carrying a piece of fatback pork and leading a young bear by a rope tied around its neck. The bear snuffled at Pappy's legs and snapped its jaws at the pork, but Pappy yanked it high above the bear's head.

"Dance, Blackie, dance," he commanded. The little bear stood on its hind legs and turned round and round trying to reach the meat.

"Bravo!" Byrnes applauded and downed the rest of his whiskey and ginger ale. His face was beginning to flush.

"Sit down, Blackie," Pappy orderd. "Down."

The bear sat on its haunches.

"May I touch him?" Byrnes asked.

Pappy held the little bear's rope while Byrnes gently patted its head.

Then Pappy prodded the sitting bear with his booted foot. "Roll over, Blackie."

The bear snarled and snapped at Pappy's foot.

"You aint gettin nothin till you roll over."

Cap suddenly grabbed Blackie and lifted him high. "Stop teasin this animal." He let the bear snatch its reward from Pappy, then set it down to gobble the meat. "Blackie's got a right to that pork. He earned it."

Pappy glowered. "He aint earned it till I say."

"That animal must weigh over a hundred pounds," Holmby exclaimed. "Yet you picked it up as though it were a small child."

Pappy handed the bear's rope to Elias. "Cappie's near as strong as I was. Why I rassled a catamount and kilt it with my bare hands when I was a boy. That's when they started callin me Devil Anse."

Cap wished Pappy would stop this. What would the Englishmen think?

"Nobody has reason to call you Devil nowadays." Floyd knew Pappy's stories as well as Cap did.

"I'm proud of bein called Devil. Shows respect. And this here's the Devil's son. Some days I'm proud of him, too." Pappy clapped Cap on the shoulder a little, too hard to be affectionate.

Cap grit his teeth.

"Mr. Hatfield, are you not a religious man?" Byrnes asked. "Don't you fear God and despise the Devil? What is your church?"

"I belong to no church unless you say I belong to the one great church of the world. If you like, you can say it's the Devil's church I belong to." Pappy roared with laughter.

Many times Cap had seen Pappy carry on like this, but this had to be the most inopportune time of all.

"But if you don't believe in God, if you align yourself with the Devil, how can you expect us to do business with you, Hatfield?" Byrnes was clearly agitated.

Pappy had done it, he'd upset the Englishmen. He could destroy any chance of a deal in a few capricious minutes.

Pappy stopped laughing and thought a moment. "I may not go to church and I like to tell a good yarn now and then, but I never tell no lies. I pay my debts. I'm a friend to any man that needs food to eat and the shelter of a roof. I aint quarrelsome nor fond of killin. Ask anybody that lives around these parts."

"I'll vouch for that," Floyd said.

"We do have a religion." Cap watched for Pappy's reaction. "Happiness is the only good we ever get, and the place to be happy is on this earth. A man's duty is to help his fellow man and look after his wife and children."

Pappy grunted. "That's Cappie's way of tellin it. He's got to use fancy words. Reads books, you know."

"Your religion fits you," Holmby replied. "A man of these vast, isolated mountains needs a free and expansive religion."

Cap was surprised at Holmby. Back in Catlettsburg, he'd thought Holmby was demanding and fussy. But out here he seemed ready to take on anything.

"Where were we before we took this unfortunate digression?" Byrnes balanced his cup on his hand like a teacup in a saucer.

I want to show you fellers some shootin," Pappy said. "Give me one of them ginger ale bottles, John Floyd. This is what I taught Cappie when he was a little tad. I'll throw a bottle up in the air, and Cappie won't draw till it's as high as that tree-top, then he'll shoot it out of the air before it drops a inch."

"I'm not a trained bear," Cap snapped.

Pappy pulled on his beard and shuffled his feet, probably working himself up to a fit.

"May I prevail upon you to shoot, Cap?" Holmby was calling him Cap for the first time. "I'd appreciate an exhibition of your marksmanship."

Impressing the Englishmen was a different matter than performing for Pappy. Cap felt for his revolver, his hand memorizing the reach. Then he dropped his hand and nodded.

Pappy threw a bottle high above them. Waiting until it began to slow as it neared its zenith, Cap snatched his gun from its holster, sighted along the barrel and fired. The bottle shattered and sprayed tiny pieces through the air.

"Bravo!" Holmby cheered. "I say. You have a very talented son here, Mr. Hatfield."

"Purty good shot aint he?" Pappy, whiskey cup dangling from his hand, was looking relaxed and congenial again. "Runs in the family."

Mama came out with a tin basin and a small towel. "Here, you fellers wash up. We're gonna have some dinner."

Pappy took the basin to the creek, filled it, and set it on a big flat rock. The Englishmen scrubbed up in the basin, but Pappy and Cap just splashed their hands and faces in the creek. The children and guards ran from the cabin and began washing, too, Elizabeth leading little Willis and Coleman to the creek, Mary bringing Rosie.

Inside, everyone crowded in together on benches at the long wooden table Mama and the girls had shoved to the middle of the room, first stacking up the chairs that had been in front of the fireplace. Nancy, Holmby, Byrnes, Floyd, Cap, the nine younger children, and six of the guards sat down, with Pappy at one end and Mama at the other.

"There 'tis. Now you fellers take hold and eat," Pappy said.

Byrnes cleared his throat. "I suppose it's not appropriate to say grace, but I propose a toast to our gracious hostess who prepared this bountiful feast." He stood up, his cup now filled with pure whiskey and drank. His eyes closed and he fell backward into his chair, toppling it into the floor, where he lay without moving.

"My word!" Holmby exclaimed. "I believe Mr. Byrnes has been overcome with exhaustion from our travels."

Pappy's eyes twinkled. "I believe he's overcome by my whiskey."

Cap took the shoulders and Pappy the legs of the now snoring Byrnes and had one of the children shove a few rifles aside so they could lay him out on a bed.

"Don't worry." Cap returned to his seat at the table. "After supper, we'll take him up to the loft and that featherbed we promised you."

"On behalf of Mr. Byrnes and myself, I extend our appreciation," Holmby said. "But with regard to our business negotiations. . ." Holmby started to press his finger tips together and missed. "We had best wait until tomorrow when Mr. Byrnes will be able to participate."

Cap wouldn't forget that he'd stayed sober while neither Holmby nor Byrnes had.

"Levicy's the cookinest woman." Pappy smiled across the table at Mama who'd sat down only after all the food had been set out. "Why if I come in from the road in the middle of the night, she'll get up and fry me some bacon and griddle cakes."

"Captain Anderson," Mama said, "I do my duty."

"Captain Anderson!" Holmby said. "You must have served in that terrible War between the States."

Pappy's face lit up. "Led a regiment. The Logan Wildcats we was called, and we served under Stonewall Jackson."

"Stonewall Jackson? Wasn't he a Confederate?"

"Sure was." Pappy sat proud and erect like a soldier. "If he'd of lived, we'd of won at Gettysburg and marched right into Washington and took old Abe prisoner."

"All that was in the sixties," Cap said. "We got better things to do than to keep on fighting an old war."

"Named one of my sons after General Lee." Pappy wasn't going to be stopped. "Robert E. Lee Hatfield."

Holmby looked perplexed. "But Lee lost the War."

"He almost won at Gettysburg," Pappy retorted. "My brother Ellison served there under General Pickett. Pickett made him major."

"If the railroad passes along the Tug in West Virginia, it'll come within twenty miles of here." Cap was determined to put an end to Pappy's war stories. "Some of our coal and timber's within a mile of the Tug."

"You know." Holmby managed to press his fingers together this time. "There's no reason why Norfolk and Western can't run spur lines to timber sites, sawmills, and coal mines once the main line is constructed. How good is the coal? How much is there?"

"Go fetch us a chunk," Cap said to Elliot who, for a change, ran off to do an errand without talking back.

"We used to own land right by the Tug," Pappy said. "Till we moved here to keep the peace. Took all our time and money to fight off some varmints by name of McCoy and Phillips comin over here from Kentucky. Takes a lot to watch out for em now even though we're fifty miles from the old place."

"Now that you'll be able to call off your guards and work without interference I'm sure your life will improve greatly," Holmby said.

Pappy's eyes narrowed. "How do you figure that?"

Just then, Elliot entered the room with a lustrous black lump of coal twice the size of a man's fist and laid it on the table next to Holmby's plate.

"That's a fine-looking specimen," Holmby said after turning the lump over in his hands to examine it.

"Doc Rutherford says it's high volatile coal." Elliot rocked back and forth from his toes to his heels and cocked his chin in the air. "That's the highest grade, and they use it to make steel and run trains. I'm named after Doctor Elliot Rutherford. He's very intelligent."

"This is all very impressive." Holmby looked pleased and proud as though he'd discovered Elliot and Elliot had discovered coal. "I'm grateful to you both, Mr. Floyd and Mr. Hatfield, for allowing me to see the wonders of West Virginia. And to you, young man, for enlightening me."

"Elliot's a smart young feller, all right, but Doc Rutherford's got him spendin most of his time readin. That aint right for a boy." Pappy glanced sideways at Mama who was dead set on educating Elliot and keeping him out of the wars, then changed the subject. "I got a few good stories about the War you might enjoy. Like the one where we was on top of this hill, surrounded by the enemy, and we was runnin out of ammunition."

Cap let his head droop till his chin was on his chest. He remembered how he and Johnse had rolled their eyes at each other whenever Pappy began this tale. He remembered how his cousin Bill Staton had loved the story so much he'd cheer and laugh every time it was told. Johnse was gone for who knew how long and Bill was gone forever.

"There was about fifty of us left on top of a hill surrounded by Union troops," Pappy began. "Them blue suits was comin up at us like a river risin in a flood. Purty soon we'd shot off every cannon ball we had, and we was down to a handful of rifle bullets. Still them blue coats kept a-comin." His face grave and severe, Pappy paused and drew on his pipe.

"The cook handed us his camp pot and we shot it off. We blasted em with every pot, pan, and kettle we had. Many of the enemy fell, but more kept comin. Our situation was desperate." Pappy frowned. "I looked around me and found one last thing to try, one last chance for us. We loaded up our company mule into the cannon and fired the miserable critter, brayin and kickin somethin fierce, right into the midst of them Union soldiers. When they seen that poor animal's flyin hooves and gnashin teeth comin at em, they turned tail and run. That mule saved the day, saved our hides. Came close to turnin around the whole way the War was goin."

Cap looked up when Pappy's voice finally stopped to see Pappy looking so proud you'd have thought the story was true. Floyd's eyelids were flickering open and shut, Holmby was staring into the fire, the children had quietly left the table, and the women had disappeared with the dishes.

As a boy, Cap had sometimes doubted many details of Pappy's stories, but he'd come to believe that the truth in them was that Pappy had the power to devastate his enemies. Now he believed Pappy told stories like a cat puffing out its fur to look more formidable.

"Enough of that old war!" Cap said. "Let's get these fellers to bed. We'll go look at the trees in the morning."

An hour later, Cap and Pappy sat facing each other in the fort, the only place where they could talk in privacy. The light of a crackling fire glinted off a row of clean, oiled Winchesters lined up in a gun rack.

"Where's my rifles and my cartridges and my dynamite?" Pappy sucked on his corncob pipe.

Cap was chewing tobacco—it always cleared his head. "Let me start at the beginning."

"Start any place you want, just get to the point, son. Where's my guns and ammunition and dynamite?"

Cap spit into the fire, then stretched his legs. "After Floyd and I got to Catlettsburg, we persuaded Sutphen to go in with us on a proposition to make crossties for the railroad. The Englishmen wanted all the figures—cost of cuttin timber, cost of cuttin crossties and deliverin em, crew wages, mill wages. Between Sutphen and me we gave em everything they wanted."

Pappy shook his head. "Never had to fuss with all that nonsense when I brung timber in."

"Norfolk and Western's a horse of a different color. It's a big corporation. Lots of money. With big stakes, they want to know right where their money's goin."

"They gonna pay us a lot?"

"If you think a hundred thousand dollars is a lot." Cap said the amount of money very slowly, knowing Pappy had never heard of such a lucrative deal. "We stand to clear about ten thousand."

"Ah!" Pappy pointed a finger at him. "You aint prankin me?"

Cap tried not to think about that finger that had accused him so many times. "Would I prank you, Pappy? Anyhow, when we gave em our price and told em how fast we could start turnin out crossties, they wanted to come out here and look at our trees and our sawmill site right away. So I said sure, come right on, we got woods full of oaks. They only use oak to make crossties. Has to be tough enough to hold the tracks in place when the trains run over em."

"You think you know all about makin railroads, don't you?"

"You bet your britches I do. When we finished talkin timber and sawmills, John Floyd took up our other problem with em."

"What problem of ours did John talk to them railroad fellers about? Can't figure no problem that'd be any of their business."

"You know we can always count on Floyd."

"He's smart from his boots up. What'd he say?"

"He told em about our troubles with the McCoys, Phillips, the posses, and Cline bein behind it all. He said we'd have a hard time gettin crossties out on a schedule if we were bein hunted. The English fellers knew who Floyd was talkin about. Cline'd been hangin around their office. Floyd told them it would be a big help if they'd get Cline to call off his dogs so's we could get to work."

"What'd they say?"

"Holmby said it was up to me and Cline to prove to them we could get along."

"'Bout as much chance of that happenin as a hound dog gettin along with a polecat."

"Hold on! Wait till you hear what I did. I made a deal with Cline. You wouldn't have thought I could, but I did. He's goin to see to it that Phillips and his men leave us be, maybe even get Buckner to withdraw the rewards. And he's goin to represent our men, make sure nobody gets lynched. The deal is we get a contract from Norfolk and Western to make crossties, he gets a contract to supply the railroad crews. He gets our men off with light jail sentences, we deed him Uncle Wall's and Plyant Mahon's land along the Tug."

"You got no business makin a deal like that behind my back!" Pappy bellowed. "And what's all this got to do with my rifles and dynamite anyhow?"

Cap tried to pick his way carefully. "If we don't keep the peace, it won't just be Phillips and his gangs after us, it'll be the militia, too. If we don't keep the peace, the railroad won't give us a contract. Don't you see that the Norfolk and Western Company has to see us as men of peace?"

Pappy took his pipe out of his mouth. "So you didn't bring what I told you to on account of these fellers was with you comin out here?"

"That's right."

"Then how're you gonna get them rifles and cartridges and dynamite out here?"

Cap licked his dry lips so the words would slide out more easily. "That's best explained by the *Catlettsburg News*." He pulled a copy of the paper out of his jacket pocket and spread it on his knees.

Pappy drummed his fingers rat-a-tat on the table.

"There's an article right here on the front page. About Henry Ragland. He was in Catlettsburg tryin to find out how the railroad construction was comin along, which side of the Tug it's comin up."

"Ragland! What in tarnation's he got to do with my guns and bullets?"

"Floyd and I saw him goin into the Catlettsburg newspaper office. He's got a feller on his payroll snoopin into everybody's business—especially who's got land for sale and who's lookin for trouble, buyin guns and ammo. Right here in this paper he sounds a warning that if anybody tries to buy up weapons in Catlettsburg he'll know about it and report it in the *Logan Banner* and the *Catlettsburg News*."

Cap would always keep his and Floyd's secret—that Floyd had talked

Ragland into threatening to report gun and ammunition purchases in his paper as a means of promoting peace.

"So you see we couldn't go in and buy a dozen rifles and four thousand cartridges. Ragland would've found out and written about it in the newspaper. One look at that paper, and Norfolk and Western would be through with us."

Pappy scowled and his beard jutted out. "And to think I passed up many a chance to put a bullet in that varmint Ragland."

"This is a chance to get what we want without using bullets."

Pappy thought a minute. "I reckon we'll have to get our supplies some place where Ragland and his spies aint watchin—Charleston or somewheres in Virginia."

"It goes against nature, Pappy, to take a hard way to get at a problem when there's an easy way." Cap explained that Cline wanted the supply contract and the land so bad that all the Hatfields had to do was keep their side of the bargain, and he'd take care of the men who were jailed in Pikeville. The raid was not only dangerously risky, but unnecessary.

Pappy scowled. "I aint trustin Cline with the fate of my men, and that's the end of it. Now where we gonna get them rifles, ammunition, and dynamite?"

Cap leapt to his feet and hammered his fists on the wall. "You're drivin me crazy! We got a chance to make some money and live in peace. My sisters can get married, Elliot can go to college, I can be a lawyer, and you're sittin there talkin about makin a wreck out of the whole thing."

"You aint got no right to contrary me! Only right a son's got is to obey his pappy. That's how sons and parents is natured."

Pappy's words exploded like gunshots in Cap's head. "Why do you have to go against me *all* the time?"

"You keep actin like you're in charge around here." Pappy's lips were pulled back so his teeth showed above his beard. "You keep forgettin I own this land. I own the place where you want that danged sawmill to go. I'm the head of this family. I'm the Captain of my men. And I say no deal!"

"You're the Captain of yesterday!" Cap roared. "The War's over, there's no Reb army anymore. Politics and law and modern business practices—those are the weapons of today. I am the Captain of today."

Pappy slammed his hand on the table and stared silently into the fire, shaking his head slowly back and forth.

Cap clasped his hands together to stop their trembling. He'd lost control, lost his temper and maybe lost hard-won ground.

"Captain of yesterday? Never thought I'd hear words like that from you." Pappy stood up and threw a couple of sticks of wood onto the fire that blazed anew to light up the rifles in their racks. "Look around you. This here's a fort, and I'm its commander." Pappy stood over Cap, forcing him to look up to talk to him.

Cap wasn't going to let this kind of bullying stop him. "You're stubborn. This fort's good protection. But it isn't goin to let our family cut and sell timber in safety, and it isn't goin to save our men in Pikeville."

"Cline aint gonna keep his side of no deal."

"He has to, to get what he wants."

"He don't have to do nothin you say."

"Don't be so contrary. Give my idea a chance."

"In the Army, if you wanted a promotion, you had to prove yourself. You want to be Captain, you got to do better'n leadin a New Year's raid, killin children and lettin the enemy escape."

Cap winced, even though this was the kind of intimidation he knew to expect from Pappy. "My education is preparin me to understand the world of today."

"Education! Books! That aint provin yourself." Pappy tugged on his beard. "You got to show me what you can do! Bring me proof Cline's doin all you say—callin off them posses, getting' our men out of jail. Get us a contract with them railroad men, get em to sign up to it. Get a dam and mill permit off Judge Harvey. Let's see you do that."

Cap hadn't gone for the mill and dam permit yet. He still had to line up the support of their downstream neighbors to set in motion the plan Beese had come up with. "I can do all that. But you got to hold off on raidin Pikeville. That'd kill the whole deal."

"I told you, and I told you. I aint gonna let them men die. There's a powerful sentiment in the McCoys and a lot of other folks over in Kentucky to do away with em."

"Yes." Cap was happy to have something he and Pappy could agree on. "I'd thought of that and so had Cline. So I proposed to Cline that he get everyone off if he can. But if someone has to hang, he'll let me know and I'll tell him who killed Allifair."

"Cotton Top done a terrible thing, shootin that girl," Pappy said. "I'll give you till the middle of May. If Cline aint takin care of business by then, I'm goin after our men. I got a right. Phillips come over here and kidnapped em and that's against the law. Think I'll try mail-orderin them rifles and cartridges— you can get em that way now. They'll just come in boxes and nobody in Logan'll be the wiser. Maybe Elias can pick up some dynamite for me in Catlettsburg."

"And the Englishmen? How about them?"

"Reckon you'll have to sign em on and get the dam and mill permit before the middle of May. You got learnin. You can do that, can't you?"

Cap grit his teeth and clenched his fists. "Do I have your word you'll call off the raid if I do all those things and Cline takes care of our men?"

Pappy thought a minute. "You have my word."

Cap sat back, exhausted. Convincing Pappy had been far harder than convincing either Cline or the Englishmen. And Pappy was only half convinced.

Chapter 45

"No posse such as you might meet up with in these parts can breach this fort." Pappy's eyes gleamed as he and Cap exhibited their prize to Holmby and Byrnes, now recovered sufficiently from yesterday's introduction to Pappy's whiskey to ride up the steep hillside.

"I imagine this fort has no equal anywhere," Floyd said.

The men began walking around the building to inspect it. "Six logs high and not a winder in it. Only them little gun ports." Pappy pried at a crack between logs. "Can't get your finger twixt em. Every log's a foot thick and double-notched at each end so's they fit together tight."

"What are those?" Holmby pointed up at the steeply angled roof with odd pieces of shingle on top.

Cap explained how from the inside a gunman could lift those shingles, which were hinged, to see who was coming and fire if necessary. He led them inside the fort.

"Look here." Cap pointed overhead, where loose-fitting poles about four inches across formed a partial ceiling. "A man can stand on those poles and look out from under the hinged shingles, poke his rifle out and take a shot if he needs to."

"You can see for yourselves, gentlemen," Floyd said. "The Hatfields are master builders. A dam and sawmill would be no problem for them."

"Indeed!" Holmby gazed at the walls, gunports and ceiling. "Excellent, well thought out. I'd wager you could hold off a small army."

"If we'd of had a few forts like this at Gettysburg, we'd of won the War," Pappy said.

Back on their horses, they rode toward Beech Creek to view the stands of oak and the site for the dam and sawmill. Cap lagged behind with Floyd so they could talk. "Last night I told Pappy he was the Captain of yesterday," he whispered to Floyd. "I practically said he's an old man, and he'd better get out of my way."

"Oh, lordy, Cap!" Floyd grunted as his horse, scrambling over large stones, bounced him around. "You couldn't have put it worse."

"He doesn't put any stock in Cline keepin our deal."

"Before your father gets into trouble he can't handle, we've got to convince him Cline is keeping his side of the deal."

"Just how are we goin to do that? Pappy's bound and determined to get our men out of jail the middle of May. That gives us about three weeks for Cline to get things turned around and for us to get proof of it. We don't even have a spy in Pikeville to tell us what's goin on."

"That's true. And who do we know who'll dare go to Pikeville?"

"How about John Sergeant? Bet he'd go see Cline if he thought it'd be worth somethin to him."

"Aah, Cap. You'll make a politician yet."

The horses rounded a last switchback and brought the riders to the top of a mountain, where they stopped to admire the view.

"There's your oaks." Cap waved his arms expansively.

Holmby whistled. "My word! A great host of them marching from horizon to horizon! Where do you propose to put the dam and sawmill?"

"Down there." Cap prodded Traveller into descending the mountain and the others followed. Soon they came to a spot where Beech Creek leveled out, then plunged steeply over rocks and boulders under overhanging trees. The men dismounted.

"We'll put the sawmill here." Cap indicated the stream below them. "The wheel for powering it goes in the falls—they're about twenty feet high and the wheel'll be twelve to fifteen feet across."

"Between you and Sutphen, you have the expertise to build the dam and mill, don't you?" Holmby gleefully walked, almost danced, alongside the creek.

"Sure do." Cap would keep to himself the fact that he didn't have a dam and mill permit yet.

Holmby looked back to where they'd left Floyd and Pappy talking to Byrnes, then suddenly turned to face Cap. "Will you run this operation or will your father?"

"I have the taste for it."

"You're the man for the job." Holmby looked him in the eye. "You're educated, you can design a mill, lay out work plans and schedules, keep the books. And you're strong as an ox. You can cut timber and run the sawmill yourself if need be."

"I can do all of that and draw up whatever contracts we need."

"You're not limited as is your father." Holmby put his hand on Cap's shoulder. "He's intelligent, but I can see he's not had the advantage of an education."

Cap had called Pappy the Captain of yesterday and here was Holmby saying nearly the same thing.

Holmby picked up a piece of coal by the creek bank and balanced it in his hand. "You've been fired in a crucible," he said. "Then tempered and refined. My talent is knowing fine steel from rough iron. You're finished steel."

Cap felt exactly as if he'd been subjected over the years to white-hot furnaces and hammering.

Holmby gazed out into the forest surrounding them. "I've grown accustomed to the thought of you being in charge." His smile flickered out and his eyes became cold.

"But you'd sign if I said I'd keep my eye on things?"

"Would your father maintain peace with Mr. Cline?"

"He's given me his word he'll keep the peace if Cline will."

"I'll sign, I think. But now is your time, Cap. In the name of all that's wonderful, use it!"

Through the mist of the waterfall, Cap saw Pappy talking and gesturing as he had years before when they'd stood with Uncle Jim by another creek and planned a sawmill. That mill had never been built. Trudging back up the hill to rejoin the others, Cap and Holmby found Pappy sitting beside the stream, feet dangling over the bank, his back against a big oak. A pile of broadbladed leaves, apparently picked from the streamside, lay around him. Pappy scowled with concentration as he plaited leaves together.

"What in heck're you doin?" Cap had an uneasy feeling about this.

"Makin a kivver for my hat," Pappy grunted.

Cap could hardly believe this. In summer heat old people liked to weave such covers and put them over the brims of their hats to shade them from the hot sun.

"It's not that hot out here. It's only April."

Pappy continued plaiting, his gnarled fingers weaving around a hole for a hat in the center and leaving loose ends of the leaves to hang out over the brim.

"Guess I feel the heat more'n I used to when I was Captain of yesterday." Pappy gazed at Cap with lackluster eyes.

Cap had never before seen Pappy plait a hat cover. As they remounted, he couldn't take his eyes off the braided monstrosity, leaf blades hanging almost to Pappy's eyes in front and down to his shoulders in back. Ornery tricks were Pappy's specialty and this had to be one of them. For sure he was out to distract everybody's attention from Cap, the trees, and the sawmill.

Chapter 46

Cap set out the next day for Logan on horseback with John Floyd, who needed to return to Charleston, and the Englishmen, who would ride to Catlettsburg without having signed a deal. Since he was soon going to meet with people to whom he'd need to identify himself, he wore no disguise.

As they approached the courthouse, Cap glanced around. Idlers in dungarees and overalls were leaning wooden chairs against the courthouse wall, sipping from jugs, spitting tobacco, and swapping stories. No good prospects for a timber crew in this sorry bunch. As Cap passed, a man looked up and waved, calling out his name. By the end of the day everyone in town would know he was back. He headed for John Sergeant's.

In his office, Cap found the same old Sergeant, hair slicked down with smelly grease, wearing a brown suit and yellow tie and looking glad to see him. Sergeant was in a good mood, and it didn't take ten minutes to persuade him to take a trip to Pikeville and determine what Perry Cline was doing to keep his end of the deal.

"No problem at all," Sergeant said. "You know how I am, how most of us in the sales professions are. Stick our noses into everybody's business, sniff out deals. I go to Pikeville so often nobody's going to think a thing of it. Besides, if peace comes to the Tug Valley the value of the land I got from you will go up. So I'll be more than happy to go. When do you want me to leave?"

Cap told him the sooner the better.

"By the way," Sergeant said. "There's a young fellow from out of town looking for the Cole and Crane timber office and asking questions about coal seams and railroad access. If I were you, I'd find out what he's up to. Always pays to check out the new players in the game."

Cap was feeling good as he walked out of Sergeant's office. Finally, something was going right. If Sergeant left the next day, April 17, he should be back in three or four days—Saturday or Sunday at the latest. Court met Monday. He'd have time to line up the neighbors downstream of the mill site—there were only two of those—and prepare the applications for the dam and mill permits. He'd also write Holmby and Sutphen. He wanted Holmby to return to Logan no later than the twenty-sixth to sign the contract. And Sutphen ought to come and look over the mill site. By the middle of May, he had a fighting chance of getting Sergeant's assurance that Cline was keeping the deal, of having the dam and mill permits in hand, and of getting Holmby to sign the contract. Maybe Sergeant could get Cline to send Pappy a message or a sign of his cooperation.

A woman's screech brought Cap out of his thoughts. He looked up and grinned at what he saw a little way down the boardwalk—two women of the idle sort trying to attach themselves to a young man dressed in a black suit and carrying a leather satchel. That was very likely the fellow Sergeant had told him about.

Fat-faced Sarah, greasy black bangs hanging down to her black shoe-button eyes, her big mouth showing gaps between black stubby teeth, stood with hands on hips, glaring at the young man.

"You aint no gen'leman," she screamed. "I was only wantin to keep you company, you bein a stranger in town. Looks like you could spare the change to buy a drink or two for my girlfriend and me." She straightened her hat loaded with bright-colored fake flowers the size and shape of cabbages and flounced her faded gingham dress that reached to the top of her muddy brogans.

"Begging your pardon, ladies." The young man moved to the edge of the boardwalk, then looked down into the deep gooey street mud and stopped. "Maybe you didn't realize I'm a married man."

Removing a corncob pipe from her mouth, Sarah's companion, a blonde in a flaming red dress, eyed him. "You aint got the married look about you."

Cap walked up to the "ladies."

"Can't you see, Sarah, this man's a preacher, not a drummer. Preachers don't drink when they're goin about the Lord's business."

The young man reacted by trying to appear serious and saintly.

Eyeing Cap and his new friend dubiously, Sarah spit into the street. "Aw, Cap, we didn't mean nothin. Come on, Ginny."

The women stomped off down the boardwalk, smoking their pipes, spitting and swearing.

Cap shook his head, partly because he remembered that as a teenager he'd chased after women like that when he'd had pocket money.

"My thanks for rescuing me from those she-devils." The young man held out his hand. "Name's Albert Holden. I'm into mining, not religion."

"Cap Hatfield." Cap wondered what Holden, who was shorter than he was, but of a husky, muscular build that showed under his suit, meant by "into mining." "Where you from, Mr. Holden?"

"Cleveland. I was looking for the Cole and Crane offices."

"Cole and Crane's a lumber company." Cap didn't mention that the office was four doors down the street.

"My interest is coal."

"If you're interested in coal, maybe you ought to talk to me."

"Be glad to," Holden replied. "Where is your office?"

Cap thought it would be better not to reveal he had no office. "Not close by. We could go sit in the bar or the hotel and have a drink, but the ladies might catch up with us there." Cap thought a minute. "I know a place where we can talk."

When they got to George Floyd's home, Cap pushed the door open and called for Floyd. No one answered, so they walked through the room that served as kitchen and bedroom and into the room full of books.

"My God!" Holden exclaimed. "I haven't seen a book since I left Cleveland. Look at this library." He walked back and forth, reading titles. "Who lives here?"

"There's just George Floyd. Guess he's out somewheres." Cap brought out a jug of whiskey and two glasses.

"And you walk right into his house? You must know him pretty well."

"All my life. Been borrowing his books for years. His son's the one that got me interested in bein a lawyer." He motioned Holden to a chair.

Holden removed his bowler and laid it on the table. "You're a lawyer?"

Dressed in blue jeans, denim shirt, and muddy mountain boots, Cap wouldn't be surprised if Holden had some doubts about him. "Went to University of Tennessee Law School in Knoxville." Cap poured them each a glass of whiskey. "This is Kentucky sour mash. It might agree with you better'n the corn whiskey they make around here."

Cap took a sip. It didn't have much taste, and it didn't take hold of you right away like the whiskey Johnse made. But Holden was smiling and looking satisfied.

"You have an interest in coal, Mr. Holden?"

"I was on my way to Cole and Crane because I was told they own timber land with coal cropping right out on the mountainside."

"So do I."

"I'd certainly like to hear about that."

"You working for anybody?"

"My father. Just got my degree from Harvard last year."

"I heard that's every bit as fine a school as the University of Tennessee."

Cap sensed Holden was trying to impress him, but had no idea where or what Harvard was. "There's a whole lot of coal out on Main Island Creek where I live. High volatile coal, the top grade. They use it to make steel and run trains." For once, Cap was glad he'd listened to Elliot.

"That's right." Holden nodded. "High volatile contains twenty-eight percent or more volatile matter. How much coal do you own?"

Cap shrugged. "No one knows. You can dig it right out of the side of the mountain above my house with a pick."

Holden took a long sip of the whiskey he appeared to be enjoying. "Just there for the taking? I'd sure like to see that."

Cap thought for a minute. If he took Holden out to Main Island Creek, there was no telling how Pappy would behave. But if he didn't take him there, Holden would find Cole and Crane and he might lose an important source of new business. "If we start now, we could get there by dark."

"I'd like that. I don't know if I could stand the Buskirk Hotel one more night."

And left on your own in Logan for a night, you might yet end up with Cole and Crane, Cap said to himself.

After borrowing a horse from Uncle Elias for Holden to use, they started out. "What kind of business is your father in?" Cap asked.

"Mining. I'm helping him modernize our operations and find new prospects."

"And coal's a new prospect for him?"

"Yes. He's in iron right now. But he'd like to lay his hands on some coal so he could supply the steel mills he sells iron to. That's why I'm here. To see how much coal you have hereabouts, test its quality, and assess the problems in transporting it to the Ohio River."

This conversation was getting really interesting. "We have a lot of high volatile out on Main Island Creek. Right now I'm about to cut timber and build a sawmill to supply crossties to a railroad that's coming up from the Ohio River to within a mile of the backside of our property." At least it would be if it was built on the West Virginia side of the Tug.

Chapter 47

Cap supposed Holden had never seen such a sight. When they rode up and had to call out for someone to let down the drawbridge, Holden watched the towering structure's slow descent in awed silence as Elliot and Elias winched it down. He held back for Cap to cross first, then followed, the clopping of their horses' hooves on the bridge bringing Pappy to the cabin door.

"Look what come over the mountain! My scalawag son and he's drug some feller all the way up this holler with him."

Cap sighed. Pappy was going to be ornery again.

"Mr. Hatfield, sir. Pleased to make your acquaintance." Holden jumped down from his horse and held out his hand. "Albert Holden here." Pappy shook hands so vigorously it looked like he was going to wrestle with Holden.

Cap climbed down from Traveller slowly, summoning determination to cope with Pappy's orneriness, trying to recall how John Floyd soothed and coaxed Pappy without confronting him, how Mama praised Pappy until he was compelled to live up to her standards, wishing their methods came naturally to him, a man of combative nature.

When two guards carrying Winchesters appeared from in back of the cabin, Cap watched for Holden's reaction and saw a fleeting look that could have been surprise. "Albert here's from Cleveland. Met him in town and brought him out to see our place and take a look at our coal."

"Guess you'd like to come in and set a spell," Pappy said to Holden. "Seeins you come all the way from Cleveland."

The three of them went inside and sat down before the fireplace where a great log smouldered. Holden's head twisted and turned, a look of incredulity coming over his face, as he took in the room with its huge stone fireplace and hearth, its log ceiling from which pegged poles full of clothes hung, and the beds stacked with rifles.

"Hope Albert aint no peddler," Pappy said. "We had a pesky peddler come by yesterday. Just wouldn't stop blatherin to your Mama about his pots and kettles. We was out by the pasture, so I turned the bull loose on him— chased that peddler clean up a tree." Pappy hee-hawed and slapped his knee. "You a peddler, Albert?"

No, no, no, Cap agonized to himself. They hadn't been here five minutes, and Pappy was already up to no good. "He's not a peddler."

"I'm not a peddler," Holden echoed, his voice calm.

"Left that peddler settin there shakin for a good while," Pappy went on. "His eyes was like to bug out of his head and his face turned yeller as a daisy."

"Why, Captain Anderson!" Mama's skirt swished as she darted across the room and set out a platter of gingerbread squares, from which an aroma rose like a warm, spicy fog. "You oughtn't to tell tales like that to our son's friend. He might believe you had a mean streak in you, not knowin you as a fine father and husband as I do, a man what always opens his home and welcomes visitors."

Pappy made no reply, but ducked his head down.

Like a bad dog caught piddling in the house, Cap thought. He silently blessed the miracle that was his Mama.

After Mama returned to her work, they helped themselves to the gingerbread and hot coffee. Holden sat back and cleared his throat.

"You seem to be under some stress here. I couldn't help noticing the armed men, and when we arrived you had the drawbridge raised." He lifted an eyebrow and looked first at Cap, then at Pappy.

"We got some troubles," Pappy replied. "Nothin we can't take care of."

Holden appeared unconvinced. "Rumors of lawless kidnappers and gunmen have caused some reluctance to invest in coal here in southern West Virginia. Nobody wants to get shot mining coal no matter how much money there might be in it."

"Take a look around at my men, Mr. Holden." Pappy pointed out the window at a sentry. "Them lawless varmints aint gonna bother us none."

"It's peaceful out here," Cap added. "Down by the border with Kentucky, that's where the trouble is." Down where the railroad was to go.

"How far away is that? My father's company is willing to take the usual risks that come with coal mining, but we're concerned about the rumors. One of my reasons for coming here is to hear the real story right from the horse's mouth."

"That's the best end of the horse to go to." Pappy hee-hawed again.

Holden laughed out loud as though he enjoyed being the butt of Pappy's joke.

"Kentucky's about forty miles away over those mountains." Cap pointed out a window. "We have a fort on the hilltop above here, always manned. No one comes this way without us seeing them."

Holden ceased grinning and got serious. "If we put a mine in near here, do you believe you can provide the security we'll need?"

"Who said you're gonna put a mine in here?" Pappy's nose hooked down and his beard jutted out.

"I apologize, Mr. Hatfield. I don't mean to give the impression we're planning anything without your approval. I know my father wouldn't go along with such presumptuousness either. But perhaps we could come up with a business proposition that would interest you. In the meantime, I certainly would like to see your coal."

Holden was being as smooth and polite as John Floyd, but how many more taunts would he put up with before he lost his temper? Cap didn't believe Holden had enough years on him to have developed a thick skin like Floyd, who could project whatever emotion would serve his purpose no matter how he was provoked. And Pappy could do some fierce provoking.

Elliot sauntered in, grabbed a chunk of gingerbread, the thick center piece Cap was eyeing, and sat in a chair in the corner.

"My son says our coal's high grade volatile." Pappy pointed to Elliot. "We can get a lot of money for it. What do we need your company for?"

"Steel mills and railroads are willing to pay good money for high volatile. If we decide we'd like to buy your land, we'd pay a good deal more than the going real estate price. Cap, however, has indicated a preference for leasing us the mineral rights."

"If *I* think sellin's the way to go, I'll do that," Pappy said. "If *I* think leasin makes more sense, I'll do that."

"You'll need a mining company to dig your coal out, and we need somebody with coal we can mine. Working together we can both profit handsomely."

"I'll show you our coal." Elliot's muffled voice came through a last mouthful of gingerbread. "I know everywhere it crops out around here."

"Good idea!" Cap roared his approval. That would get Holden away from Pappy for a while and they'd have a chance to talk. Maybe Mama would help him work on Pappy.

After Elliot and Holden had left with a pick to dig out samples, Cap hurried to explain why he was eager to do business with Holden.

"This man Holden—John Sergeant thinks he's a good bet. Looked him up in a book by some fellers named Dun and Bradstreet that makes a point of knowin how much money rich people have. His father's worth millions in iron mines and land, and he owns a newspaper—*The Cleveland Plain Dealer*. Albert's learnin the coal minin and the iron business so he can help out, take care of the business as his pappy gets older."

"Tryin to take the business away from his old man just like you." Pappy snorted.

Mama returned to sit beside Pappy. "Now, Anse, you and me've been talkin about gettin Cappie to help you more. The children and me need you here. If you're busy timberin and buildin a sawmill, you'll have to be away from home all the time again. Like the old days when you was gone day and night in them loggin camps or raftin down the river or holed up in that dadburned fort."

Cap adopted Mama's tone as best he could because he thought it had the best chance of success. "I'm only hopin to take over whatever chores are gettin in your way."

Pappy snorted. "I know what you want. You named it to me. You want to be captain of this place."

"Who else would you want to be captain around here when you and I are old, Anse?" Mama asked.

"That time's a long way down the road."

"If I take care of the crosstie deal and the mill for you and get something goin with Holden, it'll be easier for you to get ready for the raid." Cap held his breath, hoping Pappy would take the bait, fearing he'd live to regret the gamble he was taking.

"You said you was fixin it with Perry Cline so there wouldn't have to be no raid." Mama looked accusingly at Cap.

"I'm fixin it. And Pappy gave me his word he won't go if he's convinced our deal with Cline's workin. But he's not convinced yet and wants to be ready just in case."

"Did you, Anse? Did you give your word?"

"If I'm convinced, which I aint."

Cap leaned over and patted Mama's hand. "Pappy doesn't want to take a chance that something goes wrong. But it won't."

Pappy pulled at his beard. "Seein's you didn't handle your raid so good son, it's only right I should take care of this one. You get this crosstie deal goin and the mill started till I got more time for em. And see what kind of money Holden'll pay for a lease. Talk about royalties. I aint gonna sell my land."

Finally! He could go ahead with the crossties and the mill. Humble pie didn't taste too bad when it was washed down with success.

The next morning, as Nancy was packing him chunks of corn bread for the ride to Logan, he told her about Sergeant's mission to Pikeville, Holden's interest in coal, and the plan to get dam and mill permits.

"One thing bothers me," he added. "The way I talked Pappy into all this, I told him he'll have more time for getting ready for the raid if he lets me take care of the crossties and the mill for him."

"Oh no, Cap! Your mama and I've been trying to talk him out of that. She's gonna be fit to be tied."

"I know, I know. I'm takin a big chance. Now he's more fired up than ever. There'll be no holding him back if I don't have powerful evidence Cline's going to get our men out of jail."

"He might not be ready as soon as he thinks." Nancy bit lightly at her lip. "I took a chance, too."

"What? What chance?"

"You know when you didn't bring home any rifles or cartridges from Catlettsburg, he sent away for em by mail order."

Cap nodded.

"And I wrote up the order because nobody else around here can write."

Cap nodded again.

"I wrote forty cartridges instead of four thousand."

Cap laughed out loud and hugged Nancy. "Forty! That's not enough to load a repeater three times. When's it supposed to get here?"

"Maybe next week. Star Route Mail comes to Logan on Mondays and Thursdays."

"He'll be fit to be tied." Cap held his wife tightly.

"I'll tell him mail order's no good. They get their orders mixed up. Does that make you happy?" Nancy ran her hands over his chest and smiled a flirty smile up at him.

Chapter 48

Saturday night and Sergeant wasn't back yet. Everything seemed to be taking forever. Unable to sleep, Cap had left his bed at Uncle Elias's to walk the streets of Logan. He breathed in the spring air, freshened by the day's rain shower, and stretched his tight arm and shoulder muscles.

After returning Holden to Logan on Thursday and persuading him to stay with John Floyd's father, who would keep him away from Cole and Crane, Cap had ridden out to lower Beech Creek to line up his downstream neighbors before preparing permit applications. Cap laughed to himself, remembering the surprised looks on John Ferrell's and Christian and Peter Witte's faces.

"You mean you'll make us partners in this here cooperative if we let you dam Beech Creek?" They'd asked the same question over and over again, as if they couldn't believe the Hatfields wouldn't just dam the water and dare anyone to do something about it. He'd gotten them to sign an agreement that, during times when water had to be held back behind the dam, the Hatfields would pay them ten dollars a day. They'd been tickled to death to be collecting money they wouldn't have to lift a finger to get. Ferrell had agreed to come to court with Cap on Monday when the application for permits would be presented.

In addition to forming the dam and mill cooperative, he'd arranged to hire six more men for logging and gotten word from Sutphen that Holmby and Byrnes would be arriving in Logan on April 25. He'd also gotten to know Holden better; Cap believed he had him in his pocket now.

But Pappy could ruin it all in an instant. Although Cap was twenty-five, he sometimes thought he might as well be five for all the power he had over his future.

Cap waited until Sunday afternoon before setting out to look for Sergeant at Whited's boarding house where he was living. Sergeant answered Cap's knock right away and motioned him to one of two wicker bottom chairs in his sitting room, chairs made locally, unlike his fancy office furniture brought up from Ohio.

"Have I got a lot to tell you!" Sergeant laid a lit cigar in a big ash tray.

"You know what I want to hear, John. Don't you disappoint me now."

Sergeant was all smiles, his eyes gleaming. "I saw Cline. He was just as you said—all decked out in a frock coat and stovepipe hat, beard hanging to the middle of his chest."

"Good. Wouldn't want him to change a hair in that beard. I love to hate him just the way he is."

Sergeant got up and strutted around the room. "First thing I did, after stopping off at the hotel, was go see Cline in his law office. Now that's some office! Desk bigger than mine, lots of brocaded furniture and fancy draperies with tassels at the windows. Reminded me of offices I've been in in Philadelphia."

"The man's got a big weakness, needing all that show." Cap shifted his weight in his chair. It was hard to be patient, but he had to let Sergeant spin out his story.

Sergeant rubbed his hands together as though he were about to sit down to a feast. "He needs money to keep living that way. You should see his house—big three-story monster. Looks like a fortress."

Cap crossed his legs and jiggled his foot up and down. He was tired of waiting. "Did he agree to defend our men?"

"You knew he was already acting in behalf of your Uncle Wall—now he's also got the three Mahon brothers, Luke and Andy Varney, Alex Messer, Charlie Carpenter and Selkirk McCoy. I accompanied him to the jail to see them."

"How are they doing?"

"In pretty good spirits. Not too popular with the jailer and the other prisoners, though—they're up before dawn every morning, talking loud and demanding breakfast."

"Farm folks are used to getting up early. What do folks expect? Did you talk to Uncle Wall and Plyant Mahon about deeding over their land to Cline?"

"They were hesitant at first, until I read them your letter advising them to do it. Then they signed. Cline was pleased as he could be. Reached out his long, skinny arm till his bony fingers snatched up those deeds quick as a snake gulping down a mouse." Sergeant imitated Cline's grab.

"Land's important to him. I knew he'd deal."

"I admire the way you set things up, Cap, like you know how they're going to turn out." Sergeant squinted at him. "Anyway, Cline's promised to help them, but they'll all have to serve some time. He says if it looks like someone will have to hang for killing Allifair McCoy, you'll let him know which one of the men they're holding is the killer, and he's betting it was Cotton Top. So he's not going to defend him, just in case he's the one." Then Sergeant frowned. "Which brings to mind a problem. No obstacle to your enterprise, you understand. But I want you to promise you'll stay calm."

"I'm not making any promises. Out with it." Cap hoped Cline hadn't gone and done something foolish.

"It concerns Cotton Top. Evidently he's not entirely stupid. He realized Cline will be defending everyone but him, got all worked up about it and told the Pikeville prosecuting attorney some tales about some murders. Here, look at this." Sergeant held out a copy of the *Louisville Courier-Journal*.

"A Hatfield Talks: Murder and Arson." Cap read the headline aloud. The first paragraph said Cotton Top Mounts, with no lawyer except a public defender, felt abandoned by the Hatfields and, assuming his life would be spared if he talked, had consented to tell all. "I was present at the murder of the three McCoy brothers, namely, Tolbert, Phamer, and the younger Randolph McCoy." He read the supposed quote from Cotton Top to Sergeant.

Cap exploded. "Those aren't Cotton Top's words. He can't talk like that. Someone's putting words in his mouth."

"I expect you're right."

Cap read on. "It was on the night of the ninth of August 1882. . . . The three McCoy brothers were taken from a school house in Logan County, West Virginia. . . . We brought them to the Kentucky side. . . . Carpenter tied them to a pawpaw bush and hung a lantern over their heads. Anse Hatfield then said to them: 'Boys, if you have any peace to make with your Maker, you better do it.'"

Cap shook his head. Pappy never said that.

"Tolbert and Randolph began praying, but Phamer did not. However, before the boys had time to finish their prayers, Johnse Hatfield shot Phamer. . . As soon as the first shots were fired, the others followed suit, and all the bodies were riddled with bullets. The parties engaged in the shooting of the boys were Anse Hatfield, Johnse Hatfield, Cap Hatfield, Alex Messer, Charles Carpenter and Tom Wallace."

Cap searched Sergeant's face for signs of trouble, but Sergeant was good at keeping his thoughts to himself.

"Nothin like what this paper claims Cotton Top said ever happened," Cap said. "They must have got him to say it to try to save his neck."

"You don't have to justify yourself to me." Sergeant laid a hand on a ledger on a small table beside him as if to swear on it.

"I shot a few of Phillips's men when they invaded Logan County and killed my Uncle Jim and Bill Dempsey. But I'm a soldier, not a murderer, John. I want shed of these wars as much as anybody. I wrote all the newspapers around here to say I want peace. Did anybody read about that?"

"I did," Sergeant said softly.

Cap got back to reading the article aloud. "Cap Hatfield also related to me how he and Tom Chambers shot and killed Jeff McCoy whom they had arrested and allowed to escape so they would have a chance to shoot him as he tried to swim across the Tug River to Kentucky."

Cap wished he could burn the danged newspaper to the ground. Then came the part about the New Year's raid.

"When we approached the burning cabin, Allifair McCoy yelled out: 'I know you're there, Cap Hatfield. I heard your voice.' Then Cap yelled out: 'D— her! She recognized me! Shoot her!' And I did."

Cotton Top had confessed! But the way his idiot cousin had told the story, Cap feared, wouldn't put an end to his undeserved reputation as a child killer.

"As I told you before," Sergeant said. "I'm sure none of this presents an obstacle to our plans. Cline's got Frank Phillips on the county payroll guarding the jail. He's talking to the McCoys, telling them he's looking after their interests and he's handing out pieces of his railroad supply work to the right people in Pikeville. Pikeville's sewed up tight. They're on our side."

Chapter 49

On Monday morning at nine thirty, Cap and John Ferrell sat at the front table in the Logan County courtroom, awaiting the arrival of Judge Harvey. Cap was disappointed they were the only people there. He'd wanted to flaunt the dam and mill permits in front of Nighbert. And he'd wanted Nighbert to see him as a lawyer, dressed in a dark gray suit and white shirt with a stiffly starched collar, bringing his own case before the court.

The courtroom had remained unchanged since Cap's last visit—John Floyd's and Willis Wilson's portraits still up, as well as those of Robert E. Lee and Jefferson Davis. If the recount showed Fleming was in and Wilson out, Cap was sure Logan's citizens, strong supporters of Floyd and Wilson, would resist efforts to remove Floyd's and Wilson's portraits and hang Fleming's.

When Judge Harvey walked in, the jail keeper stood and announced, "Hear ye! Hear ye! The April Logan County Circuit Court, Year of Our Lord, 1889, will now come to order. The Honorable Justice John Harvey presiding. All rise."

Cap and John Ferrell stood and sat when the judge did.

"Mill and dam permit applications," Harvey muttered. "From William Anderson Hatfield."

Cap adjusted the knot in his tie to attract Harvey's eye to how splendidly he was dressed. "My application meets all the requirements with respect to suitability of location and permission of my downstream neighbors. I'd like you to meet Mr. Ferrell. He and his neighbors have entered into a cooperative agreement with me."

"That so?" Harvey barked at Ferrell.

Ferrell beamed. "Sure is. Cap's gonna cut us in on his crosstie business."

"Crosstie business," Harvey muttered. "Is Mr. Nighbert in the courtroom by any chance?" He looked around. "I see he's not." Harvey slowly read over the application again, sighed, then signed.

Cap walked out of the courtroom, jubilant. Before nightfall, he'd bet Nighbert and Ragland would know he was acting as his own attorney and planning to set up a sawmill to make crossties for the railroad.

"I got the permits," Cap said first thing after he entered the cabin.

Pappy, absorbed in whittling a handle to fit into a hoe blade, didn't react to his announcement.

"I got the permits and Cline's keepin the deal. Sergeant saw him and he's representin our men."

"What's Phillips up to?"

"Cline has him in charge of guardin the jail and seein that nobody lynches the prisoners and they don't escape."

"That don't sound like enough to keep Phillips out of trouble."

"He's busy chasin after some woman now and he needs money."

"Good." Pappy tried to jam the handle into the blade. It wouldn't fit. "Maybe we can catch him unawares when we go over there."

Cap could scarcely stand to listen to this. "That's what Cotton Top's sayin you'll do. He's told the prosecuting attorney in Pikeville it'd be just like you to ride into town, guns blazing."

"Cotton Top said that?"

"I read it in the *Courier-Journal*. He's talking, tryin to save his own neck. He's figured out Cline is defending everybody but him."

"Then maybe we'll just leave Cotton Top in that jail when we get the rest out." Pappy rammed the handle into the blade successfully this time and brandished the assembly like a weapon.

"You gave me your word you wouldn't go if Cline was keepin his side of the deal."

"If I was convinced he was keepin his side. So far I aint convinced."

"Cline's after land, money, and a contract with the railroad. And he's gettin what he wants. He'll be true to his word."

"Sergeant talk to our men?"

"He did and they're pleased as can be over what we got Cline to do for em. They told Sergeant to tell you they're mighty beholden to you for savin em from hangin."

"They figure I had somethin to do with what Cline's up to?"

"What else would they think? They know you had to be behind it. Why, you're a hero to those men."

"I'll be more of a hero when I bust em out of jail."

"Not so, Pappy. They could get killed if you try doin that, or lynched. They told Sergeant they're tired of war and they're happy you're bringin peace to these mountains."

Pappy fidgeted in his seat, looking very uncomfortable.

"You've got more admirers," Cap went on. "The Englishmen and Albert Holden."

"If they're gonna admire me, they'd best do it for the right reasons."

Mama and Uncle Elias, who was carrying a heavy crock that Mama sometimes stored cottage cheese in, entered the cabin.

"I guess you aint gonna be runnin off to Pikeville right away, Anse." Elias set the crock down with a thud. "I just come from the post office. The Star Route mail was in, but you got only forty cartridges."

"Only forty?" Pappy sputtered.

Cap tried to look as surprised as Pappy.

Elias nodded. "Nancy says them mail order places is always makin mistakes. She thinks maybe some of their help don't read all that good."

"That just about fixes it, don't it, Anse?" Mama studied Pappy as she spread the red oilcloth on the table. "You daren't ride into Pikeville without them cartridges."

"No sense in goin at all," Cap echoed, watching Mama set out a jar holding some daffodils from her new flower garden.

"I never thought that raid made sense," Elias added. "It's time to call off this foolishness, Anse."

"Them flowers is mighty pleasin to the eye, Levicy," Pappy said. "A feller could grow fond of lookin at em."

That evening, after Joey and Coleman were asleep, Cap and Nancy sat and talked before the fire. He worried that Nancy looked exhausted. She'd been planting potatoes all day and, as usual, she'd gone the extra mile to do the job right, first by looking in the almanac for the days when the moon would be dark because that was the best planting time for preventing potatoes from growing too quickly to the top of the ground and drying out, then making the effort to plant them deep to protect against a late freeze. Somehow he had to find the time to help her. Her youth seemed to be disappearing right before his eyes.

"When I'm away so much it's hard on you," Cap said. "But pretty soon I'll have the money to hire us a farm hand again."

"It'll take at least two hired hands to replace me." Nancy smiled a tired smile. "And Joey. Did you see what Joey did?" She showed him the contents of a tin half-filled with corn grits laboriously obtained by scraping ears of corn over a tin gritter.

"That must have taken him all day. Nancy, children in Knoxville don't have to grit corn to be sure they'll have enough to eat. I bet they've never even seen a gritter."

"Joey's gonna grow up to be a good worker. He'll never be a lazy, good-for-nothing."

Cap laughed. "You've been listenin to Mama." For Mama the lowest, most despicable kind of human was a "lazy, good-for-nothing" and nobody, not even Pappy, wanted her to refer to him that way.

"I almost forgot," he added. "There's bad news about Pappy's cartridge order. Uncle Elias told Pappy the mail order company made a big mistake and sent forty instead of four thousand."

"When I do a job, I do it right!"

"We got to keep workin on Pappy. Mama's against the raid, we're against it, Uncle Elias is, he's hardly got any cartridges, and now I told him our men don't want him to come for em. But he still isn't sayin he won't do it."

"You know him." Nancy sighed. "If he goes to Pikeville, then he's still in charge. If he doesn't, he's not the captain leadin his men into battle anymore and he's not takin care of his family. It's hard for that man to give up everything he's proud of. We've got to keep on him, Cap—you and me and your Mama and Uncle Elias. And you can add your brother Elliot to that list. He wants to go to college."

"John Floyd and John Sergeant are on our side."

Nancy clucked her tongue. "It always takes a whole army to deal with your Pappy."

Chapter 50

Early the next morning Cap headed for Logan, intent on returning with Holmby and Byrnes, Phineas Sutphen, John Sergeant, Albert Holden, Doc Rutherford, John Floyd and his father George Floyd, a whole army of the wealthiest and most educated men Cap could recruit, mustered for the sole purpose of dealing with Pappy. Today, Cap planned to achieve signed business deals that would profit his family for years to come and put an end to preparations to raid Pikeville. He would become the man he'd dreamed he was the day he'd led the disastrous New Year's raid, a man who would save his family from a violent, poverty-stricken life.

After he left Traveler at Uncle Elias's, the first person he spotted was John Floyd emerging from the barbershop. "Your face must be smooth as a woman's, John," he said. Floyd still got a shave once, sometimes twice, a day at Altizer's.

"Don't laugh, Cap. If Wilson loses the recount and I'm out of office, I'm planning to run for the legislature and Altizer's shop will be a necessity."

"My family will back you if you run. You can count on us."

"Thanks. Actually, I'm aiming higher this time. The legislature will choose one of its own for U. S. Senator in 1890, and I think I have a chance for it."

"Senator!" As Senator, Floyd might be able to do good things for the Hatfields.

"How are you doing with your father? Today's a big day for all of us. I hope he's not still planning that godawful raid."

"Mama, Nancy, and Uncle Elias are working on him. And today you and I and the rest— it'll take all of us together—are going to gang up on him."

They entered the lobby of the Buskirk Hotel where the Englishmen probably had spent a wretched night they were sure to complain about. Byrnes was slouched in a shabby armchair, seemingly unable to arrange either himself or his clothes suitably. Holmby's black hair, usually precisely combed, was a disheveled mess. No one else was in the lobby that doubled as a storage room with shelves of bedding, towels, basins, pitchers, and oil lamps. People didn't usually gather there until evening.

"Mr. Byrnes and I have been suffering anxieties, Hatfield." Holmby looked as though he'd eaten something disagreeable.

"I should have gotten you put up at George Floyd's or Uncle Elias's."

Cap wished he'd remembered the bad mood Buskirk's had put the English-men in the last time they were here.

"I'm not referring to this wretched hut with hotel pretenses." Holmby looked grim. "But rather to what we've read recently in the *Courier-Journal*."

Cap tried to keep a poker face. "What was that?"

"This!" Holmby slapped a copy of the paper into Cap's hand.

Cap saw it was the issue carrying Cotton Top's rants. He handed the paper to Floyd.

"Tsk, tsk." Floyd shook his head. "Newspapers! The greater the sensation they create, the greater their circulation, the more advertisements are placed in their paper, and the more the money pours in. Who can trust them to report objective facts and surround them with logic?" Cap never ceased admiring Floyd. He made it seem as though the newspaper was no more reliable than a town gossip.

"Is any of this true?" Holmby demanded.

"Look how readily Cline joined forces with the Hatfields." Floyd tossed the paper onto the chair next to him. "Would he have done this if he thought Cap was a villainous murderer?"

"Cline came to Catlettsburg to personally assure us we should pay no attention to what Mounts was saying," Holmby admitted. "He said no one in Kentucky was getting excited about the accusations. But it's all the talk in the Catletttsburg, Louisville, and Cincinnati papers."

Cap forced a small grin. "I am indebted to Mr. Cline."

"We've grown to be friends and I have a certain admiration for you, Cap," Holmby said. "But as a businessman, I must insist on assurance there'll be no interruptive warfare perpetrated by your family while you're executing your contract with us."

"You have my word."

"I mean concrete assurance, such as deposit of a bond or deed of trust for your land. Mr. Cline has deposited the deed to his home with me to show his good faith."

Cap gasped. "He did that? There's no need when you can write into our contracts that they are null if at any time we're fighting when we should be fulfilling our obligations to you."

Holmby frowned. "It's one thing for you to give up potential assets and another to forfeit current ones. I want that deed in trust and if either of you violates my terms, you both forfeit your deposits. Is that clear?"

Cap had never run into anyone so hard-nosed. He looked to Floyd for help. He'd be in a heck of a mess if he gave Holmby the deed to his land in trust and Pappy tried to rescue their men from the Pikeville jail.

"That's an unusual request," Floyd said.

"It's not a request. It's a demand."

"I'll put up the land I own with my house on it," Cap said. "Six hundred acres." He wished he could talk to Nancy before he did this. He was gambling he could keep Pappy out of Pikeville. It was a lot to risk, and she should have her say. But he had to decide now.

On the rough and rocky ride back to Main Island Creek with his colleagues and allies, Cap ran over in his mind what he hoped to see come from this meeting. Besides crosstie and coal contracts, he wanted good jobs assured for all the men in the family—not just working on timber crews or digging out coal. In those jobs, you were paid until your work was finished, then easily dispensed with. He wanted his family to be running railroad depots, constructing mines, owning stores—endeavors that would last and bring in real money. He had to make sure all the money didn't flow out of their hands into those of Norfolk and Western and Holden's father's company. He'd read a great deal of history and knew that if they let the big money out of Logan County they'd never be more than a bunch of sharecroppers, at the mercy of people who didn't care a whit about them or their way of life.

As they rounded the bend of the rocky trail leading to the drawbridge, Cap looked back from his lead position to admire the most powerful and educated group that had ever assembled in Logan County. What a contrast between these men and the "army" he'd led on the New Year's raid, hoping for a scar he could exhibit and brag about as a substitute for a captain's pin like Pappy's. What could he hope for today?

When they arrived at the edge of the creek, Cap's brothers Troy and Elias were standing on the other side, ready to let down the drawbridge and take the horses as everyone dismounted. On the way into the cabin, the men crossed a front porch swept clean of dust and dirt. Mama's windows shone and sparkled and the great wooden front door was wide open. No armed guards were in sight.

Mama, Nancy, and his sisters Nancy Belle and Mary greeted the visitors at the door with smiles on their faces, wearing new mail order dresses—shirt-waists with a long row of buttons on the front and skirts held out by several petticoats. He was surprised at how pretty his sisters could be.

Inside, chairs had been arranged in a semi-circle before the fireplace, the table used for meals having been shoved to the wall. There was not a rifle or gun rack to be seen.

Everything was perfect.

Pappy stood in front of the fireplace, dressed in a dark blue mail order suit with matching vest, a blue and yellow tie, a Confederate pin in his lapel, and a white shirt, none of it fitting exactly right, the suit coat sagging down further on one side than the other, the too-tight shirt collar unbuttoned, pants puckering where they were tucked into his mountain boots. But ill-fitting as they were, the clothes gave Pappy a certain look of authority, as Deacon Anse's suit always had when he held court.

"I believe I know most of you folks." Pappy went over to Holmby and Byrnes. "Thought you might like to see my insignia." He rubbed his finger over the gold Confederate pin, big as a silver dollar, he'd worn on his captain's hat during the War. "My rank's captain."

Cap would be grateful if this was the worst of Pappy's shenanigans today. He laid a hand on Pappy's shoulder. "First in war, first in peace, first in the hearts of his countrymen."

Pappy stood erect, a hero receiving his due, proudly displaying his danged pin. "Well now, set yourselfs down whilst my old woman and the girls get to the kitchen. They been fixin a feast for you fellers."

"That's very kind of you and your wife." Having seated himself, Holmby smiled. He appeared more relaxed now that he had the deed in trust to Cap's land in his pocket. "I anticipate a satisfying meeting."

Through a side window, Cap caught a glimpse of Elliot standing and listening. Go ahead and listen, Elliot, Cap said to himself. Your future depends on what happens in this room.

Nancy stuck her head through the kitchen door. Cap shook his head no. Not yet. He went to stand with his back to the fireplace, facing the group.

"Gentlemen, many a night I have stood watch, moonlight glinting off my rifle barrel. Many a night Pappy and I and my brothers have slept like cats, never closing both eyes at once, one ear always open for footfalls." Cap watched each man's reactions, concentrating on Pappy's.

"These wars robbed me of my boyhood," he continued. "Now that we are on the eve of peace, I look forward to giving my younger brothers and sisters and my own children a childhood full of farm life and children's play instead of guns. My father will have time to guide their lives, instead of training them to be soldiers." Cap was thrilled that someone had seen fit to clear all the rifles out of the room. It made what he said so much more believable.

Pappy nodded. "I been kept away from my wife and babies many and many a time. I don't like bein kept away from em. Levicy made clear to me she don't like me bein away neither."

"We all want to sleep in our beds with better companions than our boots and rifles," Cap continued.

"Is that your idea of it, Mr. Hatfield?" Holden asked Pappy. "Are your ideas of peace the same as your son's?" Cap wondered if Holden still had Pappy's story of setting the bull on the peddler on his mind.

"For the most part, I intend to stay here lookin after my family. We're safe here, what with the drawbridge and the fort."

Cap grimaced. He'd half expected this, no recognition at all of their success with Cline. He nodded to Nancy who was peering through the doorway. She pushed Cap's sister Rosie into the room. The little girl ran to Pappy, her golden curls bobbing to the bounce of her step. She climbed up on him, hugged his neck, and settled happily into his lap. Pappy's face softened, his eyes glowing with a pleasure he couldn't hide. Cap silently rejoiced. No trace of ferocity showed in Pappy's face or demeanor.

"An angel," Byrnes exclaimed. "A little vision of an angel."

"'Pon my word! Are you my angel?" Pappy leaned his head down and brushed his whiskers to tickle Rosie's face.

"Yes," she giggled.

Gesturing toward Pappy and Rosie, Cap continued with his well-rehearsed speech.

"We, like Augustus Caesar, having pursued and captured the dove of peace, can now look forward to a time of prosperity. The citizens of Logan County will live in peace with the dignity of a good income from their labor. Respect from the outside world will be ours." For some reason he thought of Mary White, rather than the outside world.

"And wealth for all of us," Sergeant called out.

"For Norfolk and Western's part," Holmby said, "We are cheered and heartened by the changes Anse Hatfield and his son Cap are bringing to Logan County and the entire Tug River Valley. We shall all prosper from it."

"Anse, you are about to harvest the fruit of your efforts," John Floyd said. "You have earned the right to lay down your arms and rest."

"They might be laid down for the moment, but I'm keepin em handy," Pappy retorted.

Where were the guns? Not only hadn't Cap seen a single rifle, he still hadn't glimpsed any men on lookout outside—not one.

"Mr. Hatfield, I wish to present you with a gift of appreciation," Holmby said. "From a beneficiary of your efforts to bring peace to this region."

What was this? Cap hadn't been told of a gift.

"If this don't beat all," Pappy said, looking more eager than Cap bet he wanted to.

Holmby took a small black leather box from his coat pocket, opened it and handed it to Pappy. "Why it's a gold watch!" Pappy exclaimed.

What a marvelous, clever, cunning gift. Holmby's generosity was a piece of good luck Cap had never expected.

Nancy Belle darted from the kitchen. "Let me see it, let me see it!" she coaxed.

Pappy held the box so she could look into it.

"Oh, I know how it goes!" she said. "Stand up, Pappy!"

Pappy set Rosie down and stood. Through a buttonhole in his vest, Nancy Belle pushed a gold disc attached to a gold chain that she let drape across his chest to the little vest pocket where she tucked the watch away. She stood back, eyes shining, to admire him. Pappy looked proud.

"What's this?" Nancy Belle took a little gold key from the box, holding it to the sunlight streaming through a window, turning it this way and that so it twinkled. "Look how it sparkles."

"That's a key to wind the watch," Byrnes said. "The sparkle comes from diamonds on its handle."

Cap saw Pappy's jaw drop. He had a gold watch like Nighbert always wore in his vest pocket and a diamond-studded key to go with it.

"Now this here's a thing a man can be right proud of." Pappy had never looked so pleased. "Thank you, Mr. Holmby and Mr. Byrnes."

"Oh, it's not from us, Mr. Hatfield," Holmby said. "There's an inscription on the back. Let me read it to you." Lifting the watch from Pappy's pocket, Holmby turned it so everybody could see the printing. He cleared his throat. "To Anderson Hatfield with gratitude from Perry Cline, Your Partner in Peace."

Pappy's face paled and his eyes protruded. "Cline?" Cap bet Pappy felt like Holmby had just presented him with a golden rattlesnake.

"With gratitude," Floyd said. "It says 'with gratitude' on the back."

Pappy fumbled with the watch, his lips moving but no sound coming out.

"Now do you believe me?" Cap whispered in Pappy's ear. "It's for real. Cline's our partner."

Pappy swung the watch gently back and forth on its chain. "Have to admit this looks like a sign, like he's passin me a peace pipe."

A sign! With a pang, Cap realized the lone whinny from the barn had been a sign. Why had he heard only one horse—Pappy's Queen, if he wasn't mistaken? With strange horses riding up, the whole barnful would normally have become excited. He strode over to the window where Elliot was watching. "Where's the horses?"

"Huh?" Elliot shrugged.

"Where's the horses, Elliot? They're not in the barn."

"Pappy had the guards take em up by the fort. He said to stay out of sight and keep their rifles out of sight."

"The fort!" The fort was at the head of a trail leading to Kentucky. Cap's mind raced. He turned to stare at Pappy's boots. Why hadn't Pappy worn his hard shoes today? With trembling hands, he took Rosie, clamoring to sit in Pappy's lap again, to the kitchen and handed her over to Mama.

"What's he up to?" he whispered. "Where are the guards and the horses?"

"He sent em up to the fort."

He motioned to Nancy. "The guards and the horses aren't here," he said. "What's goin on?"

"Your Pappy told the guards to go up to the fort. Wanted things to look peaceful for your meetin, I guess. A lot of armed men wouldn't look so good."

Cap's heart beat faster. "Don't need horses to go a quarter mile to the fort. We always go there on foot. Unless we're going on to somewhere else."

Alarm spread over Nancy's face. "You don't think he's got it in his head to go to Pikeville today? Without those cartridges and dynamite?"

"What better time for a raid—right after Sergeant's visit, right when Phillips and Cline are least expecting it."

"What are we gonna do, Cap?"

"I don't know. That watch from Cline took him by surprise. He nearly fainted. Look, my hands are sweaty."

Nancy took his hands in hers. "I'm so scared."

"Wouldn't surprise me if Pappy makes his move before this day's over. We got to think of something quick. It always seems like the more important a thing is to my life, the faster I got to figure it out."

Cap returned to the meeting to see everyone gathered around Pappy, inspecting and admiring the watch. Elliot was standing on his toes to get a look at it. He could use Elliot. Sidling up to his brother, Cap pulled him to the cabin doorway.

"Elliot, I want you to do somethin for me, for us," he whispered.

Elliot scrunched his face into a sneer.

"Listen! And listen good. I think Pappy's got the men at the fort ready to raid Pikeville." Elliot blinked his eyes, but didn't remove the sneer.

"If they carry out a raid, you won't be going to college. We'll be back to fighting and hiding out. Do you want that?" Cap glared sternly down at Elliot.

Elliot's sneer collapsed.

"If Pappy raids Pikeville, we'll be holed up in our houses or in the fort for good. There'll be no logging and no sawmill. And there sure won't be money for college."

"Don't let Pappy ruin everything for us, Cap," Elliot pleaded.

"I need your help."

"How?" Elliot looked unhappy and suspicious.

"I want you to run up to the fort and tell the men they're to ride down here at once with their rifles and ammo. Make something up. Tell them we think our men were taken out of the Pikeville jail down to Catlettsburg and we got to come up with a new plan quick."

"Pappy'll kill us if he finds out."

"We're dead anyway if this doesn't work," Cap whispered back. "Now get going!"

"If you're wrong about this, I'm gonna tell Pappy this was all your crazy idea and you made me do it." Elliot wheeled around and ran up the path toward the fort.

Cap returned to stand before the fireplace, holding up his hands to get the group's attention. "Let's proceed, gentlemen. I want to speak again of Augustus Caesar. Augustus turned Rome away from dark times of constant war and struggle just to survive. He turned Rome toward a golden age that was to last for centuries. Augustus gave Rome two gifts that allowed her to rise again—roads and peace."

Pappy was looking, not at him, but out the window.

"We in our time can look forward to our own golden age—Pax Romana—because we Hatfields are bringing peace, with the help of all of you in this room. Norfolk and Western is bringing us a railroad. We'll soon build roads to connect our timber camps and our mill to the railroad."

"Cap's right." Doc Rutherford looked directly at Pappy. "He's right, you know."

Fidgeting with the watch in his pocket, Pappy failed to acknowledge Rutherford's words.

"Let me tell you how I see our fortunes unfolding," Cap went on. ""First we'll do our part in building the railroad. Mr. Sutphen will help Pappy and me get a sawmill going, Mr. Sergeant will be our go-between with Cline in Pikeville and he'll help Norfolk and Western buy the easements for their tracks. If we offer timbermen good wages, say $1.50 a day, we'll have men rushing over here to work for us. No sense in spending valuable time dickering over wages. The railroad's got a schedule to meet."

His gaze fixed on the floor, Pappy didn't react.

"I quite appreciate your attention to our schedule," Holmby said. "And perhaps your work will be speeded to know Byrnes and I have decided that the railroad will indeed be built on the West Virginia side of the border. Even as we speak, tracks are being laid and a bridge is being constructed."

"We are grateful," Cap said. Grateful was putting it mildly. The tracks would pass less than a mile from their sawmill and coal field, very likely making them the most prosperous sawmill and mine operators in the mountains. "Once the railroad's in, Norfolk and Western can build spurs to Holden's mines. They'll be hauling coal from our mines out to the whole world."

"Cheap, ready transportation," Holden said. "For a magnificent source of high grade volatile. Overnight, we'll become a power to be reckoned with in the coal industry." He rubbed his hands together in anticipation.

"I say, not excessively cheap," Byrnes said. "We at Norfolk and Western, being devoted capitalists, do expect a decent profit."

"Of course, of course," Holden replied. "There's sufficient treasure for us all. But I do appreciate my great fortune in timing—commencing my coal ventures at exactly the moment dependable transportation is becoming available."

Cap, closely watching Pappy, became alarmed as the great nose hooked sharply downward and his hands tightened into fists. Pappy wasn't reacting to what was going on in the room at all. He was responding to events in his own mind.

"And my family will get our share every time Holden digs out a chunk of coal." Cap grinned at Pappy in an effort to spark a response, but to no avail. "Between the railroad ties and the coal, Pappy, you'll be able to marry your daughters to fine young men and send Elliot to college. Heck, you can send all the boys to college—Troy, Elias, Joe, Willis. Coleman, and Joey, too."

"I know you're pleased about that, Anse." George Floyd turned to Pappy. "Your children won't have the hard times you and I have seen."

"We did have some hard times," Pappy acknowledged. "That's for a truth. But we're a pair of tough old varmints, aint we, George?"

"Anse, you heard Cap say he was robbed of his boyhood." Rutherford ran his hand through a shock of white hair. "And I bet Johnse and Bobby Lee'd say the same. You want a better life for your younger children, don't you?"

"You know I do, Doc." Pappy looked with almost reverent fondness at his old friend.

"And Mama," Cap said. "You always said Mama was the workinest woman in the world. Now she won't have to work so hard. You'll be able to buy shirts for the boys and dresses for the girls so she won't have to make em anymore. You can buy Mama a cook-stove like the ones I saw in Knoxville."

"A cook-stove!" Pappy snorted. "I don't want my supper comin out of no ugly iron thing."

"My wife really likes hers," Rutherford said. "She doesn't have to bend over the fireplace all the time and it cooks real good, Anse."

"Well, Doc. I reckon if your wife's got one, my Levicy'll have to get one, too. But I aint gonna like it." He slapped his knee and hee-hawed, then stopped abruptly.

Cap was becoming increasingly edgy. Fifteen minutes had gone by since he'd sent Elliot to the fort. If he'd persuaded the men to come down, they should be here in about another ten or fifteen minutes.

"My brother Johnse is a very persuasive kind of fellow," Cap said. "He's got a good line for the men and he's not too bad with the women, either." He winked. "Any of you fellows think you'll have a place for a man who can get anyone to buy whatever he's sellin?"

"We're eager to encourage businessmen to set up stores and other establishments along the railroad," Byrnes said. "We'd like our trains to be filled with store goods when they come in as well as with coal and timber when they leave. And, of course, each town or general store will require a depot. Would your son Johnse be willing to sign on prospective customers and establish depots at strategic locations, Mr. Hatfield?"

Pappy seemed to be having difficulty focusing on what was going on in the room. "Thank you, Mr. Byrnes."

A job like that would be better than anything Johnse could ever have expected in his sorry life, Cap thought, *a drawback being that he'd probably have to learn to read and write.* But things were going well. The Hatfields were going to come out of this with high-paying jobs, sawmill profits, and coalfield royalties. There'd be no hard scrabble lives for them anymore.

That is, if Pappy didn't raid Pikeville and ruin everything.

Holden turned to Holmby and Byrnes. "With all the business I'll be bringing you, you ought to give me preferred rates."

Holmby smiled thinly. "We'll deal fairly with you, Holden. But I do recall a minute ago you were grateful to us for consenting to bring your coal to the outside world."

"If you get tough with us, we'll build our own railroad," Holden snapped. "Don't think we can't do it."

"Calm down, calm down!" Cap held up his hands. "One thing we don't need around here is to war amongst ourselves." He was beginning to be a regular peacemaker, a first for his family. He'd have his work cut out for him keeping this team of strong, ambitious men working together.

"I could use a land agent," Holden said. "To make buying and leasing arrangements for coal rights."

Cap pointed to John Sergeant who stood up and raised his hand. "At your service. I've been buying and selling in this county for twenty years."

"Aha!" Holmby pressed the fingers of both hands together. "And *our* needs?"

"You'll need 300-foot strips of bottomland between hills so there's room for tracks and sidespurs and tipples," Sergeant said. "And you'll need a rail bed with less than three percent grade. Coal trains are heavy. I think I can find what you need."

Holmby looked pleased.

"I've drawn up some papers for all of you to sign." Cap decided to plow on and hope for the best. "I have contracts between my family and the railroad, between my family and Mr. Holden, and between Mr. Holden and the railroad. And an agreement with Phineas Sutphen to help us get a mill built."

"We're ready," Holmby said. "Providing the price, quantity, and schedule are as we agreed upon in Catlettsburg. When do you expect to turn out the first crossties?"

"I'll order the band saws from Pittsburgh soon as I get back to Catlettsburg," Sutphen said. "I'm a good customer, so we should get em inside of six weeks."

"By then, Pappy and I'll have the dam built," Cap said. "Around the first of July. It'll probably take another month to get the mill set up and running. Meanwhile, the timber crew will be cutting and hauling logs so we'll have a heap of good oak trees waitin."

"That puts the first crossties in late July or first of August," Sutphen said.

Byrnes patted his stomach where his vest stretched tight. "That's just about when we hope to reach the Tug with our tracks. Providing Mr. Sergeant can get us easements in time."

"I'll get right on it," Sergeant said.

"Well, you fellers are doin such a good job here, you don't need me." Pappy stood up. "I'll just mosey off and take care of a chore I got to do."

No! Cap panicked. He had to stop Pappy.

Everybody watched in silence as Pappy pulled the gold disc through its button hole, lifted the watch from its pocket, and replaced the watch, disc, and chain in the box with the diamond-studded key. Cap opened his mouth and forced words to come out, any words.

"You can't go yet. Mama's cookin supper." He grabbed Pappy's arm.

"You fellers go right ahead and eat. Don't hold nothin up for me."

"I need you to sign papers," Cap jabbered. "A whole lot of papers."

"You sign em for me, son."

"Anse, you old goat, what are you thinking of, walking out of here now?" Rutherford huffed the words out. "This is one of the most important days of your life and your children's and grandchildren's."

"Let's get em all in here," Cap called out. "Tell em what's happening. Mama, Nancy, Nancy Belle . . . good news! Everybody get out here." Out of the kitchen came all the women and girls and little Willis. "Elias, Joey, Troy . . . All of you, come inside!" Cap yelled out a window. In a few moments, the room was filled with women and children joining the meeting.

"Gather around." Cap hung onto Pappy's arm with one hand and motioned all of them to crowd around. "Hear the good news. Go ahead, Pappy, you're the patriarch of this family. Tell them how you've led us to the Promised Land."

"Tell us, tell us!" the children shouted.

Mama's eyes, fastened on Pappy, were filled with love.

"I aint sure what all this fuss is about," Pappy said.

"Tell them, Anse," George Floyd said. "Tell them what's going on." Cap was very glad he'd brought George Floyd and Doc Rutherford along.

"Well, Levicy." Pappy turned to Mama. "Seems like we're about to do a good piece of business today. We're gonna build that sawmill I been tellin you about and make crossties for the railroad, and we're gonna sell coal to Mr. Holden."

"I'm so proud of you, Captain Anderson, I think my heart is gonna burst." Mama's hands quivered above her apron.

Pappy twisted and turned, pulling against Cap's ever firmer grip on his arm.

"And peace," Cap added. "We have peace."

"Our girls is gonna be so happy." Mama looked lovingly at Nancy Belle and Mary.

"Pappy!" Nancy Belle ran over and took his hand. "This is the best present I ever had!"

"'Pon my word, I feel right sheepish." Pappy's cheeks and nose reddened.

"Break out that whiskey, Hatfield," Holmby said. "Let's celebrate."

But Pappy, looking like he didn't know which way to turn, stood frozen.

"Whiskey! That's it!" Cap pointed to the shelf where the jug and tin cups were. Grabbing the jug, Floyd filled a cup and handed it to Pappy. The room grew quiet, waiting for Pappy to start the celebration, quiet enough to hear horses galloping in the distance.

Pappy wheeled around to look out the window.

"Cap, bar the door! I sent all the men to the fort, and they took the rifles with em. We're trapped!"

Cap dashed to the door and threw it open. "Why, Pappy, it's our own men riding up."

Pappy hurried to look outside. "What in tarnation?" By this time everyone was trying to get to the doorway.

"Your Praetorian Guard!" Holmby downed a good swig of whiskey.

"Come on in, boys," Cap shouted as twenty men, including Elliot who'd ridden in back of one of them, reined in their horses. The riders scrambled down. As Cap ushered them in, people made room for twenty men, rifles at their sides, to crowd in. Pappy opened his mouth as if to speak, but no words came out.

"Here are your men," Cap said. "They take orders only from you."

"Captain Anderson," Mama said in her quiet voice. "You must tell them the good news."

The men gawked at Pappy.

"They're waitin," Cap said.

"That's what they're s'posed to do, they're my men."

"How'd you fellers like to make $1.50 a day cuttin timber and workin in a sawmill?" Cap asked.

The men now all turned toward Cap. "You aint prankin us, are you?" one said. "I aint never made $1.50 a day in my life."

"I wouldn't have to give up my farm if I could get wages like that," another said.

"'Tention!" Pappy barked. "Quit all this palaverin and listen to me."

The men fell silent and formed a double row along one wall as best they could in the crowded room. Pappy strode before them.

"I was just about to ride up and join you fellers at the fort."

George Floyd walked up and laid his hand on Pappy's shoulder. "Well, now they're here, Anse. What're you gonna tell them?"

"I made a promise the other day," Pappy began. "And bein a man of my word I'm gonna keep it. I'm pretty well convinced there's gonna be peace around here and that my family and my men in Pikeville's gonna be taken care of. And I made a promise a long time ago to my lovin wife, Levicy, that I'd always look after her and our children. I think it's best for them and for all of us here to sign these here papers I've had my son prepare."

Had my son prepare! Cap should know better than to be surprised. Hadn't Pappy always portrayed himself as captain and Cap as his dutiful lieutenant, never mind how tired the lieutenant was of always taking orders and never giving them?

Pappy turned to his men. "I want you fellers, each and every one of you, to take your Winchesters and lay em in a pile over yonder by the winder. We aint gonna need em today."

Cap's head went giddy with joy. His trust deed was safe! A vision of a shingle reading "William Anderson Hatfield, Attorney at Law" floated before his eyes.

"We aint goin to Catlettsburg?" a man asked.

Elliot scuttled past Pappy to stand beside Cap. Cap turned and put his arm around Elliot's skinny shoulder and hugged him. Elliot wasn't such a bad little brother. The boy showed promise.

"Cap done a good job gettin all these papers ready like I told him to." Pappy strode over to stand in front of the fireplace. "Now that it's time for real work to be done, I'll be takin over."

Elliot whispered in Cap's ear. "They was gonna do it, Cap. They was gonna hold up the gun store in Pikeville and take all the cartridges they had. Dynamite, too, if they could get their hands on it."

"We had a close call, but you saved us. I'm grateful, very grateful. We're all grateful." For the first time Cap could remember, Elliot looked at him with admiration in his eyes.

"Now gather 'round." Pappy motioned the men over by him. "We got a lot of timberin to do. We're gonna build a dam and mill up here on Beech Creek so's we can make crossties for the railroad that's comin through. It's gonna be hard work."

"Sounds a whole lot better'n duckin bullets in Kentucky," Dan Dempsey said. "But what's to come of our men over there in jail?"

"Perry Cline's gettin em off," Pappy said. "He's workin for us now—us and the railroad."

"How sweet the sound!" Mama said. "The voice of my husband bringin all our troubles to an end."

Cap grimaced. That hurt, Mama not giving him credit. But hadn't she always praised Pappy above everyone else?

"I promised right from the first I'd take care of you, Levicy," Pappy said. "I was thinkin of you when I agreed to sign these papers and told these boys to lay down their guns." Pappy turned to Cap. "I want you to get that dam started right away."

Cap crossed the room to his wife and hugged her. "Out on Beech Creek?" he called out, falling easily into his old habit of deferring to Pappy for decisions.

Someday he'd tell their grandchildren how the Hatfield-McCoy feud had ended. By the time he had grandchildren, maybe he'd be head of this family at last.

AUTHOR'S BIO

Anne Black Gray

Anne Black Gray grew up in Parkersburg, West Virginia. She graduated with a degree in physics from Carnegie Institute of Technology in Pittsburgh, then went on to spend thirty-five years as an engineer and manager in the aerospace industry in Los Angeles.

She has now added a writing career to her engineering experience.

She is married, lives in Los Angeles, and has two grown daughters and two baby grandsons.

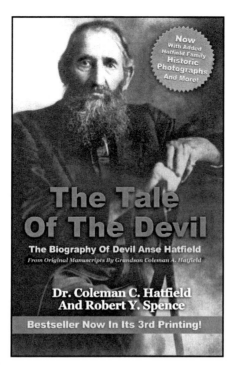

The Tale of the Devil
The Biography of Devil Anse Hatfield

By Dr. Coleman C. Hatfield and Robert Y. Spence

This collaborative effort of Coleman C. Hatfield and Robert Y. Spence, *The Tale Of The Devil,* is the factual biography of Devil Anse Hatfield, and the role he played in the infamous and brutal Hatfield and McCoy feud. Coleman Hatfield is Devil Anse Hatfield's direct descendant and brings a special and personal expertise to this project. *The Tale Of The Devil* candidly examines this figure's early life, the origins of the Hatfield and McCoy feud, its brutal toll, denouement, and ultimate conclusion -- as well as the impact it has had on subsequent generations of Hatfields and McCoys. A profound, sometimes dark, yet often insightful life story, *The Tale Of The Devil* is a very highly recommended addition to American History and Biography collections. **— Midwest Book Review**

Featured as resource material in the recent History Channel documentary, directed by Mark Cowen, on the Hatfield and McCoy feud, this book represents the first biography on the life of Anderson "Devil Anse" Hatfield, penned by great-grandson Dr. Coleman C. Hatfield and noted historian Robert Y. Spence, which also includes the historical research of C.A. Hatfield, son of Cap Hatfield. *Tale of the Devil* covers Hatfield's service in the Civil War as an officer for the Wildcats, a Confederate militia. It features in-depth coverage of the feud years, as well as the time period after the gunfire seized. In recognition of this undertaking and his exhaustive investigation of the subject matter, Dr. Coleman C. Hatfield was named Tamarack Author of the Year in 2004. Since it's first release, this book has been recognized throughout the nation by book reviewers and historians—as well as governors and dignitaries—for its exceptional content and meticulous research. ISBN: 0-9724867-1-2. 320-Pages. Handsome Hardback Edition.

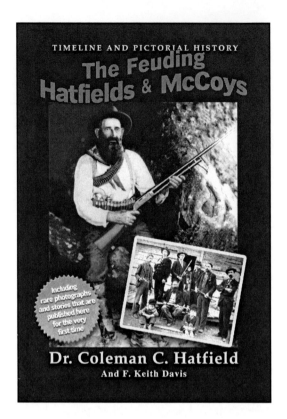

The Feuding Hatfields & McCoys

By Dr. Coleman C. Hatfield and F. Keith Davis

As a scion of one of the feuding families of the Allegheny and Cumberland hills, and one whose forebearers began their trek westward from the Virginia coast, I offer *The Feuding Hatfields & McCoys* for all who may be interested or desire to hear the facts from one who has first-hand knowledge of the people of whom he writes. **— Dr. Coleman C. Hatfield**

The Feuding Hatfields & McCoys was penned by Dr. Coleman C. Hatfield. As the great-grandson of Anderson "Devil Anse" Hatfield and grandson of Cap Hatfield, Dr. Hatfield brings a special family authenticity to this project. Its pages reflect Dr. Hatfield's unique voice and storytelling style. Assisting Dr. Hatfield was co-author and southern West Virginia historian F. Keith Davis. This volume is about two proud families, and includes a comprehensive timeline of the Hatfield family migration westward. It also faithfully documents the history before, during, and following the bloody Hatfield & McCoy feud era. Along the way, there are special family stories, which have never been published before, that add color and clarity to the period. The volume features rare and interesting photographs from both families and, besides being historically significant, *The Feuding Hatfields & McCoys* is a wonderful keepsake for those who call the Appalachian region home, or for those wanting to know more about American history. ISBN: 978-0-9793236-2-1. 192-Pages. Softcover.

w w w . w o o d l a n d p r e s s . c o m

CPSIA information can be obtained at www.ICGtesting.com
Printed in the USA
BVOW070511290312

286325BV00002B/11/P